The GOLDEN CALF

THE TWELVE CHAIRS
also by
Ilf and Petrov
is available
in the
VINTAGE RUSSIAN LIBRARY

THE *Golden Calf*

] *by* [

ILF & PETROV

Translated from the Russian by

JOHN H. C. RICHARDSON

RANDOM HOUSE NEW YORK

FIRST PRINTING

© Copyright, 1962, by Random House, Inc.

Translation dedicated to

the memory of C. S. P.

TRANSLATOR'S NOTE

(1) Even when reading a Russian work in the original, non-Russians often fail to observe the importance of the names given to the characters. Actually, they are very important, and although they tend to be chosen less subtly in humorous writings, they are nevertheless symbolic throughout.

It might perhaps add to the enjoyment of *The Golden Calf* if the reader knows the root of the names of the personages involved. Some are clear, others more vague. The following list is submitted for the reader's consideration and own interpretation.

Balaganov, from "balaganshchik"—a buffoon.
Panikovsky, from "panika"—panic.
Kozlevich, from "kozly"—the driver's seat in a coach.
Koreiko, from "koreika"—bacon.
Polykhayev, from "polykhat"—to blaze.
Skumbriyevich, from "skumbriya"—a mackerel.
Plotsky-Potseluyev, from "plot"—flesh, and "potselui"—
    kiss.
Sinitsky, from "sinitsa"—a titmouse.
Lokhankin, from "lokhanka"—a bathtub.
Berlaga, from "berloga"—a lair.
Ptiburdukov, from "ptiburduk"—a wineskin.

(2) The scene of this novel and its predecessor, *The Twelve Chairs*, is laid during NEP. The NEP (New Economic Policy) period began in 1921. During this time a limited amount of private enterprise was permitted in the Soviet Union, although the industries and all high administrative posts were in the hands of the Communists. The private traders (Nepmen) were gradually ousted by the state-owned and nationalized establishments.

CONTENTS

Part III: THE PRIVATE CITIZEN

Part : I

THE CREW
OF THE
ANTELOPE

Look both ways before crossing the street
(Highway code)

How Panikovsky
Violated the Convention

PEDESTRIANS SHOULD be loved.

Pedestrians make up the greater part of mankind. Not only that, the finer part. Pedestrians created the world. It was they who built towns, put up skyscrapers, installed drainage and plumbing, paved the streets, and lit them with electric lights. It was they who spread culture all over the world, invented printing, thought up gunpowder, built bridges across rivers, deciphered the Egyptian hieroglyphics, introduced the safety razor, abolished slavery, and discovered that a hundred and fourteen tasty, wholesome dishes could be made from beans.

And then, when everything was ready, when our planet had acquired a comparatively well-planned appearance, the motorists appeared.

It should be noted that the motor car was also invented by pedestrians. But for some reason the motorists soon forgot about that. They began to run over the meek and mild, clever pedestrians. The streets built by the pedestrians passed into the hands of the motorists. The roads were doubled in width and the sidewalks were narrowed down to the size of a tobacco wrapper. The pedestrians began to huddle against the walls of buildings in alarm.

In a large city, pedestrians lead the life of martyrs, just as though they were in a traffic-run ghetto. They are allowed to cross the street only at crossings—that is to say, at points where the traffic is heaviest and where the thread by which a pedestrian's life usually hangs may most easily snap.

In our enormous country the ordinary motor car, which the pedestrians intended to be used for peaceful purposes, has taken on the menacing aspect of a fratricidal missile. It can knock out of action whole ranks of trade-union members and their families. If, on occasion, a pedestrian just manages to skip out of the way of the silvery hood of a car, he is fined by a policeman for breaking the rules of the highway code.

Taken all around, the authority of the pedestrian has been greatly shaken. The people who gave the world such famous figures as Horace, Boyle, Mariotte, Lobachevsky, Gutenberg, and Anatole France have been forced to put on airs in the cheapest way just to call attention to their existence. What a pretty pass things have come to for the pedestrian!

There goes one along the Siberian Highway from Vladivostok to Moscow; in one hand he's carrying a banner with the words "Let us change the life of textile workers," while across his back is a stick with a spare pair of Uncle Vanya sandals and a lidless iron teapot dangling from the end.

He's a hiker who left Vladivostok as a young man and who, in his old age, will be run over at the very gates of Moscow by a large truck, the number of which no one will have a chance to catch.

Or take another, European Mohican of the pedestrian movement. He's walking round the world, rolling a barrel in front of him. He would readily have gone as he was, without the barrel, but then nobody would have noticed that he was a long-distance pedestrian, and they wouldn't have written about him in the pa-

pers. For the whole of his life he will have to keep
rolling the cursed barrel, which, by the way, is covered with large yellow letters extolling the virtues of
Driver's Dream car oil (shame, shame!).

That's how the pedestrian has been degraded.

It's now only in the smaller Russian towns that
pedestrians are still loved and respected. There they
are still the masters of the street and still light-heart-
edly stroll along the middle of the road and cross it in
any direction they like in the most intricate way.

The citizen in the white-topped peaked cap—type
usually worn by chief park attendants and M.C.'s—
undoubtedly belonged to the greater and finer part of
mankind. He wandered along the streets of the town
of Arbatov, glancing from side to side with con-
descending curiosity. He was carrying a small Gladstone bag. The town had apparently nothing with
which to impress this pedestrian in the M.C.'s cap.

He saw fifteen or so blue mignonette and white-
pink belfries; he was struck by the shabbiness of the
American gold on the church domes. A flag was flapping over an official building.

By the white turreted gates of a provincial kremlin,
two grim old women were conversing in French,
complaining about the Soviet regime and discussing
their favorite daughters. The church crypt exuded a
chilliness and a sour smell of wine. It was evidently
now a potato store.

"Verily was the temple saved by spuds," said the
pedestrian quietly.

Passing under a plyboard arch with the freshly
limed slogan "Greetings to the Fifth Regional Conference of Women and Girls," he found himself at the
beginning of a long avenue called the Boulevard of
Young Talent.

"No," he said with chagrin, "this isn't Rio de
Janeiro, this is far worse."

Practically all the benches along the Boulevard of
Young Talent were occupied by solitary young

women with open books in their hands. Perforated shadows fell on the pages of the books, the bare elbows, and the charming bangs. As the newcomer entered the cool avenue, a distinct stir ran along the benches. Hidden behind their copies of Gladkov, Eliza Orzeszko, and Seifullina, the girls cast timid glances at the young man. He marched past the interested readers and approached the executive-committee building—the aim of his visit.

At that moment a horse-cab came around the corner. A young man in a Russian-style shirt with long tails was running rapidly alongside, hanging on to the dusty, battered fender of the cab and brandishing a bulging file stamped with the word *"Musique."* He was heatedly arguing with the passenger inside. The latter, an elderly man with a pendulous bananalike nose, was gripping a suitcase between his legs and from time to time making a rude sign with his fingers at his companion outside. In the heat of the argument, his engineer's peaked cap with its band of bright green velvet slid to one side. The word "salary" was being mentioned frequently and rather loudly by both parties.

Other words were soon audible.

"You'll answer for this, Comrade Talmudovsky!" cried the long-shirt-tails, pushing away the engineer's hand.

"But I tell you that no decent specialist would agree to those conditions," Talmudovsky retorted, trying to continue making the rude sign.

"Are you on about the salary again? I shall have to report you for being too selfish."

"I don't give a damn about the salary. I'll work for nothing!" cried the engineer, excitedly describing all sorts of curves with his hand. "If I want, I can be pensioned off completely. You stop this feudalism. They write 'Liberty, equality, fraternity' all over the place and then try to make me work in that flea pit."

At this point engineer Talmudovsky quickly unclenched his fist and began counting on his fingers. "The apartment's a pigsty, there's no theater, and the salary— Cabby, take me to the station!"

"Whoa!" howled the long-shirt-tails, hastily running forward and seizing the horse by the bridle. "As the secretary of the engineers' and technicians' section . . . Kondrat Ivanovich! The plant will be left without any specialists. . . . Have a heart! The people won't allow it, engineer Talmudovsky . . . I have the minutes in my file."

And, standing with his legs apart, the section secretary began eagerly undoing the tapes of the file marked "*Musique.*"

This indiscretion settled the argument. Seeing that the coast was clear, Talmudovsky stood up and shouted as loud as he could, "To the station!"

"Where? Where?" babbled the secretary, racing after the cab. "You're a deserter from the labor front!"

Sheets of cigarette paper with the words "Action Taken" stamped in purple came flying out of the file.

The newcomer, who had followed the incident with interest, stood for a moment or two on the empty square and then said in a convinced tone, "No, this isn't Rio de Janeiro." A minute later he was knocking at the door of the executive-committee chairman's office.

"Who do you want to see?" asked the secretary sitting at a desk by the door. "What's it about?"

The visitor seemed to know the subtleties of dealing with secretaries of government, industrial, and public organizations. He was not going to pretend he had come on urgent, official business.

"A personal matter," he said dryly, without looking at the secretary, and poked his head through the chairman's door. "Can I come in?" And without waiting for an answer, he approached the desk. "Good morning—don't you recognize me?"

The chairman, a black-eyed, big-headed man in a

dark blue jacket and pants of the same color tucked into boots with thick messenger's heels, looked at his visitor in a rather vague way and said he didn't.

"Don't you really? Well, many people think I'm the image of my father."

"I'm the image of my father, too," said the chairman impatiently. "What do you want, comrade?"

"The whole point is, whose father," observed the visitor sadly. "I'm Lieutenant Schmidt's son."

The chairman looked embarrassed and half stood up. He well recalled the famous revolutionary lieutenant with his pale face and black cape with brass lion buckles. While the chairman was gathering his wits in order to ask the Black Sea hero's son a question befitting the occasion, the visitor looked closely at the office furniture with the eye of a connoisseur.

At one time, during the czars, the furnishings of government offices were made to pattern. A particular type of furniture was developed consisting of flat cupboards reaching almost to the ceiling, wooden settees with three-inch-polished seats, tables with thick billiard-style legs, and oak barriers separating the officials from the troubled outside world. During the Revolution this brand of furniture disappeared and the secret of its manufacture was lost. People forgot how to furnish the offices of administrative officials, and their premises began to be filled with objects which had until then been considered an essential part of private apartments. There appeared solicitors' sprung couches, along with a mirrored shelf for seven porcelain lucky elephants, cabinets for crockery, bookcases, extendable leather armchairs for rheumatics, and blue Japanese vases. The Arbatov executive-committee chairman's office contained, apart from an ordinary desk, two hassocks covered with tattered pink silk, a striped settee, a satin screen depicting Fujiyama and cherry blossoms, and a crudely made Slavonic cupboard with a mirror.

"That's a cupboard of the 'Hey, you Slavs' type,"

thought the visitor. "Not much to take here. No, this isn't Rio de Janeiro."

"Very nice of you to drop in," said the chairman at length. "You've come from Moscow, I imagine."

"Yes, on my way through," answered the visitor, staring at the settee and becoming more and more convinced that the executive committee's financial affairs were in poor shape. He preferred executive committees furnished with new Swedish furniture from the Leningrad Woodworking Plant.

The chairman was just about to ask the point of Lieutenant Schmidt's son's arrival in Arbatov when, unexpectedly, he smiled soulfully and said, "The churches here are wonderful. We've already had some people here from the Chief Scientific Administration. They're going to restore them. Tell me, do you actually remember the mutiny on the battleship *Ochakov?*"

"Vaguely," replied the visitor. "At that heroic time I was still extremely young. I was just a child."

"Excuse me, but what's your first name?"

"Nicholas. Nicholas Schmidt."

"And your father's name?"

"Oh, how awkward!" thought the visitor, who didn't know his father's name. "Ye-es," he drawled, avoiding a direct answer, "lots of people nowadays don't know the names of our heroes. They're befuddled by NEP. Misguided enthusiasm. Actually, I've come here quite by chance. Difficulties en route. I haven't a cent left."

The chairman was very pleased at this turn in the conversation. He was ashamed to have forgotten the name of the *Ochakov* hero. "Yes, indeed," he thought as he gazed at the hero's son's inspired face, "you get bogged down in work here and forget the great events." "What did you say? Haven't a cent? That's interesting."

"I could ask a private citizen, of course," said the visitor. "Anyone would give me something, but, you see, it's not a good thing from the political point of view. The son of a revolutionary asking a private citizen or private trader for money . . ." The words "private trader" he pronounced with a catch in his voice.

The chairman listened anxiously to the new intonation. "Maybe he's an epileptic. Then I'll never hear the end of it."

"And a good thing you didn't ask a private citizen," said the confused chairman at length.

Then, gently, without bringing pressure to bear, the Black Sea hero's son got down to business. He asked for fifty rubles. The chairman, who was restricted by the narrow limits of his local budget, could give him only eight rubles and three lunch vouchers for use in "The Stomach's Ex-Friend" cooperative cafeteria.

The hero's son put away the money and lunch vouchers in the deep pocket of his worn dapple-gray suit and was about to get up from the pink hassock when from behind the door there came the sound of stamping feet and a warning cry from the secretary.

The door opened and a new visitor appeared on the threshold. "Who's the boss here?" he asked, breathing heavily and running his lecherous eyes around the room.

"I am," said the chairman.

"Hi, Mr. Chairman!" rattled off the newcomer, offering a spade-shaped hand. "Let me introduce myself. Lieutenant Schmidt's son."

"Who?" asked the chairman, his eyes popping.

"Son of that great, immortal hero, Lieutenant Schmidt," the man repeated.

"But the comrade sitting here is Lieutenant Schmidt's son—Nicholas Schmidt." The chairman pointed in bewilderment to the first visitor, whose face had acquired a sleepy expression.

A ticklish moment had arrived in the lives of the two tricksters. At any moment the long and unpleasant sword of Nemesis might gleam in the hand of the modest and gullible chairman. Fate gave them but one second to think of something to save the situation. The eyes of Lieutenant Schmidt's second son were filled with horror.

His figure, with its *Paraguay* summer shirt, sailor's pants with a flap at the front, and blue sneakers, only a moment before sharp and angular, began to blur and lose its menacing outline; it no longer commanded respect. A nasty smirk appeared on the chairman's face.

Then, just when the second son felt that all was lost and that the chairman's terrible wrath would descend on his curly red head at any moment, salvation came from the pink hassock.

"Basil!" cried the first son, jumping up. "Basil, my own kid brother, don't you recognize me?" And he seized the second son in his arms.

"Nicky!" exclaimed Basil, catching on. "Of course I do."

Their happy reunion was accompanied by such a tumultuous show of affection and such powerful hugging that the second son of the Black Sea revolutionary emerged with his face pale with pain. His brother Nicky had crumpled him more than somewhat in his joy.

As they hugged each other, the two brothers kept glancing sideways at the chairman, whose face had not lost its vinegary expression. Owing to this latter fact, the ruse had to be developed and supplemented with details and new facts about the mutiny of 1905. Hand in hand, the brothers sat down on the hassock and, keeping their fawning eyes on the chairman, lapsed into reminiscence.

"What a remarkable coincidence!" exclaimed the first son untruthfully, inviting the chairman with his eyes to join in the family celebration.

"Yes," said the chairman in an icy voice, "it happens."

Seeing that the chairman was still in the throes of doubt, the first son stroked his brother's Irish-setter curls and asked tenderly, "When did you leave Mariopol, where you were living with Grandma?"

"Yes, I was living there," the lieutenant's second son stammered, "with her."

"Why didn't you write to me more often? I was very worried."

"I was busy," answered the redhead glumly. And, fearing that his brother might ask him what he had been doing (and what he had mainly been doing was spending his time in the workhouses of different autonomous republics and regions), Lieutenant Schmidt's second son seized the initiative and asked a question himself. "And why didn't you write?"

"I did," replied his elder brother unexpectedly, feeling a tremendous surge of gaiety. "I sent you registered letters. I've even got the receipts." And he dug into his side pocket and actually took out a number of grimy bits of paper, which for some reason he showed the chairman rather than his brother, but only from a distance.

Strange as it may seem, the sight of the bits of paper somewhat soothed the chairman, and the reminiscing of the brothers became more lively. The redhead had now fully mastered the situation and produced a fairly coherent though monotonous account of the contents of the pamphlet *Mutiny on the Ochakov.* His brother embellished the account with details which were so imaginative that the chairman, who had just begun to relax, pricked up his ears again. Nevertheless, he let the brothers go in peace, and they hurried into the street with a great feeling of relief.

Around the corner of the executive-committee building they stopped.

"Talking of childhood," said the first son, "in mine I used to kill people like you on the spot. With a catapult."

"Why?" asked the famous father's second son jubilantly.

"Such are the tough laws of life. Or, to make it shorter, life dictates its own tough laws to us. Why did you come into his office? Didn't you see that he wasn't alone?"

"I thought—"

"Oh, you thought? So you sometimes think, do you? You're a thinker. What's your name, thinker? Spinoza? Jean-Jacques Rousseau? Marcus Aurelius?"

Redhead was silent, crushed by the just accusation.

"Well, I'll forgive you. You may continue living. And now let's introduce ourselves. Whether you like it or not, we're brothers, and that imposes obligations. My name's Ostap Bender. What's yours?"

"Balaganov," said the redhead, introducing himself. "Alex Balaganov."

"I'm not going to ask your profession," said Bender courteously, "but I can guess it. Something intellectual, probably. How many times have you been in court this year?"

"Twice," Balaganov readily answered.

"That's bad. Why sell your immortal soul? People shouldn't let themselves be convicted. It's a rotten occupation. I'm talking about theft. Let alone the fact that stealing is sinful—Mom probably told you about that during childhood—it's also a waste of time and energy."

Ostap would have gone on expounding his outlook on life for some time had Balaganov not interrupted him.

"Look," he said, pointing into the green depths of the Boulevard of Young Talent. "You see that fellow there in the straw hat?"

"Yes," said Ostap haughtily. "What about him? Is he the Governor of Borneo?"

"It's Panikovsky," said Alex. "Lieutenant Schmidt's son."

A citizen was coming down the street in the shade

of the august limes, keeling slightly to one side. A hard straw hat with a ribbed brim was perched on the side of his head. His pants were so short that they showed the white ribbons of his long underwear. A gold tooth gleamed like a cigarette tip beneath the citizen's mustache.

"What, another son?" asked Bender. "This is getting ridiculous."

Panikovsky approached the executive-committee building, thoughtfully described a figure eight at the entrance, seized hold of the brim of his hat in both hands and set it evenly on his head, pulled his jacket round him, and, breathing heavily, went inside.

"The lieutenant had three sons," Bender observed: "two clever ones and one idiot. We should warn him."

"Don't bother," said Balaganov. "Next time he'll know better than to violate the convention."

"Which convention is that?"

"I'll tell you in a moment. He's just gone in!"

"I'm usually an envious person," Ostap confessed, "but there's nothing to envy here. Have you ever seen a bullfight? Let's go and watch."

The two chummy sons of Lieutenant Schmidt went around the corner and walked over to the window of the chairman's office.

Behind the misty, unwashed glass sat the chairman. He was rapidly writing something. Like all people engaged in writing, his face bore a pained expression. Suddenly he looked up. The door flew open and Panikovsky entered the room. Clasping his straw hat to his jacket, he stopped in front of the desk and moved his thick lips for some time. Then the chairman jumped up from his chair and opened his mouth wide. The friends heard a long-drawn-out howl.

With the words "Stand back," Ostap pulled Balaganov after him. They ran into the boulevard and hid behind a tree.

"Off with your hats," said Ostap, "they're bringing out the body."

He was not wrong. Hardly had the rumbling and warbling of the chairman's voice died down when two hefty-looking clerks appeared at the portals of the building. They were carrying Panikovsky. One was holding him by the arms and the other by the feet.

"The ashes of the deceased were borne by his nearest and dearest," Ostap commented.

The clerks dragged Lieutenant Schmidt's third and foolish son through the doorway and began leisurely swinging him backward and forward. Panikovsky remained silent, gazing at the blue sky.

"After a brief meeting of mourning . . ." Ostap began.

At that moment the clerks, having imparted sufficient momentum to Panikovsky's body, threw him into the street.

". . . the body was committed to the earth," Bender ended.

Panikovsky flopped on the ground like a toad. He quickly got up and, keeling over more than before, hurried off up the Boulevard of Young Talent at an incredible speed.

"Right—now you can tell me how that idiot violated the convention and what the convention is," said Ostap.

]CHAPTER[

: 2 :

The Thirty Sons
of Lieutenant Schmidt

THE BUSILY SPENT morning came to an end. Bender
and Balaganov began walking quickly away from
the executive-committee building. On the main street
two peasant carts were carrying a long steel-blue rail,
one at either end. There was such a clinking and
clattering in the street that the carter, in his canvas
fisherman's clothing, might have been carrying a
deafening musical note, rather than a rail. The sun
forced its way through the glass window of a visual-
aids shop, in which, above the globes, skulls, and the
gaily colored cardboard liver of a drunkard, two skeletons were giving each other a friendly hug. In the
more modest window of the stamp-and-seal workshop,
most of the space was taken up by enamel plates with
the inscriptions "Shut for Lunch," "Lunch Hour from
2 to 3 p.m.," "Closed for the Lunch Break," or simply "Closed," "Shop Shut," and finally a black base-
board with gold letters—"Shut for Stocktaking."
These firmly worded notices seemed to be most in
demand in Arbatov. All other everyday happenings
were summed up by the stamp-and-seal workshop in
one dark blue plate worded "Duty Nursemaid."

Then, one after the other, came three shops dealing in wind instruments, mandolins, and bass balalaikas. The brass tubes, glinting decadently, reclined in the window on tiers draped with red calico. Particularly fine was the bass helicon. It was so powerful, and warmed itself so lazily in the sun, all curled into a ball, that it shouldn't have been kept in a shop window at all but in the Moscow zoo, somewhere between the elephant and the boa-constrictor. And on holidays parents ought to have taken their children to see it and said, "And here's the helicon house, dear. The helicon's asleep at the moment, but when it wakes up, it will certainly start trumpeting." And the children would have looked at the amazing tube with wide, staring eyes.

At any other time Ostap Bender might have turned his mind to both of the freshly hewn, cottage-size balalaikas, the phonograph records curling in the sun, and the pioneer drums, whose splendid colored designs made one think of the saying "A bullet's no good, it's the bayonet that counts," but now he had no time for that. He was hungry.

"I suppose you're on the brink of financial ruin?" he asked Balaganov.

"If you're talking about money," said Alex, "I haven't had any for a whole week."

"In that case, you'll come to a sad end, young man," said Ostap warningly. "Financial ruin is the worst of all kinds. You can suffer from it all your life. Well, anyway, don't grieve. I managed to carry off three lunch vouchers in my beak. The executive-committee chairman fell in love with me at first sight."

But the foster brothers were not able to take advantage of the mayor's kindness. A large padlock covered with something that looked like a mixture of rust and porridge hung from the door of "The Stomach's Ex-Friend" cafeteria.

"The cafeteria is obviously shut for stocktaking of

the schnitzels," said Ostap bitterly. "We'll have to put ourselves at the mercy of the private traders."

"Private traders prefer money down," Balaganov objected in a dull voice.

"Well, I won't keep you in suspense. The chairman showered his blessings on me to the tune of eight rubles. But keep it in mind, my dear Alex, that I'm not going to pay for your food for nothing. For every vitamin I give you to eat I shall expect lots of small services in return."

But there turned out to be no privately owned sector in the town, so the brothers had their lunch in the co-operative summer park, where special placards informed the citizens of Arbatov of the latest novelty in public catering:

Beer Available to Trade-Union Members Only

"Let's make do with kvass," said Balaganov.

"Especially since the local kvass is brewed by a group of private traders sympathizing with the Soviet regime," Ostap added. "But now tell me what it was that thug Panikovsky did wrong. I enjoy stories about petty crooks."

Balaganov slaked his thirst, looked gratefully at his savior, and began the story. It took about two hours to tell and contained some extremely interesting information.

In all fields of human activity the supply of labor and the demand for it are regulated by special organizations. An actor will not go to Omsk until he has made quite certain that he need have no fear of competition, and that there are no other pretenders to his role of the cold lover or the butler who only says, "Dinner is served." Railroad workers run down their union newspapers, which busily publish reports that unemployed baggage-room attendants cannot count on getting work anywhere on the Syzran-Vyazma Railroad, or that the Central Asian Railroad needs four hundred women to guard level crossings. An expert salesman puts an advertisement in the paper and the whole country knows that somewhere there's an expert salesman with ten years' experience who wishes, for family reasons, to change his job in Moscow for one in the provinces.

Everything is regulated; everything moves in set channels and completes its cycle in complete conformity with the law and under its protection.

But there was one market which was in a state of chaos. Anarchy was rife among a special group of crooks who called themselves the "Children of Lieutenant Schmidt." They were no longer able to derive from their profession the advantages that their brief encounters with administrators, executives, and other officials—people who are for the most part incredibly gullible—were supposed to bring.

Throughout the country, extorting and cadging as they go, roam phony grandchildren of Karl Marx, nonexistent nephews and nieces of Friedrich Engels, brothers of Lunacharski, cousins of Klara Tsetkin, or, if the worst comes to the worst, descendants of the famous anarchist Prince Kropotkin. From Minsk to the Bering Straits, from Nakhichevan on the Araks to Franz Josef Land, the relatives of these great men and women visit executive committees, alight onto station platforms, and busily drive around in cabs. They're in a hurry. They have a lot to do.

At one time the supply of relatives exceeded the demand, and the extraordinary market was hit by a depression. A need for reform was felt. Little by little, the grandchildren of Karl Marx, the Kropotkinites, the Engelists, and their ilk organized their activity. The dissenters were the stormy "Children of Lieutenant Schmidt," who, like the Polish *Sejm*, were eternally torn by anarchy. The children who joined the group were coarse, greedy, and quarrelsome, and generally prevented each other from feathering their nests.

Alex Balaganov, who considered himself the firstborn of the lieutenant, was seriously alarmed by the

situation. He kept bumping into more and more fellow members of the corporation, who were completely ruining the fertile fields of the Ukraine and
the mountain health resorts of the Caucasus, where he
was used to working at great profit.

"And were you afraid of growing difficulties?"
asked Ostap sarcastically.

But Balaganov didn't notice the irony. Sipping his
purple kvass, he continued his story.

There was only one way out of the situation: to
hold a conference. He spent the whole winter making
preparations for it. He wrote to all the rivals whom he
knew personally. Those he did not received invita-
tions via the grandchildren of Marx whom he met on
his travels. And so, finally, early in the spring of 1928,
almost all the known children of Lieutenant Schmidt
gathered in a Moscow tavern near the Sukharevka
Tower. The quorum was extensive: the lieutenant
proved to have thirty sons, ranging in age from eighteen to fifty-two, and four daughters, who were stupid, middle-aged, and ugly.

In a brief opening speech, Balaganov expressed his
hope that the brothers would find a common language
and would eventually draft a convention, the need for
which was dictated by life itself.

Balaganov's plan was to divide up the entire Soviet
Union into thirty-four operational areas, one for each
of the assembled citizens. Each area would be placed
at the long-term disposal of a "child." None of the
members of the corporation had the right to cross
the boundary and invade someone else's area for the
purpose of earning money.

No one raised any objection to these new principles
except for Panikovsky, who declared even at that time
that he would manage without a convention. But there
were outrageous scenes when it came to the actual division. The high-contracting parties shouted at each
other from the very first moment, and, in the process,
used some choice epithets.

No one wanted to have the university centers. None of them wanted sophisticated Moscow, Leningrad, or Kharkov. The far-off, sand-blown regions of the east also had a bad reputation. They were accused of ignorance of the existence of Lieutenant Schmidt.

"What a lot of fools!" screeched Panikovsky. "Give me the Central Russian Elevation and then I'll sign the convention."

"What! The whole elevation?" Balaganov retorted. "Perhaps you'd like Melitopol thrown in as well? Or Bobruisk?"

At the mention of Bobruisk, the meeting gave a groan of misery. They were all ready to go to Bobruisk on the spot. It was considered a splendid, highly cultured place.

"Well, if not the whole elevation, at least half," insisted the greedy Panikovsky. "I'm a family man, after all. I've got two families."

But he didn't even get half.

After a great deal of shouting, it was decided to cast lots for the areas. Thirty-four pieces of paper were cut up and a geographical name put on each. Fertile Kursk and dubious Kherson, underdeveloped Minusinsk and almost hopeless Ashkhabad, Kiev, Petrozavodsk, and Chita—all the republics and administrative regions lay in someone's rabbit-fur cap with earflaps and awaited their owners.

Delighted cries, dull groans, and curses accompanied the draw.

Panikovsky's unlucky star was in the ascendent. The Volga region fell his lot. He joined the convention, seething with fury.

"I'll go there," he shouted, "but I warn you: if they don't treat me properly, I'll violate the convention and cross the boundary!"

Balaganov, who had been lucky enough to draw the Arbatov eldorado, became alarmed and declared that he would not tolerate violation of the operation acres.

In some way or other the matter was finally smoothed out and the thirty sons and four daughters of Lieutenant Schmidt departed to work in their respective areas.

"You saw for yourself, Bender," said Alex, ending his narrative, "how that idiot violated the convention. He's been sneaking around my area for quite a while, but this was the first time I'd caught him."

Contrary to the storyteller's expectations, Panikovsky's bad deed didn't arouse any criticism from Ostap. Bender leaned back in his chair, staring in front of him.

The high wall at the back of the restaurant park was painted with trees, dense-leafed and all the same height, like a picture in a textbook. There were no real trees in the garden, but the shadow cast by the wall gave a refreshing coolness and fully satisfied the citizenry. The citizens were evidently all trade-union members, as they were drinking the beer by itself and not eating.

A green car drove up to the park gates, gasping and backfiring; on its door, in white letters arranged in a semicircle, were the words "Hey, come for a ride!" Underneath were the conditions for a trip in this merry vehicle: "Three rubles an hour, and tip as agreed." There were no passengers in the car.

The visitors to the park began whispering apprehensively. For five minutes the driver stood looking hopefully through the park railings, then, evidently losing all hope of finding a fare, called out challengingly:

"The taxi's free. Please take your seats."

But none of the citizens showed any desire to take a seat in the car. Even the invitation had a strange effect on them. They lowered their heads and tried to avoid looking at the car. The driver shook his head and slowly drove away. The Arbatov inhabitants gazed sadly after him. Five minutes later the green car hurtled past the park in the opposite direction.

The driver was bouncing up and down in his seat and shouting something undecipherable. The car was as empty as before.

Ostap followed it with his eyes and said, "So, Balaganov, you're a jerk. Don't take offense. I only want to make it quite clear what place you occupy in the world."

"Go to hell!" said Balaganov rudely.

"So you're offended. Don't you think that being a son of Lieutenant Schmidt is a lousy occupation?"

"But you're a son of Lieutenant Schmidt yourself!" cried Balaganov.

"You're a jerk," Ostap repeated. "And the son of a jerk. And your children will be jerks. You baby! What happened today is not even an episode but just a pure coincidence, an artist's whim. A gentleman in search of a fast ruble. It's not in my character to play at such odds. And what kind of profession is that, God forbid! A son of Lieutenant Schmidt! I give it a year, maybe two. And then what? The moment your ginger hair appears in sight, they'll start beating you up."

"Then what's to be done?" asked Balaganov anxiously. "How can I earn my daily bread?"

"You'll have to think," said Ostap sternly. "I feed on ideas, for instance. I don't hold out my paw for a meager executive-committee ruble. I'm more ambitious. You, I see, love money. Tell me, how much would you like?"

"Five thousand," Balaganov promptly replied.

"A month?"

"A year."

"Then we don't think alike. I need five hundred thousand. And if possible, all at once, not in bits."

"But you wouldn't mind it in bits, would you?" asked Balaganov spitefully.

Ostap looked hard at his companion and answered perfectly seriously, "I wouldn't mind it in bits, but I need it all at once."

Balaganov was just going to make a joke about that remark, too, when, glancing at Ostap, he stopped himself. Sitting in front of him was an athletically built man with strong, chiseled features. Across his swarthy throat stretched a crinkly white scar. His eyes shone with menacing gaiety.

Balaganov suddenly felt an overwhelming desire to stand at attention. He even wanted to give a cough, as junior officials do when in the presence of more senior comrades. And indeed, giving a cough, he asked awkwardly, "Why do you want so much money . . . all at once?"

"Actually, I need more," said Ostap. "Five hundred thousand is my minimum—five hundred thousand genuine rubles. I want to go away, Comrade Alex, a long way away to Rio de Janeiro."

"Do you have relatives there?" asked Balaganov.

"Why, do I look like someone who has relatives?"

"No, but I—"

"I don't have any relatives, Comrade Alex. I'm alone in the world. I had a dad. He was a Turkish citizen, but he died a long time ago in terrible convulsions. But that's not the point. I've always wanted to go to Rio de Janeiro since I was a kid. I don't suppose you've ever heard of the place?"

Balaganov shook his head sadly. Apart from Moscow, the only centers of world culture he had heard of were Kiev, Melitopol, and Zhmerinka. And, anyway, he was certain the earth was flat.

Ostap threw on the table a page torn from a book. "This is taken from the *Smaller Soviet Encyclopedia*. Here's what they say about Rio de Janeiro: 1,360,000 inhabitants . . . yes . . . great number of mulattoes . . . situated in a large bay in the Atlantic . . . Here you are: 'The main streets of the city are not inferior in the richness of the shops and splendor of the buildings to the first cities of the world.' Just imagine that, Alex. Not inferior! Mulattoes, the bay, exports of coffee—coffee-dumping, so to say—a Charles-

ton called 'My girl has a little trick,' and . . . But
why talk about it? You can see yourself what it's
like. A million and a half people, and every one of
them in white pants. I want to get away from here.
I've had some serious differences with the Soviet regime over the past year. They want to build socialism,
but I don't. I'm bored by building socialism. Now
do you see why I need so much money?"

"Where will you find five hundred thousand?"
asked Balaganov quietly.

"Anywhere you like," Ostap replied. "Show me a
rich man and I'll take his money."

"How? Would you murder him?" asked Balaganov
even more quietly, and glanced around at the neighboring tables where the citizens of Arbatov were
drinking each other's health.

"You know," said Ostap, "you shouldn't have signed
the Sukharevka convention. The mental effort has evidently exhausted you. You're getting more and more
stupid before my very eyes. Kindly note that Ostap
Bender has never killed anyone. People have tried to
kill me—that has happened. But I've a clear conscience. I'm not an angel, of course. I've no wings,
but I respect the law. It's a weakness of mine."

"Then how do you expect to get the money?"

"How do I expect to get it? The appropriation or
embezzlement of money is varied according to the circumstances. Personally, I have four hundred relatively
honest ways of obtaining it. But the ways don't matter. The point is there aren't any rich people left.
Some fellows might have a go at some state-owned
establishment, but that's against my rules. You know
how I respect the Penal Code. I don't intend robbing
the collective. Give me a rather more wealthy individual, except that there aren't any."

"What do you mean?" exclaimed Balaganov.
"There are some very rich people."

"Do you know any?" asked Ostap quickly. "Maybe
you know the name and address of just one Soviet

millionaire. But there are some—there must be. Since there are currency notes circulating around the country, there must be people who have lots of them. But how do we find these shrewdies?"

Ostap actually sighed. Dreams of finding a rich individual had evidently troubled him for some time.

"How pleasant it would be," he said pensively, "to work with a legal millionaire in a well-organized bourgeois state with capitalist traditions. There, millionaires are popular figures. Their addresses are known. They live in large houses somewhere in Rio de Janeiro. You go straight to see them at their houses and there, in the hall, after the initial greeting, you take their money. And it's all done nicely and politely, mind you. 'Hello, sir. May I trouble you for a moment? All right.' Finish. And that's it. That's culture for you. What could be simpler? A gentleman doing business in a society of gentlemen. You don't need to shoot at the chandelier—that's out. But over here . . . Lordy, lordy, what a cold country we live in. Everything's hidden, everything's underground. Not even the Ministry of Finance with its super taxation machinery can find a Soviet millionaire. But there may be one sitting in this so-called summer park at this very moment at a nearby table drinking Tip-Top beer at forty kopeks a bottle. That's what's such a shame."

"So you think that if you found a secret millionaire like that—"

"Don't go on. I know what you're going to say. No, that's not it at all. I wouldn't smother him with a pillow or clump him on the head with a pistol. There wouldn't be anything foolish at all. If only we could find one, I'd organize things so that he brought me his money himself on a silver platter."

"That's very good," Balaganov sniggered believingly. "Five hundred thousand on a silver platter."

He stood up and began circling the table. He clicked his tongue plaintively, kept stopping and opening his mouth as though wanting to say something, but sat down again without uttering it, and again got up. Ostap followed his gyrations apathetically.

"Would he bring it himself?" Balaganov suddenly asked in a squeaky voice. "On a silver platter? And what if he didn't? And where's this Rio de Janeiro? Far? It can't be right that everyone there wears white pants. Stop this nonsense, Bender. On five hundred thousand you could live well even in this country."

"Of course, of course," said Ostap gaily. "But don't flap your wings for nothing. You haven't got five hundred thousand."

A deep wrinkle appeared on Balaganov's smooth, unfurrowed brow. He looked at Ostap with uncertainty and said, "I know just such a millionaire."

For a second the excitement left Ostap's face; but it immediately hardened and reassumed its chiseled outline.

"Go on with you," he said. "Don't talk such rot!"

"Honestly, M'sieu Bender."

"Listen, Alex, if you've finally switched to French, don't call me 'm'sieu' but 'citoyen,' which means 'citizen.' Anyway, what's the address of your millionaire?"

"He lives in Chernomorsk."

"Just what I thought. Chernomorsk. Even before the war, anyone there with nine thousand was called a millionaire, so nowadays . . . you can just imagine. No, that's rubbish."

"No, it isn't: let me finish. He's a real millionaire. You see, Bender, I recently had occasion to be put in the local jail . . ."

Ten minutes later the foster brothers left the summer park and the supply of beer. The smooth operator felt like a surgeon facing a very important operation. Everything was ready. The swabs and dressings were being sterilized in the electric autoclaves; a nurse in her white toga was noiselessly moving over the tiled floor; there was a glint of clinical porcelain and steel; the patient lay on a glass-topped table gazing languidly at the ceiling, while through the air-conditioned atmosphere came the medicinal smell of German chewing gum. With fingers splayed, the surgeon approaches the operating table, takes a sterilized jackknife from his assistant, and says curtly to the patient, "Okay, off with your burnoose."

"It's always the same with me," said Bender, his eyes glittering. "A million-ruble deal has to be begun with an acute lack of currency. My entire capital —basic, turnover, and reserve—amounts to only five rubles. What did you say the name of your underground millionaire was?"

"Koreiko," Balaganov replied.

"Yes, yes, Koreiko. A splendid name. And you claim no one knows about his millions."

"Nobody besides me and Pruzhansky. But Pruzhansky, as I told you, will be in jail for another three years. If only you'd seen how he fretted and wept when I was being let out. He obviously realized he shouldn't have told me about Koreiko."

"The fact that he told you his secret is nothing. That wasn't why he was fretting and weeping. He obviously foresaw that you'd tell the whole story to me. And that definitely is a loss for Pruzhansky. By the time he comes out of jail, Koreiko will only be able to console himself with that vulgar saying, 'Poverty is no vice!' "

Ostap pulled off his summer peaked cap and, waving it in the air, asked:

"Do I have any gray hairs?"

Balaganov pulled in his stomach, spread the toes of his boots to the width of a rifle butt, and replied in the voice of a right-hand marker, "No, sir."

"Well, I will have. There's great fighting ahead. You'll also turn gray, Balaganov."

Balaganov suddenly giggled foolishly. "What was

it you said? He'll bring you the money himself on a silver platter."

"On a platter for me," said Ostap, "and on a plate for you."

"And what about Rio de Janeiro? I want to wear white pants too."

"Rio de Janeiro is the crystal dream of my youth," replied the smooth operator firmly, "so keep your paws off it. Down to business. Put some markers at my disposal. The troops are to arrive in the town of Chernomorsk in the shortest possible time. Dress uniform will be worn. Sound the bugle! I'm taking the parade, or, in other words, I shall review the troops!"

] C H A P T E R [

: 3 :

The Gasoline Is Yours
and the Ideas Ours

A YEAR BEFORE Panikovsky violated the convention
by invading someone else's operational area, the first
car appeared in the town of Arbatov. The founder of
this motoring venture was a driver named Kozlevich.

It was the decision to start a new life that brought
him to the steering wheel. Adam Kozlevich's former
life had been sinful. He constantly violated the Criminal Code of the RSFSR, or, to be exact, Article 162,
which deals with the covert "appropriation" of other
people's property (theft).

This Article has a number of sections, but section
(a) (theft perpetrated without the use of technical
means) was alien to the sinful Adam. That was too
primitive for him. Section (d), which punished mal-
efactors with imprisonment for up to five years, didn't
suit him, either. He hated staying in prison for long
periods. As he was attracted to things mechanical, he
devoted himself wholeheartedly to section (c) (covert appropriation of other people's property with the
use of technical means, or on repeated occasions, or
in complicity with other persons, at stations, at docks,
on ships or trains, and in hotels).

But Kozlevich was unlucky. He was caught both while using technical means and without them. He was caught at stations, at docks, on ships, and in hotels. He was also caught in railroad carriages. He was even caught when in complete desperation he was purloining someone's property in complicity with other persons.

Having spent a total of three years in jail, Adam Kozlevich came to the conclusion that it would be much more to the point if he accumulated his own property, rather than steal other people's. This thought brought peace to his restless soul. He became a model prisoner, wrote poems denouncing others in the prison newspaper *Sunrise and Sunset,* and worked hard in the machine shop of the establishment. The penitentiary system had a good effect. Adam Kazimirovich Kozlevich, forty-six, by origin a peasant from the Chentokhov district, single, with a number of convictions, came out of jail an honest man.

After two years of work in a Moscow garage, he bought a second-hand car which was so ancient that its appearance on the market could only be due to the closing down of some veteran car museum. The rare exhibit was sold to Kozlevich for a hundred and ninety rubles. For some reason or other the car was sold together with an artificial palm in a green tub, so he had to take the palm as well. The palm was still in reasonable shape, but the car needed a lot of work. The missing parts had to be picked up at bazaars; the seats were re-covered, and the electricity system was rewired. The repairs were completed with a coat of lizard-green paint. It wasn't known what make of car it was, but Adam Kozlevich claimed it was a Lauren Dietrich. As proof he attached a plate with the Lauren Dietrich trademark to the radiator. He was then able to go ahead with the private hire which he had so long dreamt of.

On the day that Adam Kozlevich was getting ready to present his offspring to the world for the first time,

an event of great sadness for all private car owners occurred on the car market. A hundred and twenty little
black Renault taxis, looking like Browning machine
guns, arrived in Moscow. Kozlevich didn't even attempt to compete with them. He left the palm at the
Versailles cabbies' tearoom for safekeeping, and drove
off to find work in the provinces.

Arbatov, a town lacking in motor transport, appealed to the driver, and he made up his mind to
stay there for good.

Adam Kozlevich imagined how energetically, happily, and, most important, honestly he would work
in the field of private car-hire service. He imagined
himself on duty at the station in the early arctic morning, waiting for the Moscow train. Wrapping himself
in a light brown cowhide coat and pushing up his flying goggles onto his forehead, he offers the porters
cigarettes. Somewhere in the background the frozen
horse-cab drivers are huddled up with cold. They're
crying with the cold and shaking their thick dark blue
skirts. Then comes the warning sound of the station
bell, announcing the arrival of the train. Passengers
come out into the station square and stop in front of
the car with contented expressions. They hadn't realized that the idea of a car-hire service had reached
the backwaters of Arbatov. Tooting the horn, Kozlevich races his passengers to the Peasants' Club.

Enough work for the whole day; everyone is glad
to utilize the services of the mechanical carriage. Kozlevich and his faithful Lauren Dietrich are certain to
take part in all the town weddings, excursions, and
ceremonies. But most of the work comes in the summer. On Sundays whole families drive out of town in
Kozlevich's car. There's the sound of children's inane
laughter, the wind pulls at the scarfs and ribbons, the
women prattle away happily, the head of the family
looks admiringly at the chauffeur's leather-covered
back and asks him questions about the car industry in

the northern United States (was it true, for instance, that Ford buys a new car every day).

That was how Kozlevich visualized his wonderful new life in Arbatov. But in no time at all reality sent his castles-in-the-air crashing down, together with all the towers, drawbridges, weathervanes, and flags.

The railroad timetable was the first thing to let him down. Both express trains and mail trains passed through Arbatov without stopping, picking up the batons and casting off the special-delivery mail as they went. The mixed trains stopped there only twice a week. The people they brought were small-time types—peasants, and shoemakers with knapsacks, lasts, and petitions. As a rule these passengers didn't make use of the car. There were no excursions or ceremonies, and Kozlevich wasn't invited to the weddings. In Arbatov the cab drivers usually hired for wedding processions used to weave their horses' manes with paper roses and chrysanthemums, which always pleased the wedding sponsors very much.

But there were lots of out-of-town trips, though they were not always quite what Adam Kozlevich had dreamt about. There were no children, no scarfs fluttering in the wind, and no merry prattle.

On the first evening, lit by the dim kerosene street lamps, Adam Kozlevich, who had fruitlessly stood the whole day on Co-operative-Savior Square, was approached by four men. They gazed at the car in silence for some time. Then one of them, a hunchback, asked awkwardly:

"Can we all go for a ride?"

"Yes, all of you," said Kozlevich, surprised at the timidity of the Arbatov citizens. "Five rubles an hour."

The men whispered among themselves. Peculiar sighs and words reached the driver's ear: "Let's go for a drive, comrades, now the meeting's over. But is it all right? A ruble twenty-five per person isn't expensive. What's wrong with that? . . ."

And for the first time the roomy car took Arbatov citizens onto its calico lap. For a few minutes the passengers were silent, overwhelmed by the speed, the hot smell of gasoline, and the whistling of the wind. Then, saddened by some vague presentiment, they quietly began singing "Fleeting, like waves, are the days of our lives." Kozlevich changed into third gear. The somber outline of a canned-goods stall flashed past and the car hurtled into the open country along a moonlit road.

"Like the day, our path to the grave is short," crooned the passengers soulfully. They became sorry for themselves and resentful that they had never been students. They sang the chorus in loud voices:

"A wine glass each, trala bom bom, trala bom bom."

"Stop!" cried the hunchback suddenly. "Let's go back. My throat's parched."

In the town the excursionists picked up a large number of white bottles and a broad-shouldered citizenness. Out in the country they set up camp, supped on vodka, and danced the polka without music.

All the next day, exhausted by the events of the night, Kozlevich dozed at the wheel. Toward evening the same four appeared, already rather tipsy, got into the car, and drove round and round the town all night. The same thing happened again the next day. The nocturnal revelry of the merry company, with the hunchback as master of ceremonies, continued for two weeks on end. The delights of motorized transport had a strange effect on Adam Kozlevich's clients; their faces became puffy and pale and gleamed white like pillows in the darkness. With a piece of sausage hanging out of his mouth, the hunchback looked like a vampire.

They became neurotic and sometimes used to cry at the height of the fun. On one occasion, the crazy hunchback brought a sack of rice to the car by horse-cab. At dawn they took the rice to a village, traded it for hooch, and stayed out of town the whole day. They drank with the peasants, sitting on wheat sheaves, and during the night they lit bonfires and sobbed their hearts out.

In the grayish morn that followed, the Linesman railroad co-operative, at which the hunchback was manager and his gay companions members of the administration and shop committee, was closed for stocktaking. How bitter was the surprise of the auditors when they failed to find any flour, pepper, household soap, peasant troughs, cloth, or rice in the shop. The shelves, counters, drawers, and buckets were all empty. In the middle of the floor stood a pair of giant waders, size forty-two, with yellow cardboard soles, and behind the cash-desk window an automatic National cash register, the nickel-plated womanly bust of which was studded with multicolored buttons, glinted dully. In the meantime a letter was sent to Kozlevich's apartment from the public prosecutor's office summoning him to appear in court as a witness in the case of the Linesman co-operative.

The hunchback and his friends were not seen again, and the green car stood idle for three days.

The next lot of passengers, like the first, appeared under cover of night. They also began by an innocent trip into the country, but the thought of vodka in their case arose before the car had even completed half a mile. The citizens of Arbatov were evidently unable to imagine how the car could be utilized in a state of sobriety, and thought of Kozlevich's motor as a den of iniquity, in which you just had to let your hair down, make undignified noises, and generally live it up. It was only then that Kozlevich realized why the men passing his parking place each day winked at one another and smiled wickedly.

Things worked out quite differently from what Adam Kozlevich had expected. At night he raced past the neighboring copses with bright headlights, listening to the drunken revelry behind him, while in the daytime, befuddled by lack of sleep, he sat in witness boxes and gave evidence. For some reason the inhabitants of Arbatov lived it up on funds belonging to the state, to society, and to the co-operative system. And so, despite himself, Kozlevich was once more plunged into the abyss of the Penal Code, into the world of Section 3, which dealt so constructively with crimes involving the abuse of professional position.

The trials began and in each of them the chief witness for the prosecution was Adam Kozlevich. His truthful accounts of events always dumfounded the accused, and choking back their tears and sniveling, they used to admit everything. He ruined heaps of government establishments. His latest victim was the local branch of the regional film organization which had been making the historical film *Stenka Razin and the Princess*. The entire branch was put away for six years, and the film was sent to the police museum, which already contained the wading boots from the Linesman co-operative.

After this the market collapsed. People began to avoid the green motor car like the plague. The citizens made long detours around the station square where Kozlevich had put up a striped pole with the sign "Taxi Stand." For several months he hardly earned a cent and lived on what he had saved during the nightly jaunts.

It was then that he made sacrifices. On the car door he painted the white and, to his mind, very inviting inscription "Hey, come for a ride!" and lowered the price from five rubles an hour to three. But not even then would the citizens change their tactics. The driver slowly cruised around the town, approaching state-owned establishments and shouting through the windows:

"Isn't the air something? Let's go for a ride, shall we?"

The officials would poke their heads out of windows and call out, to the rattle of Underwood type-writers, "Go for a ride yourself, you thug!"

"Why am I a thug?" asked Kozlevich, almost blubbering.

"That's what you are," answered the clerks. "You'll get us convicted at the local assizes."

"You should try spending your own money!" shouted Kozlevich heatedly.

At these words the officials would exchange amused glances and shut the windows. To go driving on your own money seemed absolutely stupid to them.

The owner of "Hey, come for a ride!" quarreled with the entire town. He stopped greeting people and became neurotic and spiteful. Seeing a state-employed clerk in a long Caucasian-style shirt with puffed sleeves, he would drive up behind him and shout, laughing acidly, "Crook! I'll see that you get a show trial. Under Article 109."

The employee would shudder, indifferently adjust his belt, which was of the kind usually used to decorate cart-horse bridles, and, pretending the remarks were not meant for him, quicken his pace. But the spiteful Kozlevich would drive alongside him and tease his enemy by reading monotonously from a pocket edition of the Penal Code.

" 'The embezzlement of funds, valuables, or other property placed in a person's charge by virtue of official position is punished . . .' "

The Soviet employee would run off like a coward, his backside, flattened by long repose on an office stool, bouncing up and down as he went.

" '. . . by imprisonment,' " shouted Kozlevich after him, " 'for a period of up to three years.' "

But this only gave the driver moral satisfaction. His financial affairs were bad. The savings were running out. He had to make a decision.

It was in this inflamed state of mind that Adam Kozlevich was sitting one day in his car eying with revulsion the stupid striped pole with the sign "Taxi

Stand." He vaguely realized that his life of honesty had not been successful, that as a motorized messiah he was ahead of his time, and the citizens did not believe in him. Kozlevich was so engrossed in his sad thoughts that he didn't notice the two young men who had been admiring his car for some time.

"An unusual design," said one of them at length. "The dawn of the motor car. You see what can be done, Balaganov, with a simple Singer sewing machine. A few adjustments and you have a splendid farm sheafer."

"Go away," said Kozlevich sullenly.

"What do you mean, 'go away'? Why have you put the advertisement 'Hey, come for a ride' on that threshing machine? It's possible that my friend and I may want to make a business trip. It's possible we may want to 'Hey, come for a ride!' "

For the first time during his life in Arbatov a smile appeared on the face of the motorized martyr. He leapt out of the car and nimbly cranked the loudly rattling engine.

"Certainly—where to?"

"Nowhere, at the moment," Balaganov remarked. "We've no money. It can't be helped, comrade mechanic, we're poor."

"Get in anyway," cried Kozlevich in desperation. "I'll take you for nothing. Aren't you going to drink? Aren't you going to dance naked by moonlight? Hey, come for a ride!"

"Well, why don't we take advantage of his hospitality?" said Ostap, taking a seat next to the driver. "I see you're a man of good character. But why do you think we're likely to dance naked?"

"There are people like that here," replied the chauffeur, driving into the main street. "State-owned criminals."

He felt a desire to share his troubles with someone. It would have been better for him, of course, to recount his sufferings to his gentle wrinkled mother.

She would have been more sympathetic. But Madam Kozlevich had passed away from grief some time before when she learned that her son Adam was gaining a reputation as an inveterate thief. So the driver told his new passengers the whole story of the fall of the town of Arbatov, from whose ruins the green motor car was now struggling to free itself.

"So what am I to do?" Kozlevich ended dejectedly.

Ostap told him to slow down, gave his red-haired companion a knowing look, and said, "All your troubles result from the fact that you're a seeker of the truth. You're simply a lamb, an unsuccessful Baptist. It's sad to find such decadent feelings among motorists. You have a car, but you don't know where to go. We're far worse off. We haven't a car, but we do know where to go. Would you like to come with us?"

"Where to?" asked the driver.

"To Chernomorsk," said Ostap. "We have some small, intimate business there. There'll be work for you, too. In Chernomorsk they value antiques and enjoy riding in them. Let's go."

At first Adam Kozlevich could only smile, like a frustrated widow. But Bender laid it on thick. He unfolded magnificent vistas before the confused driver and immediately colored them sky-blue and pink.

"And you've nothing to lose by coming with us, except your spare chain. You won't starve on the way. I'll see to that. The gasoline's yours and the ideas ours."

Kozlevich stopped the car and, still resisting, said morosely, "There's not much gasoline."

"Enough for thirty miles?"

"Enough for fifty."

"In that case all's well. I've already told you I have no lack of ideas and notions. Exactly thirty-two miles from here there's a large can of airplane fuel waiting for you by the roadside. Do you like airplane fuel?"

THE CREW OF THE ANTELOPE

"Yes." Life suddenly seemed bright and easy. Adam felt an urge to drive to Chernomorsk immediately.

"And the can will be absolutely free," concluded Ostap. "I'll say more. They'll even ask you to accept the gasoline."

"What gasoline?" Balaganov whispered. "What are you driveling about?"

Ostap looked haughtily at the orange-colored freckles dotted all over his foster brother's face, and replied just as quietly, "People who don't read the papers ought to be morally slaughtered on the spot. I'm only sparing your life because I hope to re-educate you."

Ostap did not explain the connection between reading the papers and the can of gasoline by the roadside.

"I declare the grand Arbat-Chernomorsk motor race open," Ostap announced solemnly. "I appoint myself captain of the race. The driver of the car is—What's your name? Adam Kozlevich. Citizen Balaganov is nominated chief mechanic with the general duties of nursemaid. But the point is this, Kozlevich: you've got to paint out that sign 'Hey, come for a ride!' immediately. We don't want any identification marks."

Two hours later the car, with a freshly painted dark green blob on the side, rolled out of the garage and drove through the streets of Arbatov for the last time. Kozlevich's eyes shone with hope. Next to him sat Balaganov, who was zealously carrying out his new duties as chief mechanic and busily wiping the brass parts with a cloth. The captain of the race lay back in his light brown seat and surveyed his subordinates with satisfaction.

"Adam!" he shouted above the rattling of the engine. "What's the name of this jalopy?"

"Lauren Dietrich."

"What kind of name is that! A car must have its own name, like a warship. Your Lauren Dietrich possesses great speed and noble beauty of line. So I propose that it should be given the name Antelope-Gnu. Anyone object? Unanimously adopted."

The green Antelope, creaking in every joint, hurtled along the Boulevard of Young Talent and dashed into the market square. There its crew was treated to an extraordinary sight. A man with a white goose tucked under his arm was running away from the square in the direction of the highway. With his left hand he was keeping a hard straw hat on his head. A large crowd of shouting people were chasing after him. The runner kept looking back, and there was an expression of terror on his noble, actor's face.

"It's Panikovsky!" cried Balaganov.

"The second stage of stealing a goose," Ostap observed coldly. "The third stage begins when the culprit is caught. It's accompanied by a painful thrashing."

The approach of the third stage had obviously been sensed by Panikovsky, for he was running at full pelt. He was unable to drop the goose from fright, and this caused great irritation among his pursuers.

"Article 116," Kozlevich recited: " 'covert or overt theft of cattle and poultry from the land-cultivating and livestock-breeding population.' "

Balaganov roared with laughter. He was amused by the idea of the convention violator receiving his just desserts.

The car reached the highway, cutting its way through the noisy crowd.

"Save me!" cried Panikovsky as the Antelope drew level with him.

"God will look after you," said Balaganov, leaning out.

The car enveloped Panikovsky in clouds of raspberry-colored smoke.

"Take me!" howled Panikovsky with his last breath, keeping abreast of the car. "I'm a good man."

The voices of the pursuers merged into a concerted malevolent roar.

"Maybe we should take this jerk," said Ostap.

"Don't bother," Balaganov replied harshly. "Let him know next time not to violate the convention."

But Ostap had already made up his mind. "Drop the bird!" he shouted to Panikovsky, and, turning to the driver, added, "Slow down."

Panikovsky obeyed at once. The goose angrily rose from the ground, scratched itself, and walked back toward the town as though nothing had happened.

"Get in, damn you!" Ostap ordered. "But don't commit any more sins or I'll pull out your arms by the roots."

Kicking his legs, Panikovsky grabbed the side of the car, leaned over on his stomach like a swimmer getting into a boat, and fell onto the bottom of the car, his cuffs making a knocking sound as he went.

"Full speed ahead," Ostap ordered. "The hearing's continued."

Balaganov squeezed the bulb, and from the brass horn came the old-fashioned, gay staccato sound of a bugle call.

And the Antelope-Gnu hurtled into wild open country in the direction of the can of gasoline.

An Ordinary Attaché Case

THE HATLESS MAN wearing gray canvas pants, leather sandals without socks, in the style of monks, and a collarless white shirt emerged from the wicker gate of No. 16 with his head lowered. Finding himself on the bluish paving stones of the sidewalk, he stopped and said softly, "Today's Friday. I must go to the station again."

Having uttered these words, he quickly glanced around. He thought he saw a citizen behind him with the zinc-like jowls of a snooper. But Lower Tangent Street was completely deserted.

The June morning had just begun to take shape. The acacias trembled from time to time, letting cold, pewtery dew fall onto the flat stones. The street birds were abusing each other in a merry twitter. Down the street, beyond the roof tops, blazed a heavy, molten sea. Young dogs clambered onto the garbage cans, sadly looking about them and scraping with their paws. The hour of the yard attendants had passed; the hour of the milk girls had not yet begun.

It was the interval between 5 and 6 a.m. when the yard attendants, having brandished their prickly brooms to their heart's content, had retired to their dens, and it was as light, clean, and quiet in the town as in the state-run bank. At such moments you feel an urge to cry and to believe that buttermilk really is better for you and nicer than hard liquor; but then comes a distant rumble as the milk girls unload their cans from the suburban trains. They will soon be hurrying into the town to start their accustomed bickering with housewives on back-stair landings. Workers with baskets will appear for a moment and then vanish through factory gates. Smoke will pour from the factory stacks. And then, leaping up and down with fury, myriads of alarm clocks on bedside tables will sound their troika-like bells (those made by Pavel Bouret & Co. are quieter than those made by the state-owned precision-instrument plant), and the Soviet employees will start groaning, still half asleep, and falling out of their high cots. The hour of the milk girls is over, and now is the hour of the clerical staff.

But it was too early; the clerks were still asleep under the fig trees. The man in sandals walked right across town almost without meeting a soul. He walked under the acacias, which, incidentally, in Chernomorsk have civic duties to perform. Some were hung with mailboxes with the departmental arms (an envelope and streaks of lightning), while others had tin troughs nailed to them with drinking water for dogs.

The man in sandals arrived at Seaside Station just as the milk girls were coming out. Painfully colliding with their iron shoulders, he approached the baggage-room office and presented a receipt. The attendant scrutinized the receipt with that unnatural suspicion only to be found at railroad stations, and tossed the bearer his attaché case. In return, the bearer unbuttoned a leather purse, took out a ten-kopek piece with a sigh, and placed it on the baggage counter, which was made of six old elbow-polished rails.

Finding himself on the station square, the man in sandals put down the attaché case on the roadway, carefully inspected it from all sides, and even fingered its white clasp-type lock. It was an ordinary attaché case, made of wood and covered with fiber.

It is this kind of attaché case which is used by younger passengers to carry Sketch cotton socks, two clean shirts, a hair net, shorts, a pamphlet entitled *Tasks for Young Communists in the Countryside*, and three crushed hard-boiled eggs. Besides this, there should be a bundle of dirty wash in the corner, wrapped up in the newspaper *Economic Life*. Rather older passengers use this kind of attaché case to hold a two-piece suit with an extra pair of pants made from a check material, adjustable suspenders, bedroom slippers with tongues, a bottle of eau de Cologne, and a white marseilles blanket. It should be noted that in their case, too, there's something in the corner wrapped up in *Economic Life*. It's not dirty wash but a pallid boiled chicken.

Satisfied with his cursory inspection, the man in sandals picked up the case and got into a tropical-white streetcar, which took him to Eastern Station, at the other end of town. There his actions were the exact opposite of what he had done at Seaside Station. He deposited the attaché case and obtained a receipt from the attendant.

Having completed these curious operations, the owner of the attaché case left the station, just as the keener clerks were beginning to appear in the streets. He joined their disorderly ranks, whereupon his clothes lost all their originality. The man in sandals was a clerk, and the clerks in Chernomorsk always dressed according to an unwritten fashion—a nightshirt with the sleeves rolled up above the elbows, light, ready-made pants, and sneakers. Nobody wore a hat or peaked cap. Occasionally you came across a cloth cap, quite often a shock of black hair standing on end, and more often still a sun-tanned bald spot, which glimmered like a melon in a patch and made you want to write something on it in indelible ink.

The government office in which the man in sandals worked was called the Hercules and was located in a former hotel. The permanently grounded elevator served as the reception desk. A smiling woman's face was already peeping out of it. Carried forward by inertia, Koreiko stopped in front of an ancient doorman in a peaked cap with a gold zigzag on the band, and asked in a breezy voice:

"Well, old man, isn't it time for the crematorium?"

"It is, mister," the doorman answered, grinning broadly. "Time for our Soviet columbarium." He even threw up his arms. His kindly face expressed complete willingness to be consigned to the flames at any moment.

Plans were being made in Chernomorsk to build a crematorium with suitable space for the burial urns, i.e., a columbarium, and this innovation on the part of the Sub-Department for Cemeteries greatly amused the citizens for some reason or other. Perhaps they were tickled by the new words "crematorium" and "columbarium," or perhaps they were amused at the thought that people could be burnt like logs on a fire, but whatever it was, they kept teasing the old men and women on the streets with cries of "Where are you off to, old woman? Hurrying to the crematorium?" or "Let this old man go past, he's on his way to the crematorium." And, surprisingly enough, the notion of cremation greatly appealed to the old-timers, so that these jolly jests met with their full approval. What's more, the discussion of death, which up till then had been considered embarrassing and impolite, gained just as much popularity in Chernomorsk as stories about Jews and Caucasians, and was enjoyed by all.

Circumventing the naked girl in marble holding an electric light in the air at the foot of the stairs, and glaring angrily at a notice that said "The purge of Hercules is on. Down with the conspiracy of silence and back-scrubbing," the clerk went up to the sec-

ond floor. He worked in the accounts department. Although there was still fifteen minutes left before work
began, Sakharkov, Dreyfus, Tesoimenitsky, Muzy-
kant, Chevazhevskaya, Kukushkind, Borisokhlebsky,
and Lapidus, Jr., were all at their desks. They weren't
in the least afraid of the purge, or so they kept telling
each other, but for some reason had recently begun
arriving at work as early as possible. Taking advantage
of the few minutes of leisure left, they were chatting
noisily. Their voices hummed through a huge room
which at one time had been the hotel restaurant.
A reminder of this was the ceiling, with its carved
oak caissons, and the mural paintings, in which maenads, naiads, and dryads frollicked about with shocking leers.

"Have you heard the news, Koreiko?" asked Lapidus,
Jr. "Haven't you? You'll be amazed."

"What news? Good morning, comrades," said Koreiko. "Good morning, Anna Vasilevna!"

"You'll never guess," said Lapidus, Jr., delightedly.
"Berlaga the accountant is in the madhouse."

"What on earth do you mean? Berlaga? Why, he's
perfectly normal."

"He was until yesterday, but today he's abnormal,"
Borisokhlebsky joined in. "It's a fact. His brother-in-
law called me. Berlaga has a very serious mental ill-
ness—disturbance of the calcaneal nerve."

"It's a wonder we haven't all got a disturbance of
that nerve," said old Kukushkind acidly, surveying his
colleagues through nickel-rimmed spectacles.

"Stop moaning," said Chevazhevskaya. "You're always such a bore."

"A pity about Berlaga, anyway," said Dreyfus,
swinging around on his swivel stool toward them.

The others silently agreed with Dreyfus. Lapidus,
Jr., alone smirked mysteriously. The conversation
turned to the behavior of lunatics. They discussed maniacs and told some jokes about well-known madmen.

"You know, I had a mad uncle who imagined he

was Abraham, Isaac, and Jacob all at the same time!"
Sakharkov exclaimed. "You can imagine the noise he
made!"

"It's a wonder," said old Kukushkind in a tinny
voice, unhurriedly wiping his spectacles with the hem
of his jacket, "that we haven't all begun imagining
we're Abraham"—the old man snuffled—"Isaac . . ."

"And Jacob?" Sakharkov asked sarcastically.

"Yes, and Jacob," Kukushkind screeched unexpect-
edly. "And Jacob! We live in such uncertain times
. . . When I was working in the Sikomorsky and
Tsarevich Bank, we didn't have any purges."

At the word "purges" Lapidus, Jr., jerked up, took
Koreiko by the arm, and led him over to the huge window, which was inlaid with two stained-glass Gothic
knights. "You don't yet know the point about Berlaga," he whispered. "He's fit as a fiddle."

"You mean he's not in the madhouse?"

"No, he is." Lapidus gave a knowing smile. "That's
the point. He was simply scared of the purge and decided to sit out the troubled times. He's feigning madness. He's probably howling or roaring with laughter
at this moment. There's a crafty one for you! I even
envy him."

"What's wrong—are his parents suspect? Were they
private traders or a harmful element?"

"There's something wrong with his parents, and he
himself, between ourselves, used to own a chemist's
shop. Anyway, who could have seen the revolution
coming? People organized themselves as best they
could. One had a chemist's shop, another owned a
factory. I don't see anything bad about that, personally. Who could have known?"

"They should have known," Koreiko replied coldly.

"That's what I'm saying," Lapidus put in quickly.
"There's no place for such people in our office." And
giving Koreiko a wide-eyed look, he went back to his
stool.

The room was already full of clerks; pliable metal

rulers with a herring-like silvery shine, abacuses, thick registers ruled with pink and blue lines, and a heap of other major and minor office equipment had already been taken out of the drawers. Tesoimenitsky tore yesterday's date from the calendar and a new day began; one of the clerks had already sunk his young teeth into a long mutton-pâté sandwich.

Koreiko, too, sat down at his desk. Planting his sun-burned elbows on the top, he began making some entries in an account book.

Alexander Ivanovich Koreiko, one of the most insignificant clerks in the Hercules office, was at the last lap of his youth: he was thirty-eight years of age. On his red sealing-wax face there were yellow corn-colored eyebrows and white eyes. His military mustache was also like ripened grain in color. His face would have looked quite young had it not been for the coarse folds of skin traversing his cheeks and neck. At work Koreiko behaved like a supernumerary soldier: he didn't answer back and he was efficient, painstaking, and dull-witted.

"He's a shy one," the head of the department used to say about him. "He's too retiring and eager. They only have to announce a state loan and he's there with his monthly salary. The first to subscribe. And his salary's only forty-six rubles a month. I'd like to know how he can exist on that money."

Alexander Koreiko had one remarkable gift. He could multiply and divide sums of three and four figures in his head in an instant. But this didn't save his reputation as a dull-witted fellow.

"Listen, Alexander Ivanovich," a neighbor would say, "how much is eight hundred and thirty-six times four hundred and twenty-three?"

"Three hundred and fifty-three thousand, six hundred and twenty-eight," Koreiko answered after a moment's hesitation.

His neighbor didn't bother to check the multiplication, for he knew the dull-witted Koreiko never made a mistake.

"Anyone else in his shoes would have made a career for himself," the clerks used to say, "but he's such a drip. He'll spend the rest of his life earning his forty-six rubles."

Koreiko's colleagues, and the head of the department, too, and even Serna Mikhailovna, personal secretary to the head of the whole establishment, Comrade Poly-khayev—in short, all of them—would have been very surprised had they known that the attaché case that Alexander Koreiko, the meekest of clerks, had been carrying from one station to another only an hour before did not contain pants, a pallid chicken, or *Tasks for Young Communists in the Countryside,* but ten million rubles in foreign currency and Soviet bank notes.

In 1915, middle-class Alexander Koreiko was a twenty-three-year-old idler of the kind that is rightly called a "retired schoolboy." He had not graduated from high school and had no occupation. He loitered about the avenues and lived off his parents. He was exempted from military service by his uncle, clerk to the commandant, and listened to the hysterical cries of the newsboy without fear:

"Latest news! Our troops advance. Heavy casualties!"

At that period Koreiko envisaged his future as follows: he would be going along the street when he would suddenly see a cherry-colored squeaky billfold near a zinc star-spangled drain just by a wall. There would be lots of money in the billfold—two thousand, five hundred rubles . . . After that, everything would go swimmingly.

So often did he imagine himself finding the money that he even knew the exact place where it would be —on Poltava Victory Street, in an asphalt corner formed by a projecting house, in the starry drain. There it lay, his leather benefactor, half strewn with dried-up acacia flowers, just next to a squashed cigarette butt. He used to go to Poltava Victory Street every day, but to his great surprise there was no billfold. He poked about in the garbage with a riding crop and stared dully at the enamel plate hanging on the front door: "Tax Inspector Yu. M. Soloveisky." He would then go home, perplexed, throw himself onto the red velvet divan, and dream about wealth, deafened by his heartbeats and pulse. His pulse was feeble, evil, and impatient.

The Revolution of 1917 sent Koreiko running from his velvet divan. He suddenly realized he could become the happy heir to the property of many wealthy people. He saw that a huge quantity of ownerless gold, jewelry, fine furniture, pictures and carpets, fur coats, and dinner services was waiting to be picked up all over the country. There wasn't a moment to be lost.

But he was still too young and green at that time. He took over an apartment, the owner of which had sensibly fled to Constantinople on a French ship, and lived in it openly. For a whole week he lived the rich though alien life of the vanished merchant, washed down his ration of herring with wine found in the sideboard, sold various knickknacks at the market, and was greatly surprised when he was arrested.

He came out of jail five months later. He had not given up his idea of becoming a rich man, but now realized that the matter required secrecy, obscurity, and moderation. He had to don a protective skin, and it came to him in the form of high orange-colored boots, deep-seated blue breeches, and the long-tailed coat worn by food-supply officials.

At that troubled time, nothing man-made was up to the prèvious standards. The houses gave no protection from the cold, the food wasn't filling, the electricity was switched on only when there was a house-to-house search for deserters and bandits, the plumbing supplied water only to the first few floors, and the streetcar line wasn't working at all. The natural elements became more vicious and dangerous. The winters were severer than before, the winds were stronger, and the common cold, which used to send a man to bed for three days, now killed him in the same amount of time. Young men of no fixed occupation roamed the streets in gangs, singing their heads off about the devalued money.

I nip into a bar,
Though I haven't a cent,
Can you change me ten mill-ion . . .

With trepidation Alexander Koreiko watched the money he had gained by great guile turning into dust.

Typhus killed off people like flies. Koreiko sold medical supplies stolen from a warehouse. He earned five hundred million rubles from the typhus, but the rate of exchange reduced the money to five million in a month. On sugar he earned a hundred thousand. The rate of exchange reduced it to powder.

During this period one of his most successful ventures was the hijacking of a supply train on its way to the Volga. Koreiko was put in charge of the train. It was supposed to go from Poltava to Samara, but it never reached its destination or returned to Poltava. It disappeared into thin air. And so did Alexander Koreiko.

The Underworld

THE ORANGE BOOTS turned up again in Moscow at the end of 1922. Above the boots came a greenish overcoat lined with golden fox. The turned-up lamb's-wool collar, which looked like a down quilt on the inside, gave the owner's tough-looking face with its Sevastopol sideburns protection from the frost. On Alexander Koreiko's head was a magnificent curly fur hat.

It was the time in Moscow when people were already driving about in new motor cars with crystal headlights, and when the nouveau riche walked the streets in sealskin skullcaps and coats lined with striped fur. It was the fashion to wear Gothic boots with pointed toes and carry brief cases with straps and handles. The word "citizen" had begun to oust the usual word "comrade," and some of the younger set, having soon made up their minds about what made life worth living, had already begun dancing the one-step "Dixie" in restaurants, and even did a foxtrot called "The Sunflower." The city was filled with the cries of speed-crazy cab drivers, and in the large building housing the Foreign Ministry, Zhurkevich the tailor spent his days and nights making morning coats for Soviet diplomats going abroad.

Alexander Koreiko noted with surprise that his garb, which in the provinces was considered a symbol of masculinity and wealth, was looked on in Moscow as a survival of the past and revealed its owner in an unfavorable light.

Two months later a new state-run establishment called the Revenge Chemical Plant opened on Sretenka Boulevard. The plant had two rooms. In the first hung a portrait of the founder of socialism, Friedrich Engels, and under it, smiling innocently, sat Koreiko himself, dressed in a gray suit of English cloth shot with red thread. The orange boots and vulgar sideburns had gone. Alexander Koreiko's cheeks were smoothly shaven. The back room was the workshop. It contained two oak barrels with manometers and hygrometers, one on the floor and the other on a raised platform. The barrels were joined by a thin enema tube through which a liquid flowed, gurgling busily. As soon as all the liquid had passed from the top to the bottom barrel a boy in felt boots entered the workroom. Sighing in an unchildlike way, the boy scooped the liquid out of the bottom barrel with a bucket, dragged it up to the platform, and poured it into the second barrel. Having completed this complicated operation, the boy went off to the office to get warm, while the enema tube again began emitting a gurgling noise: the liquid was making a routine journey from the top container to the bottom one.

Not even Alexander Koreiko knew exactly what chemicals the Revenge produced. He had no time for chemicals. His working day was busy enough without them. He went from bank to bank, requesting loans to expand production. In the state-owned trusts he signed contracts for the delivery of chemical products and bought raw materials at a good price. The trusts also gave him loans. A lot of time was taken up by resale of the raw material to state-owned plants at ten times the price, and a lot of energy was absorbed by

currency deals on the black market at the foot of the
monument to the heroes of Plevna.

At the end of a year, the banks and trusts expressed
a desire to know how beneficial their financial aid
and material assistance to the Revenge plant had been
in the development of its business, and to know
whether or not the smart businessman required any
further help. A committee adorned with scholarly
beards arrived at the plant in three carriages. For some
time the chairman of the committee stared at the apa-
thetic face of Engels in the empty office, and tapped
the firewood counter with his stick to summon the
management and workers of the plant. The door of
the workroom eventually opened, and before the
committee stood a tearful boy carrying a bucket.

It became clear from their conversation with the
youthful representative of the plant that production
was in full swing and that the boss had not appeared
for a week. The committee did not spend long in the
workroom. The liquid which had gurgled so busily
through the enema tube resembled water in taste,
color, and chemical composition, and in fact was water. Having made this extraordinary discovery, the
chairman of the committee said "Hm" and looked at
the committee members, who also said "Hm." Then
the chairman looked at the boy with a ghastly
smile and asked:

"And how old are you, young man?"

"Just twelve," the boy replied.

And he burst into such sobs that the committee
members, pushing and jostling, fled into the street and,
getting into their carriages, left in complete confusion. As for the Revenge plant, all transactions with
it were entered in the bank and trust ledgers under
Profit and Loss, or, to be more exact, under *Loss.*

The same day that the committee had its enlighten-
ing conversation with the boy at the office of the Revenge, Alexander Koreiko emerged from a railroad

sleeping car in a small republic, fifteen hundred or so miles from Moscow.

He opened his hotel-room window and beheld a little town in an oasis with bamboo water pipes, a shabby clay fortress, and a town protected from the sands by plane trees; the air was filled with Oriental noises.

The next day he found out that the republic had begun to build an electric power station. He also found out that there was a permanent shortage of funds and that the construction work, on which the future of the republic depended, might have to be halted. And so the smart businessman decided to help the republic. Once again he donned his orange-colored boots and an Oriental skullcap, and, seizing a bulging brief case, made his way to the building administration.

He was not greeted very cordially, but he behaved in a dignified way, asked nothing for himself, and laid great stress on the fact that the idea of electrification of the backward areas was extremely near to his heart.

"You need money for your construction," he said. "I will get it." And he suggested the organization of a lucrative subsidiary enterprise at the site of the power station.

"What could be simpler? We'll sell picture postcards with views of the power station and that will bring in the funds needed for the construction. Just remember: you won't be paying out anything, only receiving."

The first requirement was capital. This had to be taken from the funds appropriated for the construction of the power station, as there was no other money in the republic.

"Don't worry," he consoled the builders: "from now on the money will come rolling in."

Alexander Koreiko slashed the air with his hand to show his determination. His words were convincing and the project was sound and profitable. Signing a contract in which he received a quarter of all profits from the postcard venture, he set to work.

First Koreiko rode out on horseback to inspect the ravine where the concrete parallelepipeds of the future power station were already in position, and in a glance sized up the panoramic nature of the porphyrian cliffs. He was followed by a truckload of photographers. They encircled the building site with jointed, spindly-legged tripods, disappeared under black shawls, and clicked away with their shutters. When everything had been taken, one of the photographers dropped his shawl and said aggressively, "It would have been better, of course, to build the station a little bit more to the left, against the monastery ruins. It would have made a much better picture."

They decided to build their own printing works to print the postcards. The money, as before, was taken from the building funds. This meant cutting down some of the work on the station. But they consoled themselves with the thought that the profits from the new enterprise would enable them to make up for lost time later on.

The printing works was set up in the ravine, opposite the station. Very soon, not far from the concrete parallelepipeds of the power station, there appeared those of the printing works. Barrels of cement, iron rods, bricks, and gravel were shifted bit by bit from one end of the ravine to the other. Then the shift across the ravine was made by the workers themselves: the pay was better at the new place. Six months later, salesmen in striped pants appeared at all railroad stops. They sold postcards showing the cliffs of the grape-growing republic, amid which the tremendous building operations were in progress. In summer parks, and in theaters, movie houses, aboard ship, and at holiday resorts, sweet little girls twirled the glass-plated drums of the charity draw. Every ticket won a prize and every prize was a postcard with a view of the electrified ravine.

Koreiko's words came true. Money poured in from all sides. But he held on to it tight. He took a quarter of it under the contract, pocketed as much again with the excuse that returns from the convoys of agents were not yet complete, and the remainder he spent on enlarging the charitable institution.

"You have to be efficient," he used to say quietly. "First let's get things organized, and then the real profits will flow in."

By this time the *Marion* excavator had been taken away from the power station and was digging a trench for the new printing works. Work at the power station was halted. The building site emptied. The only people left were the busy photographers with their black shawls.

Business flourished, and Alexander Koreiko, whose face still retained its honest Soviet smile, switched to printing picture postcards of film stars.

As happens, one evening a fully empowered committee arrived in a rickety old cab. Koreiko hadn't a moment to lose; he threw the cracking foundations of the power station and the impressive, light-filled building of the subsidiary plant a farewell glance, and made off.

"Hm," said the chairman, poking the cracks in the foundations with his stick. "Where's the power station?"

He looked at the other committee members, who also said "Hm."

There wasn't one.

Operations at the printing works, on the other hand, were in full swing. Purple lamps glowed and printing presses fussily flapped their wings. Three of them were turning out postcards of one color, while the fourth, a multicolored one, like a conjurer producing cards from his sleeve, was shooting out pictures of Douglas Fairbanks wearing a black mask over his

wide, samovar-like face, the delightful Lia de Putti,
and that splendid young fellow with the pop eyes
known as Monty Banks.

That memorable evening was followed by prolonged court proceedings, held in the open air in the
ravine, while Koreiko added another half-million to
his capital.

His feeble, evil pulse continued beating impatiently.
He felt that it was just the right moment, now that the
old economic system had rotted away and the new
one was just beginning to come in, to amass a great
fortune. But he knew well that an overt get-rich-
quick campaign in the Soviet Union was unthinkable.
With a superior smile he gazed at the private traders
nearing ruin beneath signs saying: "Sale of Wares
from Leybedev's Worsted Mills, Brocade and Accou-
terments for Churches and Clubs," or "Robinson and
Pyatnitsa Grocery Store."

Under pressure from the state-owned press, the
financial foundations of both Leybedev, Pyatnitsa, and
the owner of the "Sound of Tambourines" musical
pseudo-artel were cracking fast.

Koreiko realized that at this stage underground dealings in the strictest secrecy was the only thing possible. All the crises that rocked the young economic
system were to his advantage; everything on which
the state lost money brought him revenue. He broke
through into every market and carried off his hundred
thousand every time. He sold grain products, sugar,
textiles—in fact, everything. Yet he was alone, completely alone with his millions. He had small-time and
big-time crooks working for him all over the country,
but they had no idea whom they were employed by.
He acted through go-betweens. He was the only one
who knew the length of the chain by which the
money reached him.

Exactly at midday, Alexander Koreiko pushed back
the current account book and began his lunch. He
took a raw, peeled turnip out of a drawer and, staring

sedately in front of him, ate it. Then he swallowed a
cold soft-boiled egg. Cold soft-boiled eggs are not
very nice, and decent people never eat them. But
Alexander Koreiko only ate to live. He didn't have
lunch, but merely performed the physiological operation of letting his organism absorb the requisite amount
of fats, carbohydrates, and vitamins.

All the employees of the Hercules finished off their
lunch with tea, but Koreiko drank a cup of hot water
through a lump of sugar. Tea is a strong heart stimu-
lant, and Koreiko valued his health.

The owner of ten million rubles was like a boxer
who is carefully preparing to win his match. He con-
forms to a special diet, doesn't smoke or drink, tries to
avoid excitement, works out regularly, goes to bed
early—and all so that on the appointed day he can
emerge from the brightly lit ring as the victor. Alexander Koreiko wanted to be young and fresh on the day
when everything returned to the old way and he
would be able to come out of hiding and open his
ordinary little attaché case without apprehension.
The fact that the past would not return never entered
his mind. He was saving himself for capitalism.

And so that nobody should guess the secret of his
second and important life, he led a miserly existence,
trying to keep within the limits of the forty-six rubles
which he was paid for his miserable and dreary work
in the accounts department decorated with maenads,
dryads, and naiads.

The Antelope-Gnu

THE GREEN CRATE with the four tricksters bounded along the misty highway.

The car was experiencing the same sort of elemental forces as a bather swimming in a gale. It was suddenly jolted by bumps, sucked into pits, pitched from side to side, and enveloped in dust as red as the sunset.

"Listen, student," said Ostap, turning to the new passenger, who had now recovered from his recent shock and was sitting happily next to the captain. "How come you dared to violate the Sukharevka convention, that honorable treaty ratified by the League of Nations?"

Panikovsky pretended not to hear, and even turned aside.

"Not only that," Ostap continued, "you have itchy fingers as well. We have just witnessed an outrageous scene: you being chased by the citizens of Arbatov, from whom you pinched a goose."

"Miserable, useless people," Panikovsky muttered angrily.

"So that's it," said Ostap. "And what do you think you are? A medical officer or a gentleman? In that case, if as a true gentleman you ever decide to write notes on your cuffs, you'll have to do it in chalk."

"Why?" asked the new passenger irritably.

"Because they're absolutely black. It wouldn't be dirt by any chance, would it?"

"You're a miserable, useless person!" Panikovsky promptly replied.

"Are you saying that to me, your rescuer?" Ostap asked mildly. "Adam Kazimirovich, stop the car for a moment. Thank you. Alex, old boy, restore the status quo, would you please?"

Balaganov didn't know what a "status quo" was, but he guessed the meaning by the tone in which the words were uttered. Grinning wickedly, he seized Panikovsky under the arms, lifted him out of the car, and put him down on the road.

"Go back to Arbatov, student," said Ostap abruptly. "The owners of the goose are looking forward to seeing you. We don't need churls. We're churls ourselves. Let's go."

"I won't do it again," said Panikovsky imploringly. "I'm neurotic."

"Down on your knees!" Ostap ordered.

Panikovsky dropped to his knees faster than if his feet had been cut off.

"Good," said Ostap, "your posture satisfies me. You're accepted conditionally, until the first breach of discipline, and you are assigned the duties of general nursemaid."

The Antelope-Gnu took aboard the repentant churl and continued on its way, jolting like a horse.

Half an hour later the car turned into the wide Novy Zayats highway and, without slowing down, drove into a village. A crowd of people had gathered by a beamed house, the roof of which sprouted a knobby and crooked radio mast. A beardless man moved forward from the crowd, looking very determined. He held a sheet of paper in his hand.

"Comrades," he called out in an angry voice, "I de-

clare the ceremonial meeting open! Let me regard
your applause, comrades . . ."

He had evidently prepared the speech beforehand
and had begun reading from the sheet of paper, but,
observing that the car had not stopped, cut it short.

"Everyone to the motor highways!" he cried hurriedly as Ostap drew level with him. "Let us organize
the mass production of Soviet automobiles. The iron
steed will replace the peasant dray."

And, shouting above the crowd in the wake of the
fast disappearing vehicle, he came out with his final
slogan:

"A car is not a luxury but a means of transportation."

With the exception of Ostap, the crew of the Antelope was somewhat disconcerted by the ceremonial
meeting. They fidgeted about in the car like fledg-
lings in a nest, not knowing what to think.

Panikovsky, who never liked large gatherings of
honest people in any one place, squatted down on
the floor in alarm, so that all the villagers saw was the
crown of his dirty straw hat. Ostap, however, wasn't
the least perturbed. He took off his white peaked cap
and responded to the greetings with imperious nods
of his head to the left and the right.

"Improve your roads," he called in farewell. "*Merci*
for your reception."

And the car found itself once more on a white
highway cutting through the quiet expanses of countryside.

"They're not coming after us, are they?" Panikovsky asked anxiously. "What was the crowd for?
What happened?"

"They've simply never seen a car before," said Balaganov.

"The exchange of views is continued," Bender said.
"The driver has the floor. What do you think, Adam
Kazimirovich?"

The driver thought for a moment, hooted at a dog

which had stupidly run into the road, frightening it away, and expressed the assumption that the crowd had gathered to celebrate a church holiday. "Holidays of that sort," explained the driver of the Antelope, "are often held in the villages."

"Yes," said Bender. "Now I see quite clearly that I'm in the midst of a crowd of uncultured people— that is to say, bums without higher education. Listen, dear children of Lieutenant Schmidt, why don't you read the newspapers? You should. They quite often tell you sensible, good, and everlasting things."

Ostap took a copy of *Izvestiya* out of his pocket and in a loud voice read the crew of the Antelope a report on the Moscow-Kharkov-Moscow motor race.

"At the moment," he said smugly, "we're on the race route about ninety miles in front of the leading car. I presume you've guessed what I'm talking about?"

The lower orders of the Antelope said nothing. Panikovsky undid his jacket and scratched the bare chest under his dirty silk tie.

"So, you haven't understood? It's clear that not even reading the papers helps in some cases. Well, all right, I will explain in greater detail, though it's not usually my custom. The first thing is that the peasants mistook the Antelope for the leading car in the race. Second, we're not going to refuse that honor, and, what's more, we're going to ask all the appropriate institutions and officials for proper assistance, stressing that we are in fact the leading car. Third . . . Anyway, those two points are enough. It's quite clear that for a certain time we can keep ahead of the race picking up what goodies we can from such a highly cultured sporting event."

The smooth operator's speech had a tremendous effect. Kozlevich threw his commanding officer a look of devotion. Balaganov wiped his palms on his rust-colored curls and burst into laughter. Panikovsky shouted "Hooray," anticipating easy profit.

"Okay, that's enough emotion," said Ostap. "In view

of the approach of dusk, I declare the evening open. Halt!"

The machine stopped and tired Antelopeans got out. Among the ripening crops, grasshoppers clicked out their happy little tune. Long after the passengers had sat down in a circle by the roadside, the old Antelope continued simmering, its body creaking from time to time and its engine producing an occasional clank.

The inexperienced Panikovsky lit such a huge campfire that it looked as though the whole countryside was alight. With a snuffling sound the fire spread in all directions. The travelers battled with the column of flames, while Panikovsky, bending low, ran into a field and returned with a warm, curved cucumber. Ostap promptly took it from him with the advice:

"Don't make a cult out of eating."

Thereupon he ate the cucumber himself. They supped on salami sausage brought from home by the thrifty Kozlevich, and dropped off to sleep under the stars.

"Okay," said Ostap to Kozlevich at daybreak, "make all the necessary preparations. Your mechanical bathtub has never seen anything like the day we have ahead of us, nor ever will."

Balaganov grabbed a cylindrical pail marked "Arbatov Maternity Home" and went to the stream to get water.

Whistling to himself, Adam Kazimirovich lifted the hood of the car, dipped into the engine, and began rummaging among its brass-plated intestines.

Panikovsky leaned back against one of the wheels and, feeling depressed, stared unblinking at the cranberry-colored segment of the sun which had appeared above the horizon. Panikovsky had a wrinkled face with a whole heap of other age-induced trimmings— bags under the eyes, pulsating veins, and strawberry-red cheeks. It was not exactly the face of a man who had lived a long, orderly life, who had grown-up children, who drank health-giving Zheludin coffee in the mornings, and who wrote occasionally for a government-office newspaper under the pseudonym of "Antichrist."

"Shall I tell you how you'll die, Panikovsky?" Ostap asked suddenly.

The old man gave a shudder and turned around.

"This is how it'll happen. One day, when you return to your cold and empty room at the Hotel Marseilles—it will be somewhere in a district center where your profession will take you—you'll feel unwell. Your leg will go numb. Hungry and unshaven, you'll lie on your wooden cot, Panikovsky, and no one will come to see you. No one will be sorry for you. You haven't had any children so as to save money, and you've left all your wives. You'll suffer for a whole week. You'll be in terrible agony. You'll take a long time to die, and everyone will get fed up with you. You won't yet be quite dead when the bureaucrat in charge of the hotel will already be writing an application to the communal-services department for a free coffin— What's your name and patronymic?"

"Michael Samuelevich," answered the shocked Panikovsky.

". . . for a free coffin for citizen M. S. Panikovsky. But there's no need for tears. You'll last a year or two yet. Now, to business. We must attend to the propaganda side of our campaign."

Ostap took his Gladstone bag out of the car and put it down on the grass.

"My right hand," said the smooth operator, patting the thick sausage-colored side of the bag. "It has everything that an elegant citizen of my age and initiative may need."

Bender squatted down over the bag like a wandering Chinese magician over his magic sack, and began taking out different articles. First he pulled out a red arm band with the word "Official" embroidered on it in gold. Then came a militiaman's cap with the arms

of the City of Kiev, four decks of cards all with the
same design on the back, and a batch of documents
with round lilac-colored seals.

The crew of the Antelope gazed with awe at the
Gladstone bag. More and more new things kept appearing out of it.

"You're simpletons," Ostap continued. "You'll
never understand, of course, that an honest Soviet pil-
grim like me cannot do without a doctor's white coat."

Besides the white coat, the bag contained a stethoscope.

"I'm not a surgeon," Ostap observed. "I'm a
neurologist. A psychiatrist. I study the souls of my
patients. And for some reason I always seem to get
the stupid ones."

The next objects to be brought into the light were
the deaf-and-dumb alphabet, some charity postcards,
enamel coat badges, and a poster with a portrait of
Bender in baggy trousers and a turban.

The poster read:

Announcing the Arrival of the
HIGH PRIEST
(*Famous Bombay Brahmin Yoga*)
Son of Strongman and
Favorite of Rabindranath Tagore
Iokanaan Marusidze
(Honored Artist of the Union Republics)
Turns Based on the
Adventures of Sherlock Holmes:
Indian Fakir: Invisible Chicken:
Candles from Atlantis: Chamber of
Horrors. The Prophet
Samuel Answers the Audience's Questions.
Materialization of
Spirits and
Distribution of Elephants
TICKETS FROM 50 k. TO 2r.

The notice was followed by a filthy, much-handled turban. "That amusing little thing I use very rarely," said Ostap.

"You wouldn't believe it, but the people who mainly fall for the high-priest stunt are such progressives as railroad-club managers. It's easy but revolting work. It really sickens me to be Rabindranath Tagore's favorite. And the Prophet Samuel always gets asked the same questions, such as 'Why isn't there any lard on sale?' or 'Are you Jewish?'"

Ostap finally found what he was looking for. It was a lacquered tin box with honey paints in little porcelain dishes and two brushes.

"The car in the lead should be decorated with at least one slogan," said Ostap.

And on a long strip of yellowish calico, also taken from the bag, he laboriously painted in brown letters:

LET US USE THE MOTOR RACE TO
STRIKE AT THE LACK OF ROADS
AND SLOPPINESS

The banner was stretched above the car on two pieces of firewood. As soon as the car moved off, it billowed out and looked so splendid that there could no longer be any doubt that the motor race would deal a crushing blow at the lack of roads, sloppiness, and possibly bureaucracy into the bargain. The passengers in the Antelope swelled with pride. Balaganov pulled on a cloth cap that he constantly kept in his pocket. Panikovsky turned his cuffs to the left and let them down two more centimeters below his sleeves. Kozlevich was more concerned about the car than himself. Before they left he had given it a wash, and the sun now glittered on the Antelope's uneven sides. The captain squinted happily and made jokes about his fellow travelers.

"Village on the port side!" cried Balaganov, shading his eyes with his hand. "Shall we stop?"

"There are five first-class cars behind us," said

Ostap. "We aren't planning a rendezvous with them. It's our job to collect those goodies as soon as possible. I therefore order the next halt in the village of Udoyevo. There should be a can of gasoline waiting for us there, by the way. Step on it, Kazimirovich."

"Do we respond to the greetings?" asked Balaganov anxiously.

"Respond with bows and smiles. Kindly don't open your mouth or you'll go and put your foot in it."

The village gave the leading car a friendly welcome, but the hospitality there was of rather a strange kind. The village community had evidently been told that someone was arriving, but who it was and why they were coming they didn't know. So just in case, they brought out all the slogans and mottoes which had been made over the previous few years. Along the street stood school children with out-of-date placards of varying strength: "Greetings to the League of Time and to its founder, dear Comrade Kerzhentsev," "We're not afraid of the bourgeois ranting, let's answer Curzon's ultimatum," "Stop our children from dying by organizing nurseries."

In addition, there were a large number of posters written mainly in Church Slavonic script, all with the same greeting: "Welcome!"

Everything sped merrily past the travelers. This time they waved their hats confidently. Panikovsky was unable to restrain himself, and, despite the warning, jumped up and bawled out an incoherent, politically illiterate greeting. But no one could hear it, owing to the noise of the car and the shouts of the crowd.

"Hip, hip, hooray!" shouted Ostap.

Kozlevich opened the throttle and the car emitted a trail of blue smoke, which made the dogs chasing after the car sneeze violently.

"How's the gas?" asked Ostap. "Enough to get to Udoyevo? We only have fifteen miles to go. And there we'll take everything."

"It should be enough," said Kozlevich dubiously.

"Don't forget," said Ostap, surveying his troops sternly, "I don't permit looting. No laws are to be broken. I'm taking the parade."

Panikovsky and Balaganov looked embarrassed.

"The villagers will provide us with everything we need. You'll soon see that for yourselves. Keep some space handy for their hospitality."

The Antelope covered the fifteen miles in an hour and a half. During the final half-mile Kozlevich fussed about, pressing the accelerator and dejectedly shaking his head. But neither his efforts nor Balaganov's moral support had any effect. The brilliant finish envisaged by Adam Kazimirovich was thwarted by a lack of gasoline. The car stopped shamefully in the middle of the street a hundred yards or so short of a platform decorated with garlands of greenery in honor of the valiant motorists.

The gathered crowd noisily rushed forward to meet the Lauren Dietrich, newly emerged from the murk of past centuries. Thorns of glory pricked the noble foreheads of the travelers. They were roughly pulled from the car and thumped on the back so violently that they might have been drowning men who had to be resuscitated at all costs.

Kozlevich stayed by the car while the others were taken to the platform, where a three-hour meeting was scheduled to be held. A young man of the motoring type pushed his way through to Ostap and inquired:

"How are the other cars?"

"Left behind," said Ostap indifferently. "Punctures, breakdowns, and the enthusiasm of the country folk have all delayed them."

"Are you in the captain's car?" the motoring enthusiast persisted. "Is Kleptunov with you?"

"I dropped Kleptunov from the race," said Ostap peevishly.

"Is Professor Pechnikov in the Packard?"

"That's right."

"And the writer Vera Cruz?" asked the semi-motorist. "I'd give anything to see her! And Comrade Nezhinsky too. Is he with you?"

"I'm rather tired from the race," said Ostap.

"And you're in the Studebaker?"

"You can call my car a Studebaker if you like," said Ostap viciously, "but so far it has been called a Lauren Dietrich. Are you satisfied?"

But the motoring enthusiast wasn't satisfied. "Just a moment," he exclaimed with youthful persistence, "there aren't any Lauren Dietrichs in the race! I read in the paper there were two Packards, two Fiats, and a Studebaker."

"To hell with you and your Studebaker!" Ostap bellowed. "Who is this Studebaker, anyway? Is he a relative of yours? Is he your dad? Why pick on him? I'm telling you in plain Russian that the Studebaker was replaced by a Lauren Dietrich at the last moment and you keep on about a Studebaker."

For some time after the youth had been pushed aside by the officials, Ostap continued waving his arms and grumbling:

"Experts indeed. Those experts need shooting. I'll give him a Studebaker!"

In his speech of welcome the chairman of the reception committee linked together such an interminable chain of subordinate clauses that he took half an hour to disentangle himself. The period was one of great uneasiness for the captain. The platform was high enough for him to follow the suspicious movements of Panikovsky and Balaganov, who were darting in and out of the crowd in far too brisk a fashion. Bender glared hard at them and finally managed to signal to them that they were to stay in one place.

"I'm very glad, comrades," said Ostap in his reply, "to be able to disturb the patriarchal tranquillity of the village of Udoyevo with my motor horn. A car, comrades, is not a luxury but a means of transportation. The iron steed is replacing the peasant dray. Let us organize the mass production of Soviet automobiles. Let us use the motor race to deal a blow at roadlessness and sloppiness. That's all I want to say, comrades. After a snack we'll continue on our long journey."

While the crowd stood motionless around the platform, listening attentively to the captain's words, Kozlevich launched into great activity. He filled the tank with gasoline, which, as Bender had said, proved to be the highest grade, casually helped himself to another four cans as a reserve, changed the tires and tubes on all four wheels, and appropriated the pump and the jack to go with it. By so doing, he completely exhausted both the base store and the operational supplies of the Udoyevo branch of the motor-highways organization.

They now had the necessary supplies for the journey to Chernomorsk. There was admittedly no money, but that didn't worry the captain. The meal that the travelers had in Udoyevo was splendid.

"There's no need to think about pocket money," said Ostap. "It's lying all over the road and we'll pick it up when we require it."

Between the village of Udoyevo, founded in A.D. 794, and Chernomorsk, founded in A.D. 1794, lay a thousand years of time and two thousand miles of dirt roads and highways. In the course of this thousand years many different figures had made their way along the route from the village to the Black Sea. Traveling merchants with wares from Byzantine firms once used it. They would be met, from the stirring forest, by Solovei the Highwayman, a coarse fellow in an Astrakhan cap. He took possession of their wares and dispatched the merchants. Conquerors and their bodyguards roamed it, peasants traversed it, and wanderers hobbled along it, singing as they went.

The life of the country changed with every century. Apparel changed, weapons were improved, and the potato riots were suppressed. People began shaving their heads. The first balloon was launched.

The iron twins—the locomotive and the steamship—
were invented. Motor cars began sounding their horns.

But the road remained exactly as it was during the
time of Solovei the Highwayman.

Humped, covered with volcanic mud or coated with
dust as poisonous as flea powder, the road wound its
way past villages, towns, factories, and farms; wound
its way like a thousand-mile death trap. By its sides,
in the yellowing, defiled grass, lay the skeletons of
carts and tortured, expiring motor cars.

Perhaps Russian émigrés, driven to distraction by
selling newspapers on the asphalt fields of Paris, recall
the country roads of Russia with all the charming detail of their native landscape: the crescent moon lying in a puddle, the crickets praying loudly, and the
clanking of empty buckets tied to peasant carts.

But nowadays the light of the moon has another
function in Russia. It will soon shine just as well on
tarred roads. Motor-car horns and klaxons will replace
the symphonic music of the peasant bucket. And you
will be able to hear the crickets in special sanctuaries.
Stands will be erected, and after an introduction by a
gray-haired cricketologist, citizens will be able to enjoy the singing of their favorite insects to their heart's
content.

The Sweet Burden of Glory

THE CAPTAIN, driver, chief engineer, and general nursemaid were in splendid shape.

The morning was cool. A pearly sky entangled the pale sun. A feathered rabble chirped in the grass. Moor hens slowly crossed the road right in front of the wheels of the car.

Ostap and his companions had been traveling ahead of the race for twenty-four hours. They were met everywhere with music and speeches. Children played drums for them. Grownups plied them with spare parts procured in advance, and in one settlement brought them bread and salt on a carved oak dish in a cloth embroidered with crosses. The loaf of bread lay on the floor of the car between Panikovsky's feet. He kept picking little bits off, until he finally made a huge mouse hole in it. The fastidious Ostap immediately threw the bread out into the road.

They passed the night in a hamlet waited on by the more politically active villagers. They took away with them a large jug of boiled milk and the sweet memory of the fragrant hay on which they had slept.

"Milk and hay," Ostap remarked as the Antelope left the hamlet at dawn. "What could be better! You always think to yourself, 'There's time for that later. There'll be lots of milk and hay in my life yet.' But actually there won't be any more. So remember that! This has been the best night of our lives, my poor friends. And you haven't even noticed!"

Bender's companions looked at him with admiration. They were enchanted by the easy life that had opened up before them.

"It's good to be alive," said Balaganov. "We're on the road, we've eaten. Maybe there's good fortune in store for us."

"Do you really believe that?" asked Ostap. "Good fortune waiting for us on the roadside? Perhaps she's flapping her wings with impatience as well? 'Where is Admiral Balaganov?' she's asking. 'Why isn't he here yet?' You're a nut, Balaganov. Good fortune doesn't wait for anyone. She roams the country in long white clothes, crooning the children's song, 'Ah, America, there's a country where they enjoy themselves and drink without a meal!' You have to chase after that naïve child. You have to appeal to her, you have to woo her. You won't have an affair with her, Balaganov. You're a bum. Just look at yourself. A man dressed like you will never find good fortune. What's more, the whole crew of the Antelope is disgracefully attired. It's a wonder they still mistake us for competitors in the motor race at all."

Ostap surveyed his companions with disdain, and then continued.

"Panikovsky's hat really embarrasses me. Not what I'd call a picture of elegance. The precious tooth, the ribbons on his long underwear, the hairy chest under the tie . . . You should dress more simply, Panikovsky! You're supposed to be a respectable old man. You need a black coat and beaverskin hat. Balaganov should have a check shirt and leather leggings. Then he'll look like a student keen on gymnastics. At the moment he looks like a merchant seaman who's been drummed out for drunkenness. I won't mention our distinguished driver. The hard times inflicted on him by fate have prevented him from dressing in accordance with his calling. Surely you can see how leather overalls and a black leather cap would go with his inspired, slightly oil-be-smirched face? Yes, children, you need new outfits."

"We haven't any money," said Kozlevich, looking around.

"The driver's right," said Ostap amiably. "We certainly haven't. We have none of those little round metal discs which I love so much."

The Antelope slid down from a hillock. The fields continued to spin slowly by on both sides of the car. A large red owl was sitting by the roadside with its head on one side, its yellow unseeing eyes bulging stupidly. Alarmed by the squeaking of the Antelope, the bird spread its wings, soared up over the car, and flew off on its boring, owlish business. Nothing else eventful occurred on the road.

"Look!" cried Balaganov suddenly. "A car!"

Ostap ordered them to take down the banner just in case. As Panikovsky carried out the command, the Antelope approached the other car.

The gray Cadillac was parked at the side of the road, leaning slightly to one side. The central-Russian countryside reflected in its thick polished glass looked cleaner and pleasanter than it actually was. The chauffeur was on his knees, removing the cap from one of the front wheels. Three figures in motoring coats stood expectantly beside him.

"Had a breakdown?" asked Ostap, politely raising his cap.

The chauffeur raised a strained face, and then reimmersed himself in his work without answering.

The Antelopeans clambered out of their green milk wagon. Kozlevich walked around the beautiful car several times, sighing enviously, then squatted down beside the chauffeur and engaged him in a technical conversation. Panikovsky and Balaganov stared with childlike curiosity at the passengers, two of whom had a haughty, foreign appearance. The third, to judge by the overpowering smell of galoshes from his rubber raincoat, was a fellow countryman.

"Had a breakdown?" Ostap repeated, lightly tapping the fellow countryman's rubber shoulder and at the same time throwing the foreigners a pensive look.

The fellow countryman grumpily began an account of a burst tire, but his grumbling flew right past Ostap's ears. Here on the highway, right in the middle of European Russia, seventy-five miles from the nearest big town, were two plump foreign chickens, joy riding in their car. The fact excited the smooth operator.

"Tell me," he said, interrupting, "these two aren't from Rio de Janeiro, are they?"

"No," answered the fellow countryman, "they're from Chicago, and I'm an interpreter from Intourist."

"What are they doing here, at the crossroads, out in wild, ancient countryside, miles from Moscow, miles from the ballet *The Red Poppy*, miles from antique shops and Repin's famous painting *Ivan the Terrible Murders His Son*? I don't get it. Why have you brought them here?"

"They're a damn nuisance," said the interpreter bitterly. "For three days we've been chasing around the villages like crazy. I've never seen people like these." He waved his hand toward his ruddy-faced fellow travelers. "Most tourists run around Moscow buying peasant-made spoons or souvenirs, but these two are the end. They decided to drive around the countryside."

"That's praiseworthy," said Ostap. "The wide masses of millionaires are learning about everyday life in the new, Soviet countryside."

The citizens of Chicago haughtily watched the car being repaired. They wore silvery hats, stiff collars, and dull red shoes.

The interpreter looked at Ostap in annoyance and

exclaimed, "I like that! The new countryside! What they're after is local hooch, not countryside!"

At the word "hooch," which the interpreter strongly emphasized, the gentlemen looked around hopefully and went over to the two men.

"You see!" said the interpreter. "They can't even hear the word without getting excited."

"Yes, there's something fishy here, or else perverted taste," said Ostap. "I don't see how anyone can like hooch when there's such a huge choice of fine liquor in our country."

"It's all much simpler than it sounds," said the interpreter. "They're looking for a recipe for good hooch."

"Ah, of course," cried Ostap. "They have prohibition in their country. It's quite clear. Have you found a recipe? You haven't? I see. You should have come in three more cars. You are obviously mistaken for the authorities. You won't get a recipe, I can assure you."

The interpreter continued complaining about the foreigners. "You wouldn't believe it. They keep pestering me, 'Tell us, come on, tell us the secret of the hooch.' But I'm not a hooch brewer, I'm a member of the Union of Educational Workers. I have an elderly mother in Moscow."

"And you very much want to get back to Mother in Moscow?"

The interpreter sighed sadly.

"In that case the hearing is continued," Bender declared. "How much will your bosses pay for a recipe? A hundred and fifty rubles?"

"Two hundred," whispered the interpreter. "Have you really got one?"

"I will dictate it to you—that is to say, as soon as I get the money. Which one do you want, hooch from potatoes, wheat, apricots, barley, mulberry, or buckwheat? You can even make hooch from an ordinary chair. Some people like chair hooch. Or else you can have simple almond or plum hooch. In short, any one of a hundred and fifty varieties for which I have the recipes."

Ostap was introduced to the Americans. The air was filled for some time with politely raised hats. Then they got down to business.

The Americans chose wheat hooch, which appealed to them on account of the simplicity of preparation. The recipe was laboriously copied down in notebooks. As a bonus, Ostap informed the American pilgrims how to design a portable still that could easily be hidden in the side of a desk. The pilgrims assured Ostap that with American engineering it would not be at all difficult to manufacture the still. In turn, Ostap assured the Americans that a still of his design turned out a bucket a day of delicious hooch.

"Wow!" said the Americans.

They had heard about Russian hooch from a respectable family in Chicago, where it was given the very best references. The head of the family had at one time been with the American Occupation Force in Archangel and had drunk it there, since which time he had been unable to forget the delightful sensation he had experienced.

In the mouths of the mellowed tourists the coarse word "hooch" sounded tender and alluring.

The Americans willingly parted with two hundred rubles and shook Bender's hand for some time. Panikovsky and Balaganov were also lucky enough to shake hands with the citizens from that transatlantic country suffering from prohibition. In his joy the interpreter planted a kiss on Ostap's firm cheek and invited him to visit his house, adding that his elderly mother would be very pleased to see him. But for some reason he didn't leave the address.

The friendly travelers got into their respective cars. Kozlevich sounded the horn in farewell, and the cars shot off in opposite directions to its merry tune.

"You see," said Ostap as the American car disappeared in a cloud of dust, "it all happened exactly as

I told you. We were driving along. The money was lying in the road. I picked it up. Look, it isn't even dusty."

And he crackled the bunch of currency notes.

"Actually, there's nothing to boast about. The trick was a very simple one. But neatness and honesty are what counts. Two hundred rubles in five minutes. And besides not breaking any laws, I've even done some good. I've supplied the crew of the Antelope with funds. I've returned the interpreting son to his mother, and, last but not least, I've quenched the spiritual thirst of a country with which, despite everything, we have trade relations."

It was nearly time for lunch. Ostap pored over a map of the course torn out of a motoring magazine, and announced the approach of the town of Luchansk.

"The town's very small," said Ostap. "That's bad. The smaller the town, the longer the speeches of greeting. So we'll ask our kind hosts in the town for lunch as the first item on the agenda, and speeches as the second. Panikovsky, you're forgetting your duties. Restore the banner to its previous place."

Kozlevich, now thoroughly versed in triumphant finishes, brought the car to a spectacular halt just in front of the platform. Bender confined his address to a brief greeting. It was agreed to postpone the meeting for two hours. Fortified by a free lunch, the motorists made their way in excellent spirits to a ready-to-wear clothes shop. They were surrounded by a crowd of curious people. The Antelopeans bore the sweet burden of glory in a dignified manner. They walked down the middle of the street, holding hands and swaying like sailors in a foreign port. The red-haired Balaganov, who looked just like a young bosun, struck up a sea chantey.

The "Men's, Women's, and Children's Clothes" shop was located underneath an enormous sign covering the front of an entire two-story house. On the sign were lots of painted figures: yellow-faced men with thin mustaches in coats showing the polecat lining, ladies with muffs, short-legged children in sailor suits, Young Communist girls in red kerchiefs, and gloomy executives up to their hips in felt boots.

All this splendor was somewhat marred by a small piece of paper stuck to the entrance to the shop:

> No Breeches

"Fooh, how vulgar!" said Ostap, going in. "You can see we're in the provinces all right. They should have written 'No pants' decently and elegantly, as they would in Moscow. Citizens would then go home satisfied."

The motorists did not spend long in the shop. They found Balaganov a cowboy shirt with wide canary-colored checks and a Stetson with holes in it. Kozlevich had to be content with the promised leather cap and a short black coat, which glistened like pressed caviar. They took much longer over Panikovsky. The long clergyman's coat and soft hat which, according to Bender, should have ennobled the appearance of the violator of the convention were out from the very first. The shop could only offer a fireman's uniform, consisting of a tunic with miniature gold hosepipes on the lapel, hairy wool-mixture pants, and a peaked cap with blue braid. Panikovsky pranced about in front of the wavy mirror.

"I can't understand why you don't like the fireman's uniform," said Ostap. "It's better than looking like a king in exile, which you do now. Turn around, sonny. Splendid! I tell you straight, it suits you better than the frock coat and hat I planned for you."

They went out into the street in their new outfits.

"I need a tuxedo," said Ostap. "There aren't any here. I'll wait for better times."

Ostap opened the meeting in a good mood, not sus-pecting that there was trouble brewing for the passengers of the Antelope. He made jokes, recounted some funny motoring stories, and told Jewish jokes, which greatly amused the public. The end of his speech was devoted to an analysis of the long-overdue problem of transportation.

"A car," he proclaimed in a trumpetlike voice, "is not a luxury but . . ."

At that moment he saw the chairman of the reception committee take a telegram from a boy who had come running up.

Articulating the words "Not a luxury but a means of transportation," Ostap leaned across and glanced at the telegram over the chairman's shoulder. What he read shocked him. He thought he still had another day ahead of him. His mind instantly recalled a number of villages and towns where the Antelope had utilized other people's money and supplies.

While the chairman was wiggling his mustache, trying to fathom the contents of the dispatch, Ostap quickly leaped down from the platform in mid-sentence and pushed his way through the crowd. The Antelope shone green at the crossroads. Fortunately, the crew were already in their seats, waiting with bored expressions for Ostap to order them to load up the car with the offerings of the city, a procedure which usually took place after the meetings.

The chairman finally got the point of the telegram. He raised his eyes and beheld the captain making off. "They're frauds!" he shouted in martyred tones. He had worked the whole night on the speech of greeting, and his author's pride was now wounded. "Catch them, boys!"

The chairman's shout reached the ears of the Antelopeans. They sprang into action. Kozlevich cranked the engine and took a flying leap into his seat. The car lurched forward without waiting for Ostap. In their haste the Antelopeans completely forgot they were leaving their captain in danger.

"Stop!" cried Ostap, taking gigantic bounds. "I'll fire the lot of you when I catch up with you."

"Stop!" the chairman bellowed.

"Stop, you fool!" cried Balaganov to Kozlevich. "Can't you see you've left the boss behind?"

Adam Kazimirovich applied the brake and the Antelope screeched to a halt. The commanding officer somersaulted into the car with a desperate cry of "full speed ahead!" Despite his adaptable nature and sang-froid, he hated physical retribution. The panic-stricken Kozlevich threw the gear into third, the car gave a lurch, the door flew open, and Balaganov toppled out. It all took place in a split second. By the time Kozlevich braked for a second time, the shadow of the oncoming crowd had reached Balaganov. Large, muscular hands were already reaching out to seize him, when the Antelope backed up and the captain's iron fist grabbed hold of his cowboy shirt.

"Full speed!" Ostap roared.

It was at this point that the inhabitants of Luchansk realized for the first time the advantages of mechanical transport over horse traction. The car, creaking in every joint, shot away, carrying off the four lawbreakers from their just desserts.

For the first half-mile the tricksters breathed heavily. Balaganov, who valued his good looks, took out a pocket mirror and admired the strawberry scratches on his face caused by his fall. Panikovsky trembled inside his fireman's uniform. He was dreading the captain's revenge. And it soon came.

"Was it you who told them to drive off before I managed to get in?" asked Ostap menacingly.

"Honestly, I—" Panikovsky began.

"Come on, don't deny it! It was your doing. So you're a coward as well, are you? I've teamed up with a thief and a coward, have I? All right, I'm demoting you. So far I've thought of you as the chief of the fire brigade, but from now on you're just an ordinary fireman."

Ostap ceremonially tore the gold hosepipes from Panikovsky's lapel. After that he informed his companions of the contents of the telegram.

"Things are bad. The telegram told them to hold the green car in front of the race. We'll have to turn off the course at some point. We've had enough victories, palm leaves, and free lunches. The novelty has worn off. The only place we can turn off is the Gryazhskoye highway. That's another three hours from here. I'm sure there's a warm welcome being prepared at all the other places in the vicinity. That damned telegraph system has poles sticking up everywhere."

The captain was not wrong.

They never found out the name of the town which lay a little further along the road. The entrance to the town was barred by a hefty beam. The Antelope turned around and began nosing about like a blind puppy, looking for a side road. But there wasn't one.

"Back!" said Ostap, who had become very serious.

The tricksters suddenly heard the very distant mosquito-like hum of engines. The cars in the real race were evidently nearby. They couldn't go back, so they hurtled forward again.

Kozlevich frowned and drove the car headlong at the beam. The citizens standing around it jumped back in alarm, fearing an accident, but Kozlevich suddenly slowed down and leisurely knocked the obstacle aside. As the Antelope passed through the town, disgruntled passers-by swore at the motorists, but Ostap didn't bother to answer.

The Antelope reached the Gryazhskoye highway to the ever louder roar of the still invisible motor cars. Hardly had they turned off the highway and hidden the car behind a hillock in the approaching darkness, when, with a machine-gun-like rattle, the leading car came into view. The tricksters hid in the grass by the roadside and, with a lack of their usual aplomb, watched the passing column in silence.

Strips of dazzling light striped the road. The cars squeaked softly as they passed the dejected Antelopeans. Dust flew up from under the wheels. The klaxons wailed continually. The wind swept along from all sides. In a moment everything vanished and all that was left was the ruby tail light of the last car, jerking and dancing in the darkness.

True life had passed by, trumpeting with joy and flapping its glistening lacquered wings.

The adventurers were left with a trail of gasoline. They sat for some time in the grass, sneezing and coughing.

"Yes," said Ostap, "now I see that a car is not a luxury but a means of transportation. Aren't you envious, Balaganov? I am."

A Crisis in the Arts

BETWEEN 3 AND 4 A.M. the harassed Antelope came to a halt above a precipice. An unknown town lay below them on a plate. It was neatly sliced like a pastry. Multicolored morning mist swirled above it. The dismounted Antelopeans thought they could hear a crackling and very faint whistling. It was probably the citizens snoring. Saw-toothed forest land grew right up to the town. The road looped down along the cliff.

"A heavenly valley," said Ostap. "Such towns are nice to loot early in the morning, before the sun gets too hot. It's less tiring."

"It's early morning now," Panikovsky returned, gazing fawningly into his captain's eyes.

"Quiet, commandos!" cried Ostap. "What a one-track mind the man has. He doesn't understand jokes."

"What shall we do with the Antelope?" asked Kozlevich.

"Yes," said Ostap, "we wouldn't get very far into the town in that green bathtub. They'd arrest us. We'll have to imitate the more advanced countries. In Rio de Janeiro, for instance, they paint stolen cars a different color. It's done for strictly humane motives—so that the former owner isn't upset when he sees a stranger driving around in his car. Since the Antelope has gained a rather unfortunate reputation, we'll have to rechristen it."

They decided to walk to the town on foot and buy some paints as soon as they had found a suitable hiding place for the car outside the town limits.

Ostap quickly made his way down the road along the cliff and soon came to a sloping beamed cottage, the little windows of which reflected a riverlike blue. Behind the cottage was an outhouse which looked suitable for the Antelope.

As the smooth operator was wondering what excuse would be best to get into the cottage and make friends with its inmates, the door opened and a dignified old man in soldier's underwear with black tin buttons ran out onto the porch. His pale, paraffin-wax cheeks were adorned with respectable gray side whiskers. This kind of physiognomy was an everyday sight at the end of the last century. At that time most men grew these official, loyalist facial adornments, but now that there was no blue uniform to go with them, no Order of the Realm on a silk ribbon or tabs with the gold stars of a privy councilor, the face seemed unnatural.

"Oh Lord," mumbled the cottage dweller, stretching out his hands toward the rising sun. "Oh Lord, those dreams! Those same dreams!"

Having voiced this complaint, the old man burst into tears and, dragging his feet, went running along the path around his cottage. The common, or garden, cockerel, which was just about to crow for the third time and had emerged into the center of the yard for this very purpose, took to its heels. Having taken several steps in haste and even dropped a feather, it quickly recovered, clambered onto a wicker fence, and from that secure position informed the world that morning had come. But its voice revealed the agitation it felt at the undignified behavior of the cottage owner.

". . . dreaming about them, damn them," came the old man's voice.

Bender stared at the old man with side whiskers in surprise. Such whiskers are only seen nowadays on the ministerial faces of conservatory doormen.

In the meantime the unusual gentleman had completed his round and was back again at the porch. He slowed his pace and, with the words "I'll go and try again," disappeared through the door.

"I like old men," whispered Ostap. "You never get bored with them. I shall have to await the results of the mysterious try."

He didn't have to wait long. There soon came a plaintive wailing from the cottage, and, backside first, like Boris Godunov in the last act of Mussorgsky's opera, the old man staggered out onto the porch.

"*Pax, pax!*" he cried with Chaliapinesque tones in his voice. "That dream again! Oh! Oh!"

He turned around and, tripping over his own feet, made straight for Ostap. Deciding the time to act had come, the smooth operator came out from behind the tree and seized the old man in his powerful arms.

"What? Who are you? What's all this?" cried the restless old man.

Ostap slowly released his grip, seized the old man by the hand, and shook it cordially. "I sympathize," he exclaimed.

"Really?" asked the owner of the cottage, pressing against Ostap's shoulder.

"Of course I do," Ostap replied. "I often have dreams too."

"And what do you dream about?"

"Different things."

"What, for instance?" the old man persisted.

"Well, different things. A mixture. What they call in the newspapers 'Bits and Pieces' or 'World Report.' The day before yesterday, for example, I dreamt about the Mikado's funeral, and yesterday about the anniversary of the Sushchevka fire brigade."

"Heavens!" the old man declared. "How lucky you are! How lucky! Tell me, have you dreamt about a governor general or a minister?"

Bender was not going to be difficult. "Yes indeed," he said gaily, "of course I have. A governor general. Last Friday. I dreamt about him the whole night. And I remember there was a police chief in baggy flowered pants beside him."

"Ah, how splendid!" said the old man. "And what about the arrival of His Imperial Majesty in Kostroma?"

"In Kostroma? Yes, as a matter of fact I dreamt of that, too. Wait a moment, when was it? Yes, February the third this year. The Emperor, and there was a Count Fredericks with him—you know the one, the Court Chamberlain."

"My lord," cried the old man in delight. "Why are we standing here? Please come inside. Excuse me, you're not a Socialist, are you? You're not a Communist?"

"Good heavens," said Ostap amiably. "How could I be a Communist? I'm a non-party monarchist. Servant to the Czar and father to the soldiery."

"Won't you have some tea?" mumbled the old man, pushing Bender toward the door.

The cottage consisted of one room and an entrance hall. On the walls were portraits of gentlemen in frock coats. Judging by their badges of rank, they had all served at some time in the Ministry of Education. The bed was untidy and showed that the owner spent his most troubled hours in it.

"How long have you been living as a recluse?" asked Ostap.

"Since spring," replied the old man. "My name is Khvorobyov. I thought I'd begin a new life here, but you see what happened. You see . . ."

Theodor Khvorobyov was a monarchist and hated

the Soviet regime. He found it repulsive. A one-time senior school inspector, he had later been forced to work as the head of the methodological-pedagogical sector of the local Proletarian Culture Organization, known by the abbreviation "Proletcult." This disgusted him.

To the very end of his work he never found out what the term "Proletcult" meant, and despised it all the more on that account. A shudder of revulsion ran through him at the very sight of the members of the local committee, his colleagues, and the visitors to the methodological-pedagogical sector. He loathed the word "sector." Oh, that sector! Never had Theodor Khvorobyov, who valued everything refined and elegant, even geometry, imagined that the word "sector"—this beautiful mathematical concept, meaning part of the area of a curvilinear figure—would be so debased.

At work he was infuriated by all sorts of things: meetings, wall newspapers, loans, and so on. But even at home he was unable to find solace for his proud heart. At home there were also wall newspapers, loans, and meetings. His acquaintances talked about things which to him were the height of vulgarity, for instance, salary, which they called "wages," aid-the-children months, and the social significance of the play *The Armored Train*.

He couldn't get away from the Soviet system. Whenever the embittered Khvorobyov wandered by himself along the streets, he would catch such loathsome phrases from the strolling crowds as: ". . . then we decreed that he should be struck off the board . . ." And, gazing sadly at the notices calling upon citizens to fulfill the five-year plan in four years, he used to repeat to himself in irritation, "Struck off the board! In four years! Lousy regime!"

When the methodological-pedagogical sector switched to a seven-day work week, and instead of Sunday, Khvorobyov's day off was the fifth of every month, he applied for a pension in disgust and moved a long way out of town. He did this to get away from the regime, which had taken possession of his life and deprived him of peace and quiet.

For days on end the self-employed monarchist used to sit on top of the cliff trying to think about something nice, such as prayers on the occasion of the birthday of a highly placed person, his high school examinations, or his relatives who had served in the Ministry of Education. But, to his surprise, his thoughts immediately used to turn to things Soviet and unpleasant.

"What can be happening in that damned Proletcult?" he used to wonder. "The Soviet regime has taken everything away from me—rank, awards, honor, and money in the bank. It has even invaded my thoughts. But there's one sphere that the Bolsheviks haven't reached—my dreams. The night will bring solace. In my dreams I shall see the nice things I want to see."

The first night after this, Theodor Khvorobyov was visited by a ghastly nightmare. He dreamt he was lying in a government-office corridor lit by a kerosene lamp. He was sitting there knowing he was about to be struck off the board. Suddenly an iron door opened and clerks came running out shouting, "Khvorobyov needs more work." He wanted to run but couldn't.

Khvorobyov woke up in the middle of the night. He prayed to God, explaining that there had evidently been some misunderstanding and that a dream intended for an official, perhaps a Communist Party member, had gone astray. He, Khvorobyov, wanted to see, to begin with, the Czar leaving the Cathedral of the Assumption.

Easier in mind, he dozed off again, but instead of the adored monarch's face, he suddenly saw the chairman of the local committee, Comrade Surzhikov. The monarchist howled in his sleep. "The same dreams!"

Khvorobyov concluded in a plaintive voice. "Those damned dreams!"

"Things are in a bad way," said Ostap sympathetically. "As they say, mind reflects environment. If you live under the Soviet regime, your dreams must be Soviet ones.

"I'll help you," he said. "I've had occasion to treat some of my friends by Freud's method. A dream is just nonsense. The important thing is to remove the cause of the dream. The main cause is the very existence of the Soviet regime. But at the present moment I can't do anything about that. I just haven't time. You see, I'm a racing enthusiast and I have to make some small repairs to my car, so let me put it in your outhouse. And don't worry about the cause. I'll remove it on the way back. Let me finish the race first."

The dream-drunk monarchist willingly agreed to allow the nice, understanding young man to use the outhouse. He threw a coat over his shirt, pulled galoshes on to his feet, and followed Bender out into the yard.

"So there's hope, is there?" he asked, pattering after his early-morning visitor.

"No doubt about it," answered the captain breezily. "As soon as the Soviet regime is over, you'll get better. You'll see!"

Half an hour later the Antelope was hidden at Khvorobyov's house and left in the charge of Kozlevich and Panikovsky. Bender and Balaganov set off for town to fetch some paint.

The foster brothers walked toward the sun, making their way to the center of town. Gray doves wandered about on the cornices of houses. The wooden water-sprayed sidewalks were clean and cool.

A man with a clear conscience enjoys emerging from his house at this hour and dallying a moment or two at the gate; then, taking from his pocket a match-box with a picture of an airplane with a finger in front making a rude sign instead of a propeller and the in-

scription "The Answer to Curzon," he gives the new
pack of cigarettes a loving look and lights up, the in-
cense-like smoke frightening a bee with gold braid on
its tummy.

Bender and Balaganov were enchanted by the morning, the clean, tidy streets, and the apolitical pigeons.
For a time it seemed to them that their own consci-
ences were completely clear, that everyone liked them,
and that they were suitors on their way to see their
fiancées.

The brothers' path was suddenly barred by a man
with a folding easel and a shiny paint box in his hands.
He looked extremely agitated as though he had just
jumped out of a burning building, saving only the
easel and the paint box.

"Excuse me," he sang out, "Comrade Plotsky-
Potseluyev should have just passed by here. You
haven't seen him, have you?"

"We never see people of that kind," said Balaganov
rudely.

The artist bumped into Balaganov's chest, said
"Pardon," and raced off.

"Plotsky-Potseluyev indeed!" grumbled the smooth
operator, who had not had any breakfast. "I once
knew a midwife who was called Medusa-Gorgoner,
but I didn't make a fuss about it and run through the
streets shouting 'Have you by any chance seen Madam
Medusa-Gorgoner?' Just imagine, Plotsky-Potseluyev!"

Hardly had Bender finished his tirade when two
men with black easels and shiny portfolios made right
for him. They were both completely different. One
apparently adhered to the view that an artist should be
hairy, and by the amount of vegetation on his face, he
could have been a Russian version of Henry of Navarre. The mustache, curls, and short beard greatly
enlivened his flat face. The other was absolutely bald,
with a head as smooth and slippery as a glass lamp
shade.

"Have you seen—" said the Russian Henry of Navarre.

"Comrade Plotsky?" added the lamp shade.

"Potseluyev," cried Navarre.

"He should be somewhere around here," explained the shade.

Bender pushed aside Balaganov, who had just opened his mouth to utter an oath, and said with icy politeness, "We haven't seen Comrade Plotsky, but if this comrade really interests you, you'd better hurry. Some laborer or other, to judge by appearances, is looking for him."

The artists sped on, catching in each other's easels and bumping into one another. At this moment a horse-cab came around the corner.

Inside was a fat man, the long tails of whose blue shirt probably hid a sweaty belly. The over-all effect of the person recalled an ancient advertisement for a patent ointment, which began with the words "The sight of a naked body covered in hair produces a feeling of revulsion." It was not difficult to guess the profession of the fat man. He had his hand on a large studio easel.

"Hey!" called Ostap. "Are you looking for Potseluyev?"

"Yes, indeed," the obese artist confirmed, looking helplessly at Ostap.

"Hurry! Hurry!" cried Ostap. "There are already three artists ahead of you. What's going on? What's happened?"

But the horse, drumming its hoofs against the cobblestones, had already whisked off the fourth representative of the arts.

"What a cultured town!" exclaimed Ostap. "No doubt you've noticed, Balaganov, that out of the four citizens we've met, four are artists. Curious!"

As the foster brothers stopped outside the hardware store, Balaganov whispered to Ostap, "Aren't you ashamed?"

"Of what?"

"Of the fact that you're going to pay real money for the paint."

"Oh, you mean *that*," said Ostap. "I admit I am rather ashamed. It's a silly situation, of course. But what can you do? Should we run to the executive committee and ask for paints to hold a children's charity bazaar? They'd give it to us for sure, but we'd lose a whole day."

The powdered paints in jars, glass cylinders, sacks, barrels, and torn paper bags possessed attractive circus-like colors and gave the store a festive air.

The captain and the chief engineer painstakingly selected the colors.

"Black is too much like mourning," Ostap was saying. "Green isn't any use, either: it's the color of dashed hopes. Purple no. Let the chief of the secret police ride in a purple car. Pink is vulgar, light blue is banal, and red is too patriotic. The Antelope will have to be yellow. It'll be bright, but attractive."

"And who might you be? Artists?" asked the man behind the counter, whose beard was slightly flecked with cinnabar.

"That's right," Ostap replied. "Painters of battle scenes and seascapes."

"Then you've come to the wrong place," said the shopkeeper, removing some packages and jars from the counter.

"What do you mean, the wrong place!" Ostap exclaimed. "Where, then?"

"Opposite."

The salesman led the friends to the door and pointed to a sign on the other side of the street. It showed a brown horse's head with the words "Oats and Hay" in black letters on a light blue background.

"All in order," Ostap observed, "hard and soft fodders for livestock. But what has that to do with the likes of us artists? I don't see the connection."

But there was a connection, and a very important one. Ostap discovered it at the very beginning of the shopkeeper's elucidation.

The town had always liked painting, and the four artists, who had resided there for some time, founded a group called the Dialectic Studio Artists.

They painted the portraits of various officials and sold them to the local art museum. As time went on, the number of unpainted officials declined considerably, causing a marked reduction in the earnings of the Dialectic Studio Artists. But that was still tolerable. The years of suffering began with the arrival of a new artist in town named Feofan Mukhin.

His first work caused a great furor in the town. It was a portrait of the manager of a group of hotels. Mukhin left the Studio Artists way behind. The manager of the hotel group was not portrayed in oils, or water color, or charcoal, or tempera, or pastel, or gouache, or even lead pencil. He was done in oats, and while the painter Mukhin was taking the painting to the museum in a horse-cab, the horse kept looking around and neighing anxiously.

As time went on, Mukhin began using other cereals.

Tremendously successful were portraits made with millet, wheat, and poppy seed, bold sketches in corn and buckwheat, landscapes in rice, and *nature mortes* in lentils.

He was now working on a group portrait. The large canvas depicted a meeting of the district planning organization. Although he was doing the picture in peas and beans, in the depths of his heart he was true to the oats that had made his career and floored the Dialectic Studio Artists.

"It's cleverer in oats, of course!" Ostap exclaimed. "Rubens and Raphael were fools to use oil paints. We're also fools, like Leonardo da Vinci. Give us some yellow enamel."

While settling up with the talkative shopkeeper, Ostap inquired:

"By the way, who's this fellow Plotsky-Potseluyev? We're from out of town."

"Comrade Plotsky is a well-known official in Moscow, but he is originally from here. He's just arrived from Moscow on vacation."

"I see," said Ostap. "Thanks for the information. Good-by!"

In the street, the foster brothers suddenly caught sight of the Dialectic Studio Artists. All four were standing at the crossroads like gypsies, with sad, longing expressions. Beside them were their easels, stacked into a pyramid like piled rifles.

"What's up, lads?" Ostap asked. "Have you missed Plotsky-Potseluyev?"

"Yes, we have," groaned the artists. "He got away."

"Did Feofan get there first?" Ostap asked, displaying a sound knowledge of the subject.

"He's painting a picture in oats, the hack!" answered the deputy Henry of Navarre. "Said he was going back to his old style. He complained there was a crisis in the arts, the flour dealer!"

"And where might this smartie's studio be?" Ostap inquired. "I'd like to take a look at it."

The artists, who had a great deal of spare time, willingly took Ostap and Balaganov to Mukhin's place. The portrait painter was working in his little garden in the open air. In front of him on a stool sat Comrade Plotsky, evidently a timid man. Hardly breathing, he gazed at the artist, who, like the sower on a three-ruble note, was seizing handfuls of oats from a basket and scattering them over the canvas. Mukhin was frowning. The sparrows kept disturbing him. They impudently flew up to the picture and pecked out some of the detail.

"How much will you get for this picture?" asked Plotsky shyly.

Feofan stopped sowing, looked critically at his opus, and replied thoughtfully, "Well, the museum will give me about two hundred and fifty rubles."

"That's expensive."

"But oats are hard to get nowadays," said Mukhin in a singsong voice. "They're expensive."

"Well, how are the spring crops?" asked Ostap, poking his head through the garden railing. "I see the sowing campaign is proceeding favorably. A hundred per cent! But all that's rubbish compared to what I saw in Moscow. There was an artist there who made a picture from hair. A large painting with lots of figures and, mind you, ideologically acceptable, although he did use hair from non-party members, I admit. But ideologically, I repeat, the picture was splendid. It was called *Granddad Pakhom and His Grazing Tractor*. It was such a refractory picture that people didn't know what to do with it. Sometimes the hair on it stood on end. And then one day it went completely gray, and Granddad Pakhom and his tractor disappeared into thin air. But the artists managed to get fifteen hundred rubles for it. So don't be too pleased with yourself, Comrade Mukhin. The oats may suddenly sprout, your pictures will grow ears, and you won't be able to reap the harvest any more."

The Dialectic Studio Artists roared with laughter, but Feofan was not in the least put out. "That sounds like a paradox," he observed, renewing his broadcasting operations.

"All right, then," said Ostap in farewell, "sow what is sensible, good, and everlasting, and then we'll see. Good-by to you, too, lads. Give up oil paints. Change to mosaics made of bolts, large nails, and small screws. A portrait in nuts. A magnificent idea!"

The Antelopeans spent the whole day painting their car. By evening it was unrecognizable and shone with all the hues of the yolk of an egg. At dawn on the following day the transformed Antelope left the hospitable outhouse and set course for the south.

"A pity we didn't have a chance to say good-by to our host, but he was sleeping so soundly that I didn't want to disturb him. At this moment he may be having the dream he's been so looking forward to—Metropolitan Dvulogy blessing the officials of the Ministry of Education on the three-hundredth anniversary of the House of Romanovs."

At that very moment a familiar plaintive wailing was heard from the beamed cottage behind.

"That dream again!" screeched the old Khvorobyov. "Oh Lord, oh Lord!"

"I was wrong," Ostap observed. "He obviously hasn't dreamt of the Metropolitan Dvulogy but a general meeting of the literary group Forge and Estate. Anyway, to hell with him! Business calls us to Chernomorsk."

Another Crisis in the Arts

THE THINGS people get up to!

Parallel to the big world, in which there are big people and big things, there is a little world with little people and little things. In the big world they invented the Diesel engine, wrote *Dead Souls,* built the Dnieper hydroelectric station, and made the first round-the-world flight.

In the little world they invented squeaking dolls, wrote the song "Little Bricks," and originated ambassador-style pants. In the big world people are motivated by a desire to make man more virtuous. The little world is far from such noble aspirations. Its inhabitants have but one desire—to make ends meet somehow and not to go hungry.

The little people hasten after the big people. They realize they have to keep in tune with the times or their inferior goods won't find a market. In Soviet times, now that ideological bases have been set up in the big world, the little world is showing great activity. All the inventions of the little antlike world are now based on a solid "Communist" ideology. The squeaking doll portrays Chamberlain looking as he does in *Izvestiya* cartoons. In the latest hit song a

clever mechanic fulfills or even overfulfills his financial norm in three verses in order to win the love
of a Young Communist girl. And while the big world
heatedly discusses the new way of life, in the little
world everything is ready: there's a "Shock-worker's Dream" tie, a plaster statue entitled *The Bathing
Collective-Farm Girl,* and cork under-arm pads for
ladies sold under the trade name "Worker-Bees' Delight."

In the field of riddles, charades, conundrums, and
picture puzzles, there were new trends abroad. The
old approach was out of date. Secretaries of newspaper
and magazine sections entitled "For Leisure Moments"
or "Use Your Brains" had resolutely stopped ac-
cepting contributions lacking in ideology. And while
the great country hummed, while tractor plants were
being built and impressive grain mills were being
erected, old man Sinitsky, a poser of puzzles by profession, sat in his room and, fixing his glassy eyes on
the ceiling, thought out a new charade on the up-to-
date word "industrialization."

Sinitsky had the appearance of a gnome—the sort
of gnome that is usually shown on signs outside umbrella shops. These gnomes wear red pointed caps and
wink cheerily at the passers-by as though inviting
them to buy a silk umbrella or a stick with a dog's-
head handle. Sinitsky's long yellow beard drooped
past the table into the waste-paper basket.

"Industrialization," he whispered sorrowfully, moving his aged lips, as pale as raw pork chops. And in his
accustomed way he divided the word into charade
syllables: "Indus. Tri. Ali. Zation."

Everything was fine. Sinitsky already envisaged a
nice fat charade, full of political significance, easy to
read, and difficult to guess. Only the last part, "zation,"
caused him doubt.

"What can we do with 'zation'?" the old man wondered, racking his brains. "Now, if only it were 'sta-

tion!' Then it would fit perfectly—'industrialista-
tion.' "

After half an hour's struggle he had still not thought
of a way to deal with the capricious ending, and so,
deciding that the end would come to him by itself,
he set to work.

He wrote down his verses on a page torn from an
account book marked *Debit*.

Acacia trees in bloom, patched roof tops, and the
sharp blue line of the horizon out to sea could be seen
through the white glass door leading onto the balcony. The Chernomorsk midday filled the town with
a jellylike sultriness.

The old man thought for a moment and then scribbled down the opening lines:

> *My first is a river*
> *Which through the East flows*

"Which through the East flows," murmured the
old man with delight.

He liked what he had composed. The puzzle-poser
walked up and down the room and pulled at his beard.
Suddenly he had an inspiration:

> *My second is something*
> *That everywhere grows*

"Ali" was also easy to cope with:

> *My third wears a turban*
> *And lives in the East*

Exhausted by this last effort, Sinitsky leaned back in
the chair and closed his eyes. He was seventy years
old. Fifty of them had been spent composing riddles,
charades, picture puzzles, and conundrums. But never
before had the respectable old puzzle-poser found it so
hard to work as now. He was behind the times; he
was politically illiterate, and his younger competitors
found it easy to outdo him. They brought the editors
riddles with such a splendid ideological slant that the

old man shed tears of envy as he read them. How could he keep up with this sort of riddle, for example:

> In each of the three villages of Sparrowville, Rookberg, and Thrushtown there was an equal number of clerks. In Thrushtown there were six times as many Young Communists as in the other two places together, and in Sparrowville there were twelve more Communist Party members than at Rookberg. But there were six times as many non-party members at Rookberg than in the other two villages. How many clerks were there in each village and what was the Communist Party and Young Communist strength?

Emerging from his mournful thoughts, the old man took up another sheet of paper with the heading *Debit,* but at that moment a girl with wet, bobbed hair and a black swimsuit across her shoulders came into the room.

She went out onto the balcony in silence, draped her swimsuit over the battered railings, and glanced down below. The girl saw the same scene that she had seen for many years: a slummy courtyard strewn with broken crates, coal-soiled tomcats prowling about, and a tinsmith noisily mending a bucket. On the floor below, the housewives were discussing their hard life.

And it wasn't the first time she had heard such conversations; she also knew the cats' names, and the tinsmith, or so it seemed, had been mending that same bucket for years. Zosya Sinitsky went back into the room.

"That ideology's got me down," came the mumbling of her grandfather. "How can a riddle be ideological? Riddles . . ."

Zosya began setting the table. She moved backward and forward between the sideboard with its porthole mirrors and the table, and unloaded the crockery. A china soup tureen without handles appeared, then plates with and without flowered designs, tarnished forks, and even a stewed-fruit dish, although there wasn't going to be any stewed fruit for lunch.

Things weren't going well for the Sinitskys. The riddles and charades brought home more trouble than money. The home-cooked lunches which the old puzzle-poser prepared for citizen acquaintances, and which were his main source of income, were not going very well, either. Podvysotsky and Bomse had gone on vacation. Stulyan had married a Greek girl and was lunching at home, while Poburikhin had lost his job in a government office under Article 2, and was so upset that he also lost his appetite. He was now going about town stopping friends and acquaintances and asking the same sarcastic question: "Have you heard? I've been thrown out under Article 2." Some of his acquaintances replied sympathetically, "They certainly started something, those Marx and Engels!" while others didn't answer at all, looked askance at Poburikhin, and swept past, shaking their brief cases. Eventually, only one of the boarders was left, and he hadn't paid for a week, making the excuse that his wages were late in arriving.

Pushing back her shoulders in annoyance, Zosya went into the kitchen, and by the time she came back, the last boarder, Alexander Ivanovich Koreiko, was already sitting at the lunch table.

In the non-office atmosphere Alexander Ivanovich did not seem at all timid or subdued, but his face still maintained a guarded expression.

He was now gazing intently at Sinitsky's latest riddle. Among the various mysterious clues to it was a paper bag with lots of *t*'s spilling from it, a fir tree with the sun rising behind it, and a sparrow sitting on a musical stave. The riddle ended with an inverted comma.

"That riddle will keep you guessing," said Sinitsky, walking round and round his boarder. "You'll have to think hard."

"Yes, I will, I will," Koreiko answered with a grin.

"The only thing worrying me is the goose. What can it be? Ah, I see. Got it! 'Thou shalt gain thy right in battle,' is that it?"

"Yes," drawled the old man in disappointment. "How did you guess it so quickly? You must be very clever. You're obviously a first-grade accountant."

"Second-grade," Koreiko corrected him. "Who is the riddle for? the Press?"

"Yes."

"A complete waste," said Koreiko, looking at his beet soup, which had gold medals of fat floating in it. " 'Thou shalt gain thy right in battle' is the Social Revolutionaries' motto. It won't be any good for the Press."

"Oh Lord," groaned the old man, "I've blundered again. Do you hear, Zosya? I've blundered. What am I going to do now?"

They calmed him down. Having struggled through his lunch, he immediately got up, collected all the riddles composed during the week, put on a horsy straw hat, and said:

"Zosya, I'm going to the *Youth Herald*. I'm rather worried about the algebraic riddle, but I'll probably get some money there."

Although the Young Communist magazine *Youth Herald* usually rejected the old boy's work and criticized him for being behind the times, it still gave him money, hence it was the only source from which the old man received his thin stream of income. Sinitsky took with him a charade which began, "My first is at the bottom of the sea," two collective-farm riddles, and a mathematical conundrum, which, apart from some complicated multiplication and subtraction, sought to prove that the Soviet system was better than any other.

As soon as the puzzle-poser had gone, Alexander Ivanovich gloomily turned his attention to Zosya. He used to board there because the lunches were cheap and good. Besides that, he never allowed himself to forget that he was an ordinary clerk. He enjoyed talking about the difficulties of eking out an existence in a large town on a miserable salary. But for some reason the price and taste of the lunches had lost for him the abstract and symbolic value which he attributed to them. If he needed to—and he could have done it without batting an eyelid—he would have paid three or even five thousand rubles for them and not sixty kopeks, as he was doing now.

Alexander Ivanovich, the ascetic who willingly bound himself with the chains of financial penance, who forbade himself to touch anything that cost more than half a ruble, and yet who at the same time was peeved that he couldn't openly spend a hundred rubles for fear of losing his millions, had fallen in love with all the determination that can be shown by a man who is strong, hard, and embittered by constant frustration.

He had finally decided to declare his love for Zosya and offer his hand, with its feeble and evil weasel-like pulse, and his dream-filled heart.

"Yes," he said, "that's how it is, Zosya Viktorovna."

Having made this pronouncement, citizen Koreiko picked up from the table an ash tray on which was written the prerevolutionary slogan "Husband, don't anger your wife," and began examining it carefully.

It should be explained at this point that there are no girls in the world who do not sense an impending declaration of love at least a week in advance.

So Zosya sighed and stopped in front of the mirror. She had that sporty look that all pretty girls have acquired over the last few years. Having made certain that this was so, she sat down opposite Alexander Koreiko and got ready to listen. But Koreiko didn't say anything. He knew only two roles—the clerk and the underground millionaire.

"Have you heard the news?" Zosya asked. "Poburikhin has been purged."

"A purge has started at our place, too," Koreiko replied. "Lots of people will be thrown out. Lapidus, Jr., for instance. And Lapidus, Sr., too . . ."

Here Koreiko saw that he was following in the footsteps of the poor clerk. A leaden pensiveness overcame him once more.

"Yes, yes," he said. "We live in solitude without enjoyment."

"Without what?" Zosya asked, livening up.

"Without female affection," Koreiko remarked in a husky voice.

Not receiving any support from Zosya, he proceeded to develop the idea.

He was already old. That is to say, not all that old, but no longer young. And not only was he not so young; time was flying. The years were passing, and the passage of time made him think about certain things. Marriage, for example. Let it not be thought that he was just anyone. He was basically a good man. A very harmless man. He should be pitied. And it had even occurred to him that he could be loved. He wasn't a swank, like the others, and didn't like wasting words. Why shouldn't a girl marry him?

Having expressed his feelings in this modest way, Alexander Koreiko looked angrily at Zosya.

"Can they really purge Lapidus, Jr.?" asked the puzzle-poser's granddaughter.

And without waiting for an answer, she began a businesslike reply.

She understood everything perfectly. Time really was passing terribly quickly. She had only recently been nineteen, and now she was twenty. And in a year she would be twenty-one. She had never thought that Alexander Ivanovich was just anybody. On the contrary, she had always been certain he was a good man. Better than many. And worthy of everything, of course. But at the moment she was seeking something else; what it was, she didn't exactly know. In effect, she couldn't get married at that moment. And, anyway, what would life be like? She was seeking something. And putting it frankly and honestly, he only made forty-six rubles a month. Another thing was that she didn't love him, which, generally speaking, was important.

"What do you mean, forty-six rubles?" said Alexander Ivanovich in a terrible voice, drawing himself up to his full height. "I have . . ."

He didn't say any more. He felt afraid. The role of the millionaire had come to the fore, and that could only end in ruin. His fear was so great that he even began to stammer something about money not bringing happiness. But just at that moment there was a snuffling sound from outside the door. Zosya hurried into the corridor.

Grandfather was standing there in his large hat, glittering with straw crystals. He couldn't bring himself to come in. Grief had made his beard splay like a broom.

"Why are you back so soon?" cried Zosya. "What's happened?"

The old man raised his tear-filled eyes.

The startled Zosya seized the old man by his bony shoulders and pulled him into the room. Sinitsky lay shaking on the couch for half an hour. After much persuasion the old man told them his story.

It had all gone splendidly. He got to the editorial office of the *Youth Herald* without incident. The head of the "Brain-Teaser" section greeted him most politely.

"He shook my hand, Zosya," sighed the old man. "'Sit down, Comrade Sinitsky,' he said. And it was then he told me the staggering news. 'They're closing down our section,' he said. 'A new editor has arrived who thinks our readers don't need brain-teasers.' They need a special checkers section instead, Zosya. 'What's going to happen?' I asked. 'Nothing at all,' said the chief. 'Your stuff is unsuitable and that's it.' But he liked my charade. 'The verse is as good as Pushkin,' he said. Especially the part that went, 'My first is at the bottom of the sea, and there you'll find my second too.' "

The old puzzle-poser remained shivering on the couch for some time, complaining of the tyranny of Soviet ideology.

"This means another scene," Zosya exclaimed.

She pulled on a hat and made for the door. Alexander Ivanovich went after her, although he realized that he shouldn't do so.

On the street, Zosya took Koreiko's arm. "We can be friends anyway, can't we?"

"It would be better if you married me," Koreiko blurted out.

The open mineral-water kiosks were crowded with hatless young men in white shirts with rolled-up sleeves. Blue siphons with metal tops filled the shelves. Tall jars of syrup on rotating bases glittered with a drug-store effect. Persians with sad faces were roasting nuts on braziers. and the fumes attracted the people strolling by.

"I feel like going to a movie," said Zosya whimsically. "I feel like some nuts and an ice-cream soda."

Koreiko was ready to do anything for Zosya. He would even have broken his vows and spent five rubles on having a good time. In his pocket was a flat tin box of *Caucasus* cigarettes containing ten thousand rubles in notes. But even if he had gone mad and decided to display as much as one currency note, they wouldn't have been able to change it in any of the movie theaters.

"The wages have been delayed," he said in complete despair. "They come extremely irregularly."

At that moment a young man wearing a magnificent pair of sandals on his bare feet emerged from the passers-by. He saluted Zosya and said, "Hi. I have two free tickets for the movies. Want to come? Only make up your mind right away!"

And the young man in the wonderful sandals carried off Zosya under a dull sign which said: "Whither

Goest Movie Theater (Formerly the Quo Vadis)."

That night the clerk-millionaire did not sleep at home. He wandered around town until early morning, staring stupidly at pictures of naked babies in photographers' shop windows, kicking up the gravel on the avenue, and gazing into the darkness of the port. Invisible ships conversed together, militiamen's whistling could be heard, and the red light of a lighthouse went round and round.

"Damned country," mumbled Koreiko. "A millionaire can't even take his girl-friend to the movies."

He already thought of Zosya as his girl-friend.

Toward morning, Alexander Ivanovich, pale from lack of sleep, wandered over to the edge of town. As he went along Bessarabia Street, he heard the sound of a musical horn and stopped in surprise.

A yellow car was coming down the hill toward him. Behind the wheel, all hunched up, sat a tired-looking driver in a leather coat. A broad-shouldered young man was dozing next to him with his head on one side. He was wearing a Stetson with holes in it. In the back seat lounged two more passengers—a fireman in full-dress uniform and a well-built young fellow in a sailor's hat with a white top.

"Greetings to the first Chernomorsk citizen," Ostap called as the car shot past Koreiko, rumbling like a tractor. "Are the warm baths still going? Is the theater open? Have they declared Chernomorsk a free city?"

But Ostap didn't get a reply. Kozlevich opened up the throttle and the Antelope enveloped the first citizen of Chernomorsk in a cloud of blue smoke.

"Well," said Ostap to Balaganov, who had just awakened. "The hearing's continued. Bring on your underground Rockefeller. I'll soon take the clothes off him. Really, these princes and paupers!"

Part : II

TWO
OPERATORS

]CHAPTER[

: 10 :

A Telegram from the
Brothers Karamazov

FOR SOME TIME the underground millionaire had felt himself the object of someone's unflagging attention. At first there was nothing definite. It was just that his accustomed and peaceful feeling of solitude disappeared. Then symptoms of a more alarming nature began to manifest themselves.

One day while Koreiko was on his way to work, walking at his normal measured pace, he was stopped just outside the Hercules by a beggar with a gold tooth. Treading on the ribbons trailing from his underwear, the beggar seized Koreiko by the arm and began murmuring rapidly:

"Gimme a million! Gimme a million! Gimme a million!"

After that the beggar stuck out a thick, dirty tongue and rattled off some of the usual rubbish. He was an ordinary half-wit of the kind you often find in southern towns. Nevertheless, Koreiko went upstairs to the accounts department with a troubled heart.

Weird things began happening after that meeting.

At three o'clock in the morning Koreiko was awakened by the arrival of a telegram. With his teeth chattering from the morning chill, the millionaire tore open the envelope and read:

COUNTESS RUNNING TO LAKE
WITH CHANGED FACE

"What countess?" whispered the dumfounded Koreiko, standing in his bare feet in the corridor.

But no one answered. The messenger boy had gone. Pigeons began cooing passionately in the garden. The tenants were asleep. Alexander Ivanovich fiddled with the gray form. The address and the name were right:

ALEXANDER KOREIKO 16 CAREFREE STREET
COUNTESS RUNNING TO LAKE
WITH CHANGED FACE

Koreiko had no idea what it meant, but suddenly felt so nervous that he burned the telegram in the candle flame.

At 5:35 p.m. the same day a second dispatch arrived:

HEARING CONTINUED STOP MILLION KISSES

Alexander Koreiko paled with fury and tore the telegram into little pieces. But that night he received two more.

The first read:

LOAD ORANGES BARRELS BROTHERS
KARAMAZOV

And the second:

THINGS MOVING STOP I AM TAKING PARADE

After this a shameful incident occurred at the office. While multiplying nine hundred and eighty-five by thirteen at the request of Chevazhevskaya, Koreiko made a mistake and gave the wrong answer, something which had never happened to him before in his life.

But he couldn't be bothered with mathematics. The crazy telegrams were unnerving him.

" 'Barrels,' " he whispered, fixing his eyes on old Kukushkind. " 'Brothers Karamazov.' Someone's playing a lousy trick on me."

He tried to console himself with the thought that it was an amusing prank played on him by some friends, but the possibility was soon discarded. He had no friends. His colleagues were serious types and indulged in practical jokes only once a year, on the first of April. And on that day of jolly japes and merry mystification they always played the same trick: they typed out a phony dismissal notice for Kukushkind and put it on his desk. And every time for the last seven years the old man had nearly had a heart attack, which everyone found great fun. Anyway, they couldn't afford to waste money on telegrams.

After the telegram in which an unknown citizen announced that he was personally taking the parade, peace and quiet followed. Alexander Ivanovich was not disturbed for three days. He was just getting used to the idea that nothing that had occurred concerned him in the least, when a registered package arrived. It contained a book entitled *Capitalist Sharks* with the subtitle *Biography of American Millionaires*.

At any other time Koreiko would have bought this fascinating publication himself, but now he just winced with horror. The first sentence was circled in blue pencil and read:

"All large modern fortunes have been acquired in the most dishonest way."

Alexander Koreiko decided that, just to be sure, he would not for the moment go to the station to see how his cherished attaché case was getting on. He was in an extremely disturbed state of mind.

"The main thing," Ostap was saying as he walked up and down a large room in the Carlsbad Hotel, "is to cause confusion in the enemy camp. The enemy must be demoralized. It isn't so hard to do that. People are terribly afraid of things they don't understand. At one time I was a mystic myself and things reached the stage where I could be frightened by a mere jack-knife. Yes, we need more of the spooky stuff. I'm certain my last telegram 'together in thought' made an overwhelming impression on our counter-agent. It's all superphosphate and fertilizer for our cause. Let him worry for a bit. Our client must get used to the idea that he is going to have to part with his money. He must be morally disarmed and his reactionary acquisitive instincts must be suppressed."

Having made this speech, Bender looked hard at his subordinates. Balaganov, Panikovsky, and Kozlevich were sitting sedately in red velvet armchairs with fringes and tassels. They felt awkward. They were embarrassed by the captain's grand style of living, by the gilt lambrequins, the carpets splashed with bright colors, and the print *Christ Appears to the People*. They themselves, plus the Antelope, had stopped at a tavern, and only came to the hotel for instructions.

"Panikovsky," said Ostap, "you were given the job of meeting our client and once more asking for a million, accompanying the request with insane laughter, were you not?"

"As soon as he saw me he crossed the street," said Panikovsky smugly.

"Yes, all goes well. Our client is getting nervous. He's now going from dumb bewilderment to stark terror. I don't doubt that he jumps up at night and babbles plaintively 'Mom! Mom!' A little bit more nonsense—the last touch of the brush, so to speak—and he'll see the light. With a sob he'll stagger over to the sideboard and bring out the silver platter."

Ostap winked at Balaganov, Balaganov winked at Panikovsky, Panikovsky winked at Kozlevich, and although the honest Kozlevich had no idea what it was all about, he began winking too, with both eyes.

And for some time to come, the room at the Carlsbad was the scene of friendly winking accompanied
by chuckling, clicking of tongues, and even some
jumping up and down from the red velvet chairs.

"That's enough hilarity," Ostap ordered. "As long
as the platter with the money is in Koreiko's hands—
provided it really exists—it's an invisible platter."

Bender sent Panikovsky and Kozlevich to the tavern,
instructing them to keep the Antelope in a state of
readiness.

"Well, Alex," he said, left alone with Balaganov, "no
more telegrams are needed. The spade work can be
considered finished. Now we start the open warfare.
Let's go and watch the precious calf carrying out his
office duties."

Keeping in the transparent shade of the acacias, the
foster brothers walked through the park, in which the
wide jet of water from the fountain poured back
onto itself like a dripping candle, passed by several
mirrored beer halls, and stopped on the corner of
Mehring Street. Flower girls with red sailors' faces
were bathing their tender wares in enamel dishes. The
sun-warmed asphalt crunched under their feet. Some
citizens emerged from a blue-tiled milk bar, wiping
the yogurt off their lips as they went.

The thick macaroni-like gold letters forming the
word "Hercules" glinted alluringly. The sun played
on the sooty glass panes of the revolving door. Ostap
and Balaganov went into the vestibule and mingled
with the crowd of busy people.

The Herculeans

No MATTER HOW HARD the frequently replaced directors tried to rid the Hercules of its hotel atmosphere, they were unable to do so. However much the office managers painted over the old signs, they peeped out from everywhere. One moment the words "Private Dining Rooms" would pop up in the sales section, then suddenly a stenciled sign "Duty Chambermaid" would be noticed on the frosted-glass door of the typistry, or gold forefingers with the word "Ladies" in French would be discovered on the wall. The hotel was making itself felt.

The less important clerical staff worked in the one-ruble rooms on the fourth floor, which in their time had accommodated village priests arriving for diocesan congresses or petty commercial travelers with Warsaw mustaches. They still smelled of armpits and contained pink iron washbowls.

The rather cleaner rooms, which had been stayed in by billiard kings and provincial actors and actresses, now housed the heads of sections, their assistants, and the office manager. They were better furnished: they contained wardrobes with mirrors, and the floor was laid with light brown linoleum. In the luxury rooms with baths and alcoves nestled the directors. The white baths were strewn with files, and the dingy alcoves were hung with diagrams and charts showing the structure of the Hercules and its link with the outlying organizations. The rooms retained their stupid gilt couches, carpets, and marble-topped bedside tables. In some of the alcoves there were even heavy armorlike, nickel-plated beds with brass knobs. These were also strewn with files and any unwanted correspondence. It was an extremely convenient system of filing, as the papers were always at hand.

It was in one of these rooms, No. 5, that the famous writer Leonid Andreev had stayed in 1911. All the Herculeans knew this, and the room had a bad reputation in the office.

Every official who set up his office in it inevitably suffered some disaster. Hardly had the new inmate of No. 5 time to get into the swim of things when he was taken away and given some other job. And he was lucky if he got away without an official reprimand. Otherwise there were reprimands, sometimes criticism in the Press, and sometimes more unpleasant things which won't be mentioned.

"The hell of a room," affirmed the victims to a man. "Who would have suspected it?"

And the author of the terrible "Seven Who Were Hanged" was charged with being responsible for the fact that Comrade Lapshin gave jobs to six of his own husky brothers; that while organizing wood-bark procurements, Comrade Spravchenko had let things slide; or that Comrade Indokitaisky lost 7384 rubles, 03 kopeks in government funds playing cards, and no matter how he prevaricated, how much he tried to show that he had spent the 03 kopeks for the good of the state and could produce relevant documents, it was all no use. The shadow of the deceased writer was relentless, and one evening in the fall, Indokitaisky was taken away to serve his sentence. Room No. 5 really was a stinker.

Comrade Polykhayev, director of the Hercules, had his office in the former wintergarden, and his secretary, Serna Mikhailovna, was constantly flitting to and fro past palms and sycamores, which had somehow been preserved. There was also a table, as long as a railway platform and covered with a raspberry-red cloth, at which frequent and interminable meetings of the board were held. And of late, room No. 262, at one time the second pantry, had been the meeting place of the purge committee, which consisted of eight unprepossessing comrades with steely eyes. They arrived punctually each day and did nothing but read office memorandums.

As Ostap and Balaganov were on their way upstairs, an alarm bell rang and clerks immediately came pouring out of all the rooms. The promptness with which they carried out the operation was reminiscent of the action-stations signal aboard ship. It wasn't action stations, however, but the lunch break. Some of the clerks sped to the cafeteria so as not to miss the red-caviar sandwiches, while others promenaded along the corridors, eating as they went.

A clerk of distinguished appearance emerged from the planning department. A short, round beard hung from his pale, loving face. He was holding a cold meatball which he kept raising to his mouth, having carefully inspected it each time.

Balaganov all but sabotaged the operation by inquiring where the accounts department was.

"Can't you see I'm eating, comrade?" said the clerk, turning away from Balaganov in annoyance.

And, ignoring the foster brothers, he immersed himself in contemplation of the last piece of meatball. Having inspected it thoroughly on both sides and even sniffed it in farewell, the clerk popped it into his mouth, stuck out his chest, brushed the crumbs off his coat, and slowly went over to another clerk standing at the door of his department.

"Well, now," he asked, looking around, "how do we feel?"

"You'd better not ask, Comrade Bomse," replied the other, and, also looking around, added, "Is this really a proper life? There's no scope for individuality. It's always the same thing—the five-year plan in four years, the five-year plan in three years."

"Yes, yes," Bomse whispered. "It's simply awful. I couldn't agree more. Exactly that, no scope for individuality. No incentive, no future in anything. My wife's a housewife, you understand, and even she says there's no incentive, no future in it."

Giving a sigh, Bomse moved toward another clerk. "Well, now," he asked, smiling sadly as before, "how do we feel?"

"I came back from a trip this morning. Managed to see a state farm. It's terrific! A grain mill. You can't imagine, old boy, what the five-year plan will do."

"That's exactly what I've just been saying!" Bomse exclaimed heatedly. "The five-year plan in four years, that's the incentive which . . . Take my wife, even. She only knows housekeeping, but even she gives industrialization its due. There's a new life being born literally while you watch."

Moving aside, he joyfully waggled his head. A minute later he was clutching Borisokhlebsky by the sleeve and saying, "You're right, I think so too. Why build magnetogorsks, state farms, and the like, when there's no private enterprise, when the personality is suppressed?"

In the course of the lunch hour, Bomse, who enjoyed a spiritual communion, managed to chat with ten or so colleagues. The subject of each conversation could be judged by the expression of his face, on which distress at the suppression of the personality rapidly changed to the radiant smile of an enthusiast. But whichever feelings Bomse was expressing, his face maintained a look of innate nobility. And everyone, from the hardened comrades in the local committee to the politically immature Kukushkind, considered Bomse a man of integrity and, more important, a man of principle. Bomse himself adhered to this opinion, incidentally.

A fresh bell announcing the end of the "emergency" returned the clerks to their rooms. Work was resumed.

Actually, the words "work was resumed" bore no relation to the immediate activity of the Hercules, which, according to the book, involved various transactions in the field of timber and saw wood. For the past year the Herculeans, having discarded every notion of tiresome beams, boards, cedar for export, and other such uninteresting things, had been engaged in a most absorbing occupation: they were battling for their premises, for their own hotel.

It all began with a small piece of paper delivered in a canvas dispatch book by a sluggish messenger from the communal-services department.

"With effect from receipt of this," the note read, "you are *instructed* to vacate the premises of the former Cairo Hotel within one week and to hand it over to the hotel trust together with all the original furnishings. You are assigned the premises of the former Tin and Bacon Co. Authority: City Council Resolution dated 12/1929."

In the evening the letter was placed in front of Comrade Polykhayev, who was sitting at his desk in the electric shade of the palms and sycamores.

"What!" screeched the head of the Hercules. "They say I'm instructed! Me! Someone who's directly responsible to Moscow! Have they gone mad or something!"

"They might just have well said 'directed,'" said Serna Mikhailovna, adding fuel to the fire.

"It must be a joke!" said Polykhayev, smiling mournfully.

A very firm reply was dictated immediately. The

head of the Hercules refused point blank to quit the premises.

"Next time they'll know I'm not their nursemaid and don't need to be 'instructed,' " burbled Comrade Polykhayev, taking a rubber stamp out of his pocket and, in his nervousness, impressing his signature on the letter upside-down.

And once again a sluggish messenger, this time one from the Hercules, ambled along the streets, dallying at the kvass stalls, getting involved in all the street imbroglios, and waving his dispatch book in despair.

For the whole of the ensuing week the Herculeans discussed the situation. The clerks all agreed that Polykhayev would not allow his authority to be undermined in that way.

"They don't know our Polykhayev," said the boys from accounts. "He's not green. You can't catch him with a mere resolution."

Soon after this, Comrade Bomse left the chief's office, clutching a list of selected members of the staff. He marched from department to department, leaned over the nominated person, and whispered mysteriously, "There's going to be a small party. Three rubles a head. A farewell for Comrade Polykhayev."

"What's that?" cried the staff members in alarm. "Is he leaving? Have they fired him?"

"No. He's going to Moscow to try and settle the problem of the premises. See you aren't late. It's at seven sharp at my place."

The farewell party was a great success. The staff members gazed devotedly at Polykhayev sitting with a glass in his hand, clapped their hands in time to the music, and sang:

"Drink up, drink up!"

They drank until their beloved boss had downed a reasonable number of toasts, after which he began to sing in a quavering voice, "Along the old Kaluga highway, at the forty-ninth mile." But no one ever found out what had gone on at that mile, because he unexpectedly changed to another song:

"While streetcar nine was passing by,
A man inside saw fit to die,
Now they're bringing out his corpse,
Tum—tiddly—tum."

After Polykhayev's departure, labor productivity at the Hercules declined somewhat. It was absurd to work at full pressure without knowing whether you were going to stay in the building or whether you were going to transfer all your office equipment to the Tin and Bacon Co. But it was still more absurd to work at full pressure after Polykhayev returned. He came back, as Bomse put it, like the conquering hero. The building remained in the hands of the Herculeans, and the clerks spent their office hours jeering at the communal-services department.

The vanquished establishment then requested the transfer of at least the washbowls and armor-plated beds, but success-drunk Polykhayev didn't even bother to answer. Thereupon the battle was renewed with fresh vigor. Complaints sped to Moscow. Polykhayev went there personally to refute them. The victorious "drink up" was heard more and more frequently in Bomse's apartment, and the numbers of staff members drawn into the battle for the building grew and grew. The timber and saw wood were forgotten. Whenever Polykhayev found a paper on his desk dealing with cedar for export or plyboard, he was so startled that he was unable for a while to figure out what was required of him. He was now engaged in an extremely important task—winning over two particularly dangerous officials from the communal services for higher wages.

"You're in luck," Ostap remarked to his companion. "You're present on an amusing occasion—Ostap Bender hot on the trail. Learn something! Petty crooks

like Panikovsky would have written Koreiko a letter
saying, 'Leave sixty rubles under the garbage can in
the yard or you'll be in for it!' and would have drawn
a skull and crossbones underneath. Sonya Golden Fingers, whose virtues I do not wish to belittle in the
least, would have resorted in the long run to stealing
from him while he was in bed with her, which might
have brought her one and a half thousand. That's
women for you. And what about Lieutenant Savin?
An outstanding confidence man. As they say, he
never moves a wrong foot. What would he have
done? He would have gone to Koreiko's apartment dis-
guised as the King of Bulgaria, would have made a scene
in the housing administration and spoiled the whole
issue. But, as you see, I don't hurry. We've been here
in Chernomorsk a week, and today's our first date.
Ah, here's the accounts department! Well, engineer,
show me the patient. You're the Koreiko expert, after
all."

They entered the noisy room teeming with visitors,
and Balaganov led Bender to the corner where Chevazhevskaya, Koreiko, Kukushkind, and Dreyfus were
sitting behind a yellow partition. Balaganov had already lifted his hand to point out the millionaire when
Ostap whispered angrily:

"Why don't you just shout out 'There's the
hoarder! Catch him!' Take it easy! I'll work it out
myself."

Ostap sat down on a cool marble window ledge
and, kicking his feet as children do, began reasoning:

"The girl doesn't count. That leaves three—the red-
faced toady with the white eyes, the pig-faced old
man with iron spectacles, and the fat walrus mustache
with the serious look. Old pig-face is out. Besides the
cotton wool which he's stuffed in his ears, he has no
other valuables. That leaves two—the mustache and
the white-eyed toady. Which of them is Koreiko? Let
me think."

Ostap stretched out his neck and began comparing

the two candidates. He moved his head from side to side so quickly, it looked as if he was following a tennis match.

"You know, engineer," he said at length, "the big walrus mustache would be more suitable for the part of an underground millionaire than the white-eyed toady. Notice the uncertain gleam in the eyes of the mustache. He can't sit still, he fidgets about, he wants to run home as soon as possible and fondle the bags of cash. Yes, of course he's the gold and dollar collector. Can't you see that his big face is nothing but a democratic combination of the faces of Shylock, the Covetous Knight, and Harpagon? While white-eyes over there is simply a nonentity, a Soviet dormouse. He has a fortune, of course—twelve rubles in the savings bank—and his greatest ambition is to buy a camel-hair coat with a calfskin collar. That's not Koreiko, that's a mouse, which . . ."

But at this point the smooth operator's brilliant speech was interrupted by a male voice shouting from the depths of the room. It clearly belonged to an official who had the right to shout.

"Comrade Koreiko! Where are the figures for our debts to the communal service? Comrade Polykhayev wants them immediately."

Ostap nudged Balaganov. But the walrus mustache continued scratching away with his pen. His face, which bore the features of Shylock, Harpagon, and the Covetous Knight, remained unchanged, while the red-faced, fair-haired man with white eyes, that nonentity, that Soviet mouse obsessed by his dream of a calfskin-collar coat, showed unusual animation. He busily began banging drawers, seized hold of a sheet of paper, and hurried off to answer the call.

The smooth operator gave a croak and looked searchingly at Balaganov. Alex laughed.

"No," said Ostap after a while. "That fellow won't bring us his money on a platter. Not even if I ask him nicely. A worthy objective. Let's get out of here quickly. An amusing idea has come to mind. This evening, with the help of the good Lord, we'll give Mr. Koreiko's udder its first squeeze. You'll do the squeezing, Alex."

Homer, Milton, and Panikovsky

THE INSTRUCTIONS were very simple:

1. Meet citizen Koreiko by chance on the street;
2. Don't hit him under any circumstances and don't use physical force;
3. Remove anything found in the pockets of the citizen in question;
4. Report completion of mission.

Despite the incredible simplicity and lucidity of the instructions issued by the smooth operator, Balaganov and Panikovsky were having a heated argument. The sons of Lieutenant Schmidt sat on a green bench in the park, and threw significant glances at the entrance to the Hercules. On account of their wrangling, they hardly noticed that the wind, bending the hoselike stream of water from the fountain, was showering them with a fine spray. They just waggled their heads, stared at the clear sky, and continued arguing.

Panikovsky, who had changed his thick fireman's tunic for a calico shirt with a turned-down collar because of the heat, was conducting himself imperiously. He was very proud of the mission entrusted to him. "The only way is to pick his pocket," he declared.

"The only way is to waylay him," retorted Balaganov, who was also proud of the commanding officer's trust in him.

"You're a miserable, worthless person," declared Panikovsky, looking at his companion with disgust.

"And you're a cripple," observed Balaganov. "I'm in charge now."

"Who's in charge?"

"I am. I was put in charge."

"You?"

"Me."

"You!!"

"Yes, who do you think? Not you, I hope?"

And the conversation switched to a theme which had little in common with the original instructions. The tricksters got so heated that they began pushing each other away with the flat of their hands and shouting, one above the other, "And who do you think you are?" This kind of behavior usually precedes a free-for-all in which the adversaries throw their caps on the ground, appeal to the bystanders, and brush away the childlike tears on their stubbly visages.

But there was no fight. Just as the right moment arrived for the first slap, Panikovsky suddenly lowered his arms and agreed to consider Balaganov his immediate superior. He most likely remembered he had often been beaten up by separate individuals as well as whole groups, and that it was usually very painful.

Having seized power, Balaganov became more approachable. "Why shouldn't we rob him?" he asked, less persistently. "It isn't so difficult. Koreiko walks home at night. It's dark. I could go up to him from the left and you from the right. I punch him in the left side and you in the right side. The fool stops and cries 'Hooligan!' at me. 'Who's a hooligan?' I ask. Then you ask, 'Who's a hooligan?' and give him one from the right. Then I belt him in the— But no, we mustn't hit him!"

"That's the point. We mustn't hit him," sighed Panikovsky hypocritically. "Bender won't allow it."

"Yes, I know. Anyway, I'll grab his arms and you see whether there's anything interesting in his pockets. He'll shout for the police, which is the usual thing, and then I'll give him— But no, damn it, we mustn't hit him. Anyway, then we go home. How does it sound?"

But Panikovsky declined to give a straight answer. He took the carved hiking stick with a fork instead of a knob at the top that Balaganov was holding and, drawing a straight line in the sand, said, "Look. First, let's wait till evening. Second . . ." Panikovsky drew a wavy perpendicular from the right-hand end of the line. "Second, he may simply not come out this evening. And even if he does . . ." Here Panikovsky joined both lines by a third, so that something rather like a triangle appeared in the sand, and concluded, "Who knows? He may go about in company. How would you like that?"

Balaganov looked at the triangle with admiration. Panikovsky's arguments were not particularly convincing, but the triangle conveyed a feeling of such genuine hopelessness that Balaganov wavered. Observing this, Panikovsky didn't waste a second.

"Go to Kiev," he said unexpectedly. "Then you'll see I'm right. You must definitely go to Kiev!"

"What do you mean, Kiev?" burbled Balaganov. "Why?"

"Go to Kiev and ask what Panikovsky used to do there before the revolution. Just you ask them."

"What are you talking about?" said Balaganov grimly.

"No, you ask!" Panikovsky insisted. "Go and ask. And they'll tell you that before the revolution Panikovsky was blind. Would I really have become one of the sons of Lieutenant Schmidt had it not been for the revolution? After all, I was a rich man. I had a family and a chrome-plated samovar on the table. And where did the money come from? Dark blue glasses and a white stick."

He took out of his pocket a cardboard box wrapped with black paper with dull silver stars, and showed the dark blue glasses.

"These glasses," he said with a sigh, "fed me for many years. I used to go out to the Kreshchatik, the main thoroughfare in Kiev, and ask some decent-looking gentleman to help a blind man across the street. They used to lead me across by the arm. By the time we got to the other side, the gentleman had lost his watch, if he had one, or his billfold. Some of them used to carry billfolds."

"And why did you give it up?" asked Balaganov, gaining interest.

"The revolution," replied the ex-blindman. "I used to pay the policeman at the corner of Kreshchatik and Proreznoy Street five rubles a month, and no one touched me. He even used to see that no one was nasty to me. He was a good man. I met him recently. He's now a music critic. But nowadays! Just try contacting the militia. I've never seen a worse lot. They've become so ideology-conscious, such culture maniacs. And so, Balaganov, in my old age I've had to become a crook. But for this emergency I can bring out the old glasses. They're much more reliable than highway robbery."

Five minutes later a blindman in dark blue glasses emerged from a public lavatory surrounded by beds of tobacco plant and mint. Sticking his chin in the air and tapping his way along with the walking stick, he went toward the park entrance. He was followed by Balaganov. Panikovsky was unrecognizable. Leaning backward and placing his feet carefully on the sidewalk, he walked up to the walls of buildings, tapped his stick against window ledges, bumped into passers-by, and, looking through them, passed on. He worked so diligently that he even dented a long line of people leaning against a pole with the sign "Bus Stop." Balaganov could only gasp with admiration at the smart blindman.

Panikovsky kept up his act until Koreiko appeared at the entrance to the Hercules. Balaganov began darting about. First he moved too near the scene of the intended crime, then he ran too far back. Finally, he took up a suitable observation post by a fruit stall. He had a filthy taste in his mouth, just as though he had been sucking a brass doorknob for half an hour. But, watching Panikovsky's maneuvers, he relaxed.

Balaganov saw the blindman turn toward the millionaire, hook him around the leg with his stick, and butt him with his shoulder, after which they appeared to exchange a few words. Then Koreiko smiled, took the blindman by the arm, and helped him step onto the road. To make things more realistic, Panikovsky dug the cobblestones furiously with his stick and threw back his head as though he were muzzled. His next actions were characterized by such neatness and precision that they made Balaganov really envious. Panikovsky put his arm around his companion's waist. His left hand slid around Koreiko's left side and dwelled for a fraction of a second above the millionaire clerk's canvas pants pocket.

"Come on, come on, you old man!" Balaganov whispered.

But at that moment there was a crash of glass, the warning grunt of a horn, and a large white bus, only just keeping upright, stopped dead in the middle of the street. At the same time two shouts were heard.

"Idiot! Can't you see the bus?" screeched Panikovsky, jumping out of the way of the wheels and threatening his guide with the glasses he had just snatched off his nose.

"You're not really blind!" cried Koreiko in amazement. "You shark!"

Everything was enveloped in blue smoke as the bus moved on, and when the gasoline curtain was lifted, Balaganov saw a small group of agitated citizens surrounding the imaginary blindman. Balaganov ran closer. A hideous grin spread across Panikovsky's

face. He was curiously indifferent to what was going
on, though one of his ears was so ruby-red that it
probably would have shone in the dark and you could
have developed films by it.

Pushing his way through the crowd of citizens hurrying over from all sides, Balaganov raced to the
Carlsbad Hotel.

The smooth operator was sitting at a bamboo table
writing.

"Panikovsky's being beaten up!" cried Balaganov,
appearing in the doorway in a rather theatrical way.

"What, already?" Ostap inquired in a businesslike
tone. "That's rather soon."

"They're mobbing him," cried the red-haired Alex
in desperation. "Near the Hercules."

"Stop roaring like a polar bear in warm weather,"
Ostap sternly ordered. "How long has it been going
on?"

"About five minutes."

"Then why didn't you say so? There's a cantanker-
ous old man for you. Well, let's go and see the sight.
You can tell me about it on the way."

By the time the smooth operator arrived at the spot,
Koreiko had gone, but Panikovsky was still in the middle of the dense crowd jamming the street. Cars
quacked impatiently, digging their noses into the mass
of people. Nurses peered out of ambulance windows,
and dogs with curly, saber-like tails ran around in circles. The fountain in the park had stopped. Sighing
with determination, Ostap pushed through the crowd.

"Excuse me, madam, wasn't it you who lost a jam
coupon at the corner? Hurry up, it's still lying there.
Let the experts through, men! Let that refugee alone,
I tell you."

Applying the policy of the whip and the gingerbread, Ostap reached the middle, where Panikovsky
was imprisoned. By this time it would have been possible to develop photographs by the light of the con-

vention violator's second ear as well. Seeing his captain, Panikovsky lowered his head dejectedly.

"Is this the one?" asked Ostap curtly, thumping Panikovsky in the back.

"Yes, him," came the eager voices of truth-lovers in confirmation. "We saw him ourselves."

Ostap called upon the citizens to remain calm, took out his notebook, and, looking at Panikovsky, proclaimed authoritatively, "All witnesses please supply their names and addresses!"

It might have been thought that the citizens who showed such eagerness in apprehending Panikovsky would not have hesitated to give their evidence against the offender. But in actual fact, at the mention of the word "witnesses" all the truth-lovers lost interest and began moving slowly away. Gaps appeared in the crowd. It was disintegrating even as one watched.

"Where are the witnesses?" Ostap repeated.

Panic broke out. The witnesses elbowed their way through the crowd and a minute later the street was back to normal. The cars raced away, the ambulance windows banged shut, the dogs began carefully inspecting the bottoms of lampposts, and the fountain in the park sent up a jet of frothing water.

Making certain that the street was clear and that Panikovsky was no longer in danger, the smooth operator said in a disgruntled tone, "You worthless man! Clueless clot! Now we have another great name among the blind—Panikovsky! Homer, Milton, and Panikovsky. Good company for them. And Balaganov comes running in like a shipwrecked mariner. 'They're beating up Panikovsky,' he shouts, but he himself . . . Let's go into the park. We'll have a little scene by the fountain."

At the fountain, Balaganov immediately laid all the blame on Panikovsky, while the bedraggled blindman protested that his nerves were shattered and that the person responsible for it all was Balaganov, who was, as is well known, pitiful and worthless. At this point

the brothers started shoving each other again. Monotonous exclamations of "Who do you think you
are?" were already audible, and a large tear, the fore-
runner of the free-for-all, had already sprung to Panikovsky's eye, when the smooth operator called
"Break" and parted the opponents like an umpire
in the boxing ring.

"You can have a boxing match on your days off,"
he said. "A splendid pair: Balaganov a bantam weight,
and Panikovsky a chicken! However, my prize fight-
ers, there's as much chance of making workers out of
you as there is of making a strainer from a dog's tail.
You'll come to a sticky end. I'll fire you, especially
since you don't represent anything of social value."

Forgetting about their quarrel, Panikovsky and Balaganov began swearing and promising that they
would find Koreiko by that very evening, come what
may. Bender only laughed.

"You'll see," Balaganov bristled. "Waylaid in the
street. Under the cover of night. That's right, isn't it,
Michael Samuelevich?"

"Honestly," Panikovsky confirmed. "Alex and I
. . . Don't worry. You're dealing with Panikovsky!"

"That's just the trouble," said Bender, "though . . .
what did you say? 'Under the cover of night.' All
right, do it at night, then. Although the idea is rather
a wishy-washy one, and I doubt whether the performance will be much better."

After several hours of keeping watch on the street,
the basic prerequisites for the situation were finally
found—the cover of night and the patient himself,
who left his house with a girl from the apartment in-
habited by the puzzle-poser. The girl didn't fit into
the plan. For the time being they were forced to follow behind the couple, who went toward the sea
front.

A blazing fragment of moon hung low over the
fast cooling shore. The cliffs were ranged with black
basalt couples, locked in eternal embraces. The sea

murmured eternal love, irretrievable happiness, the madness of the heart, and other such non-topical trifles. Star spoke to star in Morse code. A tunnel of light from a searchlight joined the shores of the gulf. When it disappeared, a black streak remained on the water for some time after.

"I'm tired," Panikovsky whimpered, tottering along the cliffs after Koreiko and his girl-friend. "I'm too old. I can't do it."

He kept stumbling over gopher holes and, as he fell, clutching at dry cow claps. He was longing to get back to the tavern, to the thrifty Kozlevich, with whom it was so nice to drink tea and chat about this and that.

Just as Panikovsky had firmly made up his mind to go home and was about to suggest that Balaganov continue by himself, he heard a voice in front saying:

"How warm it is. Do you ever go swimming at night, Alexander Ivanovich? Then wait here a moment. I'll take a quick dip and be back!"

There came the sound of pebbles rolling down the cliff, the white dress vanished, and Koreiko was left alone.

"Quick!" Balaganov whispered, pulling Panikovsky by the arm. "I'll come up on his left flank, and you on the right. Only make it snappy!"

"I'm on the left," said the violator of the convention timidly.

"That's right, you're on the right. I'll give him a punch in the left side—I mean the right—and you wallop him on the left."

"Why the left?"

"You would ask that! All right, then, the right. He shouts out 'Hooligan!' and you answer 'Who's a hooligan?' "

"No, you answer first."

"All right, only I'll tell Bender. Let's go. So you come up on the right."

And the valiant sons of Lieutenant Schmidt, both scared stiff, approached Koreiko.

The plan was sabotaged from the very beginning. Instead of coming up on the right flank and punching the millionaire in the right side, according to the pre-arranged disposition, Balaganov hung back and unexpectedly asked:

"Have you got a light?"

"I don't smoke," Koreiko answered coldly.

"Oh," said Alex stupidly, glaring at Panikovsky. "Any idea what time it is?"

"About midnight."

"Midnight," Balaganov repeated. "Hm, I had no idea . . ."

"A warm evening," said Panikovsky fawningly.

There was a pause, during which the crickets chirped feverishly. The moon showed white, and in its light Alexander Ivanovich's brawny shoulders could be made out quite clearly. Panikovsky couldn't stand the strain. He went behind Koreiko's back and screeched:

"Hands up!"

"What?" Koreiko asked in surprise.

"Hands up!" Panikovsky repeated in a more subdued voice, whereupon he received a quick but painful blow in the shoulder and fell down. By the time he regained his feet, Koreiko was already entangled with Balaganov. Both were panting, as though they had just moved a grand piano. From way below came the sound of mermaidish laughter and splashing.

"Why are you fighting me?" Balaganov burst out. "I only asked you the time."

"I'll show you what time it is!" hissed Koreiko, imbuing his blows with the centuries-old hatred of the rich man for the robber.

Panikovsky crawled over to the scene of the battle on all fours and slipped both hands into the Herculean's pockets from behind. Koreiko lashed out with his foot, but it was too late. The metal *Caucasus* cigarette

box had changed places from his pocket to Panikovsky's hands. From his other pocket fell some money
and membership cards.

"Let's go!" cried Panikovsky from somewhere in
the darkness.

A few minutes later the bruised and battered
Koreiko caught a glimpse of two bluish moonlit
figures way above him. He knelt down and, lighting
matches with trembling fingers, collected his papers
from the ground. Before Zosya had time to ask him
what had happened, he had already found the receipt
for the suitcase, now reclining in the baggage-room
office between a reed basket and a flannelette brief
case.

"I dropped them," he said, forcing a smile and carefully putting away the receipt.

It was not until they were back in town that he remembered the cigarette box containing ten thousand
rubles, which he had not had time to put in the case.

In the meantime, a titanic struggle was in progress
on the shore. Ostap Bender had decided that his stay
in the hotel in full view of the whole town was un-
warranted and gave him an unduly official air. Reading an advertisement in the evening paper to the effect
that "Nice rm. let lon. intell. bach., v. of s., all mod.
con.," and realizing instantly that this meant "Nice
room to let to lonely intellectual bachelor, view of
sea, all modern conveniences," Ostap thought to himself, "I seem to be a bachelor just now. Quite recently
the Stargorod Registry Office sent me notification
that my marriage to the widow Gritsatsuyeva had
been annulled at her request, and that I'm now plain
Ostap Bender again as before. Okay, then, I'll relive
my pre-married life. I'm a bachelor, lonely, and intellectual. The room is obviously for me."

And, pulling on his cool white pants, the smooth
operator set off for the address indicated in the advertisement.

: *13* :

Vasisualy Lokhankin and His Role in the Russian Revolution

AT EXACTLY 4:40 P.M. Vasisualy Lokhankin went on a hunger strike.

He lay on an oilcloth couch with his face to its convex back, rejecting the whole world. He had on green suspenders and green socks.

Having starved for twenty minutes in this position, he groaned, turned onto his other side, and looked at his wife. His green socks described a small arc in the air as he did so. His wife was throwing her worldly goods into a colored traveling bag; they consisted of oddly shaped bottles, a rubber roller for massage, two dresses with and an old one without, a felt hat with a glass crescent, brass bullets containing lipstick, and knitted bloomers.

"Barbara!" Lokhankin called through his nose.

His wife said nothing, but breathed loudly.

"Barbara," he repeated. "Are you really leaving me for Ptiburdukov?"

"Yes," replied the wife, "I'm leaving. It has to be."

"But why, why?" asked Lokhankin with bovine passion. His nostrils, large enough as they were, distended with grief. The Pharaonic beard quivered.

"Because I love him."

"And what about me?"

"Vasisualy, I notified you yesterday. I don't love you any more."

"But I love you, Barbara."

"That's your business, Vasisualy. I'm going to Ptiburdukov. I must."

"No, you mustn't," Lokhankin exclaimed. "A person can't leave when someone loves them."

"Yes they can," said his wife irritably, peering into a pocket mirror. "And, anyway, stop fooling around, Vasisualy."

"In that case I'll continue my hunger strike!" cried the unhappy husband. "I'll starve until you come back. Whether it's a day or a week. Even if it's a year!"

Lokhankin turned over again and thrust his nose against the cold, slippery oilcloth.

"And I shall lie here in my suspenders," came his voice from the couch, "until I die. And you and Ptiburdukov will be responsible for everything!"

His wife thought for a moment, hoisted back a shoulder strap that had slipped off her white, underdone shoulder, and suddenly let fly with, "How dare you talk about Ptiburdukov in that way! He's greater than you!"

That was the last straw. Lokhankin gave a shudder, as though an electric current had gone right through him, from suspenders to green socks. "You female, Barbara," he whimpered slowly. "You tramp!"

"Vasisualy, you're a fool!" his wife replied calmly.

"A bitch is what you are," Lokhankin continued, in the same drawling voice. "And I despise you. You're leaving me to go and live with him. That worthless Ptiburdukov, you cow. You want to fornicate with him. You dirty old bitch."

Reveling in his grief, Lokhankin failed to notice that he was talking in iambic pentameters, although he had never written poetry and didn't like reading it.

"Vasisualy, stop clowning," said the cow, doing up

her bag. "Just look at yourself. You might at least wash. I'm going. Good-by, Vasisualy! I've left your bread-ration card on the table."

And, picking up the bag, Barbara made for the door. Seeing that the invocations hadn't worked, Lokhankin briskly leapt to his feet, ran across to the table, and with a cry of "Help!" tore up the card. Barbara was alarmed. She had visions of a husband withered with hunger, with a feeble pulse and cold appendages.

"What have you done?" said Barbara. "You have no right to starve yourself."

"Yes I have."

"It's stupid, Vasisualy. It's a revolt of the personality."

"And I'm proud of it," said Lokhankin in a suspiciously un-iambic tone. "You underrate the value of the personality, and the intelligentsia as a whole."

"But you'll be publicly censured."

"So what!" said Vasisualy firmly, and threw himself onto the couch again.

Barbara silently threw the bag onto the floor, hurriedly pulled off her straw bonnet, and, muttering something about "rampant male," "tyrant," and "capitalist," hastily made a mashed-eggplant sandwich.

"Eat!" she ordered, holding the food to her husband's puce lips. "Do you hear, Lokhankin? Eat this moment!"

"Leave me alone," he replied, pushing his wife's hand away.

Taking advantage of the fact that the hunger-striker's mouth opened for an instant, Barbara nimbly popped the sandwich into the cavity which formed between the Pharaonic beard and the trimmed Moscow mustache. But the hunger-striker ejected the food with a strong thrust of his tongue.

"Eat, you villain!" cried Barbara in desperation, trying to stuff the sandwich into his mouth again. "You intellectual!"

But Lokhankin kept moving his face about and moaning negatively. A few minutes later the hot and bothered eggplant-smeared Barbara gave up. She sat down on her bag and wept icy tears.

Lokhankin brushed away the crumbs which had lodged in his beard, threw his wife a crazy sidelong glance, and settled down on his couch. He didn't want to part with Barbara. Apart from a large number of defects, Barbara had two important merits—a large white bosom and a job. Vasisualy himself never went to work. A job would have prevented him from thinking about the significance of the Russian intelligentsia, the social group in which he classed himself. Actually, Lokhankin's prolonged meditation boiled down to the pleasant and intimate subject of "Vasisualy Lokhankin and his significance," "Lokhankin and the tragedy of Russian liberalism," and "Lokhankin and his role in the Russian revolution." It was easy and relaxing to think about these things while wandering up and down the room in felt boots bought with Barbara's money, and gazing at his favorite cupboard in which the backs of the Brockhaus Encyclopedia glittered with church gold. Vasisualy would stand for hours running his eyes from volume to volume.

The magnificent examples of the art of bookbinding were arranged in order of size along the shelves: the large Medical Encyclopedia, the *Life of Animals*, a tome weighing half a ton called *Man and Woman*, and Elisé Réclus' *Land and People*.

"When you stand next to such a treasury of knowledge," mused Lokhankin, "you become purer, you somehow grow spiritually."

Having arrived at this conclusion, he sighed with pleasure, dragged out some copies of *Motherland* for 1899 from under the cupboard, bound the color of sea water with foam and spray, examined the pictures of the Boer War, an advertisement by an unknown

woman—"How I increased my bust six inches"—
and various other interesting items.

If Barbara left, the financial basis on which rested
the security of this worthy representative of thinking
mankind would disappear as well.

Ptiburdukov arrived in the evening. He hesitated
for some time before entering the Lokhankins' room,
and puttered about the kitchen among the long-
flamed primuses and crisscrossing ropes on which hung
dry, plaster-like underclothing with bruiselike marks
from the bluing. The apartment came to life. Doors
banged, shadows flitted past, the tenants' eyes gleamed,
and from somewhere came a passionate sigh: a man
had arrived.

Ptiburdukov took off his peaked cap, pulled at his
engineer's mustache, and finally made up his mind.

"Barbie," he said imploringly, coming into the
room, "we agreed—"

"Just look at him, Al!" Barbara shouted, seizing
his arm and pushing him over to the couch. "There
he is. A male. A rotten capitalist. Do you realize this
feudal landowner has declared a hunger strike just
when I want to leave him?"

Seeing Ptiburdukov, the striker immediately
launched into iambic pentameter. "Ptiburdukov, I
really do despise you," he whined. "Don't dare to lay
your hands upon my wife. You're a bum and a louse,
Ptiburdukov. Where do you think you're going to
take my wife?"

"Comrade Lokhankin," said the dazed lover, pulling
at his mustache.

"Get out, get out, the sight of you's revolting,"
Vasisualy continued, rocking to and fro like an old
Jew saying his prayers. "A worthless, filthy nit is what
you are. You're not an engineer, you're just a bum, a
louse, a creep, a jerk, and a pimp to boot!"

"You should be ashamed of yourself, Vasisualy
Andreyevich," said the bored Ptiburdukov. "It's just

stupid. Think what you're doing. The second year of the five-year plan."

"You have the gall to tell me that it's stupid? You, who pinched my wife from me? Get out, or else I'll turn you into mincemeat."

"He's sick," said Ptiburdukov, striving to keep within the limits of decorum.

But for Barbara the limits were too constraining. She grabbed the rather stale sandwich from the table and marched up to the hunger-striker. Lokhankin defended himself with such desperation that anyone would have thought he was being castrated. Ptiburdukov turned away and looked out of the window at the horse chestnut blossoming with little white candles. Behind him he could hear Lokhankin's sickening whining and Barbara's cries of "Eat, you foul beast! Eat, you feudal lord!"

The next day Barbara stayed away from work, having been upset by the unexpected obstacle in her way. The hunger-striker felt worse.

"I already feel pains in my stomach," he reported with gratification. "And I'll soon have scurvy through malnutrition and loss of hair and teeth."

Ptiburdukov brought along his brother, an army doctor. Ptiburdukov the Second applied his ear to Lokhankin's torso for some time, listening to the functioning of his organs with the same attention with which a cat listens to the movement of a mouse that has crept into the sugar bowl. During the examination Vasisualy stared at his chest, as shaggy as an autumn overcoat, with tear-filled eyes. He felt very sorry for himself. Ptiburdukov the Second looked at Ptiburdukov the First and declared that the sick man did not need to diet. He could eat anything at all. Soup, for instance, meatballs, or stewed fruit. Bread, too, and vegetables and fruit. Fish was permissible, too. He could smoke, though in moderation. Drinking was inadvisable, but a glass of port might be good for the appetite. In short, the doctor was a poor judge of the

Lokhankins' spiritual drama. Pouting pompously and scraping his heels, he left, adding that the patient might well have a swim in the sea and go cycling.

But the patient had no intention of taking either stewed fruit, fish, meatballs, or anything else into his system. He didn't go swimming, but stayed on the couch, showering those around him with pejorative iambuses. Barbara felt pity for him. "He's doing it for my sake," she thought with pride. "What noble sentiment! Is Al capable of such lofty feelings?" And she cast worried glances at the replete Al, whose appearance indicated that his pangs of love did not prevent him from regularly consuming meals.

On one occasion when Ptiburdukov had gone out of the room, she even called Vasisualy "Poor little thing." This was accompanied by reappearance of the sandwich near the striker's mouth and the rejection of same. "Just a little longer," thought Lokhankin, "and my Barbara will never see Ptiburdukov again."

He listened to the voices in the next room and was delighted at what he heard.

"He'll die without me," Barbara was saying. "We'll have to wait a bit. You see I can't come now, don't you?"

That night Barbara had a terrible dream. Emaciated with lofty feelings, Vasisualy was gnawing the white spurs on the military doctor's boots. It was ghastly. The doctor's face had the same calm expression as that of a cow being milked by a village milk thief. The spurs jingled and the teeth rattled. Barbara woke up in fright.

A yellow Japanese sun was shining bright, wasting all its energy on lighting such insignificant trifles as the cut-glass top of a flask of *Turandot* eau de Cologne. The oilcloth couch was empty. Barbara moved her eyes and espied Vasisualy standing by the open door of the sideboard, with his back to the bed, munching loudly. His impatience and greed were so great that he was bending down, tapping the floor

with a green-clad foot, and making snuffling and
snorting noises. Having demolished a large can of pre-
serves, he cautiously removed the lid from a saucepan
and, dipping his fingers into the cold beet soup,
fished out a piece of meat. Even if Barbara had caught
her husband at this game at the happiest moment in
their married life, Vasisualy would have had it coming
to him. But this time his fate was sealed.

"Lokhankin!" she cried in a terrible voice.

The frightened hunger-striker let go of the piece
of meat, which plopped back into the saucepan, send-
ing up a spray of cabbage and flecks of carrot. He
rushed back to the couch with a pitiful howl. Barbara
dressed quickly and in silence.

"Barbara," said Lokhankin through his nose, "are
you really leaving me for Ptiburdukov?"

There was no answer.

"You bitch," Lokhankin declared in an uncertain
voice. "I hate the sight of you. You're leaving me for
Ptiburdukov . . ."

But it was too late. It was no use whimpering about
love and starving to death. Barbara had gone for good,
dragging with her a traveling bag containing a pair of
colored bloomers, a felt hat, fancy bottles, and other
articles in everyday use by ladies.

A period of painful thoughts and moral suffering
had arrived in the life of Vasisualy Lokhankin. There
are people who don't know how to suffer; they somehow don't manage. And even if they do, they try to
get through it as quickly as possible, unobserved. Lokhankin, however, suffered openly and majestically:
he encouraged his woes with cups of tea and reveled
in them. The great malaise gave him the chance of
pondering yet again on the meaning of the Russian
intelligentsia, or the tragedy of Russian liberalism.

"But perhaps it's necessary," he thought to himself.
"Perhaps it's atonement and I'll be purified. Isn't that,
after all, the lot of those with a sensitive make-up, like

Galileo, Milyukov, and A. F. Koni, who rise above the crowd? Yes, indeed, Barbara's right. It's necessary."

However, his depression did not prevent him from placing an advertisement in the paper to the effect that he wanted to sublet the room.

"It will be material support for me at the beginning," he decided. And he reimmersed himself in his nebulous meditation on mortification of the flesh and the importance of the soul as a source of the beautiful.

He could not even be distracted from this occupation by his neighbors' persistent exhortations to turn out the light in the toilet after use. In his emotional turmoil, Lokhankin often forgot to do so, thus infuriating the thrifty tenants.

The inmates of the large communal apartment, No. 3, in which Lokhankin lived were considered odd, anyway, and were known throughout the apartment house for their frequent bickering and squabbling. The apartment had even been nicknamed "Rooks' Row."

Prolonged cohabitation had hardened them and they knew no fear. The household balance of power was maintained by military blocks of the tenants. Sometimes they all ganged up against a tenant, and the one in question came off badly. The centripetal force of barratry seized him up, sucked him into solicitors' offices, swept him through the foggy law-court corridors like a whirlwind, and pushed him into the courtrooms. For a long time after, the rebellious tenant would peregrinate in search of truth, trying to reach the height of Comrade Kalinin, the All-Union Elder. And to his dying day the tenant used to bandy about legal jargon which he had picked up in various official establishments, where they say "correction" instead of "punishment" and "offense" instead of "crime." He no longer used "Comrade Zhukov," as he was born, but "the injured party." But most of all, and with particular relish, he would use the phrase "to file a suit." And his life, which even before was hardly one of luxury, then became a pure misery.

Some time before the Lokhankin family tragedy, a pilot named Sevryugov, who had the misfortune to live in apartment No. 3, flew over the polar circle on an urgent job for the Voluntary Defense Organization. The whole world followed his flight with excitement. A foreign expedition exploring the Pole had been reported missing, and Sevryugov was given the job of finding it. The world lived in hope of the success of the pilot's mission. Radio stations on all continents sent each other messages, meteorologists warned the valiant pilot of magnetic storms, shortwave enthusiasts filled the ether with crackling, and the Polish newspaper *Kurjer Poranny*, close to the Foreign Ministry, demanded the extension of Poland as far as the 1772 frontier. For a whole month Sevryugov flew over the desert of ice, and the roar of his engines was heard by the whole world.

Sevryugov finally did something that completely floored the newspaper close to the Polish Foreign Ministry. He found the expedition among the mountains of ice, reported its exact location, and then vanished himself. At this news the whole globe was filled with sound. Sevryugov's name was uttered in three hundred and twenty languages and dialects, including Blackfoot Indian; pictures of Sevryugov wrapped in furs appeared on every spare sheet of newspaper. In an interview with the press, Gabriele d'Annunzio declared he had just finished a new novel and was setting off by air to find the valiant flier. A Charleston called "I'm warm with my cutie at the Pole" came into vogue, and the old Moscow hacks, Uslyshkin-Werther, Leonid Trepetovsky, and Boris Ammiakov, who had been practicing literary "dumping" for years and swamping the market with their produce at dirt-cheap prices, were already writing a review called "Aren't You Cold?" In short, our planet was in the grips of a great sensation.

But the report caused an even greater sensation in apartment No. 3 at No. 8 Lemon Alley, better known as Rooks' Row.

"Our tenant's missing," said Nikita Pryakhin, a retired superintendent, as he dried a felt boot by the primus. "He's lost, the dear boy. Don't fly, don't fly. A man should walk, not fly." And he turned the boot over the hissing flame.

"He's had his stint of flying," mumbled Grandma, whose name no one knew. She lived on the mezzanine above the kitchen, and although the whole apartment had electricity, Grandma used to use a kerosene lamp with a reflector. She didn't trust electricity. "So his room's now free! There's space at last!"

She was the first to utter the word which had for some time depressed the tenants.

The missing pilot's room became the subject of everyone's conversation: citizen Gigienishvili, a Caucasian ex-prince now a working man from Siberia, and Dunya, who rented a bunk in Auntie Pasha's room, and Auntie Pasha herself, a tradeswoman and hardened drinker, and Alexander Sukhoveiko, who was once a gentleman-in-waiting at the court of His Imperial Majesty, but was now simply called Mitrich, and various other small fry headed by Lucy Pferd, who was legally responsible for the apartment.

"Well," said Mitrich, adjusting his gold-rimmed spectacles, as soon as the kitchen was full of tenants, "if the fellow has disappeared, the room should be allotted to someone. I've been due for extra space for some time."

"Why should a man need space?" objected Dunya the bunk-renter. "Though a woman does. It may never happen again in my lifetime that someone gets lost."

And for some time she wandered among the gathered tenants, putting forward various reasons why she should have the room, and frequently repeating the word "man."

At any rate, the tenants all agreed that the room should be taken over at once.

The same day the world was shaken by another sensation. The brave Sevryugov had been found. Nizhni Novgorod, Quebec, and Reykjavik heard Sevryugov's call signals. He was sitting on the eighty-fourth parallel with a dented undercarriage. The ether hummed with reports: "Brave Russian feels well"; "Sevryugov reports to Presidium of Voluntary Defense Organization"; "Charles Lindbergh rates Sevryugov best flier in world"; "Seven icebreakers go to aid of Sevryugov and expedition." In the intervals between these reports the newspapers printed photographs of ice-bound shores. The words "Sevryugov," "North Cape," "parallel," "Sevryugov," "Franz-Josef Land," "Spitzbergen," "Kings Bay," "fur-lined boots," "Sevryugov," "fuel," were endlessly repeated.

The gloom which overcame the apartment at this news was soon replaced by calm confidence. The icebreakers could only move slowly, breaking through the ice with difficulty.

"We should take the room and finish," said Nikita Pryakhin. "It's all very well for him to stay there on the ice, but Dunya here has every right to it. Especially since by law a tenant is not allowed to vacate his room for more than two months."

"You ought to be ashamed, Comrade Pryakhin!" retorted Barbara, who was still a Lokhankin at that time, waving a copy of *Izvestiya*. "He's a hero. He's at the eighty-fourth parallel!"

"Which parallel is that?" asked Mitrich vaguely. "There may not be any such parallel. We don't know. We didn't go to school."

Mitrich was telling the sober truth. He hadn't gone to school. He had been in the *Corps de Pages*.

"Try to understand," seethed Barbara, holding up a sheet of newspaper in front of the gentleman-in-waiting's nose. "Here's the article. Don't you see? 'Among the hummocks and icebergs.'"

"Icebergs!" sneered Mitrich. "That we can understand, all right. We haven't lived properly for ten
years. It's all icebergs, Weisbergs, Eisenbergs, and Ra-
binoviches of all kinds. Pryakhin's right. Let's take the
room and finish. All the more so, since Lucy Franzevna
has confirmed that it's within the law."

"Throw his damned stuff out on the stairs," exclaimed the ex-prince in a deep voice.

They all went for Barbara, and she ran off to complain to her husband.

"Maybe it's necessary," her husband answered, lifting his Pharaonic beard. "Maybe the simple peasant
Mitrich is speaking the peasant truth. Just think of the
role of the Russian intelligentsia and its significance."

On the great day that icebreakers finally reached
Sevryugov's tent, citizen Gigienishvili broke the lock
on the door and threw out the whole of the hero's belongings onto the landing, including the red propeller
hanging on the wall. The room was taken over by
Dunya, who immediately sublet it to six lodgers. The
whole night they celebrated in the newly conquered
territory.

Pryakhin played the accordion and Mitrich danced
a Russian folk dance with Auntie Pasha.

Had Sevryugov had just a fraction less of the
world-wide glory gained by his impressive flights over
the Arctic, he would never have seen his room again,
but would have been whisked away by the centripetal
force of legal wrangles, and to his dying day would
have referred to himself as the "injured party." But
this time Rooks' Row was soundly squashed. The
room was returned to him (he moved out soon afterward), while the dashing Gigienishvili was put in jail
for three months for taking the law into his own hands,
and came out like a bear with a sore head.

It was he who made the first representations to the
deserted Lokhankin about turning the light out in the
toilet after use. His eyes had a diabolical glint as
he said it. The absent-minded Lokhankin failed to as-

sess the importance of this diplomatic move by citizen
Gigienishvili and thus muffed the beginning of a conflict which soon led to an event that was both terrifying and unprecedented in housing practice.

This is how it all happened. Vasisualy Lokhankin still
kept forgetting to turn out the light in the most used
room in the apartment. Indeed, how could he be expected to remember such an unimportant thing when
his wife had gone and left him without a cent, when
he still had not come to his final conclusion on the
tremendous significance of the Russian intelligentsia.
Could he be expected to think that the miserable
bronze light emitted by the eight-watt bulb would
arouse such strong feelings among the neighbors? At
the beginning they warned him several times a day.
Then they sent him a letter, composed by Mitrich
and signed by all the tenants. Finally they stopped
warning him and sent no more letters. Lokhankin had
still not realized the significance of the situation, but
he had a vague sort of feeling that something was
brewing.

On Tuesday evening Auntie Pasha's little girl came
running along and rattled off all in one breath,
"They're telling you for the last time to turn the light
out."

But somehow or other Vasisualy Andreyevich forgot again and the light continued to glow in criminal
fashion through the cobwebs and dirt. The apartment
gave a sigh. A minute later citizen Gigienishvili appeared in the doorway of Lokhankin's room. He was
wearing blue cloth boots and a flat cap made of brown
lamb's wool.

"Come on," he said, beckoning Vasisualy with his
finger.

He seized him firmly by the arm and led him along
the dark corridor, where for some reason Vasisualy
became rather bored and tried to resist, and shoved
him into the middle of the kitchen. Clutching hold
of the wash lines, Vasisualy managed to keep his bal-

ance and looked around him in alarm. The whole apartment was gathered there. Lucy Pferd was there, standing in silence. There were violet wrinkles on her imperious face. Alongside her sat the tipsy Auntie Pasha, looking sad. Nikita Pryakhin, without his shoes, grinned at the timid Lokhankin. The ownerless grandma was leaning over the mezzanine stairs. Dunya was making signs at Mitrich, who was smiling and hiding something behind his back.

"Is there going to be a general meeting?" asked Vasisualy in a high-pitched voice.

"Yes, yes," said Pryakhin, approaching Lokhankin, "there's going to be everything. Coffee and cocoa if you like. Bend over!" he suddenly shouted, breathing a mixture of vodka and turpentine fumes on Vasisualy.

"In what sense bend over?" asked Lokhankin, beginning to tremble.

"What's the use of talking to him, the bad man," said citizen Gigienishvili, and, squatting down, he began fumbling around Lokhankin's waist, undoing his suspenders.

"Help!" called Vasisualy in a whisper, throwing Lucy Pferd a desperate look.

"You should have turned the light out!" said citizenness Pferd sternly.

"We're not like the bourgeoisie who burn electric lights for nothing," added the gentleman-in-waiting, dipping something into a bucket of water.

"I'm not guilty," squeaked Lokhankin, trying to tear himself out of the ex-prince's grip.

"None of us are guilty," mumbled Pryakhin, keeping hold of the trembling tenant.

"I haven't done anything."

"No one's done anything!"

"I suffer from mental depression."

"Everyone does."

"Don't dare touch me. I'm anemic."

"Everyone's anemic."

"My wife has left me."

"Everyone's wife has left them."

"Come on, come on, Nikita!" Mitrich said, bringing wet, glistening birch rods out into the light. "We'll be here all night with all this talk."

Vasisualy Lokhankin was placed face down on the floor. His legs were a milky white. Gigienishvili swung with all his might and the birch swished through the air.

"Mommie!" shrieked Vasisualy.

"Everyone has a mommie," said Nikita informatively, holding Lokhankin down with his knee. And then Vasisualy suddenly went quiet. "Perhaps it's necessary," he thought, jerking from the strokes and staring at Nikita's dark, armor-like toenails. "Perhaps this is atonement, purification, and great sacrifice."

And while they thrashed him, while Dunya chuckled with embarrassment, and Grandma called from the stairs "That's what he deserves, the poor boy." Vasisualy Lokhankin meditated on the significance of the Russian intelligentsia and the fact that Galileo had also suffered for the truth.

The last to take up the birch was Mitrich.

"Let me have a go," he said, raising his arm. "I'll give him a few strokes on the rump."

But Lokhankin didn't have to taste the gentleman-in-waiting's strokes. There was a knock at the back door. Dunya ran to open it. (The front door of the apartment had been boarded up some time before, as the tenants couldn't decide who should wash the stairs first. The bathroom was tightly locked for the same reason.)

"Vasisualy Andreyevich, there's a man asking for you," said Dunya, as though nothing had happened.

And they all caught sight of a man in gentleman's white trousers standing in the doorway. Vasisualy jumped up, adjusted his clothes, and turned toward the stranger with a confused smile.

"I hope I haven't disturbed you," said the smooth
operator politely, squinting hard.

"No, no," Lokhankin stammered, scraping his feet.
"You see, I was just a little busy . . . but . . . I think
I'm free now."

He glanced around him, but there was no one left
in the kitchen except for Auntie Pasha, who had dozed
off on the stove during the thrashing. The floor was
strewn with birch rods and a white cloth button with
two little holes.

"Please come this way," Vasisualy invited.

"But I'm afraid I've interrupted you anyway," said
Ostap as they went into Lokhankin's first room. "No?
Good. Well, it's about the advertisement. Does it really
have all mod. con.?"

"Yes indeed," said Lokhankin, brightening up. "It's
a wonderful room with all conveniences. And I'm
not asking much for it. Fifty rubles a month."

"I won't haggle," Ostap replied politely. "But what
about the neighbors?"

"Marvelous people," Vasisualy answered. "And it
has all conveniences and isn't expensive."

"But they seem to allow corporal punishment here."

"Ah, who knows in the long run," said Lokhankin
with great insight. "Perhaps it's necessary. Perhaps
therein lies the great peasant truth."

"Great peasant truth," Ostap repeated thoughtfully. "I see. Tell me, from which grade in school
were you kicked out for failing your exams? Sixth?"

"Fifth," Lokhankin replied.

"Very fine grade. So you didn't get as far as Kraye-
vich's physics? And have you lived an entirely intellectual life since then? It doesn't matter, anyway.
Live how you like. I'll move in tomorrow."

"What about a deposit?" asked the high-school
graduate.

"You're not in church: you won't be cheated," said
the smooth operator weightily. "You'll get your
deposit in the course of time."

The First Date

WHEN OSTAP got back to the Carlsbad Hotel and, having seen himself reflected countless times in the mirrors with which the vestibules, stairways, and corridors of establishments of this kind are so often adorned, reached his room, he was astonished at the disorder reigning inside. The red velvet chair lay with its dock-tail feet in the air, exhibiting an unsightly jute underneath. The velvet tablecloth with tassels had slid off the table. Even the picture *Christ Appears to the People* was askew and thereby lost much of the edification with which the artist had imbued it. A cool, steamship breeze blew from the balcony, rustling the currency notes strewn over the bed. A metal *Caucasus* cigarette box lay in the middle. Panikovsky and Balaganov were rolling about in silence on the carpet, locked together and kicking with their feet.

The smooth operator disdainfully stepped over them and went out onto the balcony. People were strolling past on the avenue below, the gravel crunched under their feet, and the concerted breath of a symphony orchestra wafted over the black maples. The murky depths of the port teemed with lights, and a refrigerator ship under construction clanked in the darkness. Beyond the breakwater an invisible steamer hooted a request, probably wanting to enter the harbor.

Going back into his room, Ostap saw that the foster brothers were now sitting exhausted on the floor opposite one another, pushing each other and mumbling, "And who do you think you are?"

"Haven't you divided the money?" asked Ostap, drawing the curtain.

Panikovsky and Balaganov jumped to their feet and began explaining. Each attributed complete success to himself and blackened the actions of the other. The more shameful details were automatically omitted, and instead they gave a large number of facts highlighting their initiative and bravado.

"That's enough," Ostap said. "Don't bang your bald patch against the floor. I get the picture. You say there was a girl with him. That's good. So, the little clerk carries in his pocket . . . I suppose you've counted it. How much is there? Oho! Ten thousand! Mr. Koreiko's wages for twenty years' impeccable service. A sight for the gods, as the most intelligent and advanced writers put it. But I've probably disturbed you. You were doing something on the floor, weren't you? Carry on, I'll watch."

"I was trying to divide it honestly and fairly," said Balaganov, picking up the money from the bed. "Everyone gets an equal share of two and a half thousand." And, placing the money in four piles, he modestly stood back and said, "You, me, him, and Kozlevich."

"Very good," observed Ostap. "And now let Panikovsky divide it up. He seems to have his own opinion."

The man with his own opinion went to work with gusto. Bending over the bed, he moved his thick lips, wet his fingers, and moved the notes from one pile to another like someone playing solitaire.

At the end of his manipulations there were three

mounds on the blanket—one big one, composed of
crisp, new bank notes, a second just as big, but with
rather dirtier notes, and a third, smaller one, consisting
of the dirtiest money of all.

"You and I get four thousand," he said to Bender,
"and Balaganov gets two thousand. He doesn't even
deserve that."

"What about Kozlevich?" asked Balaganov with
fury.

"Why Kozlevich?" screeched Panikovsky. "That's
robbery! Why do we have to share with him? I don't
know any Kozlevich."

"Is that the lot?" asked the smooth operator.

"Yes, that's the lot," said Panikovsky, unable to
take his eyes off the clean bank notes. "How does
Kozlevich fit in?"

"Now I'll do the dividing," said Ostap in a businesslike way. Unhurriedly, he gathered the piles into
one, put the money into the metal cigarette box, and
stuffed it into the pocket of his white pants. "The
whole of the money," he concluded, "will be returned to the victim, citizen Koreiko immediately.
Don't you think that's a good way of dividing it?"

"No, I don't," Panikovsky burst out.

"Stop kidding, Bender," said Balaganov angrily.
"We've got to divide it fairly."

"Nothing of the sort," said Ostap coldly. "And, anyway, I don't intend kidding you at this late hour."

Panikovsky clapped his purple, aged hands. He
looked with horror at the smooth operator, retired
to the corner, and became silent. Now and then his
gold tooth gave a glimmer.

Balaganov's face became moist as though it had been
baked by the sun. "What have we worked for?" he
said, breathing hard. "You can't do that. Explain . . ."

"To you, the favorite son of Lieutenant Schmidt,"
said Ostap courteously, "I can only repeat what I said
in Arbatov. I respect the law. I'm not a bag-snatcher,
but an ideological champion of currency notes.

Highway robbery isn't one of my four hundred honest ways of obtaining money. It doesn't fit in. And, anyway, we haven't come here for ten thousand. I need at least five hundred thousand."

"Then why did you send us?" asked Balaganov, cooling down. "We did our best."

"In other words, you want to ask your highly respected commanding officer if he knows why he undertook the last operation? The answer is yes, he does. The point is—"

At this moment the gold tooth stopped glimmering in the corner. Panikovsky turned around, lowered his head, and, with a furious cry of "Who do you think you are," launched himself at Ostap. Without changing his pose or even turning his head, the smooth operator returned the maddened convention-violator to his former position with a blow of his rubber fist, and then continued:

"The thing is, Alex, that it was a test. The clerk with a forty-ruble salary turned out to have ten thousand rubles in his pocket. That's rather odd and gives us a good chance, as the crooked bookies and marathon runners say, of hitting the jackpot. Five hundred thousand is certainly a jackpot. And this is how we'll get it. I'll give Koreiko back his ten thousand and he'll take it. I'd like to see a man who wouldn't take back his own money. And that'll be the end of him. He'll be destroyed by his own greed. As soon as he admits his wealth, I'll grab it with both hands. Like a clever man, he'll realize that a part is less than a whole and he'll give me a part for fear of losing the whole. And that's the point, Alex, when the silver platter appears—"

"Right!" Balaganov exclaimed.

Panikovsky sobbed in the corner. "Give me back my money," he wailed. "I'm a pauper! I haven't had a bath for a year. I'm old. Girls don't like me."

"Apply to the League for Sexual Reform," said Bender. "They may help you."

"No one likes me," Panikovsky continued, squirming.

"Why should they? Girls don't like people like you. They like young, gangly, politically literate men. Anyway, you'll soon be dead. And no one will put in the paper 'Yet another works himself to death.' Nor will there be a beautiful widow with Persian eyes sitting at your graveside. And sobbing children won't ask 'Can you hear us, Dad?'"

"Don't talk like that!" cried the panicky Panikovsky. "I'll live longer than any of you. You don't know Panikovsky. Panikovsky will buy and sell you all yet. Give me back my money!"

"You'd do better to say whether you want to go on working or not. I'm asking for the last time."

"Yes, I do," Panikovsky answered, wiping away his sluggish, old-man's tears.

Night, night, night lay over the whole country.

At the Chernomorsk docks, cranes nimbly swung around, lowered their steel claws into the deep holds of foreign vessels, and swung around again in order to drop pinewood crates of tractor equipment with caution and catlike love onto the quayside. A pink cometlike light was pouring from the high stacks of the silicate plants. The constellations marking Dnieperstroy, Magnetogorsk, and Stalingrad were ablaze. In the north rose the Krasnoputilovo star, and beyond it glowed a multitude of first-magnitude stars. They were plants, combines, power stations, and construction sites. The whole five-year plan was aglow, eclipsing in brightness an ancient sky, glimpsed in its time by the Egyptians.

And the young man sitting far too long with his girl-friend in the Worker's Club hastily switched on an illuminated chart of the five-year plan and whispered, "You see that red light? That's going to be the Sibcombine. We'll go there if you like."

And the girl-friend laughed softly and freed her hands.

Night, night, night, as we have already said, lay over the whole country. Khvorobyov the monarchist grunted in his sleep as he dreamt of an enormous trade-union membership card. Engineer Talmudovsky snored on the upper berth of a railroad carriage, on his way from Kharkov to Rostov, enticed there by a better salary. Vasisualy Lokhankin tossed on his couch, rubbing the affected parts. The old puzzle-poser Sinitsky wasted electric light compiling a picture puzzle called "Find the chairman of the general meeting of workers and employees gathered to elect the local committee of the power station" for the magazine *Plumber's Review*. As he worked he tried to avoid making a noise so as not to awaken Zosya. Polykhayev was in bed with Serna Mikhailovna. The remaining Herculeans were sleeping a troubled sleep in various parts of the town. Alexander Koreiko couldn't get to sleep, so worried was he by thoughts of riches. If he hadn't had all that wealth, he would have slept soundly. What Bender, Balaganov, and Panikovsky were doing all this time is known. And Kozlevich, the driver and owner of the Antelope-Gnu, is the only one we won't talk about just now, although a misfortune with extraordinary political implications had befallen him.

Early next morning Bender opened his Gladstone bag, took out a militiaman's peaked cap with the coat of arms of the City of Kiev, and, stuffing it in his pocket, went off to see Koreiko. On the way he teased the milk girls, for the hour of these resourceful young ladies had arrived, though the hour of the clerks had not yet come, and crooned the words of the song "And the joy of our first date no longer stirs my blood." The smooth operator was not really telling the truth. His first date with the millionaire clerk excited him. Entering No. 16 Carefree Street, he pulled on the militiaman's cap and, knitting his brows, knocked at the door.

Alexander Ivanovich was standing in the middle of the room. He was wearing a sleeveless undershirt and had just had time to pull on the typical pants of a junior clerk. The room was furnished with that exemplary austerity common before the revolution in orphanages and other such institutions patronized by the Empress Maria Fedorovna. It contained three articles—an iron hospital bed, a kitchen table with doors fitted with a wooden latch of the kind usually used to lock up garden lavatories, and a battered Viennese chair. There were two dumbbells in the corner and in-between them two large weights, the delight of weight-lifters.

At the sight of the militiaman the millionaire took a heavy step forward.

"Citizen Koreiko?" Ostap asked, smiling radiantly.

"Yes," Alexander Ivanovich answered, also expressing his joy at meeting an officer of the law.

"Alexander Ivanovich?" Ostap asked, smiling still more radiantly.

"Yes indeed," Koreiko confirmed, warming up his joy as much as possible.

After this the smooth operator could only sit down on the chair and force a supernatural smile on his face. Having done so, he looked at Koreiko. The millionaire clerk tried hard but the result was heaven knows what—pity, ecstasy, admiration, and dumb adoration all in one. And all because of meeting an officer of the law.

The foregoing build-up of smiles and emotion was reminiscent of a manuscript by Franz Liszt, in which one page is marked "presto," the second "molto presto," the third "molto piú presto," the fourth "sempre piú presto," and the fifth "prestissimo!"

Observing that Koreiko had reached page five and no further competition was possible, Ostap got down to business. "I've come to see you by request," he said, becoming serious.

"Certainly, certainly," Koreiko responded, also becoming straight-faced.

"I have some good news."

"I'm curious to know what."

And oozing with sorrow, Bender dug into his pocket. Koreiko followed his movements with a funereal face. The metal cigarette box was brought out. The cry of astonishment expected by Ostap was not forthcoming. The underground millionaire stared at the box with complete apathy. Ostap took out the money, carefully counted it, and, moving the pile toward Koreiko, said:

"Exactly ten thousand. Be so kind as to sign the receipt."

"You've made a mistake, comrade," said Koreiko very quietly. "What ten thousand? What receipt?"

"What do you mean? You were robbed yesterday, weren't you?"

"Nobody robbed me."

"Of course they did. Yesterday by the sea. And they took ten thousand rubles from you. The robbers have been arrested. Sign the receipt."

"But honestly, no one robbed me," Koreiko protested, his face suddenly brightening. "There's obviously been a mistake."

Still not realizing the profundity of his defeat, the smooth operator exhibited undue commotion, which he always recalled subsequently with shame. He insisted, he grew angry, he pushed the money into Koreiko's hands, and, as the Chinese say, he lost face. Koreiko shrugged his shoulders, smiled politely, but refused the money.

"So, then, you weren't robbed?"

"Nobody robbed me."

"And you didn't lose ten thousand?"

"Certainly not. Where do you think I'd get so much money from?"

"Quite right, quite right," said Ostap, cooling down a little. "How could a junior clerk have such a pile of cash? So in fact everything is okay."

"Everything," said the millionaire with a disarming smile.

"And is your stomach in order?" asked Ostap, smiling still more charmingly.

"Perfectly. I'm a really healthy character, you know."

"And you're not troubled by bad dreams?"

"No, I'm not."

After this the smiles started up again, just as in Liszt —presto, più presto, etc. The two parted as though they adored each other.

"Don't forget your militiaman's cap," said Koreiko. "It's on the table."

"Don't eat raw tomatoes before going to bed," advised Ostap, "or you'll have indigestion."

"All the best," said Koreiko, bowing happily and scraping his feet.

"Good-by, good-by!" Ostap replied. "You certainly are an interesting fellow. Everything is okay with you! Amazing how you can be so happy and free at the same time."

And, still keeping the forced smile on his face, the smooth operator hurried into the street. He went several blocks at full speed, forgetting that he still had on the cap with the Kievan coat of arms, completely out of place in the town of Chernomorsk. It was only when he found himself among a crowd of respectable old men, babbling away on the covered balcony of cafeteria No. 68, that he regained his wits and began summing up the situation.

While he was deep in thought, wandering absent-mindedly up and down, the old men continued doing what they did every day.

They were curious people, amusing in our time. They practically all wore white piqué vests and boaters. Some of them even wore soiled Panamas. And all of them, naturally, wore yellowed starched collars, from which rose hairy, scraggy necks. Here in cafeteria No. 68, which had previously been the famous Café Florida, was the meeting place of the flotsam of the prewar commercial Chernomorsk—officeless brokers, agents withered for lack of commission, corn brokers, and other such rabble. At one time they used to gather there to clinch their deals, but now they were drawn there, to that sunny corner, by years of habit and the need to wag their aged tongues. Each day they read *Pravda* (they didn't trust the local press), and whatever went on in the world was looked upon by the old men as a prelude to the declaration of Chernomorsk a free city. About a hundred years before, Chernomorsk had indeed been a free city, and this had been so nice and lucrative that the legend of the porto franco to this day cast a golden light on the bright corner at the Café Florida.

"Have you read about the disarmament conference?" one old piqué vest asked another. "Count Bernsdorf's speech."

"Bernsdorf, there's a brain for you!" answered the second piqué vest in a tone of voice which suggested he was basing his view on years of personal friendship with the count. "But have you read Snowden's speech to his constituents in Birmingham, that citadel of conservatism?"

"There's no doubt about it: Snowden's a clever one! Listen, Valiadis," he said, turning to a third old man in a Panama, "what do you think of Snowden?"

"I tell you straight," replied the Panama, "I wouldn't trust him an inch."

But not in the least disconcerted by the fact that Valiadis wouldn't trust Snowden an inch, the old man went on. "Whatever you say, I tell you straight, Chamberlain's really a man with a brain."

The piqué vests hunched their shoulders. They didn't deny that Chamberlain was clever. They were more consoled by Briand.

"Briand," they muttered with feeling: "there's a brain for you. With his plan for Pan-Europe . . ."

"I tell you straight, M'sieu Funt," whispered Valiadis, "it's all right. Beneš had already agreed to a Pan-Europe, but do you know on what condition?"

The piqué vests got closer together and stretched their scraggy necks.

"On condition Chernomorsk is declared a free city. Beneš is a brain! After all, he needs to sell his agricultural implements. So we'll buy them."

At this announcement the eyes of the old men lit up. They had been wanting to buy and sell for many years.

"Briand—there's a brain," they muttered, sighing. "Beneš is, too."

As Ostap emerged from his thoughts, he found an old man in a straw hat with a tattered band grasping him by the edge of his jacket. The pin-on bow tie had slipped to one side, and a brass stud stared straight at Ostap.

"I tell you MacDonald won't be caught like that!" shouted the old man into Ostap's ear. "He won't. Do you hear?"

Ostap removed the impassioned old man's hand and made his way through the crowd.

"Hoover—there's a brain for you!" the words came floating after him. And Hindenburg too."

By evening Ostap had made up his mind. He had been through all the four hundred honest ways of getting money, and though they included such gems as starting a shareholding company for salvaging a bullion carrier sunk during the Crimean War, a grand festival in aid of the victims of capital, or a concession for the removal of shop signs, none of them suited the situation in hand.

"Since it has proved impossible to take the fort by surprise attack," he thought, "we'll have to start a siege. The most important thing has been done. The client has the money. And, judging by the fact that he refused the ten thousand without batting an eyelash, quite a lot of money. So in view of the absence of agreement by the parties concerned, the hearing is continued."

He returned home, buying on the way a stiff yellow folder with bootlace-like tapes.

"Well?" asked the desire-torn Balaganov and Panikovsky in one voice.

Ostap went over to the bamboo table in silence, put the folder down in front of him, and scrawled on it in large letters: "The case of Alexander Ivanovich Koreiko. Begun June 25, 1930. Completed 193—.

The foster brothers peered at the file over Bender's shoulder.

"What's inside?" asked the curious Panikovsky.

"Aha!" said Ostap. "There's everything inside—palms, girls, express trains, the deep blue sea, a white steamer, a slightly worn tuxedo, a Japanese valet, my own billiard table, platinum teeth, socks without holes, meals cooked in pure lard, and, most important, my little friends, the glory and power which money brings."

And he opened an empty file in front of the astonished Antelopeans.

: 15 :

Horns and Hoofs

ONCE THERE WAS a poor old private trader. He was a fairly rich man and owned a notions store almost opposite the Capitol movie theater. He calmly sold his linen, lace, ties, buttons, and other such trivial though remunerative articles. One evening he returned home with his face all contorted. Without a word he opened the sideboard, took out a whole cold chicken, and greedily consumed it, pacing up and down the room. Having done this, he opened the sideboard again, took out a complete ring of Cracow sausage weighing a good half-pound, sat down on a chair, and, fixing his glassy eyes on one point, slowly chewed his way through the lot. As he reached for the boiled eggs on the table, his wife asked in alarm:

"What's happened, Boris dear?"

"A disaster," he replied, stuffing a rubbery egg into his mouth. "I've been taxed to the gills. You can't imagine!"

"Why are you eating like that?"

"Trying to take my mind off it," the private trader answered. "I'm scared."

And the whole night the private trader walked about his rooms, in which there were as many as eight sideboards, and ate. He ate up everything there was in the house. He was scared.

The next day he sublet half the store for the sale of stationery and office supplies, whereupon one of the windows displayed ties and suspenders, while in the other hung an enormous yellow pencil on two strings.

Then came even more troubled times. A third co-owner appeared in the shop. He was a watchmaker, who ousted the yellow pencil and took up half the window with a brass clock which had a figure of Psyche on it but no minute hand. And so, opposite the poor notions-store owner, who continued to smile ironically, there now sat, apart from the loathsome pencil vendor, a watchmaker with a black magnifying glass jammed in one eye.

Twice more was the notions-store owner visited by misfortune. The next addition was a plumber, who immediately lit his blowtorch, and then came a weird merchant who had decided that for some reason 1934 was the year in which the populace of Chernomorsk would rush to buy his wares—stiff collars.

And the once proud, tranquil sign outside the shop now looked utterly disgraceful:

NOTIONS B. KULTURTRIGER	CLOCK & WATCH REPAIRS— ALL TYPES GLASIUS- SHENKER	*STATIONERY* EVERYTHING FOR THE ARTIST AND SOVIET CLERK LEV SOKOLOVSKY

PIPES, SINKS, & TOILET BOWLS *REPAIRED* M. N. FANATYUK	*SPECIAL* STARCHED COLLARS FROM *LENINGRAD* KARL PAVIAJNEN

Customers and clients entered the once mellifluous shop in horror. Surrounded by tiny wheels, pince-nez,

and springs, Glasius-Shenker the watchmaker sat beneath his wares, among which was one tower clock.
The shop was frequently filled with the shrill of alarm
clocks. At the back of the building was a crowd of
school children asking for out-of-stock copybooks.
Karl Paviajnen trimmed his collars while waiting for
customers. And hardly had the courteous B. Kulturtriger time to ask a lady customer what she would like,
when Fanatyuk the plumber brought his hammer
crashing down on a rusty pipe, and soot from the
blowtorch settled on the delicate notions.

Eventually the strange co-operative of private
traders collapsed, and Karl Paviajnen disappeared into
the blue, taking with him the wares which had
proved so out of tune with the times. He was followed
into oblivion by Kulturtriger and Sokolovsky, pursued by mounted tax inspectors. Fanatyuk took to
drink. The corrugated iron blinds came down with a
bang. The fascinating sign outside vanished, too.
Glasius-Shenker went off to join the New Times nationalized watchmakers' association.

Soon afterward, however, the blinds rose again, and
over the former private traders' Noah's ark appeared
a small, neat plate which said:

> Chernomorsk Branch
> of the Arbat Office
> for the Procurement of
>
> HORNS AND HOOFS

Any idle citizen peeping into the shop would have
noticed that the original counters and shelves had
gone, that the floor had been washed, that egg-box
office desks had been installed, and that the walls were
hung with the usual government-office notices about
office hours and the harmfulness of shaking hands. The
new establishment was already bisected by the usual

barrier set up to keep out visitors, though none were
yet to be seen. At a small table, on which a samovar was letting off steam and shrilly bewailing its
samovarian fate, sat a messenger boy with a gold tooth.
As he wiped the tea mugs he crooned irritably:

> *"The times we live in,*
> *The times we live in,*
> *They don't believe in God no more . . ."*

A red-haired young tough was wandering about
on the other side of the barrier. Now and then
he walked over to a typewriter, prodded the keys
with a rigid finger, and hooted with laughter. At the
back of the office, under a sign which said "Head of
Section," sat the smooth operator, bathed in the light
of an electric table lamp.

The Carlsbad Hotel had long been left, and all the
Antelopeans, except for Kozlevich, had moved into the
room at Rooks' Row, belonging to Vasisualy Lokhankin, who was outraged by the move. He even tried
to protest, claiming he had let the room to one person, not three, and to one intelligent bachelor at that.
"*Mon Dieu*, Vasisualy Andreyevich," said the smooth
operator gaily, "don't worry yourself. After all, I'm
the only intelligent one among the three, so the condition is satisfied." In reply to the owner's further pro-
testations, Ostap used to argue, "*Mein Gott*, dear Vasisualy, maybe this is the great peasant truth." And
Lokhankin immediately calmed down, having asked
for and received twenty rubles. Panikovsky and
Balaganov settled down admirably in Rooks' Row,
and their voices rang clear and true amid the general
apartment chorus. Panikovsky even managed to get
himself accused of stealing kerosene from other
people's primuses during the night, and Mitrich was not
slow to make some caustic comments to Ostap, whereupon the smooth operator silently thumped him in
the chest.

The office for the procurement of horns and hoofs
had been opened for a number of reasons.

"The investigation of the case of Koreiko," said
Ostap, "may consume a lot of time. How much,
heaven only knows. It's a ghastly situation. It may take
a month, or it may take a year. In any case we need
some sort of front. We must mix with the courageous
masses of clerks. The office will provide all that. I've
long had a yearning for administrative work. At heart
I'm a bureaucrat and bungler. We'll procure something ridiculous, like teaspoons, dog licenses, or cheap
jewelry. Or horns and hoofs for the requirements of
the comb and cigarette-holder industry. What's wrong
with that? What's more, in my suitcase I have some
splendid blanks for all possible occasions, and a circu-
lar plastic stamp."

The money which Koreiko had refused and which
the punctilious Ostap saw fit to expend was deposited
in a current account in the bank. Panikovsky mutinied
again at this and demanded that the money be split, as
punishment for which he was given the low-paid and
ignominious job of messenger boy. Balaganov got the
responsible post of hoof agent at a salary of ninety-
two rubles a month.

At the market they bought an old Adler typewriter on which the letter *s* was missing and had to be
replaced by *z*. So the first communication sent by
Ostap to the office-supplies store ran:

Pleaze izzue the bearer, mezzenger Panikovzky of the
Chernomorzk Branch, ztationery to the zum of rz. 150
(one hundred and fifty) and credit the Head Office in
Arbatov accordingly.
Attached: Nothing attached.

"A fine hoof agent you are!" Ostap fumed. "I can't
ask you to do anything! You've bought a typewriter
with a German accent! Zo I'm the head of the zection,
am I? You zon of a bitch, Alex!"

But even the typewriter with the unusual accent couldn't dampen the smooth operator's high spirits. He was very happy with his new profession. Every hour he came hurrying in with new purchases. He brought such complicated office equipment that the messenger and representative could only gasp. There were punches, duplicators, a swivel stool, and a set of brass inkwells in the form of several little peasant houses, each one for a different-colored ink. This particular object was called "Facing the Countryside" and cost a hundred and fifty rubles. The crowning glory was a railroad punch, extorted by Ostap from the local station. Finally, he arrived with a pair of branching deer horns. Wheezing and moaning about his low wages, Panikovsky nailed them over the chief's desk. Everything was going fine, swimmingly in fact. The only hitch was the inexplicable absence of the motor car and its splendid driver, Adam Kozlevich.

On the third day of the office's existence, the first visitor appeared. To everyone's surprise, it was the postman. He brought eight packages and, after chatting with Panikovsky for a while, went away. The packages contained three notices summoning a representative of the office to an urgent meeting, and stressing in all three of them that attendance was obligatory. The other papers contained requests from unfamiliar but evidently businesslike organizations for various information, price lists, and reports in quadruplicate, and all urgent and obligatory.

"What's all this?" cried Ostap. "Three days ago I was as free as a kite hawk flapping my wings wherever I wanted, and now look—attendance obligatory. It looks as though Ostap Bender is in great demand in this town. Anyway, who would conduct this kind of correspondence with friends. I shall have to make an outlay and increase my staff. We need a knowledgeable office girl. Let her do the work."

Two hours later a new misfortune befell them. A peasant arrived with a heavy sack.

"Who gets the horns?" he asked, dropping the treasure onto the floor.

The smooth operator gave the visitor and his worldly goods a sidelong glance. They consisted of small, dirty, curved horns. Ostap surveyed them with disgust. "Are they good ones?" he asked warily.

"You just see how good they are!" cried the peasant, getting hot and bothered, and he held up a yellow horn under the smooth operator's nose. "First-grade horns. As specified."

The first-grade horns had to be bought. The peasant sat for some time drinking tea with Panikovsky and telling him about life in the countryside, thereby arousing in Ostap the natural ire of a man who has spent fifteen rubles for nothing.

"If Panikovsky lets in one more horn-bearer," said Ostap as soon as the visitor had gone, "he's finished here. I'll fire him without severance pay. Anyway, we've done enough official business for the moment. It's time to get busy."

Hainging a sign marked "Closed for Lunch" on the glass door, the smooth operator took the dossier allegedly containing the blue sea and white steamer out of a cupboard and, patting it, said, "This is what our office is going to work on now. There isn't a single page in the dossier yet, but we'll fill it up even if we have to send Panikovsky and Balaganov to the Kara Kum desert or Kremenchug to make inquiries."

At that moment the doorknob gave a rattle. Outside, stamping his feet, was an old man in a Panama hat darned with white thread and a loose silk jacket, under which could be seen a piqué vest. The old man stretched out his scraggy neck and applied a large ear to the glass.

"We're shut," Ostap called hurriedly. "The procurement of hoofs has been temporarily suspended."

But the old man continued making signs.

If Ostap had not let the old white-vest in, the main line in our plot might have taken a different turn and there might never have occurred those amazing events in which the smooth operator, his irascible messenger boy, the carefree hoof agent, and many other people, including a certain wise man of the East, a grandson of the aged puzzle-poser, a well-known public figure, the head of the Hercules, and a large number of Soviet and foreign citizens, were to play a part.

But Ostap did open the door. Smiling sadly, the old man went behind the barrier and sat down. He closed his eyes and sat in silence for several minutes. The only thing that could be heard was the short whistling noise emitted from time to time by his pallid nose. Just as the office staff had decided that their visitor would never speak again, and had begun a whispered discussion on the best way to take the corpse into the street, the old man raised his brown-colored lids and said in a low voice:

"My name's Funt. Funt."

"And I suppose you think that's a good enough reason for you to burst into a government office closed for lunch," said Ostap breezily.

"You're laughing at me," replied the old man, "but my name's Funt. I'm ninety."

"What can I do for you?" asked Ostap, beginning to lose patience.

But at this point the citizen fell silent again and stayed that way for some time. "You have an office," he said at length.

"Yes, yes, an office," Ostap said, encouraging him. "Go on, go on."

But the old man only stroked his knee. "You see these pants I've got on?" he said after a long silence. "They're Easter pants. At one time I used to wear them only at Easter, but now I wear them every day."

And despite the fact that Panikovsky slapped him on the back so that the words could come out more easily, Funt lapsed into silence again. He articulated his words quickly, but between sentences he made pauses as much as three minutes long. People who weren't accustomed to this characteristic of Funt's found conversation with him intolerable. Ostap was just about to seize Funt by his starched dog collar and show him out when the old man opened his mouth again. From then on the conversation took such an entertaining turn that Ostap became quite resigned to Funt's method of discourse.

"Do you need a chairman?" asked Funt.

"What kind of chairman?" Ostap exclaimed.

"An official one. In other words, a head of the establishment."

"I'm the head."

"Then you intend to serve your sentence yourself. Why didn't you say so in the first place? Why have you been wasting my time for the last two hours?"

The old man in Easter pants seethed with fury, but the pauses between sentences were not shortened.

"I'm Funt," he said with feeling. "I'm ninety. The whole of my life I've done time for others. That's my profession—to suffer for others."

"Oh, so you're a stand-in?"

"Yes," said the old man, tossing his head with pride. "I'm Funt, the stand-in chairman. I've spent most of my time in prison. I was in prison under Alexander the Liberator, under Alexander the Peacemaker, under Bloody Nicholas the Second."

The old man slowly bent his fingers, counting the czars.

"I went in during Kerensky's time, too. Admittedly, I didn't do anything under military communism. Commerce disappeared, and there was no work. On the other hand, I went in again during NEP. The best days of my life. In four years, I spent only three months at liberty. I married off my granddaughter, Golkonda Yeseyevna, with a grand piano, a silver bird, and eight rubles in gold coins as the dowry. But now I walk about and hardly recognize our Chernomorsk. Where's everything gone? Where's the private capital? Where's the Trust Company? Where's the Second

Mutual Credit Society, may I ask? It's scandalous!"

This short speech took about half an hour. Listening to Funt, Panikovsky was deeply moved. He led Balaganov aside and said with admiration, "You can see at once he's one of us. There are few left like that, and there soon won't be any at all." And he amiably poured the old man a mug of sweet tea.

Ostap led the old man over to his desk, ordered the door to be shut, and patiently began questioning the eternal prisoner who had given his life for his "brethren." The stand-in chairman talked with pleasure. If he hadn't rested between sentences, it might have been said that he talked the hind leg off a donkey.

"Do you by any chance know a man named Koreiko?" Ostap asked, glancing at the bootlace file.

"No," said the old man, "I don't know anyone of that name."

"Have you ever had any dealings with the Hercules?"

At the word "Hercules," the old man gave a slight start. Ostap didn't even notice the movement, but had any other piqué vest from the Café Florida been in his place—for instance, someone like Valiadis, who had known Funt for ages—he would have thought, "Funt's absolutely furious. He's beside himself."

How could Funt not know the Hercules when his last four jail sentences were directly connected with that establishment! Several private companies owed their existence to the Hercules. For instance, there was the Intensivist. Funt had been asked to be the chairman of the Intensivist. The Intensivist received a large advance from the Hercules for the procurement of something or other—the stand-in chairman didn't need to know exactly what. It went bust immediately. Someone made a fortune and Funt went behind bars for six months. After the Intensivist came the Working Cedar, a trust company, obviously under the chairmanship of the benevolent Funt. Obviously an advance was made by the Hercules for the delivery of

seasoned cedar wood. Obviously there was an unexpected crash, someone became a millionaire, and Funt
earned the chairman's rate: he went behind bars again.
After that came Timber Assistance, an advance from
the Hercules, collapse, someone made a fortune, and in
went Funt, and so on and so on.

"But who was the actual ringleader?" asked Ostap,
walking up and down the room.

The old man silently sucked tea from the mug and
kept up his eyelids with difficulty. "Who knows?" he
said bitterly. "They hid everything from Funt. I was
only supposed to go to jail. That was my profession. I
was in jail under Alexander the Second, and the Third,
and under Nicholas Romanov, and under Kerensky.
And during NEP as well . . . And now I'm out of
work and have to wear my Easter pants."

For some time longer Ostap continued to filter
words from the old man. He was like someone who
anxiously washes tons of dirt and sand in the hope of
finding a few grains of gold at the bottom. He nudged
Funt with his shoulder to keep him from falling asleep
and even tickled him under the arms. After all these
machinations, he managed to find out that in Funt's
opinion there was one person behind all the bankrupt
companies and societies. As regarded the Hercules,
many hundreds of thousands of rubles had been
squeezed out of it.

"At any rate," added the ancient stand-in, "at any
rate, this unknown man is a clever one. Do you know
Valiadis? He wouldn't trust the man an inch!"

"And what about Briand?" asked Ostap with a grin,
remembering the gathering of piqué vests at the
former Café Florida. "Would he have trusted Briand
an inch? What do you think?"

"Not in the least!" answered Funt. "Briand was a
real brain." For three minutes he worked his lips in
silence, then added, "Hoover was a brain. And Hindenburg is a brain, too. That makes two brains."

Ostap was horrified. The doyen of the piqué vests

had sunk into the mire of high-level politics. At any
moment he might start talking about the Kellogg Pact
or the Spanish dictator Primo de Rivera, and then nothing under the sun could have distracted him. His eyes
had already acquired an insane glint, and the Adam's
apple above the yellowed stiff collar had already begun to quiver, heralding the birth of a new sentence,
when Ostap unscrewed the electric light bulb and
threw it on the floor. The bulb burst like the cold
crack of a rifle shot. This was the only thing that
could distract the old man from his international affairs. Ostap quickly took advantage.

"So, you haven't seen anyone from the Hercules?"
he asked. "On the question of an advance?"

"I've only had dealings with Berlaga the accountant.
He was on their payroll. I don't know at all. They
kept everything secret. I was only required to go to
jail."

Nothing more could be squeezed out of the old
man. But what he had said was enough to begin a
search.

"I feel the Koreiko touch," thought Ostap.

The head of the Arbat Office for the Procurement of
Horns and Hoofs sat down at his desk and transferred
the speech to paper. He left out Valiadis' attitude toward Briand. The first page of the discrete investigation of the underground millionaire was numbered,
punched in the correct place, and filed away.

"Well, are you going to have a chairman?" asked
the old man, putting on his darned Panama. "I see
your office needs a chairman. I don't ask much—a
hundred and twenty a month when I'm at large, and
two hundred and forty when I'm inside. An increase
of a hundred per cent for wear and tear."

"We may take you on," said Ostap. "Send in an application to the hoof agent."

]CHAPTER[

: *16* :

Jahrbuch für Psychoanalytik

THE WORKDAY in the accounts department of the Hercules began, as usual, at nine sharp.

Kukushkind had just raised the hem of his jacket to wipe his spectacles, and inform his colleagues at the same time that working in the Sikomorsky and Tsarevich Bank had been incomparably more peaceful than in the Herculean bedlam; Tesoimenitsky had swung around on his swivel stool to the wall and stretched out his hand to tear off the day before, and Lapidus, Jr., had just opened his mouth to engulf a piece of bread spread with minced herring, when the door flew open and who should appear on the threshold but Berlaga the accountant.

The unexpected entry caused a commotion in the accounts department. Tesoimenitsky slid off his stool, and the calendar leaf, for the first time in three years perhaps, was left untorn. Lapidus, Jr., forgot to take a bite of the sandwich and worked his jaws on nothing. Dreyfus, Chevazhevskaya, and Sakharkov were flabbergasted. Koreiko got up and lowered his head, while old Kukushkind quickly put on his spectacles, having forgotten to wipe them, which had never happened before in the course of his thirty years of gov-

ernment service. Berlaga sat down at his desk as
though nothing were the matter and, ignoring a subtle remark by Lapidus, Jr., opened his ledgers.

"How are you?" asked Lapidus, unperturbed. "Cal-
caneum nerve?"

"It's all gone," Berlaga replied without looking up.
"I don't even believe there is such a nerve."

The whole department fidgeted on their stools and
cushions until lunchtime, eaten up with curiosity. As
soon as the "action-stations" signal finally sounded,
Berlaga was surrounded by the cream of the account-
ing world. But the refugee hardly answered any of
their questions. He led aside four of the most trust-
worthy and, making sure there was no one else
around, told them of his extraordinary adventures in
the madhouse. The runaway bookkeeper interspersed
his account with a large number of intricate expressions and interjections which are omitted here to
make the narrative more coherent.

THE TALE TOLD BY BERLAGA THE ACCOUNTANT IN THE
GREATEST SECRECY TO BORISOKHLEBSKY, DREYFUS,
SAKHARKOV, AND LAPIDUS, JR., OF WHAT BEFELL HIM IN
THE MADHOUSE.

As has already been stated, Berlaga the accountant
fled to the madhouse in fear of being purged. He
counted on staying in that clinical institution
throughout the time of trouble and going back to the
Hercules as soon as the storm had died down and the
eight comrades with steely eyes had moved on to
the next establishment.

The whole idea had been dreamed up by his
brother-in-law. He got hold of a book on the behavior
and mannerisms of the mentally sick, and after a long
discussion, megalomania was selected as the most entertaining idea.

"You won't have anything to do," said his
brother-in-law, egging him on. "You just have to

shout at everyone 'I'm Napoleon' or 'I'm Emile Zola,'
or even 'I'm Mohammed,' if you like."

"What about the Viceroy of India?" asked Berlaga gullibly.

"Yes, of course, a madman can be anybody."

Brother-in-law talked so knowledgeably, he might
well have been a junior intern in a psychiatric ward.
In actual fact, he was a modest agent engaged in
the distribution of the fine subscription editions put
out by the State Publishing House, and all that remained of his former commercial greatness was the
derby hat with a white-silk lining in his trunk.

Brother-in-law ran to the telephone to call an ambulance, and the new Viceroy of India pulled off his
shirt and madapolam undershirt, and, just to be certain, poured a bottle of copying ink all over his head.
Then he lay on his face on the floor and, while waiting for the orderlies, began shouting:

"I'm the true Viceroy of India! Where are my
trusty nabobs, maharajahs, my kunaks,* and elephants?"

Brother-in-law listened to this megalomania and
shook his head. He didn't feel that kunaks were part
of a viceroy's stock in trade, but the orderlies merely
wiped the accountant's ink-smeared face with a wet
cloth and, with a concerted heave, deposited him in
the ambulance. The shiny doors slammed, the siren
gave a clinical wail, and the ambulance rushed the
Viceroy off to his new possessions.

On the way, the patient waved his arms and burbled something or other, dreading at the same time his
forthcoming meeting with the real lunatics. He was
greatly afraid they would beat him up or even murder
him.

The hospital turned out to be quite different from
what he had imagined. In a long, brightly lit ward,
people clad in light blue gowns sat on couches, lay in
beds, or walked about. The accountant noticed that

* Caucasian word meaning "friend."

they hardly spoke to one another. They had no time to. They were thinking. They were thinking the whole time. They had a huge number of thoughts. They had to remember something, to remember the most important thing, on which happiness depended. But the thoughts collapsed, and the most important thing vanished with a flip of its tail. So everything had to be thought out again so as to understand what had happened, why everything was so bad when it had been so good before.

An uncombed, unhappy lunatic passed Berlaga several times. Holding his chin in his fingers, he walked in a straight line—from the window to the door, from the door to the window, back to the door. So many thoughts resounded through his poor head that he clapped the other hand to his forehead and quickened his pace.

"I'm the Viceroy of India!" cried Berlaga, glancing round at the orderly.

The lunatic didn't even look in the accountant's direction. Frowning strangely, he collected his thoughts again, thoughts which had been dispersed by Berlaga's wild cry. Then the Viceroy was approached by a squat idiot who seized him lovingly around the waist and twittered something like a bird.

"What?" the alarmed accountant inquired.

"Ene, bene, raba, quinter, finter, zhaba," the new friend articulated.

With a cry of "Ugh!" Berlaga moved away from the idiot. In so doing, he found himself near a man with a lemon-colored bald patch. The latter immediately turned from the wall and surveyed the accountant with fright.

"Where are my maharajahs?" asked Berlaga, feeling the need to maintain his reputation as a lunatic.

But at this moment someone sitting at the end of the ward rose to his spindly feet, as yellow as church candles, and cried in a martyred voice, "Let me go! Let me out! To the pampas!"

As the accountant learned later, the man asking to be allowed to go to the pampas was an old geography teacher from whose textbook the young Berlaga had in his time learned about volcanoes, capes, and peninsulas. The geographer had gone mad quite suddenly; he had once taken a look at a map of both hemispheres and not found the Bering Straits. The whole day the old man pored over the map. Everything was in place: Newfoundland, the Suez Canal, Madagascar, the Sandwich Islands with their most important city, Honolulu, even the volcano Popocatepetl, but the Bering Straits weren't there. It was there and then, while looking at the map, that the old man went off his rocker. He was a kind old lunatic and never did anyone any harm, but Berlaga was desperately afraid. The cry rent his heart.

"Let me out!" the geographer went on shouting. "To the pampas!"

He knew better than anyone what freedom was. He was a geographer and he knew about boundless expanses of land that ordinary people, concerned with their own boring affairs, had no idea of.

A young woman doctor came into the ward; she had sad blue eyes and walked straight toward Berlaga. "Well, how do you feel, sonny?" she inquired, feeling the accountant's pulse with a warm hand. "You're better, aren't you?"

"I'm the Viceroy of India," he reported, reddening. "Give me back my favorite elephant!"

"It's a delusion," said the doctor tenderly. "You're in a hospital, we'll cure you."

"Oh, oh, oh! My elephant!" cried Berlaga defiantly.

"But you must try to understand you're not the Viceroy. It's a delusion, you realize, a delusion!"

"No, it's not," objected Berlaga, who knew that he had to be stubborn above all things.

"Yes, it is."

"No, it isn't."

"A delusion!"

"It's not a delusion."

Seeing the iron was hot, the accountant decided to strike. He gave the kind doctor a shove and let forth a protracted howl, which startled all the patients, particularly the little idiot, who promptly sat down on the floor and said through dribbles:

"En, den, trois quatre, Mademoiselle Jurovatre."

Berlaga was delighted to hear the doctor say to the orderly behind him, "Put him in with the other three, or he'll frighten the whole ward."

Two patient orderlies led the obstreperous Viceroy into a small room for violent patients, in which lay three calm-looking men. It was only then that the accountant realized what real madmen were like. At the sight of the visitors, the lunatics broke into feverish activity. The fat man jumped down from his bed, got down on all fours, and, sticking out his tight, mandolin-like backside, began to yap and scratch the floor with his slippered feet. The second wrapped himself in his blanket and began shouting "You, too, Brutus, sold yourself to the Bolsheviks!" This fellow obviously imagined himself to be Julius Caesar. From time to time a valve popped open in his muddled head, and getting all mixed up, he shouted, "I'm Heinrich Julius Zimmerman."

"Go away, I'm naked," cried the third. "Don't look at me. I'm a naked woman." Actually, he was a fully dressed man and had a mustache.

The orderlies went out, leaving the Viceroy in such a state of terror that he didn't even think of asking for his elephants.

"They'll strangle me as soon as look at me," he thought, breaking into a cold sweat.

And he bitterly regretted having made such a fuss in the quiet ward. How nice it would be now to be sitting at the feet of the kindly geography teacher listening to the tender babbling of the little idiot. But nothing terrible happened. The dog-man yapped a few more times and climbed grumbling into his bed.

Julius Caesar threw off the blanket, yawned desperately, and stretched his whole body. The woman with the mustache lit a pipe, and the sweet smell of Our Capstan tobacco brought peace to Berlaga's troubled mind.

"I'm the Viceroy of India," he cried, growing bolder.

"Shut up, you son of a bitch!" answered Julius Caesar lazily. And with the forthrightness of the Romans, he added, "I'll kill you if you don't."

This remark by the bravest of emperors and warriors had a sobering effect on the fugitive Berlaga. He hid under his blanket and, sadly contemplating his trouble-filled life, dozed off.

In the morning he caught some strange words as he lay half asleep.

"They've put a real nut in with us. It was fine with just the three of us, but now . . . Just try having anything to do with him! The damned Viceroy might easily bite all of us."

Berlaga could tell from the voice that it was Julius Caesar speaking. A while later he opened his eyes and saw the dog-man staring at him with lively interest.

"This is the end," thought the Viceroy: "he's going to bite me."

But the dog-man suddenly clapped his hands and asked in a human voice, "Say, aren't you Tom Berlaga's son?"

"Yes," replied the accountant, and then, remembering himself, quickly yelled, "Give the poor Viceroy his trusty elephant!"

"Look at me," invited the dog-man. "Don't you recognize me?"

"Michael Alexandrovich!" exclaimed the accountant. "What a coincidence!"

And the Viceroy heartily embraced the dog-man. In the process their heads came together with a bang which sounded like colliding billiard balls. There were tears in the dog-man's eyes.

"Then you're not really mad?" Berlaga asked. "Why are you playing the fool?"

"But why are you playing the fool? 'Give me my elephants,' indeed! Anyway, I think you ought to know, Berlaga, the Viceroy isn't any good for a lunatic."

"My brother-in-law said it was all right," said Berlaga sadly.

"Now, take me," said Michael Alexandrovich. "It's subtle. I'm a dog-man. A schizophrenic illusion complicated by a manic-depressive psychosis and a depressed state of mind to boot, mind you. Do you think I found it easy? I had to refer to original sources. Have you read Professor Bleiler's book *Autistic Thought?*"

"N-no," answered Berlaga in the voice of a viceroy who had just been stripped of his Order of the Garter and demoted to batman.

"Gentlemen," cried the dog-man. "He hasn't read Bleiler! Come over here—don't be afraid. He's as much a viceroy as you are Caesar."

The other two inmates of the special ward for badly behaved patients came over.

"Haven't you read Bleiler?" asked Caesar in surprise. "Which books did you use, then?"

"He probably subscribed to the German journal *Jahrbuch für Psychoanalytik und Psychopatologik,*" the mustachioed man with the inferiority complex conjectured.

Berlaga hung his head in shame while the experts showered him with terms from the theory and practice of psychoanalysis. They all agreed that Berlaga was in for a bad time and that the chief medical officer, Titanushkin, who was due back from a trip any day, would see through him in no time. They omitted to enlarge on the fact that Titanushkin's return depressed them, too, just as much.

"Should I perhaps try another delusion?" asked Berlaga, growing panicky. "What about Mohammed or Emile Zola?"

"It's too late," said Julius Caesar. "It's down in your case history that you're the Viceroy, and a loony can't change his madness like a pair of socks. For the rest of your life you'll be in the silly position of Viceroy. We've been in here a week and we know the system."

An hour later Berlaga knew the full details of the true case histories of his ward mates.

The advent of Michael Alexandrovich was explained by a fairly simple everyday matter. He was a successful NEP private trader, who had inadvertently failed to pay forty-three thousand rubles income tax. This involved the possibility of an enforced trip to the north, but business urgently required the presence of Michael Alexandrovich in Chernomorsk. Duvanov, as the man pretending to be a woman was called, was evidently a petty informer, who had good reason to fear arrest. Quite different, however, was the case of Julius Caesar, who was entered on his identity card as a former lawyer Starokhamsky.

Caius Julius Starokhamsky had gone into the lunatic asylum on ideological grounds.

"In Soviet Russia," he said, draping himself in his blanket, "the madhouse is the only place where a normal man can live. Everywhere else is a super-bedlam. No, I can't live with the Bolsheviks. I would rather stay here. At least ordinary mad people don't want to build socialism. And, anyway, we're fed here. Outside in that bedlam you have to work. I'm not going to work for their socialism. I have personal freedom here. Freedom of belief, freedom of speech . . ."

Seeing an orderly passing by, Julius Caesar Starokhamsky suddenly screeched, "Long live the Constituent Assembly! Everyone to the Forum. You, too, Brutus, sold yourself to responsible officials!" And, turning to Berlaga, he added, "You see? I shout what I want. Just try doing that on the street!"

The whole of that day and most of the night the four refractory patients played Sixty-six, a cunning game which required self-control, knack, purity of heart, and clarity of mind.

The next morning Professor Titanushkin returned from his mission. He promptly examined the patients and had them thrown out of the hospital on the spot. Neither Bleiler's book, nor the depression complicated by manic-depressive psychosis, nor the *Jahrbuch für Psychoanalytik* was of any help. Professor Titanushkin was not an admirer of malingerers.

They hurried along the street, jostling the passers-by with their elbows. In front marched Julius Caesar. Behind him hurried the man-woman and the dog-man. The dethroned Viceroy came up in the rear, cursing his brother-in-law and wondering with horror what would happen now.

Having concluded his instructive story, Berlaga the accountant looked mournfully at Borisokhlebsky, Dreyfus, Sakharkov, and Lapidus, Jr., whose heads seemed to him to be shaking in the dimness of the corridor.

"So that's what you got for your mad ideas," said the hard-hearted Lapidus, Jr. "You tried to avoid one purge and got caught in another. Now you've had it. Once you've been purged from the madhouse, the Hercules will surely purge you."

Borisokhlebsky, Dreyfus, and Sakharkov said nothing. Then, having done just that, they slowly faded into the darkness.

"Chums!" cried the accountant weakly. "Where are you going?"

But the chums were making off at full pelt; their ready-made pants showed for the last time on the stairs and were gone.

"That's bad, Berlaga," said Lapidus, Jr., coldly. "It's

no use trying to involve me in your dirty anti-Soviet tricks. *Adieu!*"

And the Viceroy of India was left alone.

What have you done, accountant Berlaga? Where were your eyes, accountant? And what would your dad have said if he knew that his son became a viceroy in his old age? So that's where your strange connections with Mr. Funt, chairman of many shareholding companies with mixed and unclean capital, have got you! It's even shocking to think what the old Berlaga would have said about the misdeeds of his favorite son. But Tom's been in the Second Christian Cemetery under a stone seraph with a broken wing for a very long time, and young boys who go there to steal the lilacs are the only ones to throw an occasional glance of curiosity at the inscription above the grave: "You've come to rest. Sleep, poor fellow, loved by all." But perhaps the old man wouldn't have said anything. Well, of course he wouldn't, as his own life wasn't all that pious. He'd have advised his son to be more careful and not to rely on his brother-in-law in serious matters. Yes, heaven knows what you've gone and done, Berlaga.

The oppressive thoughts which overwhelmed this ex-vice-regent of George the Fifth were interrupted by a shout from the stairs:

"Where's Berlaga? Someone's asking for him. There he is! Come this way, citizen."

Balaganov appeared in the corridor. Swinging his arms like a guardsman, the hoof agent marched up to Berlaga and handed him a note:

"Com. Berlaga. On receipt of thiz you are requezted to report immediately to explain zome factz."

The piece of paper was marked with the stamp of the Chernomorsk branch of the Arbatov horn and hoof procurement office, and with a round seal, the emblem on which would have been difficult enough to make out even if Berlaga had tried. But the run-

away accountant was so overcome by the misfortunes
which had descended upon him that he could only
ask:

"Can I call home?"

"What do you want to do that for?" growled the
hoof agent.

Two hours later the crowd waiting by the Capitol
movie theater for the first performance and gawking
around them for want of something better to do noticed the door of the horn office open and a man come
out, clasping his heart, and slowly totter away.

It was Berlaga the accountant. At first he limply
moved his legs, then gradually began to gather speed.
Turning the corner, the accountant crossed himself
surreptitiously and raced off. He was soon at his desk
in the accounts department and staring dumfounded
at the ledger. The figures jumped and twisted in front
of his eyes.

The smooth operator snapped Koreiko's dossier
shut and looked at Funt, who was sitting under a new
sign which said "Chairman of the Board," and remarked, "Even when I was young and very poor, and
used to live by putting a fat, big-chested monk on
show as a bearded lady at the Kherson market—one of
nature's unexplained phenomena—I never descended
to such moral depths as that lousy Berlaga."

"Miserable, worthless person," Panikovsky agreed,
handing round tea to the desks. He was happy to think
there were people in the world still lower than he was.

"Berlaga isn't brainy," announced the stand-in
chairman at his usual unhurried pace. "MacDonald's a
brainy one. His idea of class peace in industry—"

"That's enough!" said Bender. "We'll hold a special
meeting so that you can expound your views on Mac-
Donald and other bourgeois statesmen. I haven't time
right now. Berlaga certainly isn't brainy, but he's
told us a few things about the life and activities of self-
exploding shareholding companies."

The smooth operator suddenly felt happy. Everything was fine. Nobody had brought any more stinky horns. The work of the Chernomorsk branch could be considered satisfactory, even though the latest batch of mail contained a heap of communications, circulars, and requests, and Panikovsky had already been to the labor office twice for a secretary.

"Wait!" Ostap cried suddenly. "Where's Kozlevich? Where's the Antelope? What kind of office is this without a car? I have a meeting to attend. I'm in great demand; they can't live without me. Where's Kozlevich?"

Panikovsky looked away and said with a sigh, "Things are bad with Kozlevich."

"Why bad? Is he drunk or something?"

"Worse," Panikovsky replied. "We were afraid to tell you. The Catholic priests have got him."

As he spoke, the messenger boy looked at the hoof agent and they both shook their heads sadly.

The Prodigal Son Comes Home

THE SMOOTH OPERATOR didn't like Catholic priests.
He took an equally dim view of rabbis, dalai lamas,
popes, muezzins, medicine men, and other such ministers of religious worship.

"I'm inclined to fool people and blackmail them
myself," he said. "At the moment, for instance, I'm
engaged in extorting a large amount of money from a
certain hard-headed citizen. But I don't accompany
my dubious acts with hymn-singing or the blare of an
organ or stupid invocations in Latin or Church
Slavonic. And, anyway, I prefer to operate without incense and astral bells."

And as Balaganov and Panikovsky, constantly interrupting each other, told of the cruel misfortune which
had befallen the driver of the Antelope, Ostap's manly
heart filled with anger and fury.

The priests had trapped Adam Kozlevich's soul at
the tavern, where, among the two-horse German
wagons and Moldavian fruit carts, the Antelope was
parked in a mess of manure. Father Kuszakowski used
to visit the tavern for pep talks with the Catholic set-
tlers. Catching sight of the Antelope, the priest
walked around it and fingered the tires. He had a con-

versation with Kozlevich and found out that he belonged to the Church of Rome but hadn't been to
confession for twenty years.

With the words "That's bad, Kozlevich," the priest
went away, lifting up the ends of his black skirt and
jumping over frothy puddles of beer.

The next day, about daybreak, as the wagoners
were taking excited petty speculators to the village of
Koshara, squeezing fifteen of them into each wagon,
Father Kuszakowski appeared again. This time he
was accompanied by another priest, named Aloysius
Moroszek. While Kuszakowski greeted Adam Kozlevich, the other priest thoroughly inspected the car,
and not only fingered the tires, but actually pressed
the horn, making it play the bugle call. At this the
priests exchanged glances, went up to Kozlevich on
both sides, and began to brain-wash him. They kept it
up all day. As soon as Kuszakowski dried up, Moroszek
took over. Hardly had he time to stop and wipe the
sweat from his brow, when Kuszakowski started off
again. From time to time Kuszakowski would point a
long, yellow forefinger at the sky, while Moroszek told
his beads. Sometimes, however, Kuszakowski would
tell the beads, while Moroszek pointed to the sky. On
several occasions the priests began softly singing in
Latin, and by the end of the first day Adam Kozlevich
had joined in. At this, both the holy fathers looked at
the car.

After a while Panikovsky noticed a change in the
driver of the Antelope. Adam Kozlevich began muttering something vague about the Kingdom of
Heaven. This was confirmed by Balaganov. Then he
disappeared for long periods and finally left the tavern
yard altogether.

"Why didn't you report it?" exclaimed the outraged captain.

They wanted to, but were afraid of the smooth operator's wrath. They had hoped that Kozlevich would
recover and come back by himself. But all hope was

now lost. Only the day before, the messenger boy
and the hoof agent had come across Kozlevich. He was
sitting in the car by the entrance to the Catholic
church. They had not had time to reach him before
Father Aloysius emerged from the church accompanied by a boy in lace.

"Just imagine, Bender," said Alex, "the whole lot of
them got into our Antelope, poor Kozlevich took off
his cap, the boy rang a bell, and they all drove off. It
was just sickening to watch our Adam. We'll never see
the Antelope again."

The smooth operator silently put on his captain's
cap with the shiny peak and strode toward the door.
"Funt," he said, "you stay here in the office! Don't accept any hoofs or horns under any circumstances. If
the mail comes, put it in the waste-paper basket. The
office girl can sort it out later. All right?"

By the time the stand-in chairman had opened his
mouth to reply (about five minutes later), the
orphaned Antelopeans were far away. At the head of
the procession, taking gigantic strides, hurried the
captain. Now and then he turned his head and mumbled, "You didn't protect poor little Kozlevich, you
melancholics. I'll unfrock the lot of you. Really, these
black and white clergy." The chief engineer walked
along in silence, pretending the remarks weren't
meant for him. Panikovsky hopped along like a
monkey, working up a feeling of hatred for Kozlevich's captors, although his heart was actually filled
with frog-cold fear. He was afraid of the black priests,
whom he knew to have magic powers.

In this order the whole of the horn and hoof procurement office arrived at the steps of the church.
The empty Antelope was parked in front of iron
railings woven from spirals and crosses. The church
was huge. It towered into the sky, spikey and pointed
like a fish bone. It stuck in the throat. The glazed red
brick, the sloping tiled roofs, the metal banners, the
buttresses, the fine stone statues sheltering from the

rain in their niches—the whole of this erect, soldier-like Gothic style overwhelmed the Antelopeans. They felt very small. Ostap climbed into the car, sniffed the air, and said with disgust:

"Pooh, disgusting! Our Antelope already stinks of candles and collections for a new church and priests' boots. Of course they find it nicer riding about in the Antelope than in a cab. And for free! Well, you're not going to, holy fathers. Our own religious rites are more important!"

With these words Ostap went into the church yard and, passing through the children playing hopscotch on the chalk-marked asphalt, went up the granite steps to the door of the church. On the thick iron reinforced doors, embossed saints, each in his own little square, were blowing one another kisses, pointing in different directions with their hands, or diverting themselves with thick books, on which the conscientious carver had even put Latin words. The smooth operator pulled the door, but it didn't budge. From inside came the humble sound of a harmonium.

"They're working on him," cried Ostap, rushing down the steps. "They're right in the middle of it. To the sweet music of the mandolin!"

"Perhaps we should go away," said Panikovsky, fiddling with his hat. "It's a house of God, after all."

But the smooth operator ignored him and, walking back to the Antelope, began impatiently sounding the horn. He kept sounding it until the rattle of keys could be heard behind the doors. The Antelopeans raised their heads. The door opened into two halves and the merry saints in their little oak squares slowly disappeared inside. Out of the darkness of the portals emerged Adam Kozlevich onto the high, light-colored parvis. He was pale. His conductor's mustachios were damp and drooped sadly from under his nostrils. He held a prayer book in his hands. On either side he was supported by the priests, Kuszakowski on the left and

Father Aloysius on the right. The holy fathers' eyes were filled with unction.

"Hi, Kozlevich!" shouted the smooth operator from below. "Aren't you fed up with it yet?"

"Hello, Adam Kozlevich!" Panikovsky called breezily, hiding behind the smooth operator's back.

Balaganov raised his hand in greeting and made a face as much as to say, "Adam, stop this rubbish."

The body of the driver of the Antelope took a step forward, but his soul, egged on from both sides by the penetrating glances of the two priests, struggled to go back inside. Kozlevich gazed sadly at his friends and hung his head.

Then began the great battle for the driver's immortal soul.

"Listen, you seraphim and cherubim," cried Ostap, challenging his enemies to a dispute, "there's no God."

"Yes there is," Father Moroszek retorted, sheltering Kozlevich with his body.

"This is hooliganism," Father Kuszakowski stammered.

"There isn't, there isn't," the smooth operator continued, "and there never was one. It's a medical fact."

"I consider this conversation out of place," Kuszakowski declared angrily.

"And is pinching our car out of place?" shouted the tactless Balaganov. "Adam, they only want the Antelope."

Hearing this, the driver raised his head and looked questioningly at the priests. The priests sprang into action, and, with their robes swishing, tried to pull Kozlevich into the church. But he resisted.

"Well, and what about God, then?" the smooth operator persisted.

The priests were forced to enter into a discussion. The children stopped hopping about on one leg and came closer.

"How can you assert that there is no God when

everything living was created by Him?" Moroszek asked in a hearty voice.

"I know, I know," said Ostap. "I'm an old Catholic and Latinist myself. *Puer, socer, vesper, gener, liber, miser, asper, tener.*"

These Latin exceptions that Ostap had learned by rote in the third grade of the Iliad private school and had lodged ever since in his head had a magnetic effect on Kozlevich. His soul rejoined his body, causing the driver to take a timid step forward.

"My son," Father Kuszakowski began, glaring at Ostap with cold fury, "you're being misled, my son. The miracles of the Lord show—"

"Priest! Stop fooling!" said the smooth operator firmly. "I have worked miracles myself. Only four years ago I had to pretend to be Jesus Christ for a few days in a small town. And everything worked out. I even fed several thousand believers with five loaves. I managed it somehow, but what a crush there was!"

The dispute continued in this strange vein. Ostap's unconvincing though lively arguments had the most revitalizing effect on Kozlevich. A redness dawned on his cheeks and the ends of his mustache slowly began to rise.

"Come on, come on," came cries of encouragement from behind the spirals and crosses of the railings, where quite a crowd of curious people had gathered. "Tell them about the Pope and the Crusade."

Ostap did. He censured Pope Alexander Borgia for bad behavior, mentioned, somewhat out of place, Seraph Sarovsky, and put great emphasis on the Inquisition and Galileo's persecution. He was so carried away that he accused Kuszakowski and Moroszek of personal participation in the famous scientist's misfortune. That was the last straw. On hearing this, Adam Kozlevich put down his prayer book on the ground and fell into the brawny arms of Balaganov. Panikovsky danced around the prodigal son and patted his bristly cheeks. Kisses of happiness filled the air.

"Pan Kozlevich!" groaned the priests, "where are you going? Come to your senses!"

But the heroes of the motor race had already taken their places in the car.

"There, you see?" cried Ostap to the chagrined priests as he took the captain's seat. "I told you there wasn't a God. It's a scientific fact. Good-by, priests! So long, holy fathers!"

Accompanied by exclamations of approval from the crowd, the Antelope drove off, and very soon the metal banners and sloping tiled roof of the church were out of sight. The Antelopeans stopped at a road-house to celebrate.

"Gee, thanks, pals," said Kozlevich, holding a large mug of beer in his hand. "I was almost a goner. They certainly worked on me. Would you believe it? They made me fast, saying that otherwise I wouldn't go to heaven."

"Heaven," Ostap chuckled. "Heaven's now in a state of desolation. It's the wrong time, the wrong age. Nowadays it's the angels who want to get down to earth."

After the eighth mug of beer, Kozlevich asked for a ninth, raised it high above his head, and, sucking his conductor's mustache, asked blissfully, "So there isn't any God, then?"

"No," Ostap replied.

"Good—then cheers."

Panikovsky drank as much as anyone else, but made no comment about God. He didn't want to get involved in that controversial subject.

With the return of the prodigal son plus the Antelope, the Chernomorsk branch of the horn and hoof procurement office gained the brilliance it had lacked. There was now a car on permanent duty in front of the doors of the former five private traders' office. The car, of course, was a long way from the blue Buicks

and long-bodied Lincolns; it was even a long way
from Ford trucks, but it was still a car, an automobile,
a motorized carriage which, as Ostap used to say,
despite all its defects, could sometimes make its way
down the street without the use of horses.

Ostap worked like mad. If he had really been trying
to procure horns and hoofs, the cigarette-holder and
comb industry would have been supplied with raw
materials for the rest of the current budget century at
least. But the head of the section was engaged in
something quite different.

Leaving aside Funt and Berlaga, whose reports
were interesting but did not lead directly to Koreiko,
Ostap planned to further the cause by getting to know
Zosya Sinitsky and between two polite kisses under
the nocturnal acacia to air the question of Alexander
Koreiko and, what was more important, his financial
doings.

But prolonged observations carried out by the hoof
agent showed that there was no love relationship between Zosya and Koreiko, and that the latter, as Balaganov expressed it, didn't stand a chance.

"When love is lacking," Ostap observed with a sigh,
"it's not done to talk about money. Let's postpone
the girl."

While Koreiko remembered with a smile the crook
in the militiaman's cap who had made a miserable attempt at third-class blackmail, the head of the section
raced around town in a yellow car and looked for
persons and personages who had long been forgotten
by the millionaire clerk, but who remembered him
only too well. On several occasions Ostap called Moscow and spoke to a private trader he knew, a well-
known figure specializing in commercial secrets. The
office then began receiving letters and telegrams,
which Ostap briskly sorted out from the general mail;
the latter, as before, contained an abundance of notices, demands for horns, and reprimands for failing
to show the necessary enthusiasm in procuring hoofs.

Some of the letters and telegrams found their way into the dossier with boot-lace-like tapes.

At the end of July, Ostap got ready to make a business trip to the Caucasus. Matters required the personal attendance of the smooth operator in a small grape-growing republic.

On the day of the chief's departure, an outrageous scene occurred in the office. Panikovsky, who had been sent with thirty rubles to the quay to buy a ticket, came back drunk half an hour later, without the ticket and without the money. He was unable to give any excuse, but merely turned out his pockets, which hung like those on a billiard table, and roared with uncontrollable laughter. Everything amused him —the captain's anger, Balaganov's look of reproach, the samovar in his charge, and Funt snoozing at his desk with his Panama hat tipped onto his nose. Panikovsky took a look at the deer horns, the pride of the office, and was convulsed with such guffawing that he fell on the floor and promptly went to sleep with a delighted grin on his violet lips.

"Now we have a proper office," said Ostap. "It has its own embezzler alias the drunkard doorman. Both these characters make all our efforts look real."

Several times during Ostap's absence the two priests appeared at the windows of the office. At the sight of them, Kozlevich hid in the farthest corner. The priests opened the door, peered inside, and called softly:

"Pan Kozlevich. Pan Kozlevich. Do you not hear the voice of the Heavenly Father? Come to your senses!"

In the process Father Kuszakowski raised his finger, while Father Moroszek told his beads. Then Balaganov made toward the ministers of the church and, without speaking, showed them his ham fist. The priests departed, sadly eying the Antelope.

Ostap came back in two weeks. He was met by the whole office. The smooth operator looked down at his subordinates from the high black hull of the docking ship with affection and love. He smelled of lamb and Caucasian wine.

In addition to the office girl hired before Ostap left, there were two young men sitting in the office. They were students sent from the livestock-breeding technical school for some practical experience.

"A fine thing!" said Ostap sourly. "A new shift. I'm afraid you'll have to work hard here, young fellows. You know of course that horns—that is to say, bony outgrowths—are covered with fur, or a hard corneous layer, are appendages of the skull, and are usually found in mammals, don't you?"

"Yes, we know that," said the students firmly. "We want to do some practical work."

The students had to be got rid of in a complicated and expensive way. The smooth operator sent them to the Kalmuk plains to organize procurement points. This cost the office six hundred rubles, but it was the only way out. The students would have interfered with the completion of a smoothly proceeding operation.

When Panikovsky found out how much the students had cost, he led Balaganov aside and whispered irritably, "They don't send me on trips, and I don't get any days off or any work clothes. No, Alex, the conditions aren't satisfactory. Anyway, the wages at the Hercules are higher, I've found out. I'll go there as a messenger boy. Honestly I will!"

That evening Ostap sent for Berlaga again.

"Down on your knees!" cried Ostap in the voice of Nicholas the First as soon as he saw the bookkeeper.

The conversation was nevertheless friendly and lasted two hours. Afterward Ostap gave orders for the car to be parked outside the Hercules the next morning.

On Land and at Sea

COMRADE SKUMBRIYEVICH appeared on the beach holding a brief case with his initials on it. Attached to the
brief case was a visiting card with one edge bent over
and a very long line of italic print which clearly indicated that Yegor Skumbriyevich had successfully celebrated five years at the Hercules.

He had the clean-cut, forthright, manly face of a
cleanly shaven Englishman in an advertisement. He
stopped for a moment at a board with the temperature
of the water chalked on it and, freeing his feet with
difficulty from the burning sand, went to look for a
nice little spot.

The bathing camp was crowded. Its flimsy huts
were put up in the morning, only to disappear
with the setting of the sun, leaving behind the refuse
of the town—shriveled melon rind, eggshells, and bits
of newspaper, which live a secret life the whole night
on the empty shore, rustling and flying about the
rocks.

Skumbriyevich made his way past tents made of
wafer-pattern towels, beach umbrellas, and sheets
stretched on sticks. Hidden beneath them were girls in
bathing suits. Most of the men also wore swimsuits,

though not all. Some of them used only fig leaves, although the Chernomorsk gentlemen didn't use them to cover their biblical parts but rather their noses. Adorned in that way, the gentlemen lay in the most uninhibited postures. From time to time they went into the water, covering their biblical parts with their hands, took a dip, and promptly hurried back to their couches indented in the sand so as not to miss one cubic centimeter of salubrious sunshine. They did this to prevent their noses from peeling.

The lack of clothing among these citizens was made up for with a vengeance by a gentleman of completely different appearance. He was wearing soft leather boots with buttons, striped dress pants, a tightly buttoned jacket with a stiff collar, a tie and a watch chain, and also a homburg. The thick mustache and cotton in his ears completed the gentleman's dress. Alongside him was a walking stick with a glass knob stuck upright in the sand.

The heat was killing him. His collar had swollen with the sweat. The gentleman's armpits felt like a blast furnace: you could have smelted ore in them. But he continued lying motionlessly.

On any beach in the world you can meet a man like that. Who he is, why he's there, and why he's lying in full regalia is not clear. But there are such people, one on each beach. They may be members of a secret League of Fools, or the remnants of a powerful Order of Rosenkreutzers, or else half-witted bachelors —who knows . . .

Yegor Skumbriyevich took his place alongside the member of the League of Fools and rapidly undressed. The naked Skumbriyevich was strikingly unlike the clothed Skumbriyevich. A wizened English head on a feminine body with sloping shoulders and a wide pelvis. Yegor approached the water, tried it with a toe, and gave a screech. Then he put the other foot in and let out another screech. Next, he took several steps backward, plugged his ears with his thumbs, used his forefingers to keep his eyes shut, the middle fingers to block his nostrils, and, giving a bloodcurdling shriek, ducked four times under the water. After this he swam forward with his arms flailing and his head turning back at every throw of his arms. And the gentle waves received Yegor Skumbriyevich, an exemplary Herculean and outstanding social worker. Five minutes later, as the tired social worker turned on his back and his round, globular belly pitched and tossed on the surface of the sea, the Antelope's horn was heard from the cliff above the beach.

Out of the car stepped Ostap Bender, Balaganov, and the accountant Berlaga, whose face expressed complete resignation to his fate. All three came down and, casually examining the faces of the bathers, began searching for someone.

"These are his pants," said Berlaga at length, stopping in front of the unsuspecting Skumbriyevich's clothes. "He's probably swum out some way."

"That's the end," exclaimed the smooth operator. "I don't intend waiting any longer. Action must be taken both on land and at sea."

He peeled off his suit and shirt, under which he had on swimming trunks, and, waving his arms, plunged into the water. The smooth operator's chest was tattooed with a picture of Napoleon wearing a three-cornered hat and holding a mug of beer.

"Balaganov!" he shouted from the water. "Undress Berlaga and get him ready. He may be needed."

And the smooth operator swam sidestroke, plowing through the water with a bronze shoulder and heading nor'-nor'west, where Skumbriyevich's mother-of-pearl stomach loomed up like a lighthouse.

Before plunging into the depths of the sea, Ostap had had to do a lot of work on dry land. An important series of clues had led him to the gold lettering of the Hercules and he spent most of his time in that establishment. He was no longer surprised by the rooms with alcoves and washbowls, the statues, and the

doorman in a peaked cap with a gold zigzag, who
liked discussing cremation.

From the confused accounts of the desperate Berlaga emerged the semi-official figure of Comrade
Skumbriyevich. He occupied a large twin-windowed
room in which there had once stayed foreign cap-
tains, lion tamers, and rich students from Kiev.

The telephones in the room jangled constantly,
sometimes alone, sometimes in concert. But no one
picked up the receiver. Still more frequently the door
opened and a shaven head poked into the room,
rolled its eyes in confusion, and vanished giving way
immediately to another head, this time not shaved,
but covered with a shock of hair or simpy bald and
lilac, like an onion. But even the bulbous skull stayed
only a short time in the doorway. The room was
empty.

When the door opened for perhaps the fiftieth time
that day, it was Bender who peered into the room.
Like everyone else, he turned his head from left to
right and then from right to left, and, like everyone
else, saw that Comrade Skumbriyevich was not in
the room. Expressing his annoyance in no uncertain
terms, the smooth operator wandered around the de-
partments, sections, sectors, and private offices, asking
if anyone had seen Comrade Skumbriyevich. But in
all places he received the same answers: "He was here
a moment ago" or "He's just gone out."

The semi-official Yegor belonged to that popular
type of clerk who "was here a moment ago" or "has
just gone out." Some of them don't even manage to
reach their offices the whole workday. At exactly
nine o'clock this type of man enters the vestibule of
the office and, full of good intentions, puts his little
foot on the first step of the stairway. He has great
things ahead of him. He has arranged seven important
appointments, and two large and one small meeting in
his office. On his desk there is a pile of papers requir-
ing immediate action. He is up to his neck in work.

And so the semi-official or official citizen smartly raises his foot toward the second step. But it's not quite so easy to put it down. "Comrade Parusinov, just a moment," says a cooing voice. "I just wanted to ask you about something." Parusinov is taken gently by the arm and led into a corner. From that moment the official is lost to the country. Hardly has he time to deal with the problem and hurry up three steps, when he's intercepted again and led to the window or into the corridor, or into some other out-of-the-way place, where the slovenly office manager has left some empty packing cases, and people try to make him understand something, or urgently insist on something being returned. By three o'clock he has got as far as the first landing. But he spends so much time on the third floor that the workday comes to an end: he goes downstairs and leaves the building so as to be in time for an interdepartmental conference. But at this moment the telephone rings in his office, the appointments are broken, and the correspondence remains unanswered. Meanwhile, the members of both the meetings drink tea and chat about the trouble they are having with the streetcar system.

In the case of Yegor Skumbriyevich, all of these features were greatly accentuated on account of his social work, to which he devoted himself with undue zeal. Skillfully and profitably, he made use of mutual and multilateral deceit which had somehow taken root unobserved in the Hercules, and for some reason was termed "social load."

The Herculeans sat at meetings for three hours on end, listening to Skumbriyevich's humiliating drivel.

They all felt like grabbing him by his fat thighs and throwing him out the window from a decent height. Sometimes they were sure that there wasn't any social work at all, nor ever had been. "The louse," they thought, glumly fiddling with pencils and teaspoons. "Damned hypocrite." But they weren't up to arguing with him or exposing him. Yegor made the right sort of speeches about the Soviet regime, cultural work, professional training and recreational activities. But his impassioned words meant nothing.

Chasing Skumbriyevich through the floors of the Hercules was a bore for Bender. The smooth operator just couldn't catch the splendid fellow. Skumbriyevich kept slipping through his fingers. In the local committee room he had just been talking on the telephone; the earpiece was still warm, and the mist from his breath was still to be seen on the mouthpiece. There on the window sill was a man who had just spoken to him. On one occasion Ostap actually caught sight of his reflection in a mirror on the stairs. He darted forward, but the mirror instantly cleared and all that it showed was a window and a distant cloud.

"Lordy, lordy," exclaimed Ostap, recovering his breath. "What banal, sickening red tape! In the Chernomorsk branch we have our weak points too. There are all sorts of things wrong in the 'testing lab,' but here in the Hercules . . . That's right, isn't it, Alex?"

The hoof agent sighed deeply. They were now back in the cool corridor on the second floor, where they had been fifteen times before that day. And for the fifteenth time they passed the wooden couch next to Polykhayev's office.

The couch had been occupied since morning by engineer Heinrich Maria Sause, a specialist from Germany, sent for at great expense. He was dressed in an ordinary European suit, and it was only the Ukrainian print shirt that suggested the engineer had been in Russia more than three weeks and had had time to visit the tourist souvenir shop. He sat motionless, leaning his head against the wooden back of the couch with his eyes closed, like a man about to be shaved. He might easily have been dozing, but the foster brothers, who had had occasion to pass him a number of times in their quest for Skumbriyevich, noticed that the color of the foreign visitor's motionless face was con-

stantly changing. Every hour it got redder and redder, and by lunchtime it had acquired the hue of a
post-office ceiling. At the start of the workday, when
the engineer took up his position at Polykhayev's
door, his face was reasonably ruddy. In all probability,
Comrade Polykhayev had only reached the second
step by this time. After lunch the color change re-
versed. The color of sealing wax changed to scar-
latina-like spots, after which Sause began to pale, and
by the middle of the afternoon, by the time the head
of the Hercules had evidently managed to storm the
second floor, the visiting specialist's face was stark
white.

"What's happening to him?" Balaganov whispered
to Ostap. "What a range of feelings!"

Hardly had he uttered these words, when Heinrich
Sause sat up straight on the couch and glowered at
Polykhayev's door, from behind which came the
lonely sound of the telephone. "Red tape!" he
screeched in a descant, and, rushing up to the
smooth operator, began shaking him by the shoulder for all he was worth.

"Genosse Polykhayev!" he cried, dancing up and
down in front of Ostap, "Genosse Polykhayev!"

He kept taking out his watch, shoving it in front of
Balaganov's face, and turning again to Bender.

Was machen Sie?" asked Ostap in a daze, revealing
a knowledge of the German language. "*Was wollen
Sie* from a poor visitor?"

But Heinrich Sause wouldn't leave them alone.
Keeping hold of Bender's left shoulder, he pulled Balaganov nearer with his right hand and made a long,
impassioned speech, during which Ostap looked
around with impatience in the hope of catching
Skumbriyevich, while the hoof agent hiccuped softly,
politely covering his mouth with his hand and staring
at the foreigner's boots.

Engineer Sause had signed a contract for a year's
work in the U.S.S.R., or, as he himself expressed it,

"in the Hercules conzern." "See here, Herr Sause," his friend Bernhard Gerngross, the Doctor of Mathematics, had warned him. "Those Bolsheviks will make you work for your money." But Sause explained that he wasn't afraid of work and had long been looking for scope to use his knowledge of mechanized forestry.

When Skumbriyevich told Polykhayev of the specialist's arrival, the head of the Hercules launched into action beneath the palm trees.

"He's needed vitally! What have you done with him?"

"He's in the hotel at the moment. Having a rest after the journey."

"What do you mean, rest!" screeched Polykhayev. "Think of the good money that's been paid for him! He must be here tomorrow at ten sharp."

At five to ten Heinrich Maria Sause, wearing gleaming coffee-colored pants and smiling at the thought of scope for activity, went into Polykhayev's office. The chief hadn't yet arrived. He was not there two hours later, either, or three hours later. Heinrich began to pine. He was only consoled by Skumbriyevich, who appeared from time to time and asked with an innocent smile:

"What, isn't Comrade Polykhayev here yet? How odd!"

Two hours later Skumbriyevich stopped the lunching Bomse in the corridor and whispered, "I just don't know what to do. Polykhayev had an appointment with the German at ten o'clock, but he's gone to Moscow to take care of the question of the building. He won't be back for at least a week. Help me out, Adolf. Sit with the German and entertain him somehow or other. Good money has been paid for him."

Bomse sniffed his daily meatball for the last time, swallowed it down, and, brushing away the crumbs, went to meet the visitor.

For a whole week engineer Sause, guided by the amiable Adolf Bomse, visited three museums, saw the ballet *Sleeping Beauty*, and sat for ten hours at a ceremonial meeting convened in his honor. After the meeting, there was a reception during which the Herculeans had a good time, tossed down their liquor, and, turning to Sause, cried "Bottoms up!"

"Dear Tilli," wrote the engineer to his girl-friend in Aachen. "I've now been in Chernomorsk ten days, but I haven't yet started work at the Hercules concern. I'm afraid they may deduct these days from my wages."

Nevertheless, on the fifteenth of the month Sause was handed his mid-month salary.

"Don't you think that I've been given the money for nothing?" said Heinrich to his friend Bomse. "I'm not doing any work."

"Away with such gloomy thoughts, colleague!" exclaimed Adolf Bomse. "Anyway, if you like, you can have a special desk put in my office."

After this, Sause wrote his girl-friend a letter sitting at his own desk:

"Dear Cutie, I'm leading a strange and unusual life. I do exactly nothing, but receive my money punctually on the agreed dates. I find it all very surprising. Tell our friend Dr. Gerngross about it. He will be interested to know."

On his return from Moscow, Polykhayev learned that Sause had his own desk, and was delighted. "That's splendid," he said. "Let Skumbriyevich put the German in the picture."

But Skumbriyevich, who was devoting his zeal to organizing a powerful accordionists' circle, passed the German on to Bomse. That didn't please Bomse, for the German prevented him from having his morning snack and generally poked his nose into Bomse's business, so he passed him on to the operations department. But this department was reorganizing its work at that time—that meant an endless shifting of desks from one place to another—so Heinrich was palmed off onto the accounts section. There, Dreyfus, Sakharkov, and the others, who didn't speak German, decided Sause was a tourist from the Argentine and spent days and days trying to explain to him the Herculean system of bookkeeping. To do so, they used the deaf-and-dumb alphabet.

A month later a very perturbed Sause cornered Skumbriyevich in the cafeteria and began shouting, "I don't want to get my money for nothing! Give me some work. If this situation continues, I'll complain to the boss."

The final part of the foreign visitor's speech displeased Skumbriyevich. He sent for Bomse. "What's wrong with the Hun?" he asked. "What's he mad about?"

"You know what," Bomse declared. "I think he's just a troublemaker. Honestly, the fellow sits at a desk, doesn't have to do a damn thing, gets a pile of money, and then complains."

"He definitely is a troublemaker even though he is German. We'll have to take him down a peg or two. I'll tell Polykhayev when I get a moment. He'll soon put him in his place."

But Heinrich made his mind up to see Polykhayev personally. But as the head of the Hercules was a representative of those officials who "were here a moment ago," the attempt merely resulted in a stay on the wooden couch and a burst of emotion, the victims of which were the innocent children of Lieutenant Schmidt.

"*Burokratismus!*" cried the German, switching to Russian in his agitation.

Ostap silently took the European guest by the arm, led him over to the suggestion box hanging on the wall, and said, as though talking to a deaf person, "In here, do you understand? In the box. *Schrieben, schrieb, geschrieben*. 'To write.' Understand? I write,

you write, he, she, it writes. You understand? We,
you, they write their complaints and put them in this
box. 'To put'! The verb 'to put.' We, you, they put in
their complaints and no one takes them out. 'To take
out.' I don't take them out, you don't take them
out . . ."

But at this point the smooth operator caught a
glimpse of Skumbriyevich's broad hips at the end of
the corridor, and, breaking off the grammar lesson,
hurried after the elusive social worker.

"Keep it up, Germany!" Balaganov called in encouragement, racing after the captain.

But to Ostap's great dismay, Skumbriyevich had
dematerialized again. "It's a conjuring trick," he said,
turning his head. "The man's here one moment and
gone the next."

The foster brothers began opening every door in
turn in their desperation. Balaganov came out of the
third room like a shot. His face was contorted
to one side.

"Oooh," groaned the hoof agent, leaning against
the wall. "Oooh!"

"What's the matter, my child?" Ostap asked. "Has
someone been beastly to you?"

"In there," Balaganov gasped, pointing with a trembling hand.

Ostap opened the door and caught sight of a black
coffin.

The coffin was resting on an office desk in the middle of the room. Ostap took off his captain's cap and
tiptoed over to the coffin. Balaganov watched his
movements with apprehension. A moment later Ostap
beckoned to him and showed him a large white inscription scrawled on the sides of the coffin.

"You see what it says here, Alex?" he said. " 'Death
to Red Tape!' Does that make you any happier?"

It was a splendid propaganda coffin which the Herculeans used to heave into the streets and carry around
town on important holidays. It was usually borne on

the shoulders of Skumbriyevich, Bomse, Berlaga, and also Polykhayev, who was a man with democratic leanings and not ashamed to march alongside his subordinates in various political processions and carnivals. Skumbriyevich greatly admired the coffin and attributed great importance to it. From time to time Yegor put on an apron and personally repainted it, freshening up the antibureaucratic slogan, while the telephones in his office grew hoarse, and all sorts of heads popped in and out of the door, sadly rolling their eyes.

Yegor just couldn't be found. The doorman in the zigzag cap told Bender that Comrade Skumbriyevich had been there a moment before and had just left to go to the commandant's beach for a swim, which always perked him up a bit, as he used to say.

Taking Balaganov along just in case, and waking up Kozlevich with a jog as he dozed at the wheel, the Antelopeans drove out of town.

It was no wonder that Ostap, infuriated by everything that had been going on, wasted no time and went straight into the water after Skumbriyevich, not in the least embarrassed that an important conversation on shady dealings was to take place in the Black Sea.

Balaganov carried out the captain's orders to a T. He undressed the meek Berlaga, led him to the water, and, holding him by the waist, waited patiently. A difficult discussion was evidently taking place at sea. Ostap was shouting like Neptune himself. It wasn't possible to make out what he was saying. The only thing they could see was Skumbriyevich heading for the shore, but Ostap cut him off and chased him further out to sea. Then the voices became louder, and odd words and phrases such as "Intensivist," "And who took it?" "It wasn't the Pope, I bet!" "What's that got to do with me?" came floating over.

Berlaga kept shifting from one bare heel to another, leaving Indian footprints in the wet sand. At last there came a shout from the sea:

"You can let him go!"

Balaganov let the accountant drop into the sea, where he dog-paddled away at remarkable speed, cutting the water with his arms and legs. At the sight of Berlaga, Skumbriyevich ducked under the water with fright.

In the meantime the hoof agent stretched out on the sand and lit a cigarette. He waited twenty minutes. Berlaga came back first. He squatted down, took a handkerchief out of his pants pocket, and, wiping his face, said:

"Skumbriyevich has confessed. There was no need for the identification parade."

"Did he squeal, the creep?" Alex asked amiably. Removing the stub with his thumb and forefinger, he clicked his tongue. As he did so, he spat out a gob as long and fast as a torpedo.

Hopping on one leg and aiming the other at his pants, Berlaga explained rather vaguely, "I didn't do it in the interests of absolute truth, just ordinary truth."

The second to arrive was the smooth operator. He threw himself down on his face and, pressing his cheek to the hot sand, looked significantly at the blue Skumbriyevich climbing out of the water. Then he took the dossier from Balaganov and, wetting the pencil with his tongue, entered some new and hard-earned details in it.

Skumbriyevich had undergone an amazing transformation. Only half an hour before, the waves had received an active social worker, a man about whom even the chairman of the local committee used to say. "Some may let you down, but never Skumbriyevich." But he had let them down. And how! What the gentle summer waves brought ashore was no longer the heavenly female form with the head of a cleanly shaven Englishman but a shapeless wineskin full of mustard and horse-radish.

While the smooth operator had been pirating on the

high seas, Heinrich Sause, having lain in wait for
Polykhayev and had an important talk with him, left
the Hercules in complete confusion. Grinning oddly,
he went to the post office and there, standing behind
a table covered with plate glass, wrote a letter to his
girl-friend in Aachen:

> "Dear girl, I hasten to tell you the wonderful news.
> At last the boss is sending me to work. My new friend
> Bomse tells me it's punishment. Can you imagine that!
> And will our dear friend Doctor of Mathematics
> Bernhard Gerngross ever understand it!"

The All-Purpose Stamp

TOWARD MIDDAY the next day the rumor went around that Polykhayev had locked himself in his hall of palms with a visitor and hadn't responded to Serna Mikhailovna's knocking or the infernal telephone calls for three hours. The Herculeans were lost in conjecture. They were more used to Polykhayev's being taken by the arm along the corridors, seated on window sills, or led under stairways, where all problems could be settled. They even wondered if the chief hadn't been dropped from the class of officials who "went out a moment ago," and joined the influential group of "recluses" who arrive at their offices early in the morning, lock themselves in, unplug the telephone, and, having thus cut themselves off from the world, compile all sorts of reports.

But work was going on; papers needed signature, replies, and resolutions. An angry Serna Mikhailovna kept going up to Polykhayev's door and listening. As she did so, the delicate pearls in her big ears trembled.

"It's unprecedented," said the secretary profoundly.

"But who's in there?" asked Bomse, who smelled of

a mixture of eau de Cologne and meatball. "Maybe someone from the inspection department?"

"No, it's an ordinary visitor, I'm telling you."

"And Polykhayev's been with him for three hours?"

"It's unprecedented," Serna Mikhailovna repeated.

"What can we do about it?" asked Bomse, getting agitated. "I need a decision urgently. I've got a detailed report on the unsuitability of the former premises of the Tin and Bacon Company for the working conditions of the Hercules. I can't proceed without it."

Serna Mikhailovna was besieged on all sides by members of the staff. They all held small or large pieces of paper in their hands. After another hour, during which the hum of conversation on the other side of the door showed no sign of abating, Serna Mikhailovna sat down at her desk and said meekly, "All right, comrades. Bring your papers over here."

From a drawer she took a wooden stand in which there were thirty-six wobbling stamps with thick shiny tops and, adroitly selecting the right ones, began stamping the papers which could not be postponed.

The head of the Hercules had long since stopped signing papers personally. Whenever necessary, he used to take a seal out of his vest pocket and, breathing on it lovingly, impressed a violet facsimile opposite his rank. This manual operation greatly pleased him and even prompted the thought that it wouldn't be such a bad thing to transfer some of the commoner decisions to rubber.

This resulted in the appearance of the first rubberized comments:

> *No objection. Polykhayev.*
> *I agree. Polykhayev.*
> *Splendid idea. Polykhayev.*
> *Go ahead. Polykhayev.*

Having successfully tried out the new arrangement, the head of the Hercules came to the conclusion that it greatly simplified his work and could do with further promotion and development. A new batch of stamps was set into action. This time the decisions were wordier:

> *Issue an official reprimand. Polykhayev.*
> *Criticize severely. Polykhayev.*
> *Transfer to outlying areas. Polykhayev.*
> *Dismiss without severance pay. Polykhayev.*

The battle being waged by the head of the Hercules and the communal-services department over the question of their premises inspired him to fresh standardized comments:

> *I don't come under the communal-services department. Polykhayev.*
> *What's the matter, have they gone crazy? Polykhayev.*
> *Don't interfere with my work. Polykhayev.*
> *I'm not your nursemaid. Polykhayev.*
> *The hotel belongs to us and that's it. Polykhayev.*
> *I know your tricks. Polykhayev.*
> *You're not getting beds or washbowls. Polykhayev.*

This series was ordered in triplicate. It looked as though the battle was going to last some time, so the clear-sighted chief had good reason to believe one set wouldn't be enough.

Next he ordered a set of decisions for internal use:

> *Ask Serna Mikhailovna. Polykhayev.*
> *Don't bother me with this sort of thing. Polykhayev.*
> *Slowly but surely! Polykhayev.*
> *Curse the lot of you! Polykhayev.*

The chief's creative endeavor was not, of course, limited solely to administrative aspects of the matter. Being a broad-minded man, he could not leave out problems of current politics. So he ordered a splendid all-purpose stamp, the wording of which took him

several days to work out. It was a wonderful rubberized thought, which could be adapted to any occasion. Besides enabling him to react immediately to
the events of the day, it also freed him from the need
to think hard each time. The stamp was conveniently
designed so that the empty space in the text had only
to be filled in to obtain an up-to-date resolution:

In reply to ....
We, the Herculeans, to a man, will respond by:
a) improving the standard of our office correspondence;
b) stepping up labor productivity;
c) intensifying the campaign against bureaucracy,
   red tape, nepotism, and bootlicking;
d) eliminating absenteeism and birthday parties;
e) reducing overheads on calendars and portraits;
f) an all-round increase in trade-union activity;
g) no longer celebrating Christmas, Easter, Whitsun,
   Lady Day, christenings, Kurban Bayram, Yom
   Kippur, Ramadan, Purim, and other religious holidays;
h) merciless eradication of bungling, rowdyism,
   drunkenness, shirking of responsibility, and spine-
   lessness;
i) joining the society Down with Routine on the
   Opera Stage;
j) changing to soyabeans, all of us;
k) switching to business correspondence in the Latin
   script, and anything else that may later be required.

Polykhayev used to fill in the dotted line himself,
whenever required.

He soon began to resort to the all-purpose stamp
more and more frequently, finding it much to his lik-
ing. He reached the stage where he used it in reply to
attacks, machinations, slights, and outrageous state-
ments by his own staff. For example, "In reply to the
impudent and outrageous conduct of accountant Ku-

kushkind in demanding payment for overtime, we will respond by . . ." or "In reply to the vile machinations and foul attacks of staff member Borisokhlebsky, who has requested compassionate leave . . ." and so on.

When they first got to know about the rubberized resolutions, some of the Herculeans became depressed. They were alarmed by the abundance of alternatives. They were particularly upset by the points on changing to the Latin script and joining the society Down with Routine on the Opera Stage. But things moved along peacefully. Admittedly, Skumbriyevich waved his arms and organized a separate circle called Down with the Opera *Khovanshchina,* but he went no further than that.

And while the voices behind the door continued to drone like fans, Serna Mikhailovna worked away briskly. The stand with the stamps from the smallest —with *No objection. Polykhayev*—to the largest— the all-purpose one—was reminiscent of one of those weird instruments seen in the circus on which a clown dressed in white with a sun on his posterior plays a serenade with sticks. The secretary selected the appropriate stamp and imprinted it on the papers. She was most drawn to the one that said *Slowly but surely!* recalling that it was her boss's favorite resolution.

Everything went smoothly. The rubber stamps were an excellent substitute for the man. Polykhayev in rubber was no inferior to Polykhayev in the flesh.

The Hercules had already emptied, and the bare-footed cleaning women were walking up and down corridors with dirty buckets; the last typist had now left, having stayed behind for an hour to type out for herself some lines by the poet Yesenin; Serna Mik-hailovna had got up, tired of waiting, and begun massaging her eyelids before going out of doors, when the door of Polykhayev's office shook, opened, and out came Ostap Bender. He looked dreamily at Serna

Mikhailovna and went past, waving a yellow file with
bootlace tapes. Behind him, out of the invigorating
shade of the palms and sycamores, staggered Polykhayev. The secretary took one look at her highly
placed boy-friend and sank onto the square pad which
softened the hardness of her chair. What a good thing
the members of the staff had already gone home and
couldn't see the boss at that moment. A diamond tear
was perched in his mustache like a bird in the
branches. He was blinking at an incredible rate and
rubbing his hands so violently that he might have
been trying to make fire the way primitives do. He
hurried after Ostap, smiling sheepishly and arching
his back.

"What's going to happen?" he babbled, running in
front of Ostap first on one side and then on the other.
"I won't be ruined, will I? Tell me, my dear young
friend, I won't be ruined, will I? I can be sure, can't I?"

He wanted to add that he had a wife and children,
Serna, children by Serna and by another woman, who
lived in Rostov on the Don, but the words stuck in his
throat.

Whimpering plaintively, he accompanied Ostap right
up to the vestibule. In the empty building they saw
only two men. Skumbriyevich was standing at the end
of the corridor. At the sight of the smooth operator,
he clutched his jaw and jumped into an alcove. Downstairs, Berlaga was peeping from behind the marble
girl with the electric torch. He bowed subserviently
to Ostap and even said "Good evening," but Ostap ignored the Viceroy's greetings.

At the door, Polykhayev seized Ostap by the sleeve
and burbled, "I've hidden nothing. Honestly! I can be
sure, can't I?"

"Complete assurance comes only to a man with an
insurance policy," said Ostap without slowing down.
"That's what any insurance agent will tell you. Personally, I don't need you any more. But there's always
the police. They may be interested quite soon."

The Captain Dances the Tango

PANIKOVSKY AND BALAGANOV were seated at a little white table in a small café which sold mineral water and had a sign outside showing blue soda siphons. The hoof agent was chewing a cream puff and trying to prevent the cream from spurting out of the other end. He washed down this ambrosia with soda and green Fresh Hay syrup. The messenger boy was consuming health-giving yogurt. There were already six empty bottles in front of him. He was carefully shaking the thick liquid out of the seventh jar into a glass. That day the new office girl had issued wages on a written order from Bender, and the friends were enjoying the cool air wafted from the Italian floor tiles, from the icebox where the wet sheep cheese was kept, from the dulled cylinders of sparkling water, and from the marble counter. A piece of ice had slid out of the icebox and lay on the floor, dissolving into water. It was pleasant to watch it after the tiring view of the street with its brief shadows, wilting pedestrians, and thirst-crazed dogs.

"A good town, Chernomorsk," Panikovsky remarked, licking his lips. "Yogurt is good for the heart."

This piece of information seemed to amuse Balaganov. He inadvertently squeezed the puff and out
spurted a thick sausage of cream, which the hoof
agent only just managed to catch in mid-air.

"You know, Alex," Panikovsky continued, "I've
somehow lost faith in Bender. He's not doing things
the right way."

"Come on, now," said Balaganov gruffly, "you
weren't asked."

"No, seriously. I greatly admire Ostap Ibragimovich,
he's really quite someone. Even Funt—and you know
how I admire Funt—said that Bender was clever. But
I tell you, Alex, Funt's an ass. Honestly, a complete
dolt. Simply a miserable, useless person. I have nothing against Bender, but there's something I don't like.
I'll tell you, Alex, as a close friend. You know, Alex"
—Panikovsky lowered his voice to a whisper—"I
greatly admire Bender, but I must tell you he's an
ass. Honestly, a miserable, useless person!"

"Come on, now," said Balaganov warningly.

"What do you mean, 'come on, now!' Just think
how he's wasting our money. Why do we need that
stupid office? Think of the expense! Funt alone gets
paid a hundred and twenty. And the office girl. And
another two people were sent to us today. I saw them
get paid today. Two kids waiting to be drafted.
What's it all for? He says it's to make the thing legal. To hell with legality if it costs that much. And the
deer horns which cost sixty-five rubles . . . And the
inkwell . . . And all those files . . ."

Panikovsky undid his jacket and the cheap dickey
buttoned on at the convention violator's neck flew up
like a roll of parchment. But he was so worked up he
didn't notice.

"Yes, and we get such lousy wages while he wal-
lows in luxury. Why, I ask you, did he have to go to
the Caucasus? On a business trip, he says. But I don't
believe it. And I had to go to the quay to get the ticket.
A first-class ticket, mind you. He's such a swell he

can't go second-class. That's where our ten thousand
is going. He makes long-distance telephone calls and
sends special-delivery cables all over the place. You
know what they cost? Forty kopeks a word. And I
have to go without yogurt, which I need for my
health. I'm old and sick. I tell you straight, Bender's
not a brain."

"I wouldn't say you were, either," Balaganov observed. "Bender made a man out of you, after all. Remember how you were running away with the goose
in Arbatov? And now you've got a job, you get
wages, and you're a member of society."

"Who wants to be a member of society!" said Panikovsky suddenly, and then, lowering his voice, added,
"Your Bender's an idiot. He's latched on to the idea of
this stupid investigation, when the money could be
had today without any trouble at all."

Here the hoof agent stopped thinking about his
darling chief and moved closer to Panikovsky, while
the latter, incessantly straightening out his recalcitrant
dickey, told Balaganov of an important experiment he
had carried out at his own risk.

The day the smooth operator and Balaganov were
chasing after Skumbriyevich, Panikovsky had handed
over the office to Funt, secretly broken into Koreiko's
room, and, taking advantage of the absence of its
owner, made a careful examination of it. He had not
found any money in the room, naturally, but he
found something better—dumbbells, huge black
dumbbells, each weighing twenty pounds.

"I'll tell you as a close friend, Alex. I discovered the
secret of those dumbbells." Panikovsky finally caught
the elusive end of his dickey, buttoned it to his pants,
and glared triumphantly at Balaganov.

"What secret can there be?" asked the hoof agent
disappointedly. "Ordinary dumbbells for weight-lift-
ing exercises."

"You know how I admire you, Alex," said Panikovsky, beginning to get heated, "but you're an ass.

They're gold dumbbells! Do you understand? Made
of solid gold. Each one weighs about twenty pounds.
When it dawned on me, you could have knocked me
down with a feather. I stood in front of the dumbbells
and laughed my head off. What a crook that Koreiko
is. He made the gold into dumbbells, painted them
black, and thought no one would notice. I tell you,
Alex, would I have let you in on the secret if I'd been
able to carry them off alone? But I'm old and sick, and
the dumbbells are heavy. So I'm asking you as a close
friend. I'm not Bender. I'm honest."

"And suppose they aren't gold?" asked the favorite
son of Lieutenant Schmidt, hoping Panikovsky would
dispel his doubt as soon as possible.

"What do you think they are, then?" asked the convention violator ironically.

"Yes, I see," said Balaganov, batting his ginger eye-
lashes. "Just think, it takes an old man to find the answer! Bender certainly isn't doing things right. He
writes reports and travels about . . . But in fairness
we'll give him a share, won't we?"

"Why should we?" Panikovsky retorted. "Let's
keep it all ourselves. We'll live off the fat of the land.
I'll get myself some gold teeth and then get married.
Honestly, I'll get married."

It was decided to purloin the precious dumbbells
without delay.

"Pay for the yogurt, Alex," said Panikovsky. "We'll
settle up later."

The conspirators left the café and, dazzled by the
sunlight, began wandering around town. They were
eaten up with impatience. They loitered on the
bridges and, leaning over the parapets, gazed down
without interest at the roof tops and the streets leading to the harbor, along which trucks were making
their way with the cautiousness of a horse. Fat, port-
bred sparrows chiseled the roads with their beaks,
while filthy cats followed their movements from

doorways. Beyond the roof tops, attic lights, and antennas could be seen the bluish water, a cutter moving at full pelt, and a yellow funnel with a large red letter on it.

From time to time Panikovsky raised his head and began counting. He was converting pounds into ounces and ounces into old-fashioned gold pieces, and each time the violator of the convention arrived at such an excting total that he gave a soft gasp.

Between eleven and midnight the foster brothers were walking in the direction of the horn and hoof procurement office, sagging under the weight of two large dumbbells. Panikovsky carried his share with both hands, sticking out his stomach and puffing with delight. He kept stopping, putting down the dumbbells on the sidewalk, and muttering, "I'll get married, honestly I will." The beefy Balaganov was carrying his dumbbell over his shoulder. Now and then Panikovsky was unable to turn the corner, as the dumbbell kept pulling him forward. At such times Balaganov had to hold him back with his free hand and maneuver him in the right direction.

They halted at the door of the office.

"We'll saw off a chunk right away," said Panikovsky eagerly, "and sell it tomorrow. I know a watchmaker named Biberham. He'll give us a good price."

It was at this point that the conspirators noticed light coming from under the green office curtains.

"Who can be in there at this time of night?" Balaganov asked in surprise, bending toward the keyhole.

At his desk, lit from the side by a strong electric light, sat Ostap Bender; he was rapidly scribbling something.

"The writer!" said Balaganov, bursting into laughter and letting Panikovsky have a look.

"He's writing again, of course," Panikovsky observed, after a good look. "Honestly, that miserable man amuses me. But where are we going to do the sawing?"

And, eagerly discussing whether or not to sell a couple of chunks of gold to the watchmaker the very next day, the foster brothers raised their loads and went off into the darkness.

In the meantime the smooth operator was finishing off his life history of Alexander Ivanovich Koreiko. The brass lids were off all the five inkwells in the "Facing the Countryside" inkstand. Ostap dipped his pen into all the inkwells indiscriminately, shifted about on the chair, and kept scraping his feet along the floor under the desk.

Everything vague had become clear. The large number of people with thin mustaches and regal beards with whom he had occasion to mix and who had left their mark in the yellow dossier suddenly moved aside, and into the foreground, sweeping everyone and everything aside, came a white-eyed, pig-faced man with wheat-colored eyebrows and heavy corporal's wrinkles on his cheeks.

Ostap put a period, blotted the life history with a silver-bear-handled blotter, and began filing the documents. He liked to keep things in order. For the last time he gazed admiringly at the neat pile of written evidence, telegrams, and miscellaneous items of information. The dossier even contained photographs and extracts from account books. The whole of Alexander Ivanovich Koreiko's life lay in the dossier, and together with it were girls, palm trees, the blue sea, a white steamer, express trains, a shining car, and Rio de Janeiro, the magic city nestling in a bay where kind mulattoes live and most of the citizens wear white pants. At last the smooth operator had found the man he had sought all his life.

"And there's no one to appreciate my magnum opus," Ostap thought sadly, standing up and lacing the bulging dossier. "Balaganov's very nice, but stupid. Panikovsky's just a crabby old man, and Kozle-

vich is an angel without wings. He still thinks we procure horns and hoofs for the cigarette-holder industry. But where are my friends' wives and children?
The only hope is that Koreiko will appreciate the great
work and give me five hundred thousand rubles because I'm so poor. No, wait: now I won't take less than
a million, or the kind mulattoes won't respect me."

Ostap came around the desk, picked up the splendid
dossier, and thoughtfully began pacing up and down
the empty office, circling the typewriter with the
German accent and the railroad punch, and almost
touching the deer horns with his head. The white scar
on his neck had pinkened. The smooth operator's
movements gradually slowed down and his feet, shod
with a pair of red shoes bought second-hand from a
Greek sailor, began noiselessly gliding over the floor.
Hardly noticeably he began moving sideways. With
his right hand he clutched the dossier to his chest as
though it were a girl, while his left hand was stretched
outward. The lubricated squeak of a Ferris wheel
floated clearly through the air. It was a high-pitched
musical sound which suddenly changed to a violinish
unison . . . and the captivating, long-forgotten tune
made all the articles in the Chernomorsk branch of the
Arbatov horn and hoof procurement office resound in
sympathy.

First began the samovar. A burning coal suddenly
popped out of it onto the tray and the samovar began
singing:

> *Beneath the skies of Argentina,*
> *Those southern skies so hot and blue . . .*

The smooth operator was dancing the tango. His
chiseled features were turned in a profile view. He
went down on one knee, quickly came up again,
turned, and, smoothly shifting his weight from one
foot to the other, glided forward again. Invisible coat
tails flared out behind him at the sudden turns.

Then the melody was taken up by the typewriter with the German accent:

> *Thoze zouthern zkiez zo hot and blue,*
> *The women make zuch pretty picturez . . .*

And the clumsy wrought-iron punch sighed heavily for times gone forever:

> *The women make such pretty pictures,*
> *Dancing the tango.*

Ostap was dancing the classical, provincial tango which they used to perform in miniature theaters twenty years before, when Berlaga the accountant wore his first derby, Skumbriyevich worked in the town hall, Polykhayev was taking his government-service entrance examinations, and stand-in chairman Funt was still a cheerful seventy-year-old and together with the other piqué vests sat in the Café Florida and discussed the terrible closing of the Dardanelles on account of the Italo-Turkish war. And the piqué vests, at that time still ruddy and smooth, sorted out the politicians of the time.

Ostap was dancing. Palm trees rustled and colored birds flew about overhead. Ocean-going steamers rubbed their hulls against the quay in Rio de Janeiro. Shrewd Brazilian merchants were engaged in dumping coffee in full view of everyone, and in the street cafés the local younger set enjoyed their liquor.

"I'm taking the parade!" the smooth operator exclaimed.

Putting out the light, he left the room and took the shortest route to Carefree Street. The pale compass-like legs of searchlights moved about the sky, dropped downward, and suddenly cut through a piece of house, revealing a balcony or glass veranda with a dazed young couple caught completely unawares. Two small tanks with round mushroom hats came around the corner toward Ostap, throbbing and crunching their caterpillar tracks. A mounted soldier, bending forward in the saddle, was asking a passer-by how to get to the Old Market. At one point Ostap's path was barred by some artillery. He jumped in between two field guns. In another place militiamen were hastily nailing a black notice with the words "Gas Shelter" to the gates of a house.

Ostap hurried. He was spurred on by the Argentinian tango.

Without paying attention to what was going on around him, Ostap went into Koreiko's building and knocked at the familiar door.

"Who's there?" came the voice of the underground millionaire.

"Telegram!" the smooth operator shouted out, winking in the darkness.

The door opened and he went inside, catching the dossier in the jamb.

As dawn came, the hoof agent and the messenger boy sat in a ravine some way out of town. They were sawing dumbbells. Their feet were bespattered with iron filings. Panikovsky's dickey lay on the ground beside him; he had taken it off because it prevented him from working. The thoughtful convention violator had spread a newspaper underneath the dumbbells so as not to miss a single speck of precious material.

The foster brothers kept exchanging knowing glances and then sawing with renewed energy. The morning still was broken only by the whistling of gophers and the rasping of the heated blades.

"What's the matter?" Balaganov suddenly said, stopping. "I've been working for three hours and there's no gold yet."

Panikovsky didn't answer. He had already realized the truth and for the last half-hour had only moved the saw backward and forward for the sake of appearances.

"Well, anyway, let's saw some more," said the ginger-haired Balaganov cheerfully.

"Of course, we must," Panikovsky said, trying to delay the terrible hour of retribution. He covered his face with his hand and through his fingers watched the rhythmic movement of Balaganov's broad back.

"I just don't get it," Alex exclaimed, finishing the operation and separating the dumbbell into two apple-like halves. "It's not gold!"

"Keep sawing, keep sawing," Panikovsky stammered.

But Balaganov, holding a wrought-iron hemisphere in either hand, slowly advanced toward the violator of the convention.

"Don't come near me with that iron," Panikovsky squeaked, jumping aside. "I loathe you."

At this point Alex drew back his arm and, grunting with the effort, let fly at the intriguer with a chunk of dumbbell. Hearing the whistle of the missile Panikovsky dropped to the ground.

The hoof agent's skirmish with the messenger boy was a brief one. The infuriated Balaganov first stamped on the dickey with great relish, then set about its owner. As he landed the punches, Alex kept repeating, "Who thought of the dumbbells? Who spent government money? Who called Bender names?" In addition, the first son also reminded him about the Sukharevka convention, which cost Panikovsky a few extra thumps.

"You'll answer for that dickey," Panikovsky cried furiously, trying to protect himself with his elbows. "I'll never forgive you for that. They don't sell dickeys like that any more."

In conclusion, Balaganov removed his opponent's tattered purse, containing thirty rubles. "That's for the yogurt, you creep!" he explained.

They returned to town.

The wrathful Alex walked in front, while behind him, limping on one foot and sobbing loudly, staggered Panikovsky.

"I'm a poor old unlucky man!" he blubbered.

"You'll answer for the dickey. And give me back my money!"

"I'll give you money!" said Alex, without turning around. "I'm going to tell Bender everything. You chiseler!"

The End of Rooks' Row

BARBARA PTIBURDUKOV was happy. Seated at a round table, she surveyed her domain. There was so much furniture in the Ptiburdukovs' room that there was hardly any space left at all. But what there was sufficed for her happiness. The lamp sent its light through the window, where a green branch quivered like a lady's brooch. On the table were cookies, candy, and pickled zander in a round iron can. The electric kettle collected the entire comfort of the Ptiburdukov nest on its curved surface. It reflected the bed, the white curtains, and the bedside table. It also reflected Ptiburdukov himself as he sat opposite his wife in blue pajamas. He was also happy. Letting the tobacco smoke filter through his mustache, he was making a toy country-style lavatory out of plyboard. It was painstaking work. He had to make the walls, add a sloping roof, install the inside equipment, put glass in the window, and fit the door with a microscopic latch. Ptiburdukov worked with zeal; he considered fretwork the best relaxation.

Finishing the work, the engineer laughed with delight, slapped his wife's fat warm back, and moved the tin of zander nearer. But at that moment there was a loud knock at the door, the lamp blinked, and the teapot shifted from the wire pad underneath it.

"Who can it be at this hour?" said Ptiburdukov, going to open the door.

On the landing stood Vasisualy Lokhankin. He was wrapped in a white marseilles blanket all the way up to his beard; below it showed his hairy legs. He was hugging a copy of *Man and Woman*, thick and gilded like an icon. His eyes rolled.

"Do come in," said the engineer in a daze. "Barbara, what's all this?"

"I've come to stay as long as you can have me," Lokhankin replied in deathlike iambics. "I hope that I can find refuge with you."

"Why refuge?" Ptiburdukov asked, growing crimson. "What do you want, Vasisualy Andreyevich?"

Barbara hurried out onto the landing. "Al, look! He's naked!" she cried. "What's happened, Vasisualy? Don't just stand there. Come in!"

Lokhankin crossed the threshold in his bare feet and, muttering the words "calamity, calamity," began scurrying about the room. He immediately dislodged Ptiburdukov's fretwork with the end of his blanket. The engineer retired to the corner with a hunch that disaster lay ahead.

"What calamity?" Barbara inquired. "Why are you dressed only in a blanket?"

"I've come to stay as long as you can have me," Lokhankin repeated in a bovine voice. His yellow heel was drumming out an anxious roll on the clean wax floor.

"What rot are you talking?" Barbara snapped at her former husband. "Go home and get some sleep. Get out of here. Go on, go home!"

"I have no home," said Vasisualy, continuing to shiver. "It was burned down to the ground. A fire, a fire has brought me here. I only managed to save this blanket and later I saved my favorite book. But if you're so hard-hearted, I'll go away, and curse you all."

Tottering with grief, he walked toward the door. But Barbara and her husband stopped him. They apologized, said they hadn't realized what had happened, and generally made a great fuss over him. A new suit, underwear, and shoes belonging to Ptiburdukov were fished out of the cupboard.

While Lokhankin was dressing, the husband and wife conferred in the corridor.

"Where can we put him up?" Barbara whispered. "We've only one room: he can't spend the night with us."

"I'm surprised at you," said the good-natured engineer. "A man's in trouble and you think only of your security."

When the two returned to the room, the victim of the conflagration was sitting at the table and eating the pickled fish straight from the tin. Moreover, two volumes of *Strength of Materials* had been pulled off the shelf and *Man and Woman* put in their place.

"Imagine the whole house burning down," said Ptiburdukov sympathetically. "How terrible!"

"I think it may have been necessary," said Vasisualy, finishing up his hosts' supper. "Perhaps I shall emerge from the flames a changed man."

But he hadn't changed.

When everything had been talked over, the Ptiburdukovs began making arrangements for the night. For Vasisualy they put down a small mattress in the only space left, which only an hour before had been enough for happiness. They shut the window, put out the light, and night invaded the room. For twenty minutes no one said a word, though they all kept twisting and turning, and breathing loudly. Then from the floor came Lokhankin's drawn-out whisper:

"Barbara: listen, Barbara!"

"What is it?" asked the ex-wife peevishly.

"Why did you leave me?" Without waiting for the

answer to this question of principle, Vasisualy went
on in a nagging tone. "You female, Barbara! You
bitch, I despise you . . ."

The engineer lay quiet in his bed, choking with
fury and clenching his fists.

Rooks' Row burned down at midnight, just as Ostap was dancing the tango in his empty office and the
foster brothers were leaving the town, doubled up
under the weight of the gold dumbbells.

The first link in the long chain of adventures
which preceded the fire in apartment No. 3 was nobody's grandma. As we know, she always used kerosene in her mezzanine because she didn't trust the
electric light. Since Vasisualy's thrashing, nothing else
of interest had happened for some time and the restless mind of Mitrich the gentleman-in-waiting suffered from enforced idleness. Musing on grandma's
habits, he grew alarmed.

"She'll burn the place down, she will," he mumbled. "What does she care? My piano alone may be
worth two thousand rubles."

Having reached this conclusion, he insured all his
effects against fire. He then felt reassured as he apathetically watched grandma hauling a huge dark-col-
ored bottle of kerosene upstairs to her room, holding it in her arms like a baby. The first person to hear
about Mitrich's shrewd move was Gigienishvili, who
immediately drew his own conclusions. He went up
to Mitrich in the corridor and, grabbing him by the
front of his coat, said menacingly:

"You'd like to set fire to the whole apartment,
wouldn't you, and collect the insurance. Do you think
I'm a fool? I see it all."

And the fiery tenant insured himself the same day
for a large amount of money. The whole of Rooks'
Row was panic-stricken at the news. Lucy Pferd ran
into the kitchen with her eyes popping.

"They'll burn us to death, the scoundrels. You do
what you like, citizens, but I'm going to insure my-

self right away. It doesn't matter if the place burns
down as long as we can collect the insurance. I'm not
going to go begging just because of them."

The next day the whole apartment insured itself,
except for Lokhankin and nobody's grandma. Lokhankin was reading a copy of *Motherland* and hadn't noticed anything, while nobody's grandma didn't believe
in insurance, just as she didn't believe in electricity.
Pryakhin brought home an insurance policy edged
with lilac and examined the water marks in the light
for some time.

"So the government's helping us, is it?" he remarked gloomily. "Well, thanks. So now we can do
what we like."

And, stuffing the policy under his shirt, Pryakhin
went away to his room. His words put such fear into
their hearts that no one in Rooks' Row slept that night.
Dunya tied her belongings in a bundle, while her
roommates went off to stay the night with friends.
During the day they all followed suit and gradually
removed their property from the house.

It was all clear. The house was doomed. It just had
to burn down. Last to come flying out of the house, already full of samovar smoke and tongues of flame, was
Lokhankin, covered in a blanket. He was shouting
"Fire! Fire!" at the top of his voice, though no one
should have really been surprised at the news. All the
tenants of Rooks' Row were there outside. The
drunken Pryakhin sat on his iron-cornered box, stared
vacantly at the flickering windows, and muttered to
himself, "We can do as we like." Gigienishvili disdainfully sniffed his hands, which smelled of kerosene, and
wiped them on his pants. A coil of fire spurted from
a ventilation window and unfurled toward the
wooden cornice, loosing a shower of sparks. The
first windowpane burst and fell out with a crash. Nobody's grandma began wailing terribly.

"Forty years that house has been there," Mitrich explained gravely, wandering in and out of the gath-

ered crowd. "Through all the regimes. It was a good house, and it burned down during the Soviet regime. It's the sad truth, citizens."

The female contingent of Rooks' Row huddled together and stared at the blaze. Flames spurted from all the windows like guns. From time to time the blaze died down and made it seem as if the now darkened house had recoiled like a cannon. Then a red-yellow cloud burst out, festively illuminating Lemon Street. It grew hot. It was now impossible to remain near the building, and the crowd moved over to the far sidewalk.

Nikita Pryakhin alone dozed on his box in the road. Suddenly he jumped up, barefoot and terrifying. "Churchgoers!" he shouted, renting his shirt. "Citizens!"

He moved back sideways from the fire, dived into the crowd, and, bawling something incomprehensible, began pointing at the blazing house. A commotion broke out amid the crowd.

"They've forgotten the baby," said a straw-hatted woman confidently.

They surged around Nikita. He elbowed his way through and raced toward the house.

"It's on the bed!" he cried wildly. "Let me through, I say."

Hot tears rolled down his face. He punched Gigienishvili, who tried to bar the way, and raced into the yard. A minute later he came out again, carrying a ladder.

"Stop him!" cried the straw-hatted woman. "He'll be killed."

"Get away, I tell you!" Pryakhin roared, placing the ladder against the wall and fighting off the young men from the crowd who were trying to catch hold of his legs. "I won't let it be lost. My throat's afire." He lashed out with his feet and made his way up to the smoking window on the second floor.

"Come back!" people cried. "Why are you going up there? You'll be killed."

"It's on the bed," Nikita kept shouting. "A whole goose and a quart of vodka. Do you think I'm going to let that go, churchgoing citizens?"

With unexpected agility, Pryakhin grabbed hold of the window and was gone, sucked inside by a rush of air. His last words were, "We'll do as we like." A silence descended on the street, broken only by the bell and siren of the fire engines. Into the yard came firemen wearing stiff canvas suits with wide blue belts.

A minute after Nikita Pryakhin's one and only brave deed in the whole of his life, a blazing beam broke away from the house and fell with a crash onto the ground. The roof came apart with a crackle and collapsed inside. A column of fire rose up to the sky just as though a cannon had been fired to the moon from within.

That is how apartment No. 3, better known as Rooks' Row, met its end. Suddenly there was a clatter of hoofs in the street and through the glare of the fire hurtled engineer Talmudovsky in a cab. At his feet lay a label-covered suitcase. Jogging up and down in his seat, he was leaning forward and shouting at the driver:

"I'm not staying here one moment on that salary! Faster, cabby, faster!"

And the greasy back of his coat, lit by the light of the fire, disappeared around a turn.

] CHAPTER [

: 22 :

I'm Taking the Parade

"I'M BORED to tears," Ostap commented. "We've been talking for only two hours, yet I'm as sick of you as though I'd known you all my life. It might be all right being a millionaire in America with an obstinate nature like yours, but a millionaire in this country should be more accommodating."

"You're crazy," Koreiko answered.

"Don't insult me," Bender snapped. "I'm the son of a Turkish citizen and therefore a descendant of the Janizaries. I won't show you any mercy if you insult me. The Janizaries spare neither women, children, nor underground Soviet millionaires."

"Go away, citizen," Koreiko cried in the voice of a Hercules bureaucrat. "It's after three and I want to go to bed. I have to be up early."

"Quite right, I'd forgotten!" Ostap exclaimed. "You mustn't be late for work or they might fire you without severance pay. Still, your two-week salary is twenty-three rubles. The way you save, you could live six months on that."

"It's none of your business. Leave me alone, do you hear? Get out of here!"

"But your economy will ruin you. It's obviously

rather risky for you to show your millions. But you try too hard. Have you thought about what will happen to you if you ever manage to spend the money? Abstinence is a dangerous thing. A French teacher I knew, Ernestine Pointcaré, never drank wine. And what happened? One evening she was given a glass of brandy at a party. She enjoyed it so much that she emptied a whole bottle and there and then, at the supper table, went crazy. The next morning there was one French teacher less. The same thing might happen to you."

"What are you trying to get out of me, damn you!"

"The same thing that my life-long friend Nicky Osten-Backen tried to get from my life-long girl-friend, Inga Zając the Polish beauty. He was after love. So am I. I want you to love me, citizen Koreiko, and as a token of your affection give me a million rubles."

"Get out," said Koreiko softly.

"There, now, you've forgotten again that I'm a descendant of the Janizaries."

With these words Ostap stood up. The two were now standing opposite each other. Koreiko's face was stormy; white fleecy clouds flashed in his eyes. The smooth operator was smiling cordially, showing white corn-on-the-cob teeth. The enemies moved nearer the table lamp, casting giant shadows on the wall.

"I've told you a thousand times," said Koreiko, restraining himself, "I haven't got any millions and never had. Do you understand? Now, get out or I'll make a complaint to the police about you."

"You'll never do that," said Ostap significantly, "but I might leave you. Except that I will hardly get as far as your Carefree Street before you come running after me in tears and start licking my Janizary heels, begging me to come back."

"And why should I do that?"

"You will. It's necessary, as my friend Vasisualy Lokhankin used to say."

The smooth operator put the dossier on the table and, slowly untying the laces, continued:

"But let's come to an agreement. No excesses! You're not to strangle me, not to throw yourself out of the window, and, most important, not to die of shock. If you decide to die suddenly here and now, you'll put me in an idiotic position. The fruit of long and assiduous work will be ruined. In other words, let's have a discussion. It's no longer a secret that you don't love me. I shall never get what Nicky Osten-Backen got from Inga Zajac, my childhood girl-friend, so I'm not going to sigh and put my arm around your waist. Consider the serenading over. The balalaikas, psalteries, and golden harps are silent. I've come to see you as one lawyer to another. Here's a bundle weighing six or seven pounds. It's for sale and costs a million rubles, the same million that you are too greedy to want to give me."

Koreiko leaned across the table and read on the dossier: "The Case of Alexander Ivanovich Koreiko. Begun June 25, 1930. Ended August 10, 1930." "What rubbish!" he exclaimed, shrugging his shoulders. "First you come to me with some money, and now you've drummed up some case or other. It's simply ridiculous."

"Well, are you going to buy it?" the smooth operator persisted. "The price isn't high. I'm only asking a hundred and fifty thousand rubles a pound for some wonderful information in the field of underground commerce."

"What information?" Koreiko asked rudely, reaching out for the dossier.

"Very interesting information," Ostap replied, politely pushing his hand away. "Information on your second and principal life, which is strikingly different from your first, forty-six-ruble, Herculean existence. From ten till four you're in favor of the Soviet regime. But your second life from four till ten is known only to me. Do I make myself clear?"

Koreiko didn't reply. A shadow fell across the corporal's wrinkles on his face.

"No," said the smooth operator firmly, "you're not descended from the ape, like all citizens, you're descended from a cow. You catch on very slowly, just like a cloven-hoofed mammal. I'm telling you that as a specialist in horns and hoofs. So, once again. According to my information, you possess seven or eight million rubles. The dossier is being sold for one million. If you don't buy it, I'll take it straight to a certain other place. There they won't give me a cent for it, but it'll be the end of you. I'm telling you that as one lawyer to another. I'll remain the same needy poet and polygamist as before, but to my dying day I will have had the pleasure of knowing that I rid mankind of a great villain."

"Show me the file," said Koreiko thoughtfully.

"Don't fuss," Bender replied, opening the dossier. "I'm taking the parade. You were informed of that earlier in a telegram. So the soldiers are on parade, and, as you see, I'm giving the orders."

Koreiko looked at the first page, and, seeing his own photograph affixed to it, smiled evilly and said, "I just don't understand what you want from me. Perhaps I'll look at it out of curiosity."

"So will I, out of curiosity," the smooth operator declared. "Let's start on the basis of that innocent motive. Gentlemen of the jury, Alexander Ivanovich Koreiko was born . . . Actually, we can leave out the happy childhood. At that innocent time little Alexander hadn't yet begun his commercial robbery. Then comes a pink boyhood. Let's skip that period. And here's adolescence, the threshold of life. Let's stop here a moment, out of curiosity. Page six of the dossier . . ."

Ostap turned over page six and read out the contents of pages seven, eight, and so on, up to and including the twelfth.

"And so, gentlemen of the jury, you have just witnessed the first major deal made by my client: to wit,
speculation in government medical supplies during
the famine and typhus epidemic, and employment in
the supply department, which led to the disappearance
of a train carrying food supplies to the famine-stricken
Volga region. These facts, gentlemen of the jury, interest us purely from the point of view of curiosity."

Ostap was talking in the execrable manner of a prerevolutionary lawyer who, having taken a fancy to
some word or other, refuses to let go of it and bandies
it about for the whole ten days of a major trial. . . .

"The fact is not altogether without interest that our
client appeared in Moscow in 1922 . . ."

Koreiko's face maintained its neutrality, but his hands
wandered over the table like those of a blindman.

"Let me ask you a question, gentlemen of the jury
—out of curiosity, of course. What profit could two
ordinary barrels of tap water bring anyone? Twenty
rubles? Three rubles? Eight kopeks? No, gentlemen of
the jury, they brought Alexander Koreiko four hundred thousand rubles zero zero kopeks. Admittedly,
the barrels bore the expressive name of 'Revenge
Chemical Plant.' But let's go further. Pages forty-two
to fifty-three. The scene is a small, gullible republic.
A blue sky, camels, oases, and swells in gold skullcaps. My client helps them build a power station. I
stress, he *helps* them. Look at his face, gentlemen of
the jury . . ."

The enthusiastic Ostap turned to Koreiko and
pointed at him. But he had no time to describe a
smooth arc with his other hand, as the lawyers used
to do. The client suddenly grabbed his arm in mid-air
and silently began to twist it. At the same time, the
client attempted to seize the lawyer's throat with his
other hand. The adversaries pounded each other for
a minute or so, shaking with the effort. Ostap's shirt
came unbuttoned and the tattoo peeped through the
gap. Napoleon was still holding the mug of beer, but

his face was red, as though he had managed to get thoroughly soused.

"Don't depress me!" said Ostap, breaking away from Koreiko and regaining his breath. "It's impossible to study."

"Villain! Villain!" Koreiko whispered. "You villain." He sat down on the floor, wincing with the pain inflicted on him by the descendant of the Janizaries.

"The hearing's continued!" Bender announced as though nothing had happened. "And so you see, gentlemen of the jury, things are moving. My client has tried to kill me. He simply wanted to find out what I have inside me. I hasten to satisfy his curiosity. Inside me I have a noble and very sound heart, excellent lungs, and a liver without any sign of stones. I request this fact to be recorded in the proceedings. And now let's go on with our game, as the editor of a funny journal used to say as he opened the latest staff meeting and sternly surveyed his colleagues."

Alexander Koreiko found the game extremely unpleasant. The business trip from which Ostap had returned reeking of wine and lamb's wool had left extensive traces in the dossier. Among them was a copy of a sentence passed *in absentia*, tracings of plans for a charity combine, cuttings from *Profits and Loss*, and also photographs of film stars and the electric ravine.

"And finally, gentlemen of the jury, we come to the third stage in the activity of my bellicose client— a modest office job in the Hercules for society and hard, clandestine work for himself. Merely out of curiosity we will mention speculation in currency, furs, gems, and other such compact articles of prime necessity. And, last but not least, let us dwell on a series of explosive shareholding companies under the colorful, co-operative names of 'Intensivist,' 'Young Forester,' and 'Timber Assistance.' And it was not Mr. Funt, the prisoner of private capital, who was behind it all, but my friend, the client."

Here the smooth operator pointed once again at
Koreiko and with the other hand described the long-
intended, effective arc. Then, in pompous language,
Ostap asked the imaginary court for permission to ask
the accused some questions, and, pausing a moment
for the sake of decorum, began:

"Has the accused had any outside dealings with
Berlaga the accountant? No. Correct! Or with Skumbriyevich? Neither. Splendid! Or with Polykhayev?"

The millionaire clerk remained silent.

"I have no more questions. Pooh! I'm tired and
hungry. Tell me, Alexander Ivanovich, you haven't a
cold meatball up your sleeve, have you? Astonishing
poverty, especially when you consider the sum of
money which you squeezed out of the good-natured
Hercules with Polykhayev's assistance. Here are Polykhayev's own explanations, the only Herculean who
knew who was hiding behind the guise of a forty-six-
ruble clerk. But he didn't really know who you were.
But I do. Yes, gentlemen of the jury, my client is
guilty. It has been proved. But nevertheless I ask for
your lenience, on condition the accused buys my dossier. I rest my case."

By the end of the smooth operator's oration Koreiko
had calmed down. Thrusting his hand into the pockets of his flimsy pants, he went over to the window.
The young day resounded through the town in the
streetcar bells.

Some volunteer soldiers went past the fence, holding their rifles at all angles, like rakes. Pigeons wandered up and down the zinc-faced cornice, making a
noise with their red willowy feet and flying away at
every moment. Koreiko, who had trained himself
well in economy, turned out the table lamp and said:

"So it was you who sent me those idiotic telegrams?"

"Yes, me," Ostap replied. " 'Load apple barrels
Brothers Karamazov.' Is that bad?"

"Rather stupid."

"And the half-witted beggar?" asked Ostap, sensing that the parade had been a success. "Any good?"

"A schoolboy's spoof! And the book about millionaires was the same. And when you came here as a Kiev militiaman, I knew at once that you were a petty blackmailer. Unfortunately, I was wrong. Otherwise you damn well wouldn't have found me."

"Yes, you were wrong. We all make mistakes, as the Polish beauty Inga Zajac said a month after her marriage to my life-long friend, Nicky Osten-Backen."

"Well, I can understand the attack on me, but the dumbbells! Why did you have to steal them?"

"Which dumbbells? I didn't take any dumbbells."

"You're simply ashamed to admit it. And, anyway, you made a whole series of mistakes."

"Possibly," said Ostap. "I'm not an angel. I have my failings. But we're talking too much. My mulattoes are waiting for me. May I have the money?"

"Yes, the money," said Koreiko. "There's a hitch with the money. The dossier is a good one, there's no doubt about it. I could buy it, but in counting up my income, you've completely forgotten my expenses and direct losses. A million is a ridiculous amount."

"Then so long," said Ostap coldly, "and, if you don't mind, stay here for half an hour. They'll come for you in a truck with a grill."

"That's not the way to do business," said Koreiko with a salesman's smile.

"Maybe," sighed Ostap, "but I'm not a financier, you know. I'm a free artist and a cold philosopher."

"Why do you want the money? I earned it, after all, but you—"

"I not only worked, I even suffered. After my talks with Berlaga, Skumbriyevich, and Polykhayev, I lost hope in humanity. Isn't faith in humanity worth a million rubles?"

"Oh, it is, it is," Koreiko assured him.

"Then let's go to the treasury," said Ostap. "I hope

you have ready cash, by the way. I don't suppose you keep it in the savings bank."

"Let's go!" said Koreiko. "You'll see when we get there."

"It's not far, is it?" Ostap asked fussily. "I have a car."

But the millionaire declined the car, suggesting they should not stand on ceremony. He courteously allowed Ostap to go first, then left, taking himself a small package wrapped in newspaper which had been lying on the table. As they went downstairs, Ostap began singing, " 'Beneath the skies of Argentina . . .' "

]CHAPTER[

: 23 :

A Chauffeur's Heart

IN THE STREET, Ostap took Alexander Ivanovich by the arm and both operators walked rapidly in the direction of the station.

"You're better than I thought," said Ostap amiably. "And that's as it should be, too. We should part easily with money, without moaning."

"A million's nothing if he's a good man," answered the clerk, listening hard for something.

As they turned into Mehring Street, the wail of a siren resounded over the town. The sound was long, warbling, and sad. It was the sort of noise that on a foggy night makes seamen feel queasy and for some reason want to ask for danger money in addition to their pay. The siren continued hysterically. It was joined by other hooters farther away and more sad. People suddenly began hurrying as though spurred on by a shower of rain. As they went, they grimaced and looked at the sky. The fat old women ran off selling sunflower seeds, sticking out their stomachs, the glass jars in their reed baskets jogging up and down. Adolf Bomse raced across the street at a slant. He managed to reach the revolving door of the Hercules safely. A platoon of reserve mounted militia galloped

past on different-colored horses. A Red Cross car
flashed past. The street suddenly emptied. Some way
ahead, Ostap noticed that a herd of piqué vests had
left the Café Florida. Waving their newspapers, boaters, and Panama hats, the old men trotted along the
road. But hardly had they reached the corner when
there was a deafening burst of gunfire; the vests bent
their heads, stopped, and fled straight back again. The
tails of their silk coats billowed out.

The behavior of the piqué vests amused Ostap. While
he was admiring their astonishing gesturing and hopping about, Koreiko managed to unwrap the package
he had brought with him.

"Miserable old men. Straight out of a comic opera!"
Ostap exclaimed, turning to Koreiko.

But he was gone. Instead the smooth operator found
himself staring at a monstrous visage with a diver's
glass eyes and a rubber trunk with a khaki-colored
cylinder dangling on the end. Ostap was so astonished
that he leaped into the air.

"What the devil's that?" he growled, reaching out
for the gas mask. "Mr. Client, I call you to order."

At that moment a group of people wearing gas
masks of the same kind came running up and it became impossible to recognize Koreiko among the dozen
or so rubber visages. Keeping a grip on his dossier,
Ostap tried looking at the legs of the monsters, but he
had hardly picked out what looked like Koreiko's
pants when he was seized by the arm and a cheerful
voice said:

"Comrade, you've been gassed."

"Who's been gassed?" cried Ostap, trying to break
away. "Let me go!"

"Comrade, you've been gassed!" repeated the ambulance man with glee. "You've entered a contaminated zone. Look, there's the gas bomb."

There was indeed a box lying in the road with thick
smoke pouring from it. The suspicious pants were
now some way away. They appeared for a moment

between two columns of smoke and then were gone. Ostap silently tried to fight his way free; he was being held by six masks.

"Furthermore, comrade, you've been wounded by shrapnel in the hand. Don't get annoyed, comrade. Be co-operative. You know the maneuvers are on. We'll bandage you in a moment and take you to the gas shelter."

The smooth operator was unable to see that it was useless to resist. He was like a player who wins the kitty at daybreak, astonishing the whole table, and then suddenly loses everything in ten minutes to a passing young man who tries his hand at the game out of curiosity. The player no longer sits there, pale and triumphant; the marathoners no longer crowd around him, begging something for luck. He goes home on foot.

A Communist Youth girl with a red cross on her apron came hurrying up. She pulled some bandages and cotton from a canvas bag and, forcing a frown so as not to laugh, bound the smooth operator's arm over his sleeve. Completing this act of mercy, the girl gave a giggle and hurried off to the next casualty, who meekly offered her his leg. Ostap was dragged over to a stretcher, which occasioned a fresh skirmish in which the rubber trunks jerked up and down and the ambulance man in charge continued to call for Ostap's co-operation and various other civic virtues in his loud lecturer's voice.

"Boys!" burbled the smooth operator as they strapped him to the stretcher. "Boys, tell my late dad, the Turkish citizen, that his favorite son, an ex-expert on horns and hoofs, gave his life for his country on the field of battle."

The last words of the battle casualty were:

"Sleep, my hearties! Nightingale, nightingale, little bird . . ."

They took Ostap away and he became silent, staring at the sky, where a great hullabaloo was in prog-

ress. Dense, heart-shaped puffs of smoke floated
about. Transparent celluloid planes moved past at a
great height. They emitted a sonorous throbbing as
though they were all tied together with iron wire.
Sirens could still be heard wailing in the brief intervals between ack-ack fire.

Ostap was forced to suffer yet another indignity. He
was carried past the Hercules. Clerks were looking
out the fourth-floor windows of the timber department. The entire accounts department stood on the
window sills. Lapidus, Jr., was teasing Kukushkind,
pretending to push him off. Berlaga's eyes opened
wide and he bowed to the stretcher. At a second-floor
window, Polykhayev and Skumbriyevich were standing in a clinch against a background of palms. Catching sight of the bound figure, they began whispering
and quickly slammed the window shut.

The stretcher-bearers stooped in front of a sign saying "Gas Shelter No. 34" and helped Ostap to stand up,
and when he tried to escape, the senior ambulance
man again asked him to be co-operative.

The gas shelter was located in a club. It was a long,
well-lit basement with a ribbed ceiling, from which
were suspended models of military aircraft and mail
planes. At the back of the club was a small stage, the
backdrop of which was painted with two blue windows, a moon and stars, and a brown door. Piqué vests,
the whole herd of whom had been seized, lounged
about by a wall inscribed with the slogan "We don't
want war, but we're ready to retaliate." A lecturer in
a green field jacket was pacing up and down the stage,
glowering at the door, through which fresh groups of
gas casualties were noisily being admitted. He was saying in clipped military accents:

"According to their effect, poison gases used in
warfare divide up into asphyxiating, blistering, irritating, and so on. Among the irritant tear gases are
chloropicrin, benzyl bromide . . ."

Ostap transferred his gloomy gaze from the lecturer to the audience. Some of the young men were either staring at the speaker or jotting the lecture in a notebook, while others were crowding around a board displaying the parts of a rifle. A girl with a sporty look was sitting by herself in the second row, gazing thoughtfully at the theatrical moon.

"Not bad," Ostap decided. "A pity I won't have the time. What is she thinking about? Not benzyl bromide, I imagine. Dear me, only this morning I could have whisked off a girl like that to the Pacific Ocean, Fiji, or Rio de Janeiro."

At the thought of his lost Rio, Ostap began moving around the shelter.

The forty piqué vests had now recovered from their shock; they had buttoned up their starched collars and were heatedly discussing Pan-Europe, the Three-Power Naval Conference, and Gandhiism.

"Have you heard?" one vest was telling another. "Gandhi has arrived in Dhandi."

"Ghandhi's a brain!" sighed the second. "And Dhandi's a brain too."

An argument arose. Some of the vests claimed that Dhandi was a town and couldn't be a brain. Others endeavored to prove the opposite with frenzied insistence. They were all agreed, however, that Chernomorsk would be declared a free city any day.

The lecturer glowered again as the door opened and two new victims came into the room—Panikovsky and Balaganov. The gas attack had caught them on the way back from their nocturnal expedition. After their work on the dumbbells they were as scruffy as alley cats. At the sight of the captain the foster brothers hung their heads.

"Where have you been? To a vicar's tea party or something?" asked Ostap gruffly. He was afraid of being asked about Koreiko, so he angrily knitted his brows and went into the attack. "Well, my fine fellows, what have you been up to?"

"Honestly," said Balaganov with his hand on his heart, "it was all Panikovsky's idea."

"Panikovsky!" said the captain sternly.

"Word of honor," cried the violator of the convention. "You know how I admire you, Bender. It was Balaganov up to his tricks."

"Alex!" said the smooth operator even more sternly.

"And you believe him?" said the hoof agent reproachfully. "Do you really think I would have taken the dumbbells without permission?"

"So it was you who took the dumbbells!" cried Ostap. "Why did you do it?"

"Panikovsky said they were made of gold."

Ostap looked at Panikovsky. It was only then he noticed that the cheap dickey was missing from under his coat and that a bare chest was revealed to the world. Without a word, the smooth operator flopped into a chair. He began to shake, thrashing the air with his arms. Then came volcanic rumblings from his throat, tears rushed to his eyes, and laughter, terrifying laughter in which could be felt the total exhaustion of the night, and all the frustration of his battle with Koreiko, so miserably parodied by the foster brothers, filled the gas shelter. The piqué vests trembled, while the lecturer began speaking more loudly and precisely about gas warfare.

Even before the laughter had stopped pricking him with a thousand soda-water needles, Ostap felt refreshed and younger, like a man who has just passed through all the stages at the barber's: close friendship with the razor, slight acquaintance with the scissors, a spray of eau de Cologne, and even combing of the eyebrows with a special brush. Caressing ocean waves lapped at his heart, and in answer to Balaganov's question he replied that everything was fine, except for the unexpected flight of the millionaire to an unknown destination.

The foster brothers did not give due thought to

Ostap's words. They were glad to have got off so easily.

"Bender, look!" cried the hoof agent. "That girl over there is the one Koreiko used to go out with."

"So that is Zosya Sinitsky," said Ostap emphatically. "That really is . . ."

Ostap pushed his way through to the stage, politely stopped the speaker, and, having found out that they were all going to be kept in the gas prison for another couple of hours or so, sat down near the stage, next to Zosya. A short while later the girl had stopped gazing at the painted window. Laughing unduly loudly, she was trying to recover her comb from Ostap. The smooth operator himself, to judge by the movement of his lips, was talking nineteen to the dozen.

Into the gas shelter came engineer Talmudovsky. He defended himself with two suitcases. His ruddy forehead was moist with perspiration and glistened like a buttered pancake.

"It can't be helped, comrade," the official in charge was saying. "The maneuvers are on and you're in a contaminated zone."

"But I was riding in a cab," seethed the engineer. "A c-a-b. I'm rushing to the station on official business. I missed the night train. Am I supposed to miss the next one as well?"

"Comrade, be co-operative."

"Why should I be co-operative when I was in a cab?" Talmudovsky fumed.

He laid great emphasis on this fact, as though expecting the cab ride to make him invulnerable and to render the chloropicrin and benzyl bromide harmless. It is not certain how much longer Talmudovsky would have gone on wrangling with the official if a new casualty had not entered the shelter both gassed and wounded, to judge by his gauze-wrapped head. At the sight of the new visitor, Talmudovsky broke off and swiftly dived into the crowd of piqué vests. But the man in the gauze had already caught sight of his corpulent figure and made straight for him.

"So I've got you at last, engineer Talmudovsky," he said ominously. "On what grounds did you quit the plant?"

Talmudovsky rolled his small, piggy eyes. Seeing there was no escape, he sat down on his suitcases and lit a cigarette.

"I went to your hotel," the gauze-wrapped man continued, "and they told me you'd gone. 'How could he have gone,' I asked, 'when he only arrived yesterday and is supposed to stay a year under the contract?' They told me you'd gone to Kazan with your bags. So I then thought that was the end and we'd have to look for another specialist, but now I've got you. And you just sit and smoke! You're a rolling stone, engineer Talmudovsky. You're disrupting production!"

The engineer leaped up from his cases and, with a cry of "It's you who are disrupting production," seized his captor by the waist, carried him off to a corner, and began buzzing at him like an enormous fly. Fragments of conversation soon came floating from the corner: "On that salary . . ." "Go and find one . . ." "And what about traveling expenses . . ." The man in gauze was looking dolefully at the engineer.

The lecturer's instructive talk was now over, the doors of the shelter were now open, and the piqué vests, holding on to one another, were off to the Florida; Talmudovsky had now rid himself of his pursuer and gained his freedom, shouting for a cab at the top of his voice, but the smooth operator was still chatting to Zosya.

"What a dame!" said Panikovsky enviously as he and Balaganov emerged into the street. "If only those dumbbells had been gold! Honestly, I would have married her."

At this reminder of the ill-fated dumbbells, Balaganov gave Panikovsky a painful thump in the ribs.

It was well timed. At that moment Ostap appeared in the doorway with the dame on his arm. He spent some time saying good-by to her, gazing languidly into her eyes. Zosya smiled a last time and went off.

"What were you talking about?" Panikovsky asked suspiciously.

"Oh, this and that," Ostap replied. "Well, my brave warriors, down to business! We must find our client."

Panikovsky was sent to the Hercules, Balaganov to Koreiko's apartment, and Ostap himself hurried off to all the stations. But the underground millionaire had vanished. At the Hercules his name had been removed from the board, he hadn't been back to his apartment, and seven long-distance trains had departed during the gas attack. But that was what Ostap expected.

"It isn't so terrible in the long run," he said gaily. "In China, though, it's difficult to find the man you want. They have a population of four hundred million. Here it's easy: we only have a hundred and sixty million. That makes it three times easier than in China . . . if we had the money, and we have."

However, Ostap came out of the bank carrying thirty-four rubles.

"That's all that's left out of ten thousand," he announced with ineffable sadness. "I thought we had another six or seven thousand in our account. How did that happen? Everything was merry and bright, we procured horns and hoofs, life was heavenly, and the globe was turning just for us, then suddenly . . . I know! Overheads! The office ate up all our money."

He surveyed the foster brothers reprimandingly. Panikovsky shrugged his shoulders as much as to say, "You know how I admire you, Bender. I've always said you were an ass." Balaganov stroked his curly hair in dismay and asked:

"What are we going to do?"

"What do you mean?" cried Ostap. "What about the office? The equipment? Any establishment would be glad to give a hundred rubles for the inkwells alone.

Then there's the typewriter. The punch, the deer horns, the tables, the barrier, and the samovar—all that stuff can be sold. Then we always have Panikovsky's gold tooth in reserve. It's not as big as a dumbbell, of course, but it's still a molecule of that noble metal, gold.

The friends stopped at the office. The young leonine voices of the two livestock students back from their trip, Funt's sleepy mumbling, and some other unfamiliar basses and baritones of a clearly agricultural timbre came floating through the open door.

"This is a corpus delicti!" cried the students. "We were surprised even when we first arrived. They've only procured twenty-five pounds of horns and hoofs over the whole season."

"You'll go to court," thundered the basses and baritones. "Where's the head of the section? Where's the hoof agent?"

Balaganov began trembling.

"The end of the office," Ostap whispered, "and we aren't needed here any more, either. We'll take the sun-kissed road, while Funt is taken away to that red brick building, the windows of which, through some strange whim of the architect, have bars on them."

The ex-chief was not wrong. The fallen angels had gone only three blocks when they heard the rattle of a cab behind them. It was Funt. He would have been just like a kind old granddad on his way to see his married grandson after lengthy preparations had it not been for the fact that he was being held by a militiaman standing on the step.

"What are we going to do now?" Balaganov asked.

"Kindly don't forget that you're living in the same age as Ostap Bender," replied the smooth operator sadly. "Kindly remember that he has a wonderful Gladstone bag containing everything necessary for earning pocket money. Let's go home to Lokhankin."

A fresh blow awaited them in Lemon Street.

"Where's the building gone?" exclaimed Ostap. "Surely there was a building here last evening?"

But the building was gone. An insurance agent was stepping over the charred beams. Finding an empty kerosene can in the yard, he sniffed it and shook his head dubiously.

"Now what?" asked Balaganov, smiling nervously.

The smooth operator didn't answer. He was staggered by the loss of his bag. Gone was the magic sack with its Indian turban, its poster advertising "The High Priest Has Arrived," its doctor's white coat and stethoscope.

"So," he said at length. "Fate plays with man as man plays the flute."

They wandered along the streets, pale, dejected, and grief-stricken. They were jostled by the passers-by, but didn't even notice. Panikovsky, who had hunched his shoulders during the bank fiasco, just left them where they were. Balaganov pulled at his ginger locks and sighed bitterly. Bender walked behind them, his head down, murmuring "The day of fun is over, shoot, my little Zouave." In this mood they reached the inn. The Antelope shone yellow at the back, under a canopy. By the front entrance they found Kozlevich. He was sipping tea from a saucer, puffing out his cheeks with enjoyment. His face was like a round red pot. He was blissfully happy.

"Adam!" called the smooth operator, stopping in front of the chauffeur. "We have nothing left. We're beggars, Adam. Accept us, we're ruined."

Kozlevich stood up. The captain stood humiliated and penniless, with his head bare. Adam's light-colored Polish eyes glistened with tears. He came down from the porch and gave each of the Antelopeans a hug.

"The taxi's free!" he cried, choking back his tears of pity. "Please be seated."

"But we may have to go a very, very long way,"

said Ostap. "Perhaps to the edge of the world, or even farther. Think about it."

"Wherever you like," answered the faithful Kozle-vich. "The taxi's free!"

Panikovsky wept, covering his face with his fists and whispering, "What a heart! Honestly, what a heart!"

The Weather Was Right

for Love

EVERYTHING that the smooth operator did during the days following his move to the inn was regarded by Panikovsky with great disfavor.

"Bender's crazy!" he told Balaganov. "He'll be the ruin of us."

And indeed, instead of trying to make the last thirty-four rubles stretch as far as possible by using them solely for the purchase of food, Ostap went to the florist and for thirty-five rubles bought an enormous bouquet of trembling roses. He borrowed the extra ruble from Balaganov. In-between the blooms he put a note saying, "Can't you hear my big heart beating?" Balaganov was told to deliver the flowers to Zosya.

"What do you think you're doing?" Balaganov asked, brandishing the bouquet. "What's all the fancy stuff for?"

"We've got to, Alex," Ostap replied. "Can't be helped. I have a big heart. Like a bullock's. And it's the thought that matters, anyway, not the money."

Thereupon Ostap got into the Antelope and asked Kozlevich to drive him somewhere or other out of town.

"I've got to ponder a little in solitude on what has

happened and make the necessary decisions for the future," he said.

The whole of that day faithful Adam drove the smooth operator along the white coastal roads past rest homes and sanitoriums, where the residents shuffled about in slippers, whacked balls with croquet mallets, or jumped up and down at volley-ball nets. The telegraph wires hummed like violoncellos. Vacationers lugged around carpetbags full of eggplants and melons. Young men with handkerchiefs over their hair, still wet from swimming, impudently stared at the girls and paid them compliments, of which every male in Chernomorsk up to the age of twenty-five possessed a complete set. Whenever two girls were walking together, the boys would say, "Gee, the one on the outside is a cutie!" The remark was accompanied by hearty laughter. They were amused that the girls never knew to which of them the remark referred. If a girl came along by herself, the young wits used to stop as though thunderstruck and make kissing noises to show they were feeling pangs of love. The girl would turn red and hurry across the road, dropping her blue eggplants and evoking Homeric laughter from the lady-killers.

Ostap sprawled against the Antelope's cushions and thought. It hadn't been possible to squeeze any money out of Polykhayev or Skumbriyevich: they had both gone on vacation. The mad accountant Berlaga didn't count. He wasn't likely to yield very much milk. But Ostap's plans and his big heart required his presence in Chernomorsk, though he would have found it difficult to say exactly for how long.

Hearing a familiar sepulchral voice, Ostap looked at the sidewalk. A middle-aged couple was walking along arm in arm under a rank of poplar trees. The husband and wife were evidently going to the beach. Behind them trailed Lokhankin. He was carrying a ladies' parasol, from which protruded a thermos bottle and a beach blanket.

"Barbara," he whined. "Listen, Barbara."

"What is it, pain in the neck?" asked Mrs. Ptiburdukov without turning around.

"I want to sleep with you, Barbara!"

"Really, how scandalous!" Mr. Ptiburdukov observed, also without turning around.

And the odd family disappeared in Antelopean dust.

When the dust had settled, Bender found himself looking at a large glass building which stood against a background of sea and gardens with flowers. The building gave off a disturbing smell of essence of pears. Ostap sniffed the air and told Kozlevich to stop. He got out of the car and began inhaling the invigorating odor. Plaster lions with chipped muzzles sat at the foot of a broad flight of steps.

"How could I not have guessed at once?" Ostap muttered, dawdling by the entrance.

He glanced at the sign which said "First Chernomorsk Film Studios," patted a plaster lion on its warm mane, and, muttering "Golconda," drove back quickly to the inn.

The whole night he sat by the window sill and wrote by the light of a kerosene lamp. The wind blowing through the window spread the closely written sheets. A rather unattractive landscape unfurled before the writer. A delicate moon lit up some odd kind of huts. The inn breathed, stirred, and snored in its sleep. Invisible horses tapped messages to one another from their dark corners. The petty dealers were asleep in their carts, with their miserable wares beneath their heads. A horse freed from its halter roamed the yard, stepping carefully over the cart shafts, dragging the broken bridle behind it, and pushing its muzzle into the carts in search of barley. It wandered over to the writer's window and, resting its head on the sill, looked at him sadly.

"Go away, horse," said the smooth operator, "this is my idea!"

Just before dawn, as the inn was beginning to stir and a young boy walked among the carts with a pail of water calling in a high-pitched voice "Any horses need watering?" Ostap finished his work, took a clean sheet out of the "Koreiko" file, and scrawled the title:

THE NECK
A full-length feature film
Scenario: O. Bender

At the First Chernomorsk Film Studios there reigned the kind of hugger-mugger that is found at horse markets just at the moment when the crowd is trying to catch a pickpocket.

A soldier was sitting at the entrance. He sternly asked all newcomers for their passes, though he still let them through even if they didn't show him one. People in blue berets collided with people in overalls, hurtled up different stairways, and slowly came down again. In the foyer they described a circle, stood for a moment staring in a dazed way in front of them, then went upstairs again at the same trot, as though whipped along from behind with a wet rope's end. Extras, consultants, experts, managers, directors and their young-lady assistants, lighting men, scene-shifters, elderly women script writers, officials in charge of commas, and keepers of the Grand Seal hurtled past.

Ostap, who had just begun to stroll about the studios at his usual pace, soon noticed that he was completely unable to tune in to this swirling world. No one answered his questions; no one even stopped.

"I shall have to adopt the enemy's tactics," he thought.

He started running slowly and immediately felt relief. He was even able to exchange a few words with a young-lady assistant. Then the smooth operator began running at top speed and soon noticed he had caught the rhythm. He was now racing along nostril to nostril with the head of a script department.

"Want a script?" he shouted.

"What kind?" asked the head, keeping up a fast trot.

"A good one," replied Ostap, half a length ahead.

"I'm asking what kind. Silent or sound?"

"Silent."

Nimbly kicking up his thick stockinged legs, the head overtook Ostap at the corner and shouted, "Don't need it!"

"What do you mean, you don't need it?" asked the smooth operator, breaking into a fast gallop.

"Just that! Silent films are finished. Try the sound people."

They both halted for an instant, looked at each other in dismay, and then raced off in different directions. Five minutes later Bender was waving his manuscript again and moving in the appropriate company in between two trotter consultants.

"Want a script?" Ostap inquired, panting.

The consultants turned toward him, pulling various levers. "What kind of script?"

"Sound film."

"Don't need it," the consultants answered, increasing speed.

The smooth operator lost the step again and sheepishly began galloping. "What do you mean, you don't need it?"

"Just what we say. We aren't making sound films yet."

In the course of a hard-spent half-hour of trotting, Bender got to the bottom of the tricky situation at the First Chernomorsk Film Studios. The point was that silent films weren't being made any more on account of the arrival of the sound-film era, and sound films weren't yet being made because of organizational hitches in liquidating the era of silent films.

At the height of the workday, as the race of the extras, consultants, experts, managers, and directors reached the speed of the once famous runner named Strongman, a rumor went around that somewhere in one of the rooms there was a man who was urgently organizing a sound film. Ostap nipped into the relevant office at full pelt and stopped short in amazement at the silence. A little man with a Bedouin beard and a gold pince-nez on a cord was sitting sideways behind a desk. Bending down, he was struggling to get one of his shoes off.

"Good day, comrade!" said the smooth operator loudly.

The man didn't answer. He got the shoe off and began shaking the sand out of it.

"Good day!" Ostap repeated. "I've brought a script."

The man with the Bedouin beard leisurely replaced his shoe and silently began lacing it up. Having done so, he turned to his papers and, shutting one eye, began scrawling something in spidery twirls.

"Why don't you answer?" Ostap bellowed, so loudly that the telephone on the film director's desk gave a tinkle.

The director then raised his head, looked at Ostap, and said, "Speak more loudly, please. I can't hear."

"Write him a note," advised a consultant in a bright-colored vest who happened past. "He's deaf."

Ostap sat down at the desk and wrote on a piece of paper, "Do you make sound films?"

"Yes," answered the deaf man.

"I've brought a sound-film script. Called *The Neck*, a popular tragedy in six parts," Ostap wrote quickly.

The man looked at the note through his gold pince-nez and said, "Splendid! We'll take you on immediately. We need new blood."

"Glad to help. What about an advance?" Ostap wrote.

"*The Neck* is exactly what we want!" said the deaf man. "Wait here a moment. I'm just coming back.

Don't go away." The deaf man grabbed the script
and disappeared through the door.

Ostap sat there for an hour and a half, but the deaf
man didn't come back. It wasn't until he went out into
the corridor and took up the rhythm that Ostap found
out the deaf man had driven off in a car and wouldn't
be back that day. Actually, he wasn't ever coming
back, because he'd been transferred to Uman to carry
out cultural work among the carters. But the most
awful thing was that he'd carried off Ostap's script of
the film *The Neck*. The smooth operator broke away
from the runners, sank down onto a bench, and rested
his head against the doorman who was already sitting
there.

"So that's the way it is," said the doorman suddenly,
apparently developing a thought which had been running through his head for some time. "The director's
assistant told me to grow a beard. You can play Nebuchadnezzar or Balthazar in a film, I don't remember
the name. So I grew a beard, a real priest's beard.
And what am I going to do with it now? The assistant
director said they weren't making any more silent
films, and there's no chance of my acting in sound
films, because he told me my voice was horrible. So
here I am with a beard, damn it, just like a goat. I don't
want to shave it off and yet I'm ashamed to wear it.
That's how I'm living, like a goat."

"But aren't you shooting anything here?" asked
Bender, gradually recovering his senses.

"How can we shoot anything?" replied the bearded
doorman self-importantly. "Last year they made a film
about life in ancient Rome and the law suit is still in
progress."

"Why is everyone running about?" inquired the
smooth operator, pointing to the stairs.

"Not everyone here runs about," replied the
doorman. "Comrade Suprugov doesn't run about,
for instance. He's a businesslike fellow. I keep wondering whether I shouldn't go and see him about pay-

ment for my beard, whether it's going to be the normal way of payment or by special order . . ."

At the word "payment," Ostap went off to see Suprugov. The doorman was not wrong. Suprugov
didn't gallop through the floors, didn't wear an alpine
beret or even foreign plus-fours. He was a sight for
sore eyes.

He greeted the smooth operator extremely curtly.
"I'm busy," he said in a peacock's voice. "I can only
give you two minutes."

"That's quite sufficient," Ostap began. "My script
for *The Neck*—"

"Make it snappy," said Suprugov.

"Script for *The Neck*—"

"Come to the point."

"*The Neck*—"

"Make it snappy. How much are you due?"

"Some deaf fellow—"

"Comrade! If you don't tell me how much you are
due, I shall ask you to leave. I have no time."

"Nine hundred rubles," mumbled the smooth operator.

"Three hundred!" Suprugov stated categorically.
"Take this and go. And note that you've stolen two
extra minutes." In bold handwriting he dashed off a
note to the accounts department, handed it to Ostap,
and grabbed the telephone.

As he emerged from the accounts department and
stuffed the money into his pocket, Ostap remarked,
"Nebuchadnezzar's right. There's only one businesslike man in here and that's Suprugov."

Meanwhile, the racing up and down stairs, turning
circles, and screeching and babbling at the First Chernomorsk Film Studios had reached a peak. The
young-lady assistants snarled. The assistant directors
brought in a black goat, admiring its photogenic qual-
ities. The consultants, experts, and keepers of the Grand
Seal collided with one another and cackled hoarsely.
A messenger girl shot past with a broom. The smooth

operator even thought he glimpsed a producer in blue
pants soar up over the heads of the crowd, circle the
chandelier, and land on the cornice. At that moment
the vestibule clock began chiming.

"*Boing!*" went the clock.

Shrieks and screams shook the glass building. Consultants, experts, and montage editors came hurtling
down the stairs. A mad scramble began at the doors.

"*Boing! Boing!*" went the clock.

Silence stole out from the corners. Gone were the
keepers of the Grand Seal, the officers in charge of
commas, the managers and lady assistants. The messenger girl's broom flashed past for the last time.

"*Boing!*" went the clock for the fourth time.

There was now no one left in the studios, except for
an assistant producer in blue pants who, having caught
his pocket on the doorknob, squealed plaintively and
pawed the marble floor by the door.

The workday was over.

A cock could be heard crowing in the fishermen's
huts by the shore.

As soon as the Antelope's cash box was replenished
with the film money, the captain's reputation, which
had been slightly tarnished by Koreiko's escape, was
restored. Panikovsky was given a small sum to
spend on yogurt and a promise of gold-filled jaws.
For Balaganov, Ostap bought a jacket and a billfold as
squeaky as a saddle to go with it. Although the billfold was empty, Alex kept taking it out and looking
inside. Kozlevich got fifty rubles to buy gasoline.

The Antelopeans led a pure, moral, almost bucolic
life. They helped the innkeeper to keep the place in
order and learned about the price of barley and cream.
From time to time Panikovsky would go into the yard,
carefully open the mouth of the nearest horse, look at
its teeth, and mutter, "There's a good colt," though
he was actually looking at a good mare.

The captain alone disappeared for days on end, and

returned to the inn lovesick and happy. He sat down with his friends, who were drinking tea on the dirty glass veranda, rested a red-booted foot on his other knee, and said affably, "Isn't life just wonderful, Panikovsky, or am I imagining it?"

"Where is it you go gallivanting about?" asked Panikovsky jealously.

"You're old. The girl's no good to you," Ostap answered.

Here Balaganov roared with sympathetic laughter and inspected his new billfold, while Kozlevich sniggered into his chauffeur's mustachios. He had had many an occasion to drive the captain and Zosya along the coastal highway.

The weather was right for love. The piqué vests claimed that there had never been such an August in the franco porto. The night displayed a clear telescopic sky, while the day rolled refreshing waves up to the shore. The yard attendants stood at their gateways selling striped, monastery-size watermelons, and the citizenry nearly ruptured themselves squeezing the poles of the melons and bending their ears to hear the hoped-for crackling. Every evening, football players came home sweaty but happy from the practice fields with young boys running after them, kicking up the dust. They pointed to their famous goalkeeper, and sometimes even carried him on their shoulders.

One evening the captain informed the crew of the Antelope that the next day there was to be a grand outing with presents for everyone.

"In view of the fact that there will only be one girl at our children's outing," said Ostap importantly, "I would like to ask you, gentlemen volunteers, to wash your faces, get yourselves cleaned up, and, most important, not to use filthy language during the trip."

Panikovsky became very excited and asked the captain for three rubles; he nipped down to the public baths and spent the whole night washing and scrubbing himself like a soldier before a parade. He got up before everyone and kept urging Kozlevich to get a move on. The Antelopeans looked at Panikovsky in astonishment. He was smoothly shaven and had on so much powder that he looked like a retired M.C. He kept pulling his jacket into shape and turning his neck with difficulty in the Oscar Wilde collar.

During the pleasure trip he behaved most sedately. When introduced to Zosya, he bowed gracefully, but was so embarrassed that even the powder on his face turned red. While sitting in the car, he tucked his left leg underneath the right so as to hide the hole in his shoe and the toe sticking out of it. Zosya was wearing a white dress embroidered in red. She liked the Antelopeans very much. She was amused by Balaganov, who kept combing his hair all the time. Now and then he picked his nose, after which he always took out a handkerchief and flourished it sadly. Adam Kozlevich showed Zosya how to drive the Antelope, which also won her affection. She was slightly put out by Panikovsky and felt that he was too proud to talk to her. But most of all, her eyes rested on the chiseled features of the smooth operator.

At sundown, Ostap distributed the promised presents. Kozlevich was given a small compass for his watch chain, which matched his silver watch very well, Balaganov got a *Book of Poetry for Recitation* in a leatherette binding, and Panikovsky was given a pink tie with blue flowers.

"And now, my friends," said Ostap as they drove back to town, "Zosya and I will go for a little walk, while you go back to the inn. 'Bye-'bye!'"

The inn had long since gone to sleep, and Balaganov and Kozlevich were playing arpeggios with their noses, but Panikovsky in his new tie still roamed about the yard between the carts, clenching his fists in silent longing.

"What a dame!" he whispered to himself. "I love her like a daughter."

Ostap and Zosya were sitting on the steps of the

Ancient History Museum. Young men strolled about the cobblestone square, making complimentary remarks and laughing. The windows of the International Seamen's Club glimmered behind a rank of plane trees. Foreign sailors in soft hats strode about in twos and threes, exchanging brief, unintelligible comments.

"Why have you fallen in love with me?" asked Zosya, fondling Ostap's arm.

"You're sweet and wonderful," replied the captain. "There's no one like you in the whole wide world."

For a long time they sat in silence in the dark shadow of the museum columns, thinking of their own little happiness. It was as warm and dark as between cupped hands.

"Do you remember my telling you about Koreiko?" asked Zosya suddenly. "The one who proposed to me?"

"Yes," said Ostap absent-mindedly.

"He's terribly amusing," Zosya continued. "Do you remember my telling you how unexpectedly he went away?"

"Yes," said Ostap, a little more attentively. "He's an amusing man."

"Well, just imagine, I got a letter from him today, a very amusing—"

"What?" the lover-boy ejaculated, getting to his feet.

"Are you jealous?" asked Zosya slyly.

"Er . . . er . . . just a little. What did that jerk say in the letter?"

"He's certainly not a jerk. He's just a very poor, unhappy man. Sit down, Ostap. Why are you standing up? Honestly, I don't love him a bit. He asked me to join him."

"Where? Join him where?" cried Ostap. "Where is he?"

"I'm not going to tell you. You're jealous. You'll go and kill him."

"Don't be silly, Zosya," said Ostap warily. "I'm simply curious to know where such people find jobs."

"Oh, a long way away. He writes that he's got a very good job. He wasn't paid much here. He's now employed building the Eastern Railroad."

"Whereabouts?"

"Honestly, you're much too curious! You mustn't be such an Othello!"

"Really, Zosya, you amuse me. Do I look like a stupid old Moor? I just want to know whereabouts on the Eastern Railroad people find jobs."

"I'll tell you if you want. He's working as a time-keeper at the northern track-laying settlement," said the girl abruptly. "But it's only called a settlement. It's actually a train. He wrote me a very interesting description of it. The train lays track, do you see, and then goes along it. And there's another train of the same kind coming from the south. When they finally meet, there'll be a joining-up ceremony. It's all in the desert, he says, with camels and things. Interesting, isn't it?"

"Extremely interesting," said the smooth operator, pacing rapidly up and down under the columns. "Zosya, it's time we went. It's late and cold. Let's go!"

He helped her get up, led her into the square, and there hesitated.

"Aren't you going to see me home?" asked the girl anxiously.

"What? Oh, home! The point is—"

"All right," said Zosya curtly, "good-by! Don't ever come to see me again, do you hear?"

But the smooth operator heard nothing. Having run all the way down the block, he stopped. "Sweet and wonderful!" he murmured.

Ostap turned back after his beloved. For a minute he raced along under the dark trees, then he stopped again, pulled off his peaked cap, and began stamping his feet. "No, this isn't Rio de Janeiro!" he said at length.

He took two more wavering steps, stopped again, pulled on his cap at an angle, and made for the inn with his mind made up.

The same night the Antelope, its headlights shining palely, drove out of the gateway to the inn. The sleepy-eyed Kozlevich turned the wheel with difficulty. Balaganov had already managed to fall asleep in the car during the hasty preparations for the departure, while Panikovsky sadly rolled his eyes, shivering in the night chill. His face still showed traces of the festive powder.

"The masked ball is over!" cried the captain as the Antelope rattled under a railway bridge. "We're back to the daily routine."

And in the puzzle-poser's room, by a bouquet of roses, there wept a sweet and wonderful creature.

]CHAPTER[
: 25 :

Three Roads

THE ANTELOPE wasn't well. She kept stopping on even the gentlest slopes and helplessly running backward. The engine was making a woofing and wheezing noise just as though someone was being strangled under the yellow hood. The car was in fact overloaded. Besides the crew, it carried large reserves of fuel. The cans and bottles occupying all the free space were filled with gurgling gasoline. Kozlevich shook his head, stepped on the accelerator, and looked dejectedly at Ostap.

"Adam," said the captain, "you're our father and we're your children. Head for the east! You have a splendid navigation instrument—the compass on your watch chain. Don't fly off course!"

The Antelopeans had now been driving for three days, but other than Ostap, no one had any idea of the aim of the new journey. Panikovsky looked longingly at the tousled corn fields and lisped rather timidly:

"Why are we on the go again? What's it all about? It was so nice in Chernomorsk." And, recalling the fabulous dame, he sighed convulsively. Besides, he was hungry and there was nothing to eat; the money had gone.

"Forward!" Ostap answered. "Stop complaining, man. There are gold jaws, a plump little widow, and a bucket full of yogurt waiting for you. For Balaganov I'll buy a sailor suit and send him to grammar school. There he'll learn to read and write, which is essential at his age. And Kozlevich, our own loyal Adam, will get a new car. . . . What kind would you like, Adam Kazimirovich? A Studebaker or a Lincoln? A Rolls Royce or a Hispaño-Suiza?"

"An Isotta-Fraschini," said Kozlevich, reddening.

"All right, you shall have one. It'll be called 'Antelope the Second' or 'Daughter of Antelope,' whichever you prefer. There's no point in getting depressed. I'll provide you with food. I grant you, my Gladstone bag was destroyed in the fire, but my ideas are fireproof. If the worst comes to the worst, we'll stop in some sunny little town and fix up a Seville-style bullfight. Panikovsky will be the piccador. That alone will be enough to attract the morbid interest of the public, so the takings will be tremendous."

The car was crossing a wide, beaten track covered with tractor marks. The chauffeur suddenly jammed his foot on the brake.

"Which way?" he asked. "There are three roads."

The passengers climbed out of the car and, stretching their aching legs, walked a little way ahead. At the division of the roads stood a stone pillar with a fat crow perched on top. The squashed sun was setting behind the tousled corn. Balaganov's slim shadow stretched toward the horizon. The ground was tinged with a darkish color, and an early star signaled the approach of night in good time.

Three roads lay in front of the Antelopeans—a highway, an asphalt road, and a country lane. The asphalt was still yellow in the sun, and a blue haze hung over the highway, but the country lane was completely dark and vanished into the fields just beyond the sign post. Ostap shouted at the crow, which grew very alarmed but didn't fly away, wandered up and down in deep thought, and said:

"I declare the conference of Russian warriors open! Present are: Ilya Muromets, alias Ostap Bender, Dobrynya Nikitich, alias Balaganov, and Alyosha Popovich, alias our much-respected Michael Panikovsky."

Kozlevich, taking advantage of the halt, had crawled underneath the Antelope with a spanner and therefore wasn't included among the warriors.

"Dobrynya, dear boy, will you stand on the right, please," Ostap officiated. "M'sieu Popovich, take your place on the left. Shade your eyes with your hand and scan the horizon."

"What are you playing at this time?" asked the indignant Alyosha Popovich. "I'm hungry. Let's get on as quickly as possible."

"Shame on you, Alyosha," said Ostap. "Stand over there like an ancient warrior should. And think hard. Look how Dobrynya is behaving. Why, you could write a folk tale about him here and now! And so, my warriors, which road do we take? Which one is strewn with the money we need for current expenses? I know Kozlevich would take the asphalt: drivers like good roads. But Adam's an honest man and doesn't know much about life. The asphalt road's no good to warriors. It probably leads to a giant grain mill. We'd be lost in the roar of the machinery. We'd be run over by a caterpillar tractor or a combine. Dying underneath a combine would be a bore. No, we warriors won't take the asphalt road. Now the highway. Kozlevich wouldn't object to that, either, of course. But believe me, the highway won't suit us, either. Let them accuse us of being out of date, but we won't take that road. I have a hunch we'd meet indiscreet farmers and other such model citizens. Anyway, they wouldn't want us. They already have quite enough literary and musical teams wandering over their nationalized estates, collecting material for agricultural poetry and horticultural cantatas. We're left with the

country lane, citizen warriors! There it is—the
ancient, fairytale path which the Antelope will
traverse. It's the real Russia! There you'll still find the
firebird, and people of our profession can still pick up
a few golden feathers. There you'll still find the rich
ogre-peasant Kashchey sitting on his boxes of money.
He thought he was immortal, but now he's horribly
aware that the end is coming. Nevertheless, we may
pick up something from him if we introduce ourselves
as itinerant monks. From the point of view of transportation, this elfin path is disgraceful. But we have
no other course left. Adam, we're off!"

Adam sadly drove his car into the country lane,
where it immediately began to describe pretzel-
shaped patterns, tilt to one side, and bounce the passengers high in the air. The Antelopeans clung to each
other, swore softly, and banged their knees against the
hard cans of gas.

"I'm hungry," groaned Panikovsky. "I want some
goose! Why did we have to leave Chernomorsk!"

The car gave a squeal, tried to free herself from a
deep rut, but fell back again.

"Keep going, Adam!" cried Bender. "Keep going,
whatever happens. If the Antelope can only take us as
far as the Eastern Railroad, we'll reward her with gold
tires and swords and bunting."

Kozlevich wasn't listening. The feverish jolting kept
pulling the steering wheel out of his hands. Panikovsky
was still suffering.

"Bender," he suddenly squawked, "you know how
I admire you, but you don't understand a thing! You
don't know what a goose is. My, how I love that bird!
It's a superb, juicy bird, honest it is. Goose, Bender!
The wing. The neck. The leg. Do you know how I
catch geese, Bender? I kill them with one blow, like a
toreador. It's like an opera when I catch a goose. It's
like *Carmen!*"

"We know," Bender observed. "We saw you doing
it in Arbatov. I don't recommend a second try."

Panikovsky became silent, but a minute later, as a fresh buffet threw him against Bender, his heated whisper could be heard again. "Bender, it's walking along the road. A goose! That superb bird is walking along and I just stand and pretend I'm not interested. It comes toward me. It's just going to hiss at me. Those birds think they're very strong, and that's their undoing, Bender, that's their undoing . . ."

The convention violator was now practically singing.

"It comes toward me and hisses like a phonograph. But I'm not the type to be easily scared, Bender. Anyone else would have taken to his heels, but I stand there and wait. So it comes up to me and sticks out its white, goosey neck with its yellow beak. It's going to bite me. Notice, Bender, I have the moral advantage. I'm not attacking it, it's attacking me. And then in self-defense I grab . . ."

But Panikovsky hadn't time to finish his story. There was a terrible, sickening crunch and the Antelopeans found themselves lying in the road in the weirdest positions. Balaganov's legs were protruding from a ditch. On the smooth operator's stomach lay a can of gasoline. Panikovsky was groaning under the weight of a spring. Kozlevich stood up and staggered a few steps.

The Antelope was no more. In the road lay a ghastly pile of pistons, cushions, and springs. Brass entrails glinted in the moonlight. The battered body had slid into a ditch and lay beside Balaganov, who was just recovering his senses. The chain slithered into a rut like a snake. In the ensuing silence, there was a tinkle: a wheel which had evidently been flung some way by the shock came rolling down a slope. The wheel turned a circle and came to rest at Kozlevich's feet.

It was only then that the driver realized it was all over. The Antelope had perished. Adam sat down on the ground and buried his face in his hands. A few moments later the captain touched him on the shoulder and said in a low voice:

"Adam, we must go."

Kozlevich stood up and immediately sat down again.

"We must go," Ostap repeated. "The Antelope was a loyal car, but so are plenty of other cars in the world. You'll soon be able to choose any one you like. We must hurry. We must find a place to spend the night, have a meal, and get hold of some money for tickets. We've a long way to go. Come on, Kozlevich. Life is wonderful, ignoring its shortcomings. Where's Panikovsky? Where's that goose-lifter? Alex, take Adam with you!"

Kozlevich was helped along by the arm. He felt like a cavalry soldier whose horse had been killed through his own negligence. He felt he would now be the laughingstock of all pedestrians.

The end of the Antelope made life rather more complicated. They had to spend the night in the fields. Ostap fell asleep at once; so did Kozlevich and Balaganov; but Panikovsky sat by the fire all night and shivered.

The Antelopeans rose with the dawn but were not able to get to the nearest village until the afternoon. Panikovsky trailed behind the whole way. He was limping slightly. His eyes had acquired a catlike gleam from hunger and he never stopped bemoaning his fate and cursing the captain as well.

In the village, Ostap ordered the crew to stay put on Third Street, while he himself went to the village Soviet on First Street. He returned soon after.

"It's all arranged," he said in a relieved voice. "They're just going to find us an apartment and give us a meal. After supper we'll snuggle in the hay. Do you remember hay and milk? And this evening we'll give a performance. I've already been given fifteen rubles for it. Alex, you'll have to recite something from the *Book of Recitations*, I'll show them some antireligious card tricks, and Panikovsky . . . Where is Panikovsky? Where's he got to?"

"He was here a moment ago," said Kozlevich.

At that moment, from behind the fence beside which the Antelopeans were standing, came the gaggling of a goose and the shrill cries of a woman, feathers came flying through the air, and into the street ran Panikovsky. The toreador's hand had evidently failed him and in self-defense had hit the goose the wrong way. After him came a housewife waving a rolling pin.

"Miserable, worthless woman!" Panikovsky shouted, making off at top speed.

"What a silly fool!" Bender exclaimed, unable to hide his annoyance. "That devil has fouled up our show. Let's get out of here before they take the fifteen rubles back."

Meanwhile, the housewife had caught up with Panikovsky and was thrashing him with the rolling pin. The convention-violator collapsed onto the ground but quickly jumped up again and tore off at incredible speed. Having completed her act of retribution, the housewife turned back with satisfaction. As she hurried past the Antelopeans, she shook the rolling pin at them.

"Our career as artists is over now," Ostap remarked, striding rapidly out of the village. "The food and rest are down the drain."

They found Panikovsky a mile farther on. He was lying in the roadside ditch and cursing loudly. He was pale with fatigue, fear, and pain, and the patches of red had left his aged face. He looked so pitiful that the captain revoked the punishment he was about to mete out.

They all looked at Panikovsky in disgust. And once again he trailed along at the rear of the column, moaning and muttering:

"Wait for me, don't go so fast. I'm old and sick. I

don't feel well. . . . A goose. A leg. Neck. What a
dame! Miserable, worthless people!"

But the Antelopeans were so used to the old man's
complaining that they paid no attention to him. Hunger spurred them on. Never had they been in such dire
straits. The road stretched on endlessly, and Panikovsky dropped farther and farther behind. The
friends were already down in a narrow yellow valley,
while the convention violator was still a black sil-
houette on the hilltop against a greeny, twilight sky.

"The old man's become impossible," said the hungry Bender. "We'll have to fire him. Alex, go and
bring the old malingerer here."

Balaganov, disgruntled, went off to carry out the
order. By the time he got to the top of the hill, Panikovsky's figure had disappeared.

"Something's happened," said Kozlevich after a few
moments, looking at the hilltop from which Balaganov was semaphoring with his arms.

The captain and the driver went up.

The violator of the convention lay in the middle
of the road as still as a doll. A pink strip of tie lay
across his chest. One arm was twisted behind his back.
His eyes stared at the sky. He was dead.

"Heart attack," said Ostap, just for something to
say. "I can diagnose it without a stethoscope. Poor old
man!" He turned away.

Balaganov couldn't take his eyes off the body. Suddenly his face contorted and he stammered out, "And
to think I hit him because of the dumbbells. And had
a fight with him before that, too."

Kozlevich remembered the fallen Antelope, looked
at Panikovsky with horror, and began singing a Latin
hymn.

"Cut it out, Adam," said the smooth operator. "I
know exactly what you want to do. After the psalm
you'll say, 'What God gives, God takes,' and then,
'We all walk in the shadow of God,' and then something else quite meaningless, such as 'He's now better

off than we are.' We don't need any of that, Adam
Kazimirovich. We have one simple problem, namely:
we must bury the body."

It was quite dark when the violator of the convention found his last resting place. It was a natural grave,
hollowed out by the rains at the base of an upright
stone slab. The slab had evidently stood by the roadside for some time. It might once have been embellished with the inscription "Land owned by Major
George Volk-Lisitsky Ret." or it might simply have
been a boundary mark dating from the time of Po-
tëmkin, not that it really mattered. They put Panikovsky in the hole, dug the earth with sticks, and
covered him over. Then the Antelopeans applied
their shoulders to the time-loosened slab and pushed
it in place. That was the grave.

In the light of matches the smooth operator
scrawled an epitaph on the tombstone with a piece
of brick:

Here lies
Michael Samuelevich Panikovsky
a man without papers

He took off his captain's cap and said, "I was often
unjust to the deceased. But was the deceased a moral
man? No, he wasn't a moral man. He was an ex-blindman, imposter, and goose-lifter. He devoted all his
time and energy to living off society, but society
didn't want him to do so. And Michael Samuelevich
couldn't tolerate this difference of outlook because he
was very quick-tempered. That's why he died. That's
all."

Kozlevich and Balaganov were displeased by Ostap's graveside oratory. They thought it would have
been more to the point for the smooth operator to
perorate on the deceased's philanthropic actions, his
aid to the poor, his considerate nature, his love for
children, and all those things that are usually attributed to the dead. Balaganov even took his stand by

the grave so as to say all these things himself, but the captain put on his cap and began walking quickly away.

As the remnants of the Antelopean band crossed the valley and topped another hill, they came face to face with a small railroad station.

"Ah, here's civilization," said Ostap. "There may be a café and some food. We can sleep on benches. In the morning we'll move on to the east. What do you think?"

The engineer and the driver were silent.

"Have you lost your tongues like suitors?"

"I'm not going, Bender," said Balaganov at length. "Don't be offended, but I don't believe it'll work out. I don't know where to go. We'll all be lost over there. I'm staying here."

"I feel the same way," Kozlevich said in support.

"As you wish," said Ostap with sudden terseness.

There was no snack bar at the station. A kerosene lamp was alight. Two peasant women were dozing on sacks in the waiting room. The entire station staff wandered up and down the plank platform, anxiously peering at the signal in the predawn darkness.

"Which train is it?" asked Ostap.

"Long-distance," the stationmaster nervously answered, adjusting his red cap with its silver emblem. "A special train. It's two minutes late. It's been held up at the crossing."

There came a roar, the wire quivered, out of the roar protruded two wolfish eyes, and a short, shiny train hurtled into the station. The large windows of the first-class cars were ablaze with light; bunches of flowers and bottles of wine in the restaurant car shot past the noses of the Antelopeans; conductors carrying lamps jumped off while the train was still moving, and the platform was suddenly filled with the merry sound of Russian and foreign tongues. The cars were decorated with garlands of greenery and slogans: "Greetings to the Hero Builders of the Eastern

Railroad." The train was taking its passengers to the opening of the new railroad.

The smooth operator disappeared. He came back again in a few moments and whispered, "I'm going. How, I don't know, I only know I'm going. Do you want to come with me? I'm asking for the last time."

"No," said Balaganov.

"I won't go," said Kozlevich. "I can't go on any more."

"What are you going to do?"

"What can I do?" Balaganov answered. "I'll become one of the sons of Lieutenant Schmidt again and that's all."

"I'm thinking of putting the Antelope together again," said Adam miserably. "I'll go and have a look. I can probably repair it."

Ostap was about to say something when a long whistle stopped him. He pulled Balaganov toward him, patted him on the back, kissed Kozlevich, waved his hand, and ran for the train, the cars of which were already bumping each other from the first tug of the locomotive. But before he reached it, he turned back, pushed into Kozlevich's hand the fifteen rubles given him for the performance, and jumped onto the step of the moving train.

Looking back, he caught sight of two small figures making their way up the embankment into a lilac-colored haze. Balaganov was returning to the troubled camp of Lieutenant Schmidt's sons. Kozlevich was going off to find the remains of the Antelope.

Part : III

THE PRIVATE
CITIZEN

Passenger in a Special Train

A SHORT SPECIAL TRAIN waited by the asphalt platform at Ryazan Station in Moscow. It had only six cars: a baggage car, which, contrary to normal usage, was not intended for luggage but for keeping food supplies on ice; a restaurant car, from which a white cook kept poking his head; a government Pullman, and passenger cars in which a delegation of shock-workers, and foreign and Soviet correspondents were allowed to spread themselves on couches with austere striped covers.

The train was leaving for the ceremonial joining-up of the Eastern Railroad. A long journey lay ahead. The shock-workers stuffed picnic baskets with little black padlocks dangling on the end of iron rods into the compartment cupboards. The Soviet Press raced up and down the platform, brandishing lacquered plyboard suitcases.

Foreigners kept their eyes on the porters carrying their thick leather cases, trunks, and cardboard boxes with the brightly colored labels of different travel agencies and steamship companies.

The passengers had managed to stock up with copies of the booklet *The Eastern Railroad,* the cover of which showed a camel sniffing a rail. The booklet was being sold on the spot from a baggage trolley. The author of the booklet, a journalist named Palamidov, had already walked past the trolley several times, looking hopefully at the purchasers. He was considered an expert on the railroad and was on his way there for the third time.

Departure time arrived, but the farewell scene was quite unlike the departure of any ordinary passenger train. There weren't any old women on the platform, and no one thrust a baby out of the window so that it could take a last look at its granddad; neither were there any granddads, whose dim eyes reflect their usual fear of railroad drafts. Obviously no one was being kissed good-by, either. The shock-workers' delegation had been brought to the station by union officials who hadn't yet had time to work out the problem of farewell kisses. The Moscow correspondents were seen off by editors who were more used to shaking hands on such occasions. And the foreign correspondents, thirty of them in all, were on their way to the opening in full strength, with wives and phonographs, so there was no one to see them off.

As befitted the occasion, the members of the expedition talked louder than usual, kept taking out notebooks needlessly, and upbraided those seeing them off for not wanting to go with them on such an interesting journey. A journalist named Lavoisian was particularly boisterous. He was young in spirit, though a bald patch shone through his curly hair like a moon through the jungle.

"What a sorry sight you all are," he shouted to his companions. "Don't you realize what the Eastern Railroad means?"

If the heated Lavoisian's hands hadn't been engaged in holding an enormous typewriter with a watchman's oilcloth cover, he might even have biffed one of his friends with it, so eager was he and so devoted to Press reporting. He already felt the urge to send a telegram to his editor, but there was nothing to write about.

Ukhudshansky, a trade-union newspaperman, had been one of the first to arrive at the station and was now leisurely wandering up and down the platform. He was carrying a book entitled *The Region of Turkestan: A Complete Geographical Survey of Our Country; a Bedside or Travel Book for Russians*, compiled by Semenov-Tian-Shan, 1903. He stopped several times alongside groups of passengers and their friends, and said with a slightly satirical ring to his voice, "Traveling? Well, well!" Or: "Staying behind? Well, well!"

In this manner he reached the top of the train, stared at the locomotive for some time with his head thrown back, and then said to the engineer:

"Working? Well, well!"

After that the reporter went back to his compartment, unfolded the latest issue of his trade-union newspaper, and proceeded to read his own article, which bore the title "Improve the Work of Shop Committees." The article contained a report of a meeting, and the writer's attitude to the occasion could well be summed up by the phrase "Holding a meeting? Well, well!" Ukhudshansky continued reading right up to the train's departure.

One of the bystanders, a man with a squashed, pink nose and velvety temples, made a prophesy which scared everyone beyond measure. "I know all about these trips," he declared. "I've been on them myself. I know what's going to happen to you. There are about a hundred of you here. You'll be traveling for about a month in all. A couple of you will get left behind on some small out-of-the-way station without any money or papers, and won't catch up with the others for maybe a week, arriving tired and in rags. Somebody's suitcase is bound to be pinched. And the victim will moan the whole way and keep borrowing his neighbor's shaving brush. He'll give the shaving brush back unwashed and lose the mug. One passenger will die, of course, and his friends, instead of going to the joining-up ceremony, will be forced to bring his dearly beloved ashes back here to Moscow. Carrying ashes is a terrible bore and nasty, to boot. In addition to all that, people will start bickering on the way. Believe me! Someone, whether it's Palamidov or Ukhudshansky, will do something antisocial. And for a long time you'll all sadly take him to task, while he screeches and moans that it wasn't his fault. I know all about it. You're going off in caps and hats, but you'll come back in Oriental skullcaps. The biggest fool among you will buy a full set of armor from a Bukhara Jew—a velvet cap edged with jackal fur and a thick padded blanket made in the style of a gown. And it goes without saying that you'll be singing "*Stenka Razin.*" Not only that, the foreigners will sing "Down Mother Volga; *Sur Notre Mère Volga.*"

Lavoisian was furious and aimed a blow at the prophet with his typewriter. "You're just envious!" he said. "We won't sing."

"Yes you will, boys. You're bound to. I know it all."

"We won't!"

"You will, and if you're honest, you'll immediately write me a postcard about it."

At that moment there was a subdued cry and Menshov, a Press photographer, fell off the top of the baggage car. He had clambered up there to take some shots of the train's departure. He lay on the platform for a few moments holding his camera in the air, then got up, anxiously inspected the shutter, and clambered up on the car again.

"Falling off?" asked Ukhudshansky, poking his head and the newspaper out of the window.

"That's nothing!" said the photographer disdainfully. "You should have seen me fall off the spiral slide in the amusement park."

"Well, well!" commented the trade-union Press

representative, and disappeared through the window.

Having climbed onto the roof and knelt down on one knee, Menshov continued working. He was being watched with the greatest satisfaction by a Norwegian writer, who had already arranged his things in the compartment and was now taking a walk along the platform. He had light, boyish eyes and a large Viking nose. He was so delighted with Menshov's photo-adventurousness that he felt the urge to share his feelings with someone. He marched up to an elderly shock-worker, prodded the old man in the chest with his forefinger, and exclaimed in a piercing voice, "You! !" Then he pointed to his own chest and cried just as piercingly, "Me!!"

Thus exhausting his entire Russian vocabulary, the writer smiled pleasantly and hurried back to his compartment, as the second bell had just rung. The shock-worker hurried off, too. Menshov climbed down onto the ground. Heads began to nod, the final smiles appeared, and a humorist in a coat with a black velvet collar ran past. As the end of the train wound past the up-track switch, two brother correspondents came flying out of the snack bar. One of them had a Wiener schnitzel clamped between his teeth. Leaping about like puppies, the brothers tore along the platform, jumped down onto the oil-patched ground, and there, amid the sleepers, finally realized that there was no chance of catching up with the train.

Meantime, the train, now on its way out of a Moscow under construction, had already begun its deafening song. It banged with its wheels, roared with diabolical laughter under the bridges, then calmed down a little on reaching the suburban woods, and gathered full speed. The train had yet to describe a fair curve across the globe, had yet to traverse several provincial climates, to change from the inland coolness to the hot desert, to pass through plenty of small towns and big cities and gain four hours on Moscow time.

Toward the evening of the first day, two messengers of the capitalist world appeared in the Soviet correspondents' car. They were Herr Heinrich, who was representing an independent Austrian newspaper, and an American named Hiram Berman. They came to introduce themselves. Herr Heinrich was small in stature. Mr. Berman wore a soft hat with a curled brim. He spoke Russian fairly well. They all stood for a while in the corridor surveying each other with interest. To break the ice, they talked about the Arts Theater. Heinrich praised the theater, while Mr. Berman observed slyly that, being a Zionist, he was more interested in the Jewish problem in the U.S.S.R.

"There is no such problem here," said Palamidov.

"How is that possible?" Berman asked in astonishment.

"It doesn't exist."

Mr. Berman was upset. All his life he had written articles for his paper on the Jewish question and it would be painful for him to part with it. "But surely there are Jews in Russia?" he asked warily.

"Yes, there are," Palamidov replied.

"Then you have a Jewish problem."

"No, there are Jews, but no Jewish problem."

The electric atmosphere accumulating in the coach corridor was somewhat discharged by the appearance of Ukhudshansky. He was going to the toilet with a towel over his shoulder. "Talking?" he asked, swaying from the rapid motion of the train. "Well, well!"

By the time he came back, clean and cheerful, with drops of water on his temples, the argument had involved the whole corridor. From the compartment emerged Soviet newspapermen, from the neighboring car came some shock-workers, and then came another two foreigners, an Italian correspondent with a Fascist emblem, and a German Orientalist who was traveling to the joining-up ceremony at the invitation of the Cultural Relations Society. The theme of the dispute was very elastic and stretched from building socialism in the U.S.S.R. to men's berets now in fashion in the West. There were divided opinions on all those topics.

"Arguing? Well, well!" said Ukhudshansky, retiring to his compartment.

It was only possible to make out bits and pieces in the general hurly-burly.

"If that's the case," Herr Heinrich was saying, holding a citizen named Suvorov, from Putilovo, by the collar, "why have you merely been blathering about it these last thirteen years? Why don't you organize the world revolution you're always talking about? It's clear you can't. Then stop blathering about it."

"But we're not going to make a revolution in your country. You'll do that yourselves."

"Who, me? I'm not going to make a revolution."

"They'll do it without you: you won't be asked."

Mr. Berman stood leaning against the stamped-leather partition wall and looked apathetically at the factions. The Jewish question had lodged in a polemical cleft at the very outset of the discussion, and the other topics left him cold. A writer of humorous verse who wrote under the name Gargantua detached himself from the group in which the German professor was reacting positively to the advantages of the Soviet marriage system over church matrimony. He walked up to Hiram Berman, now lost in thought, and began explaining something heatedly. Hiram listened attentively but soon realized that he couldn't make out a single word. In the meantime, Gargantua kept adjusting some part or other of Hiram's clothing, first straightening his tie for him, then flicking off a speck of dust, then undoing and doing up a button, and all the time talked rather loudly and even distinctly, or so it seemed. Actually he had some subtle speech defect which turned his words into complete twaddle. Matters were made worse by the fact that he liked to jaw, though he required confirmation of what he was saying after each sentence.

"It's true, isn't it?" he said, wagging his head as though he were about to peck some birdseed with his large, fine nose. "It's right, isn't it?"

These were the only comprehensible words in Gargantua's jabbering. The rest merged into a marvelously persuasive rumble. Mr. Berman agreed out of politeness and promptly fled. Everyone agreed with Gargantua, and he considered himself a man able to convince anyone of anything.

"You see," he said to Palamidov, "you don't know how to converse with people, but I do. I have just proved to him, and he agreed, that we have no Jewish problem here. It's true, isn't it?"

Palamidov didn't catch a word, and, nodding his head, began listening to a discussion between the German Orientalist and the conductor. The conductor had long been dying to join in the conversation, but had only just found a free listener on his own level. Having first asked the profession and name of his interlocutor, the conductor put down his broom and began smoothly:

"Professor, you may not have heard that in Central Asia there is an animal called a camel. It has two humps. I once knew a railroad worker—you might have heard about him: his name was Dolzhnostyuk, he used to work in the baggage-room. One day he got onto this camel between the humps and lashed it with his crop. The camel was vicious and tried to crush him between its humps. It nearly killed him. Dolzhnostyuk managed to jump clear. He was quite a kid: you might have heard about him. Then the camel spat all over his tunic, and the tunic had only just come back from the laundry. . . ."

The vesperal discourse was dying away. The collision between the two worlds had ended happily. There was no quarrel. The coexistence of the two systems, capitalist and socialist, on the special train had to

go on for a month willy-nilly. Herr Heinrich, the
enemy of world revolution, told a traveler's chestnut,
after which everyone went to the dining car to have
supper, crossing from coach to coach over the shaky
iron plates and screwing up their eyes on account of
the rush of air. In the dining car, however, the passengers sat apart. The foreign contingent, represented
by the correspondents of the most important newspapers and telegraph agencies in the world, reached
sedately for the vodka and stared with awful courtesy
at the shock-workers with their knee boots and the
Soviet journalists who had made themselves at home
and appeared in slippers and collar buttons without
ties.

The people in the dining car were of all kinds: there
was the provincial-minded Mr. Berman from New
York; the Canadian girl who had arrived from abroad
only an hour before the special train departed and
was still twisting her head in a daze over the cutlet in
a long metal plate; the Japanese diplomat and another, slightly younger Japanese; Herr Heinrich,
whose yellow eyes were for some reason sparkling; a
young English diplomat with a slender tennis waist;
the German Orientalist, who had listened so patiently
to the conductor's story of a weird animal with two
humps; an American economist; a Czech; a Pole; four
other American correspondents, including a prelate
who wrote for a YMCA paper; and a true-blue
American woman from an old pioneering family with
a Dutch name, who was famous for the fact that she
had been left behind the year before at Mineral Waters
Station and for some reason had hidden in the snack
bar to get publicity, which caused a great furor in
the American Press. For three days there were articles
with such lurid headlines as "Girl from old family in
hands of wild Caucasian hillmen" or "Held for ran-
som," and many other ones. Some of the foreigners
were hostile to everything Soviet, others hoped to
fathom the mysterious Asiatic soul in next to no

time, while yet others really tried hard to understand what was going on in the Soviet land.

The Soviet side made plenty of noise at their tables. The shock-workers had brought food with them in paper bags and reached for the tea glasses in their white metal holders. The more solvent journalists gave their orders to the writer, and Lavoisian, who suddenly had a fit of Pan-Slavism, decided not to grovel in the dirt in front of the foreigners but to order sautéd kidneys. He didn't eat the kidneys because he had disliked them since childhood, but he nevertheless puffed with pride and threw challenging looks at the infidels. The people were a variety of types on the Soviet side as well: there was a worker from Sormovo sent on the trip by a general meeting; a builder from the Stalingrad Tractor Works, who had lain for ten years in the trenches opposite Wrangel on the same field where there now stood a giant tractor; and a weaver from Serpukhovo, interested in the Eastern Railroad because it would speed up the delivery of cotton to the textile regions.

There were metal workers from Leningrad, miners from the Donbas coal fields, a machine operator from the Ukraine, a delegation leader in a white Russian-style shirt with the large Star of Bukhara received for fighting the Emir. How surprised the tennis-waist diplomat would have been if he had known that the polite little poet Gargantua had been captured eight times by Cossack headmen, and at one time had even been shot by supporters of Mahno, but didn't like to talk about it, as he had unpleasant memories of climbing out of a common grave, shot through the shoulder.

Even the YMCA representative might have gasped if he had known that the gay Palamidov was a representative of an Armenian tribunal, while Lavoisian had dressed up as a woman in the interests of news reporting and got into a meeting of Baptists, about which he wrote a long antireligious dispatch; or that none of the Soviet citizens present had christened their children, or that among the friends present there were four writers.

The people in the dining car were of all kinds.

On the second day the words of the velvet prophet came true. As the train crossed the Volga, panting and puffing, passengers began singing a song in tuneless voices. As they did so they tried not to look one another in the eye. In the next car the foreigners, who didn't know where or what they were supposed to sing, enthusiastically began the folksong "Hey, the box is full, is full!" with the chorus, just as quaint, from the "Volga Boatman." No one sent a postcard to the man with the squashed nose: they felt too ashamed. Ukhudshansky alone was standing firm. He didn't sing with the others, and when the unholy row enveloped the whole car, he alone sat in silence keeping his lips tightly shut and pretending he was reading the *Complete Geographical Survey of Our Country*. He was severely punished. He had a musical fit that night, way beyond Samara. At the midnight hour, as the train slept, Ukhudshansky's quavering voice could be heard from his compartment singing "There is a cliff along the Volga, that with moss is overgrown." The journey had got the better of him.

And later still, when even Ukhudshansky had gone to sleep, the outside door of the car opened, there was a free squeal of wheels for a moment, and into the brightly lit corridor, looking around him, came Ostap Bender. For a moment he hesitated, then sleepily waved his hand and opened the first compartment door. Gargantua and the photographer Menshov were sleeping by the light of a blue bulb. The fourth bunk, one of the top ones, was empty. The smooth operator wasted no time. His legs were aching so much from his arduous peregrinations, irretrievable losses, and a two-hour stand on the footplate of the car, he climbed straight into the bunk. There he had a magnificent vision—a white, boiled chicken lying on the table by the window with its legs in the air like a wheelbarrow. "I'm following in Panikovsky's uncertain footsteps," he whispered to himself.

With these words he seized the chicken and consumed it without bread or salt. The bones he stuffed behind the hard canvas bolster. He fell asleep, happy and contented, to the creak of the roof, inhaling the inimitable smell of railroad paint.

"May a Hireling of Capital Come In?"

IN A DREAM that night Ostap saw Zosya's sad, dim face, and then Panikovsky himself appeared. He was wearing a cab driver's cap with a feather and kept saying as he wrung his hands, "Bender, Bender! You don't know what a chicken is! It's a delicious, juicy bird!" Ostap failed to understand and grew angry.

"What bird? I thought your specialty was goose!" But Panikovsky went on insisting "Chicken! Chicken!"

Bender woke up. Low overhead he saw a ceiling as curved as the lid of grandma's trunk. Right in front of the smooth operator's nose jiggled the rack. It was very light in the compartment. Through a half-lowered blind poured the hot air of the Orenburg plains.

"The chicken!" said a voice below. "Where's the chicken gone? There's no one here except us. Wait a minute, whose feet are those?"

Ostap covered his eyes with his hand and then remembered that that was what Panikovsky used to do whenever trouble was in store for him. Taking his hand away, the smooth operator saw two heads appear at the level of his bunk.

"Sleeping? Well, well!" said the first head.

"Tell me, man," said the second head in a friendly way, "was it you who ate my chicken? It's true, isn't it?"

Menshov the photographer was sitting below with both arms elbow deep in a black photographer's bag. He was changing the plates.

"Yes," said Ostap warily, "it was."

"Gee, thanks," Gargantua exclaimed unexpectedly. "I just didn't know what to do with it. It might have gone bad in the heat. I didn't want to throw it away. That's right, isn't it?"

"I'm delighted to have done you that small service," said Ostap cautiously.

"What paper are you from?" asked the Press photographer, continuing to rummage in the bag with a sad smile. "Did you get on in Moscow?"

"You're a photographer, I see," said Ostap, evading a direct answer. "I once knew a provincial photographer who even opened cans of food in red light, he was so afraid they might be spoiled."

Menshov laughed. The new passenger's joke amused him. And the whole of that morning no one else asked the smooth operator any awkward questions. He jumped down from the bunk and, stroking his cheeks, which in three days had become covered with piratical stubble, looked quizzically at the kind Gargantua. The humorist unpacked his case, took out his shaving gear, and, handing it to Ostap, proceeded to explain something at length, pecking invisible bird-seed and incessantly demanding confirmation of what he was saying.

While Ostap washed and shaved, Menshov, decked with photographic straps, spread the news around the car that there was a new correspondent from the provinces in his compartment who had caught up with the train by air during the night and had eaten Gargantua's chicken. The story of the chicken caused quite a stir. Almost all the correspondents had brought food from home for the journey—meatballs, bread, and hard-boiled eggs. None of them had eaten their food, as they all preferred to go to the dining car.

Bender hardly had time to complete his ablutions when a portly writer in a child's soft woolly appeared in the doorway. He put twelve eggs down on the table in front of Ostap and said, "Have them. They're eggs. As long as they're here, someone ought to eat them." The writer then leaned out of the window, looked at the warty plains, and commented bitterly, "Desert is useless. But once it's there, we have to consider it."

He was a philosopher. Having received Ostap's thanks, the writer shook his head and went off to finish a story. Being a punctual man, he had firmly made up his mind to write one story each day. He carried out this resolution with the assiduity of a pupil at the top of his class. He was evidently inspired by the thought that once the paper was there, someone ought to write on it.

Other passengers followed the philosopher's example. One brought some stuffed peppers in a jar, Lavoisian brought meatballs with strips of newspaper sticking to them, and another brought some herring and gingerbread. Others came too, but Ostap refused to receive them.

"I can't, I really can't, friends," he said. "I did someone a favor, and now you all come rushing."

He liked the correspondents very much. He was ready to oblige, but had stuffed himself so full that he was no longer in a position to have any feelings about it. He clambered onto his bunk with difficulty and slept practically the whole day.

It was the third day of the journey. The passengers were longing for something to happen. There was still a long way to go to the Eastern Railroad, nothing spectacular had happened, and the Moscow correspondents, wearied by their enforced idleness, began squinting suspiciously at each other.

"Has anyone found out anything and sent a cable to his editor?"

Lavoisian finally broke down and sent a telegraphic report:

PASSED ORENBURG STOP LOCOMOTIVE FUNNEL BELCHING SMOKE STOP IN GOOD SPIRITS COMMA EASTERN RAILROAD SOLE SUBJECT OF CONVERSATION IN PASSEN-GER CARS STOP CABLE INSTRUCTIONS ARAL SEA LAVOISIAN

The secret was soon out, and at the very next station a line formed at the telegraph window. They all sent brief reports on their good spirits and the loco-motive funnel, still belching smoke.

Immediately after Orenburg the foreigners were presented with plenty of scope for activity when they saw their first camel, their first tent, and their first native with a pointed fur cap and a whip in his hand. At the local station, where the train was accidentally delayed, at least twenty cameras were leveled at the camel's snout. This was the beginning of things exotic—the ships of the desert, the freedom-loving sons of the plains, and other such romantic beasts of burden.

The American lady from the family that went way back came into the corridor in dark glasses. She was further protected from the sun by a green parasol. She was photographed for some time in this get-up by a gray-haired American with an Aimo movie camera. First she stood next to the camel, then in front of it, and finally got on top of it, settling herself between the humps, which the conductor had described so lovingly. The small, bitchy Heinrich darted in and out of the crowd and whispered to everyone:

"Keep an eye on her or she'll get left behind at the station and there'll be another sensation in the Ameri-can Press. The headline will be, 'Valiant woman correspondent in grips of crazed camel.'"

The Japanese diplomat stood two paces away from the Kazak. They both glared at one another. They had identical, slightly squashed faces, stiff mustaches, yellow lacquered skin, and eyes that were narrow and slightly bulging. They could have passed for twins had not the Kazak been wearing a sheepskin coat belted with a calico sash, whereas the Japanese wore a gray London-made suit, and had not the Kazak just learned to read, whereas the Japanese had graduated from two universities, Tokyo and the Sorbonne, twenty years earlier. The diplomat took a step backward, bent over the view finder, and clicked the shutter. The Kazak laughed, got onto his rough steed, and rode off into the plains.

Ostap woke up just before sundown. The train was still traveling through plains. Lavoisian wandered along the corridor, suggesting to his comrades that they should publish a special train newspaper. He had even thought up the name *Full Speed Ahead* for it.

"What a name!" Ostap exclaimed. "I once heard of a fire-brigade newspaper called *There's Never Smoke without Fire*. Much to the point!"

"You're a born writer," cried Lavoisian. "Why don't you admit you're just too lazy to write for the mouthpiece of the train populace?"

The smooth operator didn't deny that he was a born writer. In case of need he could have explained without any difficulty which paper he represented on the train. Actually, it was the *Chernomorsk Times*. Anyway, there was no need of this, as the train was a special one and wasn't patrolled by disgruntled ticket inspectors with chrome-plated clippers. But Lavoisian was already sitting in the shock-workers' compartment with his typewriter, where his suggestion for a train newspaper caused general confusion.

That evening a large crowd of newspapermen gathered in the compartment occupied by Gargantua, Menshov, Ukhudshansky, and Bender. They sat close together with six people on each bunk. Heads and legs hung over the sides. The brisk night refreshed the journalists, who had suffered so much from the heat all day, while the drawn-out rhythm of the wheels which had not abated for three days made for a friendly atmosphere. They talked about the Eastern Railroad, editors, and secretaries, discussed amusing slips of the pen, and all of them teased Ukhudshansky for his lack of journalistic verve. Ukhudshansky drew himself up and said in a superior voice:

"Talking twaddle? Well, well."

At the height of the merriment Herr Heinrich appeared. "May a hireling of capital come in?" he said gaily.

Heinrich set himself down on the lap of the portly writer, making him grunt and think stoically, "I suppose if I've got knees, someone might as well sit on them."

"Well, and how is the construction of socialism going?" the representative of the independent paper asked impudently.

For some reason or other, all the foreigners on the train were addressed politely, with the addition of "Mr.," "Herr," or "Signor" before their names, but the correspondent of the independent paper was simply called Heinrich, considered a blatherer, and not taken seriously. So, in answer to the forthright question, Palamidov replied:

"Heinrich, why don't you pipe down? You're going to start running down the Soviet system again. It's boring. Anyway, we can hear that sort of thing from any bitchy old woman standing in a market line."

"You're quite wrong," said Heinrich, "I was just going to tell you the biblical story of Adam and Eve. Will you let me?"

"Listen, Heinrich, how come you know Russian so well?" someone asked.

"I learned it in Odessa when I occupied that wonderful city with General von Beltz's Army in 1917. I was a lieutenant at the time. You've probably heard of Von Beltz?"

"Not only heard, but seen him," Palamidov answered. "Your Von Beltz lay in his gilt office in the palace of the officer commanding the Odessa Military District with a hole in his head. He shot himself when he found there'd been a revolution in your country."

At the word "revolution," Herr Heinrich gave an official smile and said, "The general was loyal to his oath."

"Why haven't you shot yourself, Heinrich?" asked someone on the top bunk. "How did you get around the oath?"

"Well, do you want to hear the biblical story or not?" asked the freethinker peevishly.

They went on railing at him with questions about the oath for some time until he finally soured completely and started to go; then they agreed to listen to the story.

HERR HEINRICH'S STORY OF ADAM AND EVE

"Once there was a young man in Moscow, gentlemen, a member of the Communist Youth. His name was Adam. And in that city there was a girl named Eve, also in the Communist Youth. One day these youngsters went for a walk in Moscow's Garden of Eden, the Park of Culture and Rest. I don't know what they talked about. Our young people talk about love. But your Adam and Eve were Marxists, so they may have talked about world revolution. At any rate, it happened that while strolling through the former Amusement Park they sat down under a tree. I don't know what kind of tree it was. It might have been the tree of knowledge. But as you know, Marxists don't like mysticism. They probably thought it was simply an ash. As Eve was talking, she pulled a twig off the tree and gave it to Adam. At that point there suddenly appeared a man whom the unimaginative young couple mistook for a park attendant. Actually he was an angel with a sword of fire. Grumbling and arguing, the angel took Adam and Eve to an office and charged them with damaging park property. This insignificant and routine event distracted the lovers from their high politics, and Adam beheld the gentle Eve standing in front of him, while Eve could only see the manly Adam standing in front of her. And the young couple fell in love. Three years later they had had two sons."

Having reached this point, Heinrich suddenly dried up, tucking his soft striped cuffs into his sleeves.

"Well, what then?" asked Lavoisian.

"Just that one son was called Cain and the other Abel, and that after a while Cain killed Abel, Abraham begat Isaac, Isaac begat Jacob, and the whole of the Bible starts again and no Marxism can stop it. Everything repeats itself. There'll be a flood, Noah with his three sons, and Ham will offend Noah, and there'll be a Tower of Babel, which never gets built, gentlemen, and so on. There won't be anything new in the world. So you're getting excited over a new life for nothing." And Heinrich leaned back in satisfaction, squashing the fat and kindly writer with his narrow, herring-like back.

"All that would be fine," said Palamidov, "if it were supported with some evidence. But you can't prove anything. It's just wishful thinking. There's no need to stop you from believing in miracles. Believe in them—pray if you like."

"And have you any proof that things will be different?" exclaimed the representative of the independent paper.

"Yes," Palamidov answered. "You will see some of it the day after tomorrow at the joining-up ceremony."

"There you go again!" groaned Heinrich. "Construction! Plants! Five-year plans! Don't give me that stuff about steel. It's the spirit that counts. Everything repeats itself. There'll be a Thirty Years' War and a Hundred Years' War, and they'll burn people who say

the world is round. And the Wandering Jew will roam
the world again . . ."

"The Wandering Jew will never roam the world
again!" the smooth operator said suddenly, looking
around at the assembled company with a happy expression on his face.

"And you can prove it in two days, I suppose?"
squeaked Heinrich.

"Now if you like," Ostap answered affably. "If
the present company will permit, I'll tell you the
story of what happened to the so-called Wandering
Jew."

The present company willingly agreed. They all
settled down to hear the new passenger's story, while
Ukhudshansky muttered, "Telling a story? Well,
well!"

And the smooth operator began.

OSTAP BENDER'S STORY OF THE WANDERING
JEW

"I won't bother you with the long and boring life
story of the Wandering Jew. I'll just say that for about
two thousand years the old fogy loafed around the
world, avoiding registering at hotels and driving
citizens crazy with his complaints about the high railroad fares, which forced him to go about on foot. He
was seen hundreds of times. He was present at the historic meeting at which Columbus failed to give an
account of the advance he had been given to discover
America. While still a young man, he had seen Rome
burn. He lived a hundred and fifty years or so in India,
astonishing the yogis by his tenacity and obstreperous
nature. In short, the old man could have described
many interesting things had he written his memoirs at
the end of each century. But the Wandering Jew
was illiterate and also had a memory like a sieve.

"Not so long ago the old man was living in the
beautiful city of Rio de Janeiro, drinking refreshing
drinks, gazing at the ocean-going steamers, and stroll-

ing under the palm trees in his white pants. He had bought the pants second-hand in Palestine eight hundred years before from a Crusader and they were like new. Then suddenly the old man became restless. He felt an urge to go to Russia and see the Dnieper. He had been everywhere—on the Rhine, the Ganges, the Mississippi, the Yangtze, the Niger, and the Volga. But he hadn't seen the Dnieper. You see, he wanted to take a look at this huge river.

"Exactly in 1919 the Wandering Jew, wearing his Crusader's pants, crossed the Rumanian frontier illegally. It need hardly be said that under his shirt he had seven pairs of silk stockings and a bottle of Parisian perfume, which a lady from Kishinev had asked him to take to her relatives in Kiev. At that stormy time smuggling was called 'Wearing a poultice.' They had soon taught the old man how to do it in Kishinev. As the Wandering Jew was standing on the bank of the Dnieper, having accomplished his mission, dangling his unkempt green beard, a Cossack with yellow-blue braid on his pants came up to him and rapped out:

" 'You a Yid?'

" 'Yes,' replied the old man.

" 'Let's go,' ordered the man with the braid.

"And he took him to the Cossack chief.

" 'We've caught a Yid,' reported the soldier, frog-marching the old man along.

" 'You a Yid?' asked the chief with amused surprise.

" 'Yes,' answered the wanderer.

" 'Put him against the wall,' said the chief affectionately.

" 'But I'm the Wandering Jew,' screeched the old man.

"For two thousand years he had patiently awaited death, but now he wanted to live.

" 'Quiet, you lousy Yid,' cried the thick-lipped chief with delight. 'Give him the works, men.'

"And that was the end of the Wandering Jew.

"That's all," Ostap concluded.

"I imagine, Herr Heinrich, as a former officer in the Austrian Army you know all about the ways of your friends, the supporters of Petlyura," Palamidov remarked.

Heinrich said nothing and went outside. At first everyone thought he was offended, but the next day it was found out that he had gone straight to Mr. Hiram Berman and sold him the story of the Wandering Jew for forty dollars. And at the very next station Hiram cabled Bender's story to his newspaper.

]CHAPTER[

: 28 :

The Sweaty Wave
of Inspiration

ON THE MORNING of the fourth day the train turned eastward. Roaring past snowy peaks—the Himalayan spurs—and casting fleeting shadows on the mountain streams, the special train sped through a settlement under the plane trees and for some time wound its way alongside a huge snow-clad mountain. Unable to make the top in one go, the train approached it first from the left, then from the right, then turned back, puffing and blowing, and returned again, grazing the mountain with its dusty green sides, and finally escaped to freedom. With its wheels working hard, the train came to a dashing halt at the last station before the beginning of the Eastern Railroad.

A locomotive the color of spring grass was standing bathed in marvelous sunlight against a background of aluminum hills. It was a present from station workers to the new railroad.

For quite some time the presentation of gifts on ceremonial occasions and anniversaries of different kinds has not been very well handled. The usual present is either a tiny, cat-sized model locomotive or else —the other extreme—a chisel bigger than a telegraph pole. This tiresome transformation of small objects into big ones and vice-versa takes up a lot of time and money. The useless model locomotives grow dusty on office shelves, while the giant chisels, which have to be carried on two separate carts, weirdly and needlessly grow rusty in the back yard of the celebrating establishment.

But locomotive *OV*, which had undergone a general overhaul in record time, was completely normal in size, and it was clear that any chisel used for the overhaul had been an ordinary one. The fine gift was immediately harnessed to a train, and Ovechka,* as they usually call locomotives of this series on the right of way, bearing the placard "To the Join-up," arrived at the southern branch of the railroad, Mountain Station.

The first blue-black rail, produced by the Ural Plant, had been laid there two years before to the day. Since that time the rolling mills of the plant had churned out a continuous flow of flaming strips of rail. More and more were needed for the track. The track-laying camps, which were moving toward one another, challenged each other to a contest, and had worked at such a pace that the suppliers were hard put to find enough material.

The evening party at Mountain Station, illuminated with red and green rockets, was so pleasant that if there had been some old-timers there, which there weren't, they would have said that they'd never forget that evening. Luckily, there weren't any. Even back in 1928 there had been neither old-timers, station buildings, railroad track, nor the wooden triumphant arch with fluttering slogans and flags near which the special train had stopped.

While a political meeting was held in the light of kerosene lamps and the whole population crowded around the platform, Menshov the Press photographer cruised around the arch with two cameras, a tripod, and a flashlight. The arch seemed a suitable subject to

---

* Ovechka means "a little sheep," ironically enough. Trans.

the photographer, and he thought it would come out well. But the train twenty paces away would be too small. If he took the shot from the train, however, the arch would be too small. On such occasions Mohammed usually went to the mountain, perfectly well aware that the mountain wouldn't come to him. Menshov, however, did what seemed to him the simplest thing. He asked for the train to be moved up under the arch in the same casual way that people ask you to move up in a streetcar. In addition, he insisted that the funnel of the locomotive should belch thick white smoke. He further demanded that the engineer should look fearlessly into the distance from his little window, shading his eyes with his hand. The railroad workers were confused, but, thinking it was really necessary, granted his wish. The train clanked its way up to the arch, the desired smoke belched from the funnel, and the engineer, sticking his head out of the window, made a grim face. Then Menshov produced such a flash that the earth shook and dogs began barking for miles around. Having taken the photograph, he curtly thanked the railroad staff and slipped back to his coupe.

Late that night the special train was actually traveling on the new railroad. As the company prepared for bed, Menshov emerged into the corridor and said bitterly, addressing no one in particular:

"That's odd! I seem to have taken that damn arch with an empty plate. Nothing's come out."

"Don't worry," said Lavoisian sympathetically, "just ask the engineer and he'll put the train in reverse. In only three hours you'll be back at the station and you can take the shot again. The join-up can be postponed for a day!"

"I'm damned if I can take it now," said Menshov sadly. "All my magnesium is used up: otherwise we'd go back, of course."

The journey along the Eastern Railroad afforded great pleasure to the smooth operator. Every hour brought him nearer the northern track-laying camp, where Koreiko was to be found. Ostap also liked the passengers on the train. They were young, happy, and didn't suffer from the bureaucratic befuddlement which so marked his acquaintances at the Hercules. The only thing needed for complete happiness was money. He had eaten all the food presented to him, and the dining car required cash. At first, whenever his new friends dragged him off to have a meal, Ostap got out of it by saying he had no appetite, but he soon found out he couldn't go on like that. For a while he watched Ukhudshansky, who spent the whole day in the corridor gazing at the telegraph poles and the birds flying down from the wires. A satirical smile played on his lips, and throwing back his head, he whispered to the birds:

"Flitting about? Well, well!"

Ostap indulged his curiosity as far as actually reading Ukhudshansky's article, "Improving the Work of Shop Committees." After that, he looked the curious journalist up and down, smiled craftily, and, feeling the familiar excitement of a marksman, locked himself in the compartment. He came out three hours later, holding a large ruled sheet of paper.

"Writing?" asked Ukhudshansky listlessly.

"Especially for you," replied the smooth operator. "I notice you're eternally in the throes of creation. It is very difficult to write, I grant you. As an old progressive and brother writer, I can testify to that. But I've invented a little gimmick which will free you from the need to wait until the sweaty wave of inspiration hits you. Here it is: take a look."

And Ostap passed Ukhudshansky a sheet on which was written:

COMPREHENSIVE GUIDEBOOK AND ESSENTIAL AID
FOR THE COMPOSITION OF
ANNIVERSARY ARTICLES, HUMOROUS
WRITINGS FOR SCHOOL MAGAZINES,
AND ALSO FESTIVE VERSE, ODES, AND ANTHEMS

Part 1. Vocabulary

Nouns

1. Cries	11. Hour
2. Working people	12. Enemy
3. Dawn	13. March
4. Life	14. Wave
5. Beacon	15. Sands
6. Errors	16. Leaps (bounds)
7. Banner (flag)	17. Steed
8. Baal	18. Heart
9. Moloch	19. Past
10. Lackey	

Adjectives

1. Imperialist	5. Industrial
2. Capitalist	6. Steel
3. Historic (al)	7. Iron
4. Last	

Verbs

1. Blaze	6. Complete
2. Plow up	7. Sing
3. Reveal	8. Slander
4. Redden	9. Grind (teeth)
5. Flutter	10. Threaten

Epithets

1. Malicious	2. Fanged

Miscellaneous parts of speech

1. Tenth	4. May!
2. Twelfth	5. Forward!
3. Let!	

(*Interjections, prepositions, conjunctions, dots, exclamation marks, and quotation marks, etc.*)

NB: *Commas are placed before subsidiary clauses; dots, exclamation and quotation marks wherever possible.*

Part 2. Creative Section

(Composed entirely of words in Part 1)

Section 1. Leading Article

TENTH WAVE

The Eastern Railroad is an iron steed which, as it plows up the sands of the past with steel leaps and bounds, completes the march of history, revealing the latest grinding of teeth by the slandering enemy, toward whom the tenth wave is racing, threatening the lackeys of the imperialist Moloch and capitalist Baal with their twelfth and final hour; but, despite the errors, let the banners redden and also flutter at the beacon of industrialization, blazing to the cries of the working people, to whom the dawn of a new life is revealed: forward!

Section 2. Humorous Sketch

LET!

Forward!
It blazes to the cries of the working people . . .
It lights the dawn of a new life.
  The beacon!
Industrialization!
Let there be some errors. Let it happen. But see how the banners redden . . . how they race along . . . how they flutter! Those flags!
  But the lackeys are already threatened with:
  The last wave!
  The tenth hour!
  The twelfth Baal!
Let them slander us. Let them grind their teeth. Let the malicious, fanged enemy be revealed!
A historic march is being made. The sands of the past are plowed up by the leaps and bounds of steel.

It's an 'iron steed!'
"It's the
      Eastern!
      Railroad!
"Hearts sing . . ."

Section 3. Poetry

(a) The Thirteenth Baal

Hearts sing to the rumble of days
Like the dawn the beacon glows
Let the lights of industry
Make tremble our slandering foes

The iron steed hurtles ahead
With historic bounds on steel
While our working family
Advances to errors reveal

Arrived is the ultimate hour
And the tenth wave's reddish hue
Shows the clock has chimed twelve
For Moloch and Baal, yes, for you!

(b) Eastern Version

Uryuk blooms to the rumble of days
Like the dawn the kishlak glows
Through the aryks and alleyways
A donkey walking goes.

Asiatic Local Color

1. Uryuk (apricots)
2. Aryk (canal)
3. Ishak (ass)
4. Plov (food)
5. Bay (nasty man)
6. Basmach (nasty man)
7. Shakal (animal)
8. Kishlak (village)
9. Piala (cup)
10. Ichigi (shoes)
11. Medrese (seminary)
12. Shaitan (devil)
13. Arba (cart)
14. Shaitan-Arba (Central Asian Railroad)
15. Me no un'erstan'
16. Vely small (expression)

Addendum

Using the material in the first section, on the basis of the methods contained in the second section, you can also compose: novels, short stories, poems in prose, sketches from everyday life, feature articles, chronicals, exposes, plays, political reviews, radio addresses, and so on.

When Ukhudshansky had examined the contents of the document, his eyes, dim until then, lit up. A man who had up to that time struggled along with reports of meetings suddenly found himself within reach of dazzling stylistic heights.

"And all for twenty-five Mongolian rubles," said the ravenous smooth operator impatiently.

"I haven't any Mongolian rubles," said the trade-union newspaperman, keeping hold of the *Comprehensive Guidebook*.

Ostap agreed to take ordinary rubles, invited Gargantua, whom he was already calling "ward and benefactor," to accompany him, and went to the dining car. He was brought a decanter of vodka glistening like ice and mercury, a salad, and an enormous cutlet as heavy as a horseshoe. After the vodka, which made him slightly dizzy, the smooth operator secretly informed his ward and benefactor that at the northern camp he hoped to find someone who owed him a small sum of money. He would then treat all the correspondents to a feast. Gargantua replied to this with a long, convincing speech, which, as usual, was completely incoherent. Ostap called over the attendant and asked whether he carried champagne, how many bottles were available, what other delicacies he had, how much he had, and added that he needed the information because he was going to give a banquet for his confreres in a couple of days' time. The attendant said he would do his best: "In accordance with the laws of hospitality," he added for some reason.

As they approached the site of the join-up, more and more nomads were to be seen. They came down from the hills to meet the train, dressed in caps like Chinese pagodas. Chugging along, the train disappeared into purple rocky cuttings, passed over a new triple-span bridge, the last girder of which had been fixed in position only the day before, and began taking the famous Crystal Ridge. It had been made famous by the railroad builders, who had completed all the blasting and laying operations in three months instead of the scheduled eight.

The train absorbed the local ways. The foreigners, who had left Moscow in collars so stiff they looked as though they were made of porcelain, and heavy silk ties and wool suits, began to unbend. The heat was overpowering. The first to change his style of dress was one of the Americans. Grinning sheepishly, he emerged from his compartment in a curious outfit. He had on thick yellow shoes, plus-fours with stockings, horn-rimmed spectacles, and a Russian-style shirt buttoned at the neck and embroidered with little crosses. And the hotter it got, the less faithful the foreigners remained to their notion of European dress. Russian-style shirts, Apache shirts, Geisha shirts, lavishly embroidered shirts, long-tailed shirts, pseudo-long-tailed shirts and semi-long-tailed shirts, Odessa sandals, and slippers entirely transformed the newspapermen from the capitalist world. They acquired a striking similarity to the old-type Russian clerks, and one felt an overpowering urge to ask them whether before 1917 they were bureaucrats or bunglers, and whether they were safe on account of their relatives.

The hard-working locomotive decked with slogans and garlands drew the train into Jingling Spanner Station late that night. The cameramen lit Roman candles. Through their white glare the construction boss could be seen excitedly looking at the train. There was no light in the cars. Everyone was asleep. It was only the government Pullman which had its large square windows lit up. A door quickly opened and a member of the government jumped down onto the ground.

The construction boss took a step forward, saluted, and reported the completion of the railroad a year ahead of schedule.

As soon as this formality was over, the two not-very-young and not-very-sentimental young men gave each other a hug.

All the correspondents, both Soviet and foreign, including Lavoisian, who had in his impatience sent a telegram about smoke belching from the funnel, and the Canadian girl who had crossed the ocean at break-neck speed, were all asleep. Palamidov ran about the embankment looking for a telegraph office. He had worked it out that if he sent a special-delivery tele-gram right away, it would appear in the morning edi-tion. And in the black desert he found a hastily flung-together telegraphist's hut.

"In starlight," he wrote, getting furious with his pencil, "report given on completion of railroad stop present at historic hug of railroad boss and member government palamidov."

The editors accepted the first part of the telegram but left out the hug. They said it wasn't decent for members of the government to hug people.

: 29 :

Jingling Spanner

THE SUN ROSE above the desert hills at 0502 hours, 46 seconds. Ostap got up one minute later. The Press photographer had already draped himself with bags and straps. He put his cap on back to front so that the peak wouldn't get in the way while he was looking into the view finder. He had a busy day ahead of him. Ostap was also hoping for a busy day, and jumped down from the railroad car without even washing. He took the yellow file with him.

Trains which had arrived with visitors from Moscow, Siberia, and Central Asia made up the streets of the camp. Freight cars approached the stand on all sides, locomotives chugged, and white smoke hovered over the long linen slogan—"The Railroad Is the First Child of the Five-year Plan."

Everyone was still asleep, and a cool breeze was making the flags flap on the empty stand, when Ostap noticed that the clear horizon beyond the broken terrain was suddenly darkened by clouds of dust. Riding in wooden saddles and urging on their hairy mounts, thousands of horsemen were racing toward the wooden arrow marking the exact spot which had been chosen two years before as the joining point.

The nomads were coming in whole villagefuls. The heads of the families were in the lead, then came the women, riding like the men, and then came the children, three in a group, on their own ponies; even the bitchy mothers-in-law were there, digging their horses with their heels. The mounted bands raced through the swirling dust carrying their red banners, stood up in the saddle, and, turning sideways, gazed with curiosity at the wonders around them. The wonders were plentiful—trains, rails, dashing cameramen, a lattice cafeteria, which had suddenly mushroomed into being in an empty space, and loud-speakers from which a young voice could be heard saying "Testing, testing, one, two, three . . ." Two track-laying camps, two construction sites on wheels with storehouses, baths, living quarters, offices, and cafeterias faced each other in front of the stand, separated by only seventy yards or so of sleepers, on which the rails had not yet been fixed in place. That was the site where the last rail would be laid and the last spike driven in.

Ostap hurried over to the cars of the northern camp, but they were deserted. All the inhabitants had gone to the stand, in front of which the musicians had already taken their seats. Scorching their lips on hot metal mouthpieces, they were playing an overture.

The Soviet journalists took their places on the left-hand side of the stand. Leaning over, Lavoisian was trying to persuade Menshov to take a shot of him in the "execution of his duties!" Menshov couldn't be bothered, however. He was taking the railroad shock-workers, first in groups, then separately, making the plate-layers brandish their hammers and the diggers wave their shovels. The foreigners sat on the far right-hand side. Red Army soldiers checked invitation cards at the entrance to the stand. Ostap had no card. The train commandant had distributed them from a list which did not mention the name of O. Bender, representing the *Chernomorsk Times*. Gargantua kept beckoning the smooth operator onto the stand, calling out "It's true, isn't it? It's right, isn't it?" but it was no good. Ostap shook his head and ran his eyes along the stand, which was jam-packed with heroes and visitors.

Alexander Koreiko, timekeeper at the northern track-laying camp, was calmly sitting in the first row. To protect his head from the sun, he was wearing a paper hat. He had turned one ear forward slightly to hear more clearly the first speaker, now making his way to the microphone.

"Alexander Ivanovich!" Ostap called, cupping his hands to his mouth.

Koreiko glanced down and jumped up. The musicians began the "International," but the wealthy time-keeper paid little heed to the anthem. The smooth operator's menacing figure running through the clearing made ready for the final rails rid him of all peace of mind. He looked over the heads of the crowd, wondering in which direction to escape.

Fifteen thousand horsemen rocked backward and forward unceasingly, forded the cold river dozens of times, and then at the beginning of the meeting lined up behind the stand. Some of them, shy and proud, spent the whole day silhouetted on the hilltops, hesitating to ride any nearer the roaring and raving of the crowds.

The builders of the new railroad were celebrating their victory noisily and happily, with shouting, music, and cheers for their favorites. The last rails were dropped onto the track with a clang. In a moment they were in position, and the plate-layers, who had already hammered thousands of spikes into place, gave their rights to the last few blows to their superiors.

"In accordance with the laws of hospitality," said the buffet attendant, sitting on the roof of the dining car alongside the cooks.

The speeches began. Each time they were made

twice, once in Russian and once in the Kazak language.

The correspondents could no longer complain of a lack of events. The speeches were recorded. Engineers were seized by the waist and asked for information with exact figures. It was hot, dusty, and businesslike. The meeting began to smoke like an enormous bonfire. Having scribbled a few lines, Lavoisian ran to the telegraph office, sent off a telegram, and then began scribbling something else. Ukhudshansky didn't jot down anything and didn't send any telegrams. In his pocket lay the *Comprehensive Guidebook,* which enabled him to concoct a splendid dispatch in five minutes with Asiatic local color. His future was assured. And that was why he said to his colleagues with more of a satirical note in his voice than usual:

"Trying? Well, well!"

The foreigners' cameras were clicking away. Throats were parched from the speeches and the sun. The crowd kept looking more and more at the cold river, at the cafeteria, where the striped shadow of the awning lay on long banquet tables set with green bottles of mineral water. Next door were the stalls, where the visitors hurried from time to time to have a drink. Koreiko was desperately thirsty, but stood firm under his three-cornered paper hat. The smooth operator jeered at him from the distance, brandishing the yellow file and a bottle of lemonade in the air.

The meeting had ended. On the deserted stand amid the cigarette butts, torn-up notes, and sand from the desert sat Koreiko by himself. He couldn't make up his mind to come down.

"Come down, Alexander Ivanovich!" called Ostap. "Don't torture yourself. Have a swig of cold mineral water. Well, don't torture me, then. I'm hungry. I'm staying here anyway. Perhaps you'd like me to sing you Schubert's Serenade. I know it."

But Koreiko wasn't going to wait for that. It was

clear enough without that that he would have to give up the money. Hunched and halting at every step, he came down from the stand.

"So, you have a three-cornered hat on," Ostap joked. "And where's the gray field jacket? You can't imagine how I've missed you. Well, how are you, how are you? Shall we rub noses? Let's go straight to the treasury, to the secret cave where you keep your Mongolian rubles."

"Let's eat first," said Koreiko, whose tongue was dry and scratched like a rasp.

"We could eat, I suppose, but no funny business this time. Anyway, there's no chance. My boys are waiting behind the hills," Ostap lied, just in case. And then, remembering his boys, his spirits fell somewhat.

The dinner given for the builders and their guests was in Eurasian style. The Kazaks sat on rugs with their legs tucked under them, which is what everyone does in the East and only tailors do in the West. The Kazaks ate *plov* from white dishes and washed it down with lemonade. The Europeans sat at tables.

In two years of work the builders of the Eastern Railroad had suffered many trials and tribulations, but the official dinner in the middle of the desert had caused them quite a lot of trouble too. The menu, both the Asiatic and European versions, had been the subject of long discussion. The problem of hard liquor evoked a prolonged argument. For several days the building-administration office looked like the United States just before a presidential election. The supporters of prohibition and those against it fought in pairs. Finally the Communist cell spoke against liquor. Then a new difficulty arose: what about the foreigners, diplomats, and Muscovites? They had to be wined and dined with elegance. After all, in their own Londons and New Yorks they were used to culinary excesses. And so an elderly expert from Tashkent named Ivan Osipovich was sent for. At one time he had been a head waiter at the well-known restaurant Martynov's in Moscow and was now living out his days as manager of the caterers'-union cafeteria at the Chicken Bazaar.

"So don't let us down, Ivan Osipovich," they said to him at the administration office. "There'll be foreigners present. It's got to be done showily and stylishly."

"Believe me," mumbled the old man with tears in his eyes, "the people I've catered for! I once catered for the Prince of Württemberg! You needn't pay me any money. How can I refuse to cater for people at the end of my days. I'll feed them and then die!"

Ivan Osipovich was worked up. When he found out that liquor had finally been rejected, he almost had a heart attack, but he was determined that Europe should not go without a dinner. The estimate he submitted was sharply curtailed, so, mumbling "I'll feed them and die" under his breath, the old man added sixty rubles from his own savings. On the day of the banquet he arrived in a frock coat smelling of mothballs. While the meeting was in progress, he fussed about, kept looking at the sun and shouting at the nomads, who, from idle curiosity, were trying to ride their horses into the cafeteria. The old man flicked a napkin at them and squeaked:

"Get out of here, you dogs, can't you see what's going on? Oh, my God, the *sauce piquant* will be spoiled. And the consommé with eggs isn't ready."

The hors d'oeuvres were already on the table. Everything was served with extreme elegance and great skill. Stiff napkins sat upright on glass plates, bud-shaped pats of butter lay on ice, and the herrings held a sprig of onion or an olive in their mouths; there were flowers, and even the ordinary gray bread looked most presentable.

The guests finally sat down at the table. They were covered with dust, red from the heat, and very hungry. None of them looked like the Prince of Württemberg. Ivan Osipovich suddenly sensed the approach of disaster.

"I ask your pardon," he said unctuously: "just five minutes more and we can start. I have a personal favor to ask you. Please don't touch anything until we start, so that everything is as it should be."

He rushed away to the kitchen for a moment, prancing affectedly. When he returned, however, carrying a dish of some kind of festive fish, a ghastly scene of looting met his eyes. It was so unlike the ceremony of consuming food which he had planned that he stopped dead. The Englishman with the tennis waist was gaily chewing bread and butter, while Heinrich, leaning across the table, was plucking olives out of the herring mouths. Everything on the table was all over the place. Having satisfied their initial hunger, the guests were gaily comparing notes.

"What's all this?" asked the old man in a fallen voice.

"Where's the soup, daddio?" cried Heinrich with his mouth full.

Ivan Osipovich didn't answer; he merely flicked his napkin and went away. All further worries were passed on to his subordinates.

As the two operators reached the table, a fat man with a nose as pendulous as a banana was making the first after-dinner speech. To Ostap's great astonishment, it was engineer Talmudovsky.

"Yes, we're heroes," Talmudovsky was exclaiming, holding up a glass of mineral water. "Here's to you, builders of the railroad. But what about the conditions under which we work, citizens! I could mention salaries, for instance. I don't say that the salaries on the railroad aren't better than in other places, but what about the cultural facilities? There's no theater. It's desert. There's no drainage. No, I can't work like that."

"Who's he?" the builders asked each other. "Any idea?"

In the meantime, Talmudovsky had already pulled out his suitcase from under the table. "I don't give a damn about the contract!" he cried, making his way to the exit. "What, give back the traveling expenses? I'll go to court first!" And, banging the guests with his suitcase as he went, he wildly shouted, "I'll go to court first!" instead of "I beg your pardon."

Late that night he was off on a motor trolley, having joined some track-layers on their way to the southern branch of the railroad. Talmudovsky sat on top of his suitcase and explained to the track-layers the reason why an honest specialist couldn't work in that hole. Ivan Osipovich, the head waiter, went with them. In his grief he hadn't even had time to take off his frock coat. He was completely drunk.

"Savages!" he shouted, sticking his head out into the cutting wind and shaking his fist in the direction of Jingling Spanner. "Everything wasted on those dirty pigs! To think I once catered for Chekhov and the Prince of Württemberg! I'll go home and die. Then they'll remember Ivan Osipovich. Prepare a banquet for eighty-four people, they'll say, the lousy sons of bitches. But there'll be no one to do it. He'll be dead. Gone to a better world where there's no sickness, no sadness, no sighing, but everlasting life. Let us never forget him!"

And while the old man was singing his own requiem, the tails of his frock coat flapped in the wind like a pennant.

Without giving Koreiko time to finish his stewed fruit, Ostap dragged him away from the table and took him off to settle their account. The two operators went up the ladder steps to the freight car which housed the office of the northern camp and contained the timekeeper's linen bed. They locked themselves in.

Alexander Ibn Ivanovich

THE AIR in the warm and dingy freight car was thick and stagnant like that in an old shoe. There was a smell of leather and feet. Koreiko lit a conductor's lamp and began rummaging under the bed. Sitting on an empty macaroni box, Ostap watched him thoughtfully. Both the operators were tired by their battle and now took an attitude of official resignation to the event that Koreiko had feared so much and that Ostap had waited for all his life. The whole scene might well have taken place in a co-operative shop, with the customer asking to see some hats and the salesman casually throwing a tousled soft cap the color of cobblestone onto the counter. He couldn't care less whether the customer bought it or not, while the customer himself wasn't too keen, and only said "Maybe you have some others" to salve his conscience. The reply that usually comes is, "You'd better take that one, or it will soon be gone," and they both look at each other in complete apathy. Koreiko rummaged under the bed for some time, apparently undoing the top of a suitcase and feeling for something inside.

"Hey, you down there on the hold!" cried Ostap languidly. "What a bit of luck you don't smoke. To

ask an old meany like you for a cigarette would be absolute torture. You'd never offer your pack in case
people took several butts instead of one. You'd fum-
ble in your pocket trying to open the pack and then
finally bring out a miserable bent cigarette. You're a
nasty man. What's the point of pulling out the whole
case?"

"Anything else?" Koreiko snapped, breathing hard
under the bed. He didn't like being compared to a
miserly smoker. Just at that moment he drew some
thick bundles out of the case. The nickel-plated
tongue of the lock scratched his arms, bare to the
elbow. To make it easier, he lay on his back and went
on working like a miner at the coal face. Powder, bits
of straw, and whisps of corn fell into the millionaire's
face.

"This is terrible," thought Alexander Ivanovich:
"terrible and terrifying. He may strangle me and take
the lot. It would be so easy. He'll cut me up into bits
and send them to different places by slow freight.
And pickle my head in a barrel of cabbage."

Koreiko broke into a clammy sweat. In fear, he
peered out from under the bed. Bender was dozing
on his box, leaning his head against the conductor's
lamp.

"Maybe I should send him by slow freight . . ."
Alexander Ivanovich thought, continuing to take out
bundles and still feeling terrified, "to different places.
Strictly confidentially."

He peered out again. The smooth operator
stretched and gave a huge yawn, like a Great Dane.
Then he picked up the lamp and, waving it to and fro,
called out:

"Khatsepetovka Station! All change, citizens. We've
arrived. By the way, I quite forgot to tell you. In case
you're thinking of trying to do away with me, you
should know I'm against the idea. Someone tried it
once before. A crotchety old man named Kisa Voro-
byaninov, from a good family. Used to be a marshal

of the nobility and then became a registry-office clerk. We were seeking a fortune to the tune of a hundred and fifty thousand rubles. And then, just before we were to divide the booty, the idiotic old marshal slashed my throat with a razor. How disgusting it was, Koreiko. Disgusting and painful. The surgeons only just saved my life. I'm deeply grateful to them."

Koreiko finally emerged from under the bed, pushing the bundles of money toward Ostap's feet. Each bundle was neatly wrapped in white paper and tied with string. "Ninety-nine bundles," he said morosely. "Each one contains ten thousand rubles in twenty-five-ruble notes. You don't need to check it: I keep things in the same order as they do at the bank."

"But where's the hundredth bundle?" asked Ostap eagerly.

"I've deducted a thousand—as per the robbery on the seashore."

"That's a lousy trick. The money was spent on you, after all. Don't be such a stickler for formality!"

Koreiko passed over the missing money with a sigh, and in return received his *curriculum vitae* in the yellow file. The file was immediately burned in the iron stove, which had a pipe sticking through the roof. Ostap took one of the bundles at random and, breaking the wrapper, made certain that Koreiko had not tricked him; he pushed it into his pocket.

"Where's the foreign currency?" Ostap nagged. "Where are the Mexican dollars, the Turkish liras, where are the pounds, rupees, pesetas, centavos, Rumanian lei? Where are the Baltic latas and zlotys? Give me some of the currency, at least!"

"Take what you have," Koreiko answered, sitting in front of the stove and watching the documents writhing in the flames. "Take it or that will soon be gone too. I don't keep foreign currency."

"So now I'm a millionaire!" Ostap exclaimed in pleasant surprise. "An idiot's dream come true!"

Ostap suddenly felt depressed. He was struck by his

humdrum surroundings; he felt it wrong that the world hadn't changed that second, and that nothing, absolutely nothing, had taken place. And though he knew that secret caves, crocks of gold, and Aladdin's lamps were not allowed in our austere times, he still felt sad for some reason. He felt bored, like Roald Amundsen, who, when passing over the Pole in his airship *Norge* after a lifetime of endeavor, said to his companions without any enthusiasm, "Well, here we are!" Underneath was broken ice, crevices, cold, and emptiness. The secret was discovered, the goal achieved, and there was nothing left to do except change professions. But the sadness was momentary, for glory, honor, and respect lay ahead: the choirs were singing, the schoolgirls stood in ranks in their white cloaks, the aged mothers of the polar explorers eaten by their companions during the expedition were in tears, the national anthems were played, rockets were set off, and the old king hugged the explorers to his prickly orders and stars.

The moment of weakness passed. Ostap threw the bundles into a sack kindly offered by Alexander Ivanovich and, taking him by the arm, rolled back the heavy door of the freight car.

The celebrations were almost over. Rockets were cast into the air like golden fishing rods angling for little red and green fishes; a cold fire splashed into people's eyes, and pyrotechnic suns went into orbit. Behind the telegraph hut, a performance was being given for the nomads. Some of them sat on benches; others watched it from the saddle. Horses kept neighing. The special train was illuminated from front to rear.

"Yes," Ostap exclaimed, "the feast in the dining car—I'd forgotten. How terrific! Let's go, Koreiko, I'll treat you. I'll treat everyone. According to the laws of hospitality. Brandy with a piece of lemon, chicken dumplings, fricandeau with mushrooms, champagne . . ."

"Fricandeau, fricandeau," said Koreiko viciously, "and then jail. I don't want any publicity."

"I promise you a heavenly supper on a white table-cloth," Ostap persisted. "Let's go. And, anyway, you should give up living like a hermit, drink up your share of hard liquor and eat your twenty thousand cutlets, otherwise outsiders will descend on you and grab your share. I'll fix you up in the special train—I know the boys there—and tomorrow we'll be in Moscow, a comparatively cultural center. There with our millions . . . Alexander Ivanovich."

The smooth operator felt an urge to make everyone good and happy. Koreiko's face made him despondent. He began trying to convince Koreiko. He agreed that there was no point in drawing attention to themselves, but why should they starve? Ostap wasn't quite certain why he wanted the timekeeper happy, but, having once started, he couldn't stop. Finally he actually resorted to threats.

"You'll be sitting on your suitcase one fine day when a bony old man with a scythe will appear. Do you think that will be entertaining? Hurry up, Alexander Ivanovich, the cutlets are still on the table. Don't be so pig-headed."

Since his loss of a million rubles, Koreiko had become milder and more receptive. "Maybe I should have a fling," he said uncertainly. "A trip to Moscow. But modestly, without all the splash."

"Where's the splash! Two medical officers are just going to Moscow to visit the Arts Theater and to see the mummy in the Fine Arts Museum. Pick up your suitcase."

The millionaires walked to the train. Ostap swung his sack about carelessly, like an incense bowl. Alexander Ivanovich was grinning in the most moronic way. The passengers sauntered about, keeping as near as possible to the cars, as the locomotive had just been connected. The white pants of the correspondents glimmered in the darkness.

A stranger was lying under the sheet on Ostap's bunk in the compartment and reading the paper.

"Okay, down you come," said Ostap in a friendly tone. "I'm the occupant."

"It's my place, comrade," said the stranger. "I'm Lev Rubashkin."

"Lev Rubashkin, don't make me lose my temper. Come down from there." The smooth operator was being provoked into battle by Koreiko's puzzled look.

"That's news to me," said the correspondent haughtily. "Who might you be?"

"It's none of your damn business. I'm telling you to get down, so get down!"

"If every drunk in here started making a scene—"

Ostap silently grasped the correspondent by his bare foot. The whole car came running in at Rubashkin's cries. Koreiko retired to the end of the corridor just in case.

"Fighting?" said Ukhudshansky. "Well, well!"

Ostap had managed to clump Rubashkin on the head with the sack, and was now being restrained by Gargantua and the fat writer in the child's woolly.

"Make him show his ticket!" roared the smooth operator. "Make him show his reservation card!"

Rubashkin jumped about from one bunk to another stark naked, and shouted for the train commandant. Ostap, who had by now lost his sense of reality, also insisted that the management be called. The row ended most unpleasantly. Rubashkin produced both a ticket and a reservation card, after which he asked Bender in a tragic voice to do the same.

"I'm not going to on principle!" cried the smooth operator, hastily leaving the scene. "I have my principles."

"Cheat!" screeched Rubashkin, prancing into the corridor with nothing on. "Note that, comrade commandant, there's a bilker on the train!"

"Where's the bilker?" exclaimed the commandant, his eyes acquiring a hunter's gleam.

Hidden behind the jutting stand, Alexander Koreiko peered into the darkness, unable to make out anything clearly. Figures were moving about by the train, lights from cigarettes jogged up and down, and voices could be heard saying "Be so good as to show your ticket," "I tell you I'm not going to on principle," "Rowdy!" "It's true isn't it?" "You think somebody has to travel without a ticket?" The buffer plates clanked, air from the brakes hissed out just above the ground, and the bright lights of the cars began moving off. Ostap was still bristling with fury as the striped couches, luggage racks, conductors with lamps, bunches of flowers, and ceiling fans of the dining car slid past. Gliding away was the champagne feast, fresh caviar, and vintage Hungarian wine; escaping into the night were the chicken dumplings. The fricandeau, the tender fricandeau, which Ostap had described with such gusto, had left Jingling Spanner. Alexander Koreiko came up.

"I shall not let the matter rest," Ostap grumbled. "They've abandoned a Soviet correspondent in the desert. I'll cause a public scandal. Koreiko, we'll leave by the first mail train. We'll buy all the seats in the international coach!"

"What do you mean, mail train? There are no trains from here. The railroad isn't scheduled to begin operating until two months' time."

Ostap raised his head. He saw a black Abyssinian sky with weird stars and realized what had happened. But Koreiko's timid reminder of the feast gave him new strength. "There's an airplane behind the hill," he said. "One that came for the ceremony. It's not leaving until dawn. We still have time to get on."

In order to save time, the millionaires walked at a fast dromedary's pace. Their feet sank into the sand, and carrying the suitcase and the sack was not only difficult but extremely irritating. While they were

scrambling up the hill on the near side of Jingling
Spanner, dawn came to meet them from the far side
with the roar of propellers. Bender and Koreiko went
running down the far side, fearing the plane might
take off without them.

Some tiny mechanics in leather coats were walking
about under the high, rooflike, strutted wings. Three
propellers were spinning slowly, ventilating the desert. Velvet curtains with velvet pompons jerked up
and down behind the square portholes of the passenger cabin. The pilot was leaning against the aluminum
steps, eating a pastry and drinking mineral water
from a bottle in-between bites.

"We're passengers," Ostap shouted, out of breath.
"Two first-class tickets!"

No one answered. The pilot threw the bottle away
and started putting on his gauntlets.

"Aren't there any seats?" Ostap said, catching the
pilot by the arm.

"We don't take passengers," said the pilot, taking
hold of the step rail. "It's a special flight."

"I'll buy the plane," said the smooth operator
promptly. "Wrap it up in paper."

"Out of the way!" shouted the engineer, following
the pilot up the steps.

The propellers disappeared in a whirl. Shaking and
pitching from side to side, the plane began turning
into the wind. Blasts of air thrust the millionaires back,
toward the hill. Ostap's cap flew off and rolled in the
direction of India at such speed that it might well
have reached Calcutta within three hours. It might
well have rolled into the main street of Calcutta,
arousing by its mysterious appearance the interest of
circles close to the Intelligence Service, had not the
aircraft taken off and the gale abated. In the air the
plane flashed its struts and whizzed off into the sunlight.

"Road transport is out of the question. We've had
a row with the railroad. The plane won't take us.

Shall we go on foot? It's two hundred and fifty miles. Not an inspiring thought. There's only one thing to be done—embrace Islam and ride on camels."

Regarding Islam, Koreiko kept silent, but he liked the idea of the camels. The alluring sight of the dining car and airplane had confirmed his desire to go on a medical officer's jaunt, but of course without the splash, though not without a certain dash.

The nomads who had come to the ceremony had not yet dispersed, and the camels were bought not far from Jingling Spanner. The ships of the desert cost a hundred and eighty rubles each.

"How cheap!" Ostap whispered. "Let's buy fifty of them. Or a hundred!"

"That's splurging," said Alexander Ivanovich with a frown. "What would we do with them? Two's enough."

The Kazaks noisily set the travelers between the humps and helped them to attach the suitcase, sack, some refreshment for the journey—a wineskin with kumiss—and also two sheep. The camels first rose to their hind legs, then to their front legs, making the millionaires bow low, and then began striding along the railroad track. The sheep, which were attached by rope, trotted along behind, dropping globules and letting out heart-rending bleats.

"Hey, Sheik Koreiko!" Ostap called. "Alexander ibn Ivanovich! Isn't life grand!"

The sheik didn't answer. He had been given a dud camel and was furiously whacking its balding rear with a cane.

Baghdad

FOR SEVEN DAYS the camels carted the newly created
sheiks across the desert. At the outset of the journey,
Ostap had a marvelous time. Everything was fun: seeing Alexander ibn Ivanovich pitching up and down
between the humps, his puny ship of the desert,
which was shirking its duties, and the million-ruble
sack, which Ostap used from time to time to encourage
the rebellious sheep. Ostap thought of himself as Law-
rence of Arabia.

"I'm the Emir Dynamite!" he cried, swaying on a
high hilltop. "If we don't find any decent food within
the next two days, I shall incite the tribes to revolt.
Honestly, I will! I'll appoint myself the agent of the
Prophet and declare a sacred war, a jihad. On Denmark, for instance. Why did the Danes torment their
Prince Hamlet? Given the present political set-up, even
the League of Nations would be satisfied with that as a
motive for war. Honestly, I'll buy a million rubles'
worth of rifles from the British—they like selling fire-
arms to tribesmen—and we'll march on Denmark.
Germany will let us through as part of the reparations.
Can you imagine the tribesmen invading Copenha-
gen? With me on a white camel at the front? What a

pity Panikovsky's not here. He'd have liked a Danish goose!"

But a few days later, when all that was left of the sheep was rope and the kumiss had all been drunk, even the Emir Dynamite's spirits fell.

Both sheiks had become extremely thin and ragged, their faces were covered with stubble, and they looked like dervishes from a rather poor parish.

"Hold on a bit longer, ibn Koreiko, and we'll come to a city just as good as Baghdad. Flat roofs, native musicians, nice little eating-places in the eastern style, sweet wine, fabulous girls, and forty thousand skewers with all sorts of shish kebab. And, of course, a railroad."

On the eighth day the travelers approached an ancient graveyard. The rows of semicircular tombstones stretched in petrified waves as far as the eye could see. The bodies were not buried. They were left on the ground under a covering of stones. A terrifying sun shone down on the ashen city of the dead. The ancient Orient lay in these scorched graves.

The two operators whipped on their camels and soon after came to an oasis. For a long way around, the city was lit by the green torches of the plane trees, reflected by the square, flooded rice fields. The elms stood in solitude, shaped exactly like gigantic globes on a wooden leg. They began to meet asses carrying fat riders and bundles of clover.

Koreiko and Ostap rode past native shops selling green tobacco powder and smelly cone-shaped soap that resembled the top of a shrapnel shell. Artisans with snowy muslin beards were busy with copper sheets, turning them into bowls and narrow-necked pitchers. Cobblers dried small ink-dyed skins in the sun. The dark blue, yellow, and light blue tiles of the mosques glistened like liquid glass.

For the rest of that day and night the millionaires slept soundly in a hotel, and in the morning they bathed in white bathtubs, shaved, and went into the city. The millionaires' sunny mood was somewhat spoiled by the necessity of carrying the sack and suitcase wherever they went.

"I consider it my first duty," said Bender swankily, "to acquaint you with a terrific little dive called 'By Moonlight.' I was there five years ago and gave a lecture on the anti-abortion campaign. What a place! Dim lights, cool air, an owner from Tiflis, native musicians, chilled vodka, and dancing girls with tambourines and cymbals. We can stay there the whole day. Medical officers have their little weaknesses, after all, don't they? I'll treat you. The golden calf pays for everything." And the smooth operator shook his sack.

The little dive By Moonlight had gone, however. To Ostap's surprise, not even the alley where the tambourines and cymbals had once echoed was left. In its place was a straight European street which was being built up on both sides. There were fences running the entire length of it, an alabaster dust hung in the air, and trucks heated up the scorching atmosphere even more. Looking for a moment at the gray-brick frontages with horizontal windows, Ostap nudged Koreiko and led him to the other end of the city, where, as he claimed, there was another place, run by a man from Baku.

But that spot too no longer had the sign in verse composed by the dive owner from Baku.

> Respect yourself
> Respect us
> Respect the Caucasus
> Visit us.

A cardboard sign written in Arabic and Russian met the sheiks' eyes instead:

CITY MUSEUM OF FINE ARTS

"Let's go in," said Ostap sadly. "At least it's cool in there. Anyway, a visit to the museum is part of the medical officers' schedule."

They entered the large whitewashed room, dropped their millions on the floor, and wiped their burning foreheads with their sleeves. There were only eight exhibits in the museum: a mammoth's tooth presented to the museum by the City of Tashkent; an oil painting entitled *A Clash with Basmach Bandits;* two emirs' robes; a goldfish in an acquarium; a glass case with a dried-up locust; a china statuette from the Kuznetsov works; and, last, a model of the obelisk that the city intended to erect on the main square. At the foot of the model lay a tin garland with ribbon. It had recently been brought from a neighboring republic, but as the obelisk had not been ready (the appropriations had been spent on building a bath, which was required more urgently), the delegation had made their speeches and laid the garland at the foot of the model.

The visitors were immediately approached by a youth with a Bukhara skullcap on his shaven head. "Your impressions, comrades?" he asked as nervously as a kitten.

"Not bad," said Ostap.

The young fellow was the curator of the museum and without delay began explaining the difficulties which his creation was undergoing: funds were lacking; Tashkent had given them only a tooth, whereas in fact they had so many treasures, both artistic and historical, that there just weren't enough people to collect them; no expert had been sent, either.

"If I only had three hundred rubles," exclaimed the curator, "I'd make this place into a Louvre!"

"Tell me, do you know the city well?" asked Ostap, winking at Alexander Ivanovich. "Could you show us some of the sights? I used to know your city, but it seems to have changed."

The curator was delighted. Insisting that he should show them everything personally, he locked up the museum and took the millionaires to the same street

where half an hour before they had been searching
for the dive By Moonlight.

"Socialism Boulevard!" he cried, inhaling the alabaster dust with satisfaction. "What marvelous air!
The way this place will look in a year's time! Asphalt!
Buses! An irrigation institute! A tropical institute! If
Tashkent doesn't send us some scientific personnel,
then— You know, they have so many mammoth
bones, yet they only sent me one tooth. And there's
such an interest in natural history in the republic."

"Is that so?" asked Koreiko, looking reproachfully
at Ostap.

"And you know," the curator added in a whisper,
"I suspect that it isn't a mammoth's tooth at all.
They've palmed off an elephant's tooth on me!"

"How are the . . . eastern-style bars—you know,
the ones with drums and flutes?" the smooth operator hurriedly asked.

"All gone," the youth answered without feeling.
"They ought to have exterminated that disease long
ago. The last dive like that was pulled down last
spring. It was called 'By Moonlight.'"

"Was it suppressed?" gasped Koreiko.

"Honestly, it was. On the other hand, they've
opened a cafeteria with European food. The plates
are washed and dried by electricity. The graph showing stomach ailments has dropped sharply."

"The things that go on!" exclaimed the smooth operator, covering his face with his hands.

"You haven't seen anything yet," said the young
curator, giggling shyly.

They got into a cart with a festooned canvas awning and drove off. Along the way the friendly guide
kept making them peer around the awning and look
at the buildings already constructed, the buildings under construction, and the sites where they were going
to be constructed. Koreiko glared furiously at Ostap.
Ostap kept turning around and saying:

"What a marvelous little native bazaar! Just like Baghdad!"

"They start demolishing it on the seventeenth," said the young man. "There's going to be a hospital and a co-operative center there."

"But aren't you sorry at losing all this exotic environment? It's like Baghdad!"

"It's very quaint," sighed Koreiko.

The young man was annoyed. "It may be quaint for you as tourists, but we have to live here."

In the large cafeteria, surrounded by tiled walls and flypaper hanging from the ceiling, the travelers consumed pearly soup and little brown rissoles. Ostap inquired about wine and received the delighted reply that a mineral spring had recently been discovered not far from the city. As proof, a bottle of the new water was ordered and drunk in deathly silence.

"And how's the prostitution graph?" asked Alexander Ivanovich hopefully.

"It shows a sharp drop," replied the relentless youth.

"My, the things that are going on!" cried Ostap with a false laugh.

But in actual fact he knew nothing of what was going on. When they got up from the table, they discovered that the young man had paid for them. He utterly refused to take their money, assuring them he would be paid in two days' time and would get by somehow till then.

"But what about amusement? How does the city entertain itself?" asked Ostap, no longer quite so ecstatic. "Where are the drums and cymbals?"

"Don't you know?" cried the astonished curator. "Last week the city philharmonic opened. It's a large symphonic quartet named in honor of Babel and Paganini. Let's go there now. How could I have forgotten!"

As he had paid for the meal, on ethical grounds it was impossible to refuse to go to the concert. As they left, Alexander Ivanovich said in a superintendent's voice:

"City philharmonic!"

The smooth operator flushed.

As they were on their way to the hotel, the young man suddenly stopped the cart, set down the millionaires, took them by the hand, and, walking on tiptoe with pent-up delight, led them over to a small railed-off foundation stone. "This is where there will be an obelisk to Marxism," he said significantly.

As he said good-by, the young man invited them to come again. The good-natured Ostap promised to come again and said he'd never had such a wonderful day in his life.

"I'm going to the station," said Koreiko as soon as he was left alone with Bender.

"Let's go and live it up in another town," said Ostap. "We could spend three happy days or so in Tashkent."

"I've had enough," Koreiko answered. "I'm going to the station to leave my suitcase, and then I'll take a job here somewhere as a clerk. I'll wait for capitalism and then have a good time."

"Well, you can wait, then!" said Ostap rather rudely. "I'm going. Today was a silly misunderstanding: things went too far. The golden calf still has some power left in our country."

At the railroad station they caught sight of a crowd of correspondents from the special train who were making a trip to Central Asia after the joining-up ceremony. They were milling around Ukhudshansky. The possessor of the *Comprehensive Guidebook* was smugly showing his acquisition to all and sundry. He was wearing a velvet cap trimmed with jackal fur and a robe cut from a quilt.

The prognostications of the velvet prophet continued to come true.

The Gates of Great Opportunity

ON THAT SAD though bright autumn day when the gardeners in Moscow squares cut the flowers and distribute them to children, the first son of Lieutenant Schmidt, Balaganov, lay asleep on a bench in the waiting room at Ryazan Station. His head was resting on a wooden block. His crumpled cap was pulled down over his nose. From all appearances, the hoof agent and chief engineer of the Antelope was down and out. A piece of eggshell was stuck to his unshaven cheek. The sneakers had lost their shape, and their color was more like that of the rawhide shoes worn by Moldavians. Swallows swooped about under the high waiting-room ceiling.

Through the two rows of large, unwashed windows could be seen switches, signals, and various other gadgets required for running the railroads. Porters started moving about, and a line of newly arrived passengers soon stretched across the room. The last one to leave the platform was a passenger in new clothes. Under his unbuttoned macintosh he wore a suit with a very fine kaleidoscopic check pattern. His pants cascaded onto his patent-leather shoes. The foreign appearance of the passenger was further accentuated by a soft hat tipped very slightly onto his forehead. The services of a porter were deemed unnecessary, and he carried his bag himself. The passenger walked leisurely through the deserted waiting room and would certainly have found himself in the vestibule had he not suddenly noticed the miserable figure of Balaganov. He narrowed his eyes, went over, and looked hard at the sleeping man. Then, with two gloved fingers, he carefully raised the cap from the chief engineer's face and smiled.

"Arise, Count, you are summoned to the underworld," he said, jogging Balaganov.

Alex sat up, wiped his face with his hand, and finally recognized the passenger. "Captain!" he cried.

"No, no," Bender said, warding him off with his hand, "don't hug me, I'm snooty nowadays."

Balaganov danced about in front of the captain. He hardly recognized him. Not only was the suit different; Ostap had got thin and his eyes were dulled with dissipation. His face had a colonial tan.

"You're bronze, bronze," said Balaganov delightedly. "How bronze you are!"

"Yes, I'm bronze," said Bender in a dignified manner. "Look at these pants: European, first-class! The middle finger of my left hand is ornamented with a diamond ring—four carats. Well, and what have you been doing? Are you still a son?"

"Yes, in a way," said Balaganov sheepishly. "I get along on small jobs."

In the snack bar, Ostap ordered white wine and biscuits for himself and beer and a sandwich for the chief engineer.

"Tell me honestly, Alex," asked Ostap, "how much money do you need for happiness? But include everything."

"A hundred rubles," Balaganov replied, regretfully tearing himself away from his salami sandwich.

"No, you don't understand. Not just for today, but

in general. For your happiness. So that you can enjoy life."

Balaganov thought for some time, smiling shyly, and finally declared that for complete happiness he would need six thousand, four hundred rubles, and that he would enjoy life very much with that amount of money.

"All right," said Ostap, "here's fifty thousand."

He opened the square traveling bag on his knees and pushed over five white packages tied with string. The chief engineer immediately lost his appetite. He stopped eating, stuffed the money in his pocket, and kept his hand on it.

"Did you really get the platter?" he asked blissfully.

"Yes, the platter," Ostap answered without feeling. "A silver platter. The client brought it in his teeth. He wagged his tail for some time before I consented to take it. Now I'm taking the parade. I feel marvelous."

He uttered these last words with uncertainty. To tell the truth, the parade was not working out, and the smooth operator was talking nonsense when he claimed he felt marvelous. It would have been truer to say that he felt a certain awkwardness, but he didn't care to admit it, even to himself.

A month had passed since he parted with Alexander Koreiko at the baggage-room office where the underground millionaire had given him his bag. In the first town where the smooth operator had gone, feeling like a conqueror, he was unable to get accommodation in any of the hotels.

"I'll pay as much as you like," said the smooth operator haughtily.

"Won't do any good, citizen," answered the porter. "There's a congress of soil specialists here to see the experimental station. Everything's reserved for the scientists."

And the polite porter's face expressed his respect for the congress. Ostap felt an urge to shout out that he was more important, that he, too, should be respected, and that he had a million rubles in his bag, but thought it better to restrain himself, and left the hotel in extreme vexation.

The whole day he drove around town in a horse-cab. In the best restaurant he stood for an hour and a half waiting for the soil specialists, there in full strength, to leave the tables. On that day the theater was open only to the soil specialists, and, anyway, they wouldn't have let Ostap into the auditorium with the bag. So as not to have to spend the night (in the interests of science) on the streets, Ostap left by train the same evening, sleeping in the international car.

In the morning, Bender got off at a large town on the Volga. Translucent yellow leaves spiraled down from the trees. The river breathed the wind. There were no rooms in any of the hotels.

"And don't count on any," said hotel managers with beards, ones without beards, ones with mustaches, and clean-shaven ones, "until they've installed the third generator at the power station, in a month's time. Everything's reserved for specialists. Then there's going to be a Young Communist congress. We can't do anything about it."

Once more Ostap spent the day in a cab, impatiently waiting for the mail train, in which he would be able to wash up, relax, and read the paper.

The smooth operator spent fifteen nights in different trains, going from town to town in search of accommodation. At one place they were building a blast furnace, at another a refrigeration plant, and at a third a zinc works. Everywhere was filled with busy people. At the fourth place, Ostap was thwarted by a pioneer's rally, and the room where the millionaire might have spent an entertaining evening with a girl-friend was full of chattering children. He got so used to journeying that he bought a suitcase for the money, some traveling accessories, and generally equipped himself for the road. He was already considering a long and restful journey to Vladivostok, figuring that the trip would take three weeks from door to door, when he suddenly felt that if he didn't get off the train immediately he would die of some mysterious railroad disease. Then he began doing what he always used to do while the possessor of empty pockets. He began assuming false identities, such as engineer, medical officer, or tenor, and telegraphing in advance that he was due to arrive. To his surprise, there were always rooms in hotels for persons arriving on business, and he began to recover somewhat from the train sickness. On one occasion he had to pretend to be a son of Lieutenant Schmidt to get a room. The episode plunged the smooth operator in gloomy thoughts.

"Is this the life for a millionaire!" he wondered bitterly. "Where's the respect? Where's the honor? Where's the glory? Where's the power?"

Even the European suit, hat, and shoes which Ostap showed off to Balaganov were bought in a secondhand shop, and despite their excellent quality, they suffered from the one defect that they were not his but off someone else's back. He was also hurt that the government paid no attention to the disastrous state of millionaires and did not distribute the good things in life on a planned basis. Not only that . . . Station masters refused to salute him, as they used to do to every merchant with fifty thousand rubles, the elders of the town refused to come to his hotel to present themselves, and not only did the Press *not* come rushing over to interview him, they took pictures of some shock-workers or other who earned only a hundred and twenty rubles a month.

Each day Ostap counted his million, but it never seemed to change. He did his best; he had several meals a day, drank wine, left excessive tips, and bought a ring, a Japanese vase, and a polecat-lined coat. The vase and the fur coat were given away to the chambermaid, as Ostap hated encumbering himself on his travels. Anyway, if need be, he could buy himself plenty more coats and vases. Nevertheless, he had only spent six thousand rubles in the course of a whole month.

No! The parade certainly hadn't been a success, though everyone was in his place. The markers had fallen in at the right time, the troops had arrived on schedule, and the brass band had struck up. But the soldiers weren't looking at him, they weren't cheering him, and the bandmaster wasn't conducting for him. Ostap didn't give in, however. He based all his hopes on Moscow.

"But what about Rio de Janeiro?" asked Balaganov excitedly. "Shall we go?"

"To hell with it!" cried Bender in a sudden fit of viciousness. "It's all made up. There isn't any Rio de Janeiro, or any America or Europe, or anything else. The last town is Shepetovka, and the Atlantic waves lap against its shore."

"My!" gasped Balaganov.

"A doctor once explained it all to me," Ostap continued. "Foreign countries are like the myth of life after death. Once you get there, you never come back."

"It's as good as the circus!" exclaimed Balaganov, though he had no idea what Ostap was talking about. "My, how I'm going to start living! Poor old Panikovsky! He did violate the convention, of course, but let him be! He would have been delighted."

"I propose a minute's silence in memory of the deceased," said Bender.

The foster brothers stood in silence for a minute, staring down at the broken biscuits and half-eaten sandwich.

The oppressive lull was broken by Balaganov.

"Do you know what happened to Kozlevich?" he asked. "It's as good as the circus! He managed to put the Antelope together again and he's now working in Chernomorsk. He sent me a letter. Here it is. . . ."

The chief engineer took a letter out of his cap.

"Dear Alex," wrote the driver of the Antelope, "how are things? Are you still a son of Lt. S.? I'm pretty well, except that I don't have any money, and since the car was repaired, it has been behaving queerly and only works for an hour a day. I spend all my time mending it. I'm absolutely worn out by it. The passengers get huffy. Perhaps you could send me an oil pipe, Alex, old friend. It needn't be a new one. You can't get a thing at the local market. Look for one at the Smolensk market at the place where they sell old locks and keys. If things aren't going well, come over here, we'll manage together somehow. I park at the corner of Mehring St., at the taxi stand. Where's O.B.? Yours, Adam Kozlevich. I forgot to tell you, the priests Kuszakowski and Moroszek came to see me at the taxi stand. We had a terrible row. A.K."

"I'll go and get the pipe now," said Balaganov anxiously.

"Don't bother," Ostap replied. "I'll buy him a new car. Let's go to the Grand Hotel. I reserved a room there by telegram for a symphony-orchestra conductor. And you need tidying up, washing and general repairs. You are at the gates of great opportunity, Alex."

They went out onto Kalanchev Square. There were no taxis. Ostap refused to go in a horse-cab.

"They are the carriages of the past," he said squeamishly; "you can't go very far in them. Anyway, there are small mice in the upholstery."

They had to take the streetcar. It was packed. It was one of those strife-ridden streetcars which often cruise around the capital. The row is usually begun by some spiteful old woman in the early minutes of the rush hour. Gradually all the passengers are drawn into the quarrel, even those who got in half an hour after the incident began. The vicious old crone has long since got off, and the cause of the quarrel has been forgotten too, but the exchanges of abuse and shouting continue, and more and more new passengers join the fray. The row goes on until the early hours of the next morning.

The bustling passengers quickly squeezed between Ostap and Balaganov, and the foster brothers were soon dangling at different ends of the car, buffeted by bosoms and baskets. Ostap was hanging on a strap and only just managing to keep hold of his case, almost swept away by the stream.

A woman's shriek was suddenly heard above the normal streetcar bickering from the end where Balaganov was standing. "Thief! Hold him! He's standing there!"

Everyone turned his head. Enthusiasts began pushing their way to the scene of the crime, panting with curiosity. Ostap caught sight of Balaganov's dazed expression. The chief engineer himself hardly knew what had happened. Someone was gripping him by the hand in which he was tightly clasping a woman's cheap bag with a small brass chain.

"Bandit!" cried the woman. "I only turned away and he . . ."

The possessor of fifty thousand rubles had stolen a bag containing a tortoise-shell compact, a trade-union membership card, and one ruble, seventy kopeks. The streetcar stopped. The enthusiasts dragged Balaganov to the exit. As he passed Ostap, he whispered remorsefully:

"What came over me? I did it mechanically . . ."

"I'll give you mechanically!" said an enthusiast wearing a pince-nez and carrying a brief case, punching the chief engineer with great relish.

Through the window, Ostap saw a militiaman stride up to the car and march off the criminal down the road.

The smooth operator turned away.

The Indian Visitor

FROM THE enclosed quadrilateral courtyard of the
Grand Hotel came a kitchen clatter, the hissing of
steam, and cries of "Two teas for room sixteen," while
in the white corridors it was as bright and still as in
the control room of a power station. The soil congress
was sleeping in a hundred and fifty rooms; thirty
rooms were set aside for foreign businessmen seeking
an answer to the urgent question, can we or can we
not trade with the Soviet Union to advantage, the best
four-room suite was occupied by a celebrated Indian
poet and philosopher, and in a small room set aside for
the symphony-orchestra conductor lay Ostap Bender.

He lay on a velvet spread, fully dressed, hugging
the case to his chest. During the night the smooth operator inhaled all the oxygen available in the room,
and the chemical elements left in it could be called
nitrogen only for the sake of politeness. There was a
smell of sour wine, infernal cutlets, and something
else indescribably filthy. Ostap groaned and turned
over. The case slipped onto the floor. Ostap promptly
opened his eyes.

"What on earth happened?" he muttered, making a
face. "A splurge in a restaurant. Fooh, I behaved like

an out-of-town tourist. Heavens, I hope I didn't offend the diners. Some fool called out 'On your feet, soil specialists!' and then started dancing and swearing he was a soil specialist at heart, too. Of course, it was me! Why on earth did I do it? . . ."

Then he remembered that the day before he had decided to begin living a proper life, and had ordered a private house to be built for him in Mauritian style. The morning was spent in ambitious dreams. He had visions of a house with minarets, a doorman with a face like a statue, a small drawing room, a billiard room, and a conference room. In the local estate office they explained to him that he could have a piece of land, but in the construction department all his hopes were dashed. Down fell the doorman, his stone jowls clinking, the gilt conference room began to totter, and the minarets came crashing down.

"Are you a private citizen?" they asked the millionaire.

"Yes," Ostap replied. "A distinct individual."

"Unfortunately, we only build for groups and organizations."

"Co-operative, social, and industrial organizations?" asked Ostap bitterly.

"Yes, for them."

"And me?"

"You can build a house yourself."

"Yes, but where do I get the stones, window bolts, and plinths?"

"You'll manage . . . although it's difficult. All supplies have already been issued for the requirements of industry and the co-operatives."

In all probability this was his reason for the evening splurge.

Still in a lying position, Ostap took out his notebook and began working out his expenditures since the receipt of the million rubles. On the first page was the memorable entry:

CAMEL	....	rs.	180
SHEEP	....	rs.	30
KUMISS	....	rs.	1.75

The next entries were no better: fur coat; railroad ticket; another ticket; three turbans, bought for a rainy day; cabs; a vase; and various other kinds of junk. Except for the fifty thousand given to Balaganov, which hadn't done the latter much good, the million was still intact.

"They won't let me make any capital investments," said Ostap in disgust. "They just won't let me. Maybe I ought to lead an intellectual life like my friend Vasisualy Lokhankin. After all, I've amassed my material wealth: now I should try to acquire some spiritual wealth. I must find out right away what the meaning of life is."

He remembered that all day the foyer had been full of girls who wanted to talk to the visiting Indian philosopher on the problem of the soul.

"I'll go and see the Indian," he decided, "and find out what it's all about. I admit it's pretty feeble, but there's nothing else I can do."

Keeping the case with him, Ostap went down to the first floor as he was, in his crumpled suit, and knocked on the door of the great man's room. It was opened by the interpreter.

"Is the philosopher receiving?" asked Ostap.

"Depends who," the interpreter answered politely. "Are you a private individual?"

"No, no!" cired the smooth operator in horror. "I'm from a co-operative organization."

"Are you with the group? How many people are there? It's difficult for the teacher to receive people individually, you know. He prefers to talk to—"

"A group?" Ostap interjected. "That's the point. The group has authorized me to ask about an important question regarding the meaning of life."

The interpreter went away and came back five minutes later. He pulled aside the curtain and announced pompously, "Enter the co-operative organization wishing to know the meaning of life!"

The great philosopher and poet was sitting in a chair with a high, uncomfortable carved back, dressed in a brown robe and a cap of the same color. His face was swarthy and gentle and his eyes were as black as those of a junior officer. A broad white beard covered his chest like a dickey. A girl stenographer sat at his feet, and two interpreters, an Indian and an Englishman, were arranged on either side of him.

At the sight of Ostap and his case, the philosopher began fidgeting and whispered anxiously to the interpreter. The stenographer hastily began jotting something down, and the interpreter turned to the smooth operator.

"The teacher wishes to know whether the newcomer's case contains either songs or sagas, and whether the newcomer intends to read them aloud, because the teacher has already heard many songs and sagas and doesn't want to hear any more."

"Tell the teacher I have no sagas," Ostap replied respectfully.

The black-eyed ancient became even more agitated and, talking excitedly, began pointing in terror at the suitcase.

"The teacher is asking whether the newcomer intends moving into this room, because no one has ever come here before carrying a case."

It was only after Ostap had reassured the interpreter and the interpreter had reassured the philosopher that the tension was relieved and the discussion could proceed.

"Before answering your question with regard to the meaning of life," said the interpreter, "the teacher would like to say a few words on education in India."

"Tell the teacher," said Ostap, "that the problem of education has been of interest to me since childhood."

The philosopher closed his eyes and began speaking

at a leisurely pace. For the first hour he spoke in English and for the second in Bengali. From time to time he broke into song in a soft, tuneful voice, and at one point stood up and executed some dance movements, which evidently represented games played by schoolboys in the Punjab. Then he sat down again and shut his eyes, while Ostap listened to the long translation. At first Ostap politely nodded his head, then gazed sleepily out of the window, and finally began looking for something to amuse him: he fiddled with the things in his pockets, looked lovingly at his ring, and even winked rather openly at the pretty stenographer, whereupon she began scratching away more quickly.

"And what about the meaning of life?" asked the millionaire when he got a moment.

"First the teacher would like to acquaint the newcomer with extensive material collected while studying the state of education in the U.S.S.R.," the interpreter explained.

"Tell the teacher I have no objection," Ostap replied.

And the phonograph was wound up again. The teacher spoke, sang pioneer songs, showed a wall newspaper which had been presented to him by the children of the 146th trade school, and even burst into tears at one point. The interpreters rattled away their duet, the stenographer wrote on, and Ostap absent-mindedly cleaned his nails.

At length the smooth operator gave a loud cough. "You don't need to translate any more," he said. "I'm beginning to understand Bengali. When he gets around to the meaning of life, you can start translating."

When they told the philosopher Ostap's urgent request, the black-eyed ancient became excited.

"The teacher says that he himself has come to your great country to find out the meaning of life," the interpreter declared. "It is only where education is organized on such a high level that life becomes meaningful. The group—"

"Good-by," said the smooth operator quickly, "and tell the teacher that the newcomer asks permission to leave."

But the philosopher was already singing the Budënny March in a gentle voice, so Ostap left without permission.

"Krishna!" cried the smooth operator, running back to his room. "Vishnu! What's happening in the world? Where's the great truth? Maybe I'm a fool who understands nothing, and my life's gone by in a stupid, systemless way. A real Indian knows all about our country, whereas I, like the Indian in the opera can only keep singing 'The Song of India.' What a lousy state of affairs!"

That day Ostap had a meal without vodka and left his case in his room. Then he sat on the window sill and surveyed with interest the ordinary people who were jumping in and out of buses like squirrels.

In the middle of the night the smooth operator woke up and sat up in bed. It was quiet, though a melancholy boston from the restaurant filtered through the keyhole.

"How could I have forgotten?" he said angrily.

Then he laughed, put on the light, and quickly drafted a telegram:

> Chernomorsk. Zosya Sinitsky. Made mistake of my life stop ready to fly to Chernomorsk on wings of love cable reply Grand Hotel Moscow Bender.

He rang and asked for the telegram to be dispatched immediately.

Zosya didn't answer. Nor was there any answer to the other telegrams worded in the same desperate and lyrical style.

Friendship with Teen-Agers

THE TRAIN was on its way to Chernomorsk.

The first passenger took off his jacket, hung it on one of the curly hooks of the luggage rack, then pulled off his shoes, alternately lifting his plump legs right up to his face, and put on slippers with tongues.

"Have you heard the one about the surveyor from Voronezh who turned out to be a relative of the Mikado?" he asked, grinning in advance.

The second and third passengers moved closer. The fourth passenger was lying on the top bunk under a prickly, raspberry-colored blanket, glowering at an illustrated magazine.

"Haven't you really? It was the talk of the town at one time. He was an ordinary surveyor. He had a wife, one room, and a salary of a hundred and twenty rubles. His name was Bigusov. He was an ordinary, absolutely undistinguished fellow, and if you want to know the truth, he was rather a hick. One day he came home from work to find a Japanese sitting in his room. The Jap was wearing a splendid suit, spectacles, and, if you want to know, snakeskin shoes, the latest thing. 'Is your name Bigusov?' asked the Jap. 'Yes,' said Bigusov. 'And your other names?' Bigusov told him. 'That's right,' said the Jap. 'In that case, kindly take off your shirt, will you, I want to see your torso.' 'Sure,' says Bigusov. And if you want to know, the Jap didn't even need to inspect the torso: he made straight for the birthmark. Bigusov had a mark on his side. The Jap looked at it through a magnifying glass, turned pale, and said, 'Congratulations, citizen Bigusov, and allow me to present you with this parcel and package.' His wife opened the parcel, of course. And inside, if you want to know, packed in shavings, was a double-edged Japanese sword. 'What's the sword for?' asked the surveyor. 'You read the letter. It'll tell you everything. You're a samurai.' At this point Bigusov turned pale as well. Voronezh, if you want to know, isn't exactly a large city. What sort of attitude could they have there toward the samurai? Extremely negative, of course. Anyway, there was nothing to be done. Bigusov took the letter, broke the fourteen wax seals, and read it. And what do you think? It seems that exactly thirty-six years before, a Japanese half-prince had traveled incognito through the province of Voronezh. Well, naturally, if you want to know, his highness had got involved with a local girl and became the father of a child, incognito. He even wanted to marry her, but the Mikado forbade him to in a coded telegram. The half-prince had to leave, and the offspring was illegitimate. And Bigusov is that child. So, after quite a few years the half-prince began to die. But he had no legitimate children, there was no one to be his heir, and, what's more, the famous dynasty was dying out, which is the worst possible thing for a Japanese. Then he remembered Bigusov. What a bit of luck! They say he's in Japan nowadays. The old man died. And Bigusov's now a prince, a relative of the Mikado, and, if you want to know, has been given a million yen in cash. A million! To that fool!"

"If they gave me a million rubles," said the second

passenger, twisting his feet about, "I'd show them what to do with it."

The fourth passenger's head appeared in the space between the two top bunks. He looked hard at the passenger who knew exactly what to do with a million rubles, and then went back to his newspaper.

"Yes," said the third passenger, breaking open a package containing two individualized rusks, "all sorts of things happen in the realm of financial transactions. The uncle of a girl living in Moscow died in Warsaw and left her a million rubles, but she didn't even know about it. But over there, in Poland, they found out, and a month later a rather polished foreigner appeared in Moscow. The young beau had decided to marry the girl before she found out about the legacy. But she was already engaged in Moscow, to a good-looking young fellow from the Weights and Measures Office. She was very fond of him and naturally didn't want to marry the other one. But the foreigner went absolutely mad about her and sent her flowers, candy, and silk stockings. It turned out that the foreigner had not come of his own accord but on behalf of a shareholding company which had been formed solely for the exploitation of the uncle's legacy. They even had eighteen thousand zlotys basic capital. Their agent was to marry the girl at all costs and take her back to his country. Very romantic story! Imagine the agent's position. What responsibility! After all, he'd been given an advance but couldn't justify spending it on account of the Soviet fiancé. Just imagine the mess in Warsaw! The shareholders waiting and getting nervous, the shares dropping . . . Anyway, it was all a fiasco. The girl married her Soviet fiancé. So she never got to know about the legacy at all."

"There's a stupid girl for you," said the second passenger. "They ought to give me a million." And in his agitation he even seized the rusk out of his neighbor's hand and nervously began eating it.

The occupant of the top bunk gave a sarcastic

cough. The conversation was evidently preventing him from sleeping. They became quieter below. The passengers were now sitting together cheek by jowl, and, breathing hard, went on in a whisper.

"The International Red Cross recently put an advertisement in the paper to the effect that they were looking for the relatives of an American soldier called Gary Kovalchuk, who died in active service in 1918. There's a legacy of a million. It was actually less than a million, but the interest made it up. . . . And then in some little village in the back of beyond . . ."

The raspberry-colored blanket on the top bunk was threshing about. Bender was sick. He was sick of the railroad car, sick of the top and bottom bunks, and sick of the whole jogging world of travel. He would readily have given away his million rubles in order to sleep, but the whispering down below kept on.

"You see, an old woman turned up at the Women's Loan Co-operative and said, 'I've found a pot in my cellar, I don't know what's in it, so be good enough to come and see.' The officials from the co-operative took a look at the pot and found that it contained a million gold rupees—"

"Silly old woman! She *would* have to go and tell someone. If they'd given me that million, I'd—"

"If you want to know, money's everything—"

"In a cave near Mozhaisk . . ."

There was a groan from above, the meaty, full-blooded groan of a deteriorating personality. . . .

The storytellers were embarrassed for a moment, but the magic allure of sudden riches oozing from the pockets of Japanese princes, Warsaw relatives, and American soldiers was so great that they began digging each other in the knees again and whispering:

"And when they opened the remains, they found, if you want to know, a million rubles' worth . . ."

In the morning, still overcome with sleep, Ostap caught the sound of a blind being unhooked and a voice saying:

"A million, a whole million . . ."

That was the last straw. The smooth operator glared downward. But the passengers of the day before had gone. They had got off at dawn in Kharkov, leaving behind them crumpled bedclothes, a dirty piece of graph paper, meatballs and breadcrumbs, and a piece of string. The passenger standing by the window looked apathetically at Ostap and, addressing his two companions, continued:

"A million tons of pig iron—by the end of this year. The committee has ascertained that the combine can provide that amount. And the ridiculous thing is that Kharkov had confirmed it."

Ostap found nothing ridiculous about that statement, but the new passengers all began hooting with laughter. As they did so, the rubber mackintoshes all three were wearing began creaking.

"How about Bubeshko?" asked the youngest of the passengers eagerly. "I suppose he's having an easy time."

"No longer. He made a fool of himself. He first got into a fight . . . you know what he's like. Eight hundred and twenty-five thousand tons and not a ton more . . . Then there was a serious business. Deliberately underrating possibilities . . . It's a fact . . . He should have admitted his mistake right away . . ."

Ostap had long finished washing, but the passengers were still laughing. When he returned, the compartment had been swept, the beds made, and the conductor was on his way out with an armful of sheets and blankets, holding them in position with his chin. The young men, who were not afraid of drafts, opened the window, and an autumn wind came bounding into the compartment like a wave that had been kept locked in a drawer.

Ostap flung his suitcase with the million onto the luggage rack and settled himself on the lower bunk, looking amiably at his new neighbors, who had entered into the spirit of traveling by railroad with great zeal: they kept looking at themselves in the mirror of the door, jumping up and down on the bunks, testing the springs, admiring the red polished woodwork, and pressing various buttons. From time to time one of them would disappear for a moment and have a whispered conversation with his comrades when he got back. Finally a girl appeared in the doorway wearing a man's beaver coat and schoolgirl slippers with laces wound round her ankles like an ancient Greek.

"Comrades!" she said firmly. "This is a rotten trick. We want to travel in luxury, too. We'll have to change places at the next station."

Bender's traveling companions broke into an uproar.

"Why should we? We all have the same rights as you. We've already cast lots. Tarasov, Parovitsky, and I came up. Push off to the third class!"

From the din that followed, Ostap learned that the train was carrying a group of polytechnic students on their way back from a summer practical course. There wasn't enough room for them in the third-class cars, so three of them had to buy international tickets, the difference being split by the whole group.

As a result, the girl stayed in the compartment, while the three newcomers retired with belated decorum. Tarasov and Parovitsky arrived to replace them. They immediately began jumping up and down on the springs and pressing buttons. The girl busily jumped up and down with them. Not half an hour had passed before the original threesome returned. A longing for lost splendor had driven them back. They were followed by another two with embarrassed grins, and then a third boy with a mustache. The mustached youth's turn to ride in luxury wasn't due for a day or so, but he just couldn't wait. His arrival gave rise to a fresh uproar, which immediately brought the conductor.

"What's going on, citizens?" he said in an official voice. "What's the whole gang of you doing here?

Go back, those of you from the third-class compartment, or I'll tell the commandant."

The gang was intimidated.

"They're visiting," said the girl in a fallen voice. "They only came to sit in here for a while."

"It's not allowed," the conductor declared. "Go back!"

The mustache was already backing toward the door when the smooth operator entered the conflict.

"What's the matter with you, dad?" he said to the conductor. "You shouldn't condemn passengers without reason. Why abide by the law so closely? You should be hospitable, like they are in the East. Come with me: I'll explain it to you."

After his talk with Ostap in the corridor, the conductor became so imbued with the spirit of the East that he put aside the idea of chasing away the gang and even brought them nine glasses of tea in heavy glass holders and a whole stock of rusks. He even refused to take their money.

"According to Eastern custom," Ostap told the whole company, "and in accordance with the laws of hospitality, as a certain official in the culinary sector used to say."

The service was rendered with such grace and simplicity that it couldn't be refused. There was a crackle as the packages of rusks were opened. Ostap handed round the tea like a host and was soon a friend of all the eight boy students and one girl student.

"I've been interested in the problem of general, equal, and secret education for some time," he prattled away happily. "I was recently talking to an amateur philosopher from India on this point. He was a man of very great wisdom. So much so that whatever he said was immediately recorded on phonograph records. And since old people like jawing—it's a weakness—he filled about eight hundred freight cars with records, and now they're already making them into buttons."

Having begun with this adlib, the smooth operator picked up a rusk.

"This rusk," he said, "is only one step away from the grindstone, and that step has been made."

The friendship, warmed up by this type of joke, developed very quickly and in short order the whole gang, conducted by Ostap, was singing the ditty:

> *Peter the Great*
> *Has no one near to him*
> *A horse and a snake*
> *Are the only things dear to him.*

By evening Ostap knew them all by name. But a great deal of what the teen-agers talked about was incomprehensible to him. He suddenly felt terribly old. He was sitting opposite the youth of the day, slightly coarse, forthright, and somehow shamefully unsophisticated. Ostap had been quite different at the age of twenty. He realized that at their age he had been much more experienced but worse as a person. He had never laughed, only grinned. But these kids were laughing heartily.

"What can these thick-skulled kids be so pleased about?" he wondered in sudden irritation. "Honestly, I begin to envy them."

Although Ostap was the center of attention of the whole compartment and his conversation flowed smoothly, and although his companions treated him in the best possible way, he felt the lack of Balaganov's hero worship, Panikovsky's timid submission, and Kozlevich's devotion. The students seemed to feel the same superiority that an audience feels toward an M.C. The audience listens to the M.C. in tails, laughs from time to time, applauds lazily, and then finally goes home without giving him another thought. Then the M.C. goes to the actor's club after the show, sits down sadly in front of a meatball, and complains to a fellow member of the Artists' Trade Union, a comic-opera clown, that he's misunderstood by the public and underrated by the government. What is there to misunderstand about him? His gags are stale, his gimmicks are stale, and it's too late to learn new ones. It's all only too clear.

The story of Bubeshko, who deliberately underrated his quotas, was retold for Ostap's sake. He went with his new friends to the third-class car to try and persuade Lida the student to come and visit them, and used such pretty turns of speech that the bashful Lida came and joined in the general uproar. They all got on so well that toward evening, while sauntering along the platform of a large junction with the girl in the man's beaver coat, the smooth operator led her to practically the last up-track signal and, unexpectedly for himself, poured out his heart to her in rather trashy language.

"You see," he explained, "the moon was shining like the queen of the heavens. We were sitting on the steps of the history museum when I suddenly felt I loved her. But I was due to leave that evening and so the whole thing was upset. She seemed to be offended. In fact she *was* offended."

"Were you sent on a business trip?" asked the girl.

"Hm . . . yes, sort of. Well, not exactly a business trip, but something urgent. Now I'm suffering. I'm suffering nobly and stupidly."

"That isn't too bad," said the girl. "Why don't you channel some of your excess energy into some form of labor? Like sawing wood, for instance? There's a trend toward that nowadays."

Ostap promised to channel his energy, and although he couldn't see how he was going to replace Zosya by sawing wood, nevertheless he felt greatly relieved. They returned to the car with a mysterious expression and then went out into the corridor several times to whisper about eternal love and the latest trends in that domain.

In the compartment, Ostap continued to go all out to amuse the gathered company. He was finally ac-

cepted by the students as one of them. And the rough
and ready Parovitsky thumped him on the shoulder
and cried:

"Come and join our technical school. You'll get a
grant of seventy-five rubles. You'll live like a king. We
have a cafeteria with meat dishes every day. Later on
we'll be going to the Urals for practical experience."

"I'm already a graduate in arts," said the smooth operator hurriedly.

"And what are you doing now?"

"Well, I'm connected with finance."

"Do you work in a bank?"

Ostap suddenly looked at the student ironically and
said, "No, I don't work. I'm a millionaire."

Obviously the statement committed Ostap in no
way at all and could indeed have been turned into a
joke, but Parovitsky roared with such mirth that Ostap felt insulted. He was seized by a desire to astound
the students and make them admire him still more.

"How many millions do you have?" asked the girl
in schoolgirl slippers, hoping for an amusing answer.

"One," Ostap replied, pale with pride.

"That isn't much," said the mustache.

"Not enough, not enough!" they all cried.

"It's enough for me," said Bender triumphantly.

With these words he took hold of his case, clicked
open the nickel-plated locks, and poured the contents
onto the bunk. Slabs of money formed a slithery pile.
Ostap bent one of them and the wrapping tore apart.

"There's ten thousand in each pack. Isn't that
enough? A million near enough. All intact. Signatures,
lines, and water marks."

In the ensuing silence, Ostap scooped up the money
into the case and threw it onto the luggage rack with
a gesture he considered majestic. He sat down again,
leaned back, spread his legs wide, and looked at the
gang.

"As you see, the arts are also worth while," he said,

inviting the students to enjoy the situation along with him.

The students were silently examining various buttons and hooks on the ornamental walls of the compartment.

"I live like a king," Ostap continued, "or a half-king, which is the same thing in the long run."

After a while the smooth operator began fidgeting and asked in the same friendly tone:

"What are you so depressed about, damn you!"

"Well, I'm going," said the mustache after a moment. "I'm going back to my compartment to see what's going on." And he hurried off.

"A remarkable thing, an incredible thing," Ostap said. "Only this morning we still hadn't got to know one another, yet now we feel we've known each other ten years. What's happened: is it the fluids working?"

"How much do we owe for the tea?" Parovitsky asked. "How much did we drink, comrades? Nine or ten glasses? I'll go and find out from the conductor."

He was followed by four more people who expressed a desire to help Parovitsky settle up with the conductor.

"Perhaps we should sing something," Ostap suggested. "Something about iron. For instance 'Sergius the Priest.' Do you feel like it? I have a splendid Volga bass voice."

Without waiting for an answer, the smooth operator started singing "Down the river, down the Kazanka, there's a gray-blue drake swimming . . ." When it came time for the chorus, Ostap began beating time with his foot and moving his arms in choirmaster style, but the deafening chorus wasn't forthcoming. Lida alone, in her shyness, squeaked "Sergius the Priest," then suddenly broke off and ran out.

The friendship was breaking up there and then. Soon the only person left in the compartment was the kind and considerate girl in gym shoes.

"Where have they all gone?" asked Bender.

"I wonder," said the girl. "I'd better find out."

She headed for the door, but the smooth operator seized her by the arm.

"I was kidding," he stammered. "I'm a worker. I conduct a symphony orchestra. I'm the son of Lieutenant Schmidt. My father was a Turkish citizen. Believe me . . ."

"Let me go!" hissed the girl.

The smooth operator was left alone.

The compartment rocked and creaked. The spoons swung about in the empty glasses and the whole herd of tea things slid slowly toward the edge of the table. The conductor appeared in the doorway, holding an armful of sheets and blankets in position with his chin.

]CHAPTER[

: *35* :

He Was Loved by
Housewives, Maids,
Widows, and Even a
Female Dental Technician

IN CHERNOMORSK the roofs creaked and drafts roamed the streets. The force of an unexpected northeaster which hit the town banished the gentle Indian summer to the garbage cans, gutters, and eves of the houses. There it slowly died amid charred maple leaves and torn streetcar tickets. Cold chrysanthemums sank down in the pots of the flower women. The green shutters of the kvass stalls flapped in the wind. The pigeons cooed "I'm through, I'm through." Sparrows kept warm by pecking hot manure. Chernomorsk citizens walked against the wind with their heads lowered like bulls. The piqué vests were the worst off. The wind blew off their boaters and Panamas and rolled them down the road toward the boulevard. The old men pursued them, grunting and groaning. Sidewalk eddies bowled along the pursuers with such force that from time to time they overshot their hats, only realizing it when they collided with the wet legs of the bronze statue of one of Catherine's favorites in the middle of the square.

At its parking place, the Antelope was clanking like a ship. Whereas earlier Kozlevich's car had given rise to amused surprise, it now only evoked pity: the left mudguard at the rear was tied with string, a fair portion of the windshield was replaced by plyboard, and instead of the rubber bulb which used to play the bugle call, there hung a chairman's nickel-plated bell on a piece of string. Even the steering wheel, on which Adam's honest hands used to rest, was slightly bent to one side. The smooth operator stood on the sidewalk alongside the car. Leaning his elbows on the side, he was saying:

"I cheated you, Adam. I can't buy an Isotta Fraschini, or a Lincoln, or a Buick, or even a Ford. I can't buy you a new car. The State doesn't recognize me as a purchaser. I'm a private person. The only thing possible would be to answer an advertisement in the paper and buy some old jalopy like the antelope."

"Why so?" Kozlevich objected. "My Lauren Dietrich is a good car. If I only had a second-hand oil pipe, I wouldn't need Buicks or anything."

"I've brought a pipe," said Ostap. "Here it is. And it's the only thing I can do for you, my dear Adam, as far as mechanized transport is concerned."

Kozlevich was delighted with the pipe. He fiddled with it for some time and then began fixing it in position. Ostap jogged the bell, which gave a conference-room tinkle, and said hotly:

"Did you know, Adam, that the atmosphere exerts a pressure of four hundred and seventy pounds on every citizen?"

"No," said Kozlevich. "What about it?"

"What do you mean, 'what about it!' It's a scientific fact. And it's been depressing me of late. Just think! Four hundred and seventy pounds. Twenty-four hours a day. Especially at night. I sleep badly. . . . What?"

"Nothing, I'm listening," Kozlevich answered gently.

"I'm not well, Adam. My heart is too big."

The driver of the Antelope gave a grunt. Ostap prattled away.

"An old woman came up to me in the street yesterday and tried to sell me a primus needle that would never wear out. You know, Adam, I didn't buy it. I don't want an everlasting needle; I don't want to be everlasting; I want to die. I have all the rotten symptoms of being in love—no appetite, insomnia, and an obsession for writing poetry. Listen to what I jotted down last night in the flickering light of an electric lamp: 'I remember a wonderful moment; your figure before me appeared; you resembled a transient vision; a spirit of beauty most pure.' Good, isn't it? Talented stuff. Then at dawn, when I'd just completed the last lines, I remembered that it had already been written by Pushkin. What a blow from the classics, eh? . . . What?"

"No, no, go on," said Kozlevich sympathetically.

"So that's how I'm living," Ostap continued with a tremor in his voice. "My body's registered at the Hotel Cairo, while my soul is absent and doesn't even want to go to Rio de Janeiro. And the atmospheric pressure is killing me, into the bargain."

"Have you been to see Zosya?" asked the forthright Kozlevich.

"I'm not going," said Ostap. "Out of proud bashfulness. The Janizaries are raging inside me. I sent that bitch three hundred and fifty rubles worth of telegrams from Moscow and I didn't even get a half-ruble reply. Me, who has been loved by housewives, maids, widows, and even a female dental technician. No, Adam, I'm not going there. Good-by!"

The smooth operator went back to the hotel and dragged out the million-ruble case from under the bed, where it was lying next to a pair of worn shoes. He stared at it for some time rather vaguely, then

picked it up by the handle and went out into the
street. The wind seized Ostap by the shoulders and
pulled him toward the Seafront Boulevard. It was deserted there; no one was sitting on the white benches,
carved during the summer with amorous inscriptions.
A small freighter with broad, upright masts was moving into the outer sea lane, around a lighthouse.

"I've had enough," said Ostap. "The golden calf
isn't for me. Let anyone who wants have it. Let him
play the millionaire to his heart's content."

He looked around and, making certain no one saw
him, threw the case on the ground.

"It's all yours," he said, addressing the black maple
trees, and he clicked his heels.

He went off down the boulevard without looking
back. At first he just strolled along, then put his hands
in his pockets because they suddenly began getting in
his way, and finally quickened his pace in order to
overcome his vacillation. He forced himself to turn
the corner and even began humming a tune, but a
minute later he was running back. The suitcase was
still in its place, but from the other side a middle-aged
citizen of commonplace appearance was approaching
it with outstretched hands.

"What are you up to?" Ostap bellowed, still some
way away. "I'll teach you to pinch other people's suitcases. You can't leave anything alone for a moment.
It's outrageous!"

The citizen shrugged his shoulders sulkily and retired. Bender moved away again with the golden calf
in his arms.

"What'll I do now?" he wondered. "What's to be
done with this damned jackpot which has brought me
nothing but anguish? Should I burn it, perhaps?"

The smooth operator mulled over the thought with
satisfaction.

"There's a fireplace in my room at the hotel. I could
burn it there. How magestic! Worthy of Cleopatra.
Into the flames, bundle by bundle. Why should I

bother any more about it? But no, that's stupid. Burning money is a cheap trick. Too showy! But what can I buy with it except for the NEP grub? An idiotic situation. The museum curator wanted to set up a Louvre on three hundred rubles. On a million, any group of hydraulic engineers or co-operative dramatists could build a semi-skyscraper with a flat roof for open-air lectures. But Ostap Bender, a descendant of the Janizaries, can't do a flaming thing. So that's what class distinction does to a poor self-employed millionaire!"

Still wondering what to do about the million, the smooth operator hurried along avenues, sat down on concrete parapets, and glared at a steamer pitching on the far side of the breakwater.

"No, I must give up the idea of a bonfire. Burning money is cowardly and not very elegant. I must think up some effective gesture. Should I start a Balaganov foundation for correspondence-course students in radio engineering? Or buy five hundred thousand silver spoons, melt them down, and make a statue of Panikovsky for his grave? Or encrust the Antelope with mother-of-pearl? Or maybe . . ."

The smooth operator jumped down from the parapet struck by a new idea. Without wasting a moment, he left the boulevard and, stoically resisting the onslaught of frontal and lateral winds, went to the post office.

At his request they sewed a burlap covering onto his case and bound it with string. The result was an unpretentious parcel of the kind in which citizens send their relatives suet, jelly, or apples in the thousands.

Ostap picked up an indelible pen and, waving it excitedly in the air, wrote: "To the Minister of Finance, Moscow." And the parcel, flung by the hand of a hefty post-office worker, landed with a bang on a pile of oval bales, packages, and crates. Stuffing the receipt into his pocket, Ostap suddenly saw his million to-

gether with the other freight being carted away on a
trolley into the next room by a lazy-looking old man
with white lightning, the post-office emblem, in his
lapels.

"The hearing's continued," said the smooth operator, "this time without the presence of O. Bender,
representative of the Crazy Agrarians."

He stood for some time under the post-office arch,
half regretting his action and half approving it. The
wind penetrated under his mackintosh. He felt cold
and then remembered with chagrin that he hadn't yet
managed to buy a fur coat.

A girl stopped in front of him for a moment. Tossing her head back, she looked up at the gleaming face
of the post-office clock and then went on. She was
wearing a shaggy cloth coat, which came above her
skirt, and a child's blue beret with a pompom. With
her right hand she held down the side of her coat, bil-
lowing in the wind. The captain's heart began thumping even before he recognized Zosya, and he strode
after her along the wet pavement, keeping some way
behind. At times passers-by blocked his view, whereupon he moved into the road, keeping watch on her
from the side and thinking up the approach he should
use in his forthcoming explanation.

Zosya stopped on the corner by a drapery stall and
began examining some brown socks hanging from a
string. Ostap patrolled nearby.

At the very edge of the sidewalk two men with
brief cases were having a heated discussion. They were
both wearing light overcoats under which could be
seen white summer pants.

"You left the Hercules just in time, Ivan Pavlovich,"
said the first man, hugging his brief case to his chest.
"They're right in the middle of a drastic purge."

"The whole town's talking about it," sighed the second man.

"Yesterday they fired Skumbriyevich," said the first
man with relish. "He couldn't do anything. Every-

thing was very civilized at first, and Skumbriyevich told them about his background so well that they applauded. 'I was born between the anvil and the hammer,' he said. He wanted to stress the fact that his father was a blacksmith. Then someone present shouted, 'Say, do you remember a trading house called "Skumbriyevich and Son, Hardware?" Was that Skumbriyevich you?' And the silly fool went and said, 'No, it was my father.' Just imagine what'll happen now. He'll be caught under Article one.

"Yes, Comrade Weintorg, they're pretty strict. And who's being purged today?"

"It's a great day today! Today they're purging Berlaga, the one who tried to hide in the madhouse. And then Polykhayev, and that bitch Serna Mikhailovna, his morganatic wife. She never gave anyone in the Hercules a chance to breathe. I got there today two hours before the beginning, but you just couldn't get through. Incidentally, Bomse . . ."

Zosya had gone on, so Ostap never found out what happened to Bomse. Not that it really worried him, though. The opening ploy for his conversation was now ready. The captain quickly caught up with the girl.

"Zosya," he said, "I've come and the fact cannot be ignored."

The sentence was uttered in a shockingly off-hand manner. The girl gave a start, and the smooth operator realized he had started on the wrong note. He changed his tone; he talked at length; he complained of his fate, and said that his youth had not been what he had hoped for in early childhood, that life had turned out hard and low like a bass clef.

"Did you know, Zosya," he said at the end, "that everyone, even Communists, are subjected to an atmospheric pressure of four hundred and seventy pounds? Haven't you noticed?"

Zosya didn't answer.

At this moment they were passing the Capitol movie

theater. Ostap took a quick sidelong glance at the spot where his office had stood during the summer, and let out a soft gasp. A broad sign stretched right across the building. It said:

STATE HORN AND HOOF ASSOCIATION

Typewriters and portraits of government officials could be seen through all the windows. A fine-looking young messenger boy, not the least bit comparable to Panikovsky, was standing by the entrance with a triumphant smile. Three-ton trucks piled with high-grade horns and hoofs were rattling in through an open gateway bearing the sign: "Warehouse." From all appearances, Ostap's brainchild had taken the right path.

"There's class distinction for you," said Ostap mournfully. "They've even used my scatterbrained idea to their own ends. And I'm out of it. Do you hear, Zosya? I'm out of it and unhappy."

"The sad lover," said Zosya, turning toward Ostap for the first time.

"Yes, I'm a typical Eugene Onegin, alias the knight disinherited by the Soviet regime."

"Where does the knight come in?"

"Don't be sore, Zosya. Take the atmospheric pressure into account. I have the impression that it presses on me much more than on other citizens. That's because of my love for you. Besides, I'm not a trade-union member. That also accounts for it."

"And also because you talk more rubbish than other citizens."

"It's not rubbish. It's a law of physics. Though there may not be any pressure at all, and I may only be imagining it."

Zosya stopped and peeled off a dove-gray glove.

"I'm thirty-three," Ostap hastily added. "The same age as Jesus Christ. And what have I done up to now? I haven't created any faith. I've fleeced my disciples,

I haven't resurrected the deceased Panikovsky, and you alone—"

"Good-by," said Zosya, "I'm going to the cafeteria."

"I should eat something too," declared the smooth operator, glancing at the sign which said "Demonstration Kitchen of the Factory School attached to the Chernomorsk State Academy of Spatial Arts." I'll try some demonstration cabbage soup attached to the academy. It may bring me relief."

"It's only for trade-union members," Zosya warned him.

"Then I'll just sit down."

They went down the three steps. At the back of the demonstration kitchen, in the green shade of a palm, sat a dark-eyed young man; he was gazing in a dignified manner at the menu.

"Pericles!" called Zosya from some way off. "I've bought you some socks with reinforced heels. . . ." She introduced the young man as Pericles Phemides. The young man cordially shook hands.

"Bender-Zadunaysky," replied the smooth operator gruffly, realizing at once that he had arrived too late for the wedding reception, and that the socks with reinforced heels were not just the output of a pseudo-disabled persons' co-operative, but a symbol of a happy marriage, legalized in the registry office.

"What! Are you Zadunaysky as well?" asked Zosya in amusement.

"Yes, I am, and judging by the socks, you're no longer just Sinitsky."

"I'm Sinitsky-Phemides."

"Just twenty-seven days," said the young man, rubbing his hands.

"I like your husband," said the disinherited knight.

"So do I," Zosya burst out.

While the young newlyweds consumed their navy-bean soup, lifting their spoons high in the air and exchanging glances, Ostap squinted sulkily at the slogans decking the walls. One of them read:

Do not converse during meals. It prevents the proper
secretion of stomach juices.

There was nothing to be done. He wanted to leave,
but a sudden and inexplicable shyness prevented him.

"This navy-bean soup," said Ostap with an effort,
"is full of flotsam and jetsam!"

Both the Phemides laughed good-heartedly.

"What field are you working in, actually?" Ostap
asked the young man.

"Actually, I'm the secretary of the iso-group of railroad artists," Phemides answered.

The smooth operator slowly began to get up. "Aha,
a group representative. I might have guessed. Anyway,
I won't distract you with conversation. It'll prevent
you from secreting the proper stomach juices, so essential for your health."

He left without saying good-by, walking straight
toward the door and brushing against the corners of
the tables.

"They've taken away my girl!" Ostap muttered in
the street. "Taken her right from the stall. Phemides!
Nemides! Phemides the group representative has taken
away from a self-employed millionaire . . ."

At this point Ostap remembered with appalling lucidity that he no longer possessed a million rubles.
Even before the thought was complete, he was running along, parting the passers-by with his arms like a
swimmer trying to break a world record.

Slipping twice on the tiled floor of the post office,
the smooth operator ran up to the window, in front of
which was a short line of grim, silent people. Ostap
was just about to stick his head through the window
when the first citizen in the line neurotically raised his
bony elbows and forced the newcomer back. The second citizen, like a clockwork doll, did exactly the
same, and Ostap found himself even further from the
longed-for window. In complete silence other elbows

went to work until the impudent line-jumper ended up at the very tail.

"I only want . . ." Ostap began.

But he broke off. It was pointless talking. The gray, stony line was as uncrushable as a Greek phalanx. Each one knew his place and was ready to die for his own little rights.

It wasn't until forty-five minutes later that Ostap placed his head against the window and eagerly asked for his parcel back. The clerk returned the receipt apathetically.

"We don't give back parcels, comrade."

"But the parcel's mine," said Ostap sweetly. "Mine, you see. I sent it off and now I want it back. I forgot to put in a jar of jelly. Heavenly apple jelly. I'd appreciate it very much. My uncle will be terribly hurt. You see—"

"We don't give back parcels, comrade."

Ostap looked around him helplessly. Behind him was a line of grim and silent people who knew all the rules, including the one that parcels are not given back.

"I want to put in the jar of heavenly apple jelly."

"Send it in a separate parcel," said the clerk, more amenably. "Nothing'll happen to your uncle."

"You don't know my uncle!" cried Ostap hotly. "Anyway, I'm a poor student, and don't have any money. I appeal to you as a social worker."

"Where could I possibly find it?" said the clerk in a plaintive voice. "There are three tons of parcels over there."

At this point the smooth operator began burbling away in such a pitiful tone that the postal worker went off into the next room to look for the poor student's parcel. The line, silent until then, immediately broke into an uproar. All kinds of abuse was hurled at the smooth operator for not knowing the post-office regulations, and one citizen actually pinched him in her wrath.

"Never do this again," said the clerk severely, throwing Bender his suitcase.

"I never will," cried the captain. "Student's word of honor!"

The wind made the roofs creak and the lampposts sway; shadows moved across the ground, and the rain cut through the projected rays of car headlights.

"Enough of these psychological excesses," said Bender with delight. "I've had enough suffering and mortification. It's time to begin a working-class bourgeois life. In Rio de Janeiro! I'll buy a plantation and send for Balaganov as a monkey. Let him pick bananas for me."

: *36* :

The Knight of the Order
of the Golden Fleece

A STRANGE-LOOKING man was walking one night near the river Dniester flats. He was enormous and shapelessly fat. He was wearing canvas overalls with a raised hood. The weird-looking man tiptoed through banks of reeds beneath straddling fruit trees as though he were walking through a bedroom. Now and then he stopped and sighed, whereupon there was a metallic clank from inside the overalls. Each time this was followed by a high-pitched, delicate tinkle. At one point the weird man tripped over a slippery root and fell flat. There was the same loud crash as though a suit of armor had fallen on the ground. The weird man stayed down on the ground for some time, peering into the darkness.

The March night was noisy. Full-sized pharmacy dew-drops dripped from the trees and plopped onto the ground.

"Damned dish," whispered the man.

He got up and made his way to the river Dniester without further incident. He raised the ends of his overalls, clambered down from the bank, and, almost losing his balance on the slithery ice, ran across toward Rumania.

The smooth operator had been making preparations the whole winter. He bought up American dollars with effigies of presidents in white wigs, gold watches, and cigarette cases, engagement rings, diamonds, and other jewelry.

He was now carrying seventeen mighty cigarette cases with various monograms, eagles, and engraved dedications:

> To the Director of the Russian-Carpathian Bank and Benefactor Yevsei Nitwitoff on his silver wedding anniversary from grateful employees.

> To Privy Councilor M. I. Svyatotatsky on completion of the Senatorial Inspection from members of the Chernomorsk Town Administration.

His pockets were stuffed with bagel-like bunches of engagement rings, signet rings, and bracelets. Across his back were three rows of gold watches on strong string. Some of them emitted an irritating tick, and Bender felt as though insects were crawling up his spine. Among them were presentation samples, one of which had the inscription:

> To my darling son Sergei Kastraki in recognition of his academic prowess.

Someone had scratched out the word "academic" and put "sexual" above it. It had probably been done by Sergei's friends, who were really just as much dunces as he was. For a long time Ostap refused to buy this indecent watch, but had finally done so, as he was determined to turn the whole of his million into jewelry and other such valuables.

As a whole, the winter had been a difficult one. The smooth operator could only get four hundred thousand rubles' worth of diamonds, and the currency, including some dubious Polish and Balkan money, had only cost fifty thousand. His remaining funds had been spent on the heavier items. It was particularly

difficult to move about with a gold dish strapped to
your stomach. The dish was a large oval one, like an
African chieftain's shield, and weighed twenty
pounds. The captain's mighty neck was bent under
the strain of an archbishop's crucifix bought from an
ex-deacon. On top of the crucifix, on a superb piece of
ribbon, hung the Order of the Golden Fleece—a cast
ram.

The Order had been sold to him with great reluc-
tance by an old gaffer who might have been a prince;
on the other hand, he might have been just a prince's
valet. The old man had kept haggling about the price
with the excuse that there were only a few such orders
in existence, and that most of them were worn by
crowned heads.

"The Golden Fleece," mumbled the old man, "is
only awarded for the greatest valor."

"Then it's just right for me," replied Ostap, "and,
anyway, I'm buying it because it's gold scrap."

But the smooth operator was pretending. He liked
the look of the Order very much and had decided to
keep it for good as the "Order of the Golden Calf."

Spurred on by fear, and expecting to hear rifle shots
at any moment, Bender reached the middle of the
river and stopped. The gold in the dish, cross, and
bracelets pulled him down. His back itched from the
watches strung across it. The hem of his overalls was
soaked and weighed several tons. With a groan Ostap
flung off the overalls and hurried on. Underneath he
was wearing a fur coat, an enormous, almost unbe-
lievable coat, probably the most expensive item in Ostap's wardrobe. It had taken him several months to
make it, and he had designed it as he would a house,
making blueprints and traveling far afield to buy the
materials. The coat was reversible, with brown-black
fox fur on one side and genuine sealskin on the other.
But the collar was made of sable. An extraordinary
coat indeed! A supercoat with chinchilla pockets

stuffed with coastguards' medals, crucifixes, and gold
bridges, the latest thing in dentistry. The smooth
operator's head was crowned with a hat. Not a hat,
but rather a tiara of beaver.

The whole of his magnificent collection was intended to ensure an easy, carefree life on the shores
of the warm ocean among the palms.

At three a.m. the refractory descendant of the Janizaries reached the Rumanian bank. It was dark and
quiet. It was spring there, too, and the drops dripped
from the trees. The smooth operator burst out laughing.

"Just a few formalities with the understanding Ru-
manians and the way is clear. I reckon two or three
medals for life-saving should brighten up their dull,
border-line lives."

He turned around toward the Soviet side and, waving a thick sealskin glove into the melting darkness,
called out:

"Everything should be done by forms. Form number five is for saying good-by to one's country. Well,
then, *adieu*, my fine country. I don't like being first in
the class and getting good marks for attention, dili-
gence, and behavior. I'm a private citizen and not ob-
liged to take an interest in silo pits, trenches, and
tractors. I'm not very much concerned about the
Socialist transformation of men into angels and savings-
bank depositors. Just the opposite. I'm interested in the
urgent problem of care for lonely millionaires. . . ."

At this point the farewell according to form No. 5
was interrupted by the appearance of several armed
frontier guards. The smooth operator bowed with dig-
nity and carefully uttered the phrase he had learned
for the occasion.

"*Trajascu Romania mare!*"

He peered lovingly into the faces of the guards,
barely visible in the darkness. He thought he saw the
guards grinning.

"Long live great Rumania," he repeated in Russian. "I'm an old professor on the run from the secret police in Moscow. Honestly, I only just managed to get away. Allow me . . ."

One of the guards walked right up to Ostap and silently grabbed his fur cap. Ostap reached out for the cap, but the guard pushed his hand away, again in silence.

At the same time another guard began unbuttoning Ostap's supercoat with the skill of an experienced lover. The captain lunged forward. As he did so, a large bracelet fell out of his pocket and rolled along the ground.

"*Branzuletka!*" shrilled a frontier-guard officer in a short greatcoat with a dog-fur collar and large metal buttons on his protruding bottom.

"*Branzuletka!*" cried the others, pouncing on Ostap.

Encumbered by his coat, the smooth operator was thrown to the ground and could feel the dish being pulled out of his pants. Rising to his feet again, he saw the officer weighing the dish in his hands with a savage leer. Ostap grabbed hold of his property and wrenched it out of the officer's hands, whereupon he received a stunning blow in the face. Events developed at a military pace. The smooth operator's coat was in his way, and for a while he had to attack his enemies on his knees by hurling the life-saving medals at them. Then he suddenly experienced an inexplicable relief which had enabled him to deal the enemy a number of hard smacks; they had evidently managed to pull off his rather expensive coat.

"What a way to treat me!" howled Ostap, wildly looking around him.

There was a moment when he stood leaning against a tree, bringing down the glittering dish with a crash on his attackers' heads. There was a moment when they tore the Order of the Golden Calf from his neck, making him shake his head like a horse. There was a moment when, raising his archbishop's crucifix high in the air, he shrieked hysterically:

"Exploiters of the working class! Leeches! Hirelings of capital! Bastards!"

Pink spittle was dribbling from his mouth. He fought for his million like a gladiator. He flung aside his adversaries and got up from the ground with grim determination each time they pushed him over.

He came to on the ice with a face reduced to pulp, with one boot, without his coat, engraved cigarette cases, watches, dish, currency, crucifix, and jewelry, and without his million. Gazing down at him from the high bank was the officer with the dog-fur collar.

"Damned aristocrats!" cried Ostap, raising a bare foot. "Parasites!"

The officer slowly drew his revolver and cocked it. The smooth operator realized the interview was over. Bending low, he hobbled back to the Soviet side.

A white, cigarette haze hung above the river. Unclenching his fist, the smooth operator saw in his palm a flat medal, a lock of somebody's thick hair, and the Order of the Golden Calf, miraculously saved during the struggle. He looked stupidly at his trophies and the remnants of his wealth and continued moving, slithering into pits in the ice and wincing with pain.

A long, loud boom like a gunshot shook the icy surface. The warm wind blew for all it was worth. Bender looked down and saw a huge green crack in the ice. The icy platform on which he was standing gave a lurch and one end went under the water.

"Things are moving!" cried the smooth operator in horror. "Things are moving, gentlemen of the jury!" He began jumping from one piece of floating ice to another, making as fast as he could for the country which he had abandoned so imperiously an hour before. The mist rose slowly and sedately, revealing the naked flats.

Ten minutes later a weird-looking man, hatless and

with only one boot, clambered onto the Soviet bank. Addressing no one in particular, he said:

"You don't need to applaud! I didn't make a Monte Cristo. I'll have to change my profession to apartment-block superintendent."

ILYA ARNOLDOVICH ILF (*1897-1937*)
and YEVGENII PETROVICH KATAYEV (*1903-1942*)

The writers who used the pen names "Ilf" and "Petrov" were
natives of Odessa. Ilf, born into a poor Jewish family named
Fainzilberg, worked as a machine-shop assembler, bookkeeper,
and stable manager before becoming a journalist. He began as
a humorist in 1919, at the height of the civil war. Not long
afterward he joined the staff of the *Train Whistle* in Moscow,
forming his partnership with Petrov, another staff member. Still
another member of the *Train Whistle* was Petrov's brother, the
famous novelist Valentin Katayev. Subsequently Ilf and Petrov
joined *Pravda*, winning an audience of millions for their satires
against bureaucratism written under the pen names Tolstoy-
evsky and the Chill Philosopher. They wrote film scenarios
as well as *The Golden Calf* and *The Twelve Chairs*. In 1936
the two made a 10,000-mile automobile tour through the
United States collecting material for their book *One-Storey-
High America*. Ilf died of tuberculosis in 1937 in Moscow,
where his body was cremated. Petrov edited several humorous
periodicals, as well as the popular *Little Flame*, a weekly which
contributed toward making the U.S.A. and Great Britain better
understood by the Russians. During World War II he was a
correspondent at the front, and was killed at his post in 1942
during the defense of Sebastopol. Concerning the official Soviet
attitude toward Ilf and Petrov, Bernard Guilbert Guerney has
said: "The most painstaking research shows no indication that
these two satirists ever received as much as a slap on the wrist
throughout their careers." [See *An Anthology of Russian Lit-
erature in the Soviet Period*, edited by B. G. Guerney in The
Vintage Russian Library.]

JOHN H. C. RICHARDSON, born in 1926, was educated at British
private schools and London University. He has been an interpreter and translator both at the British embassy, Moscow, and
at the United Nations, New York. He has also taught Russian
at London University. Since 1957 John Richardson has lived in
New York City.